RUSH OF RAVENS

TIL KINGDOM COME
BOOK ONE

ABIGAIL BRIER

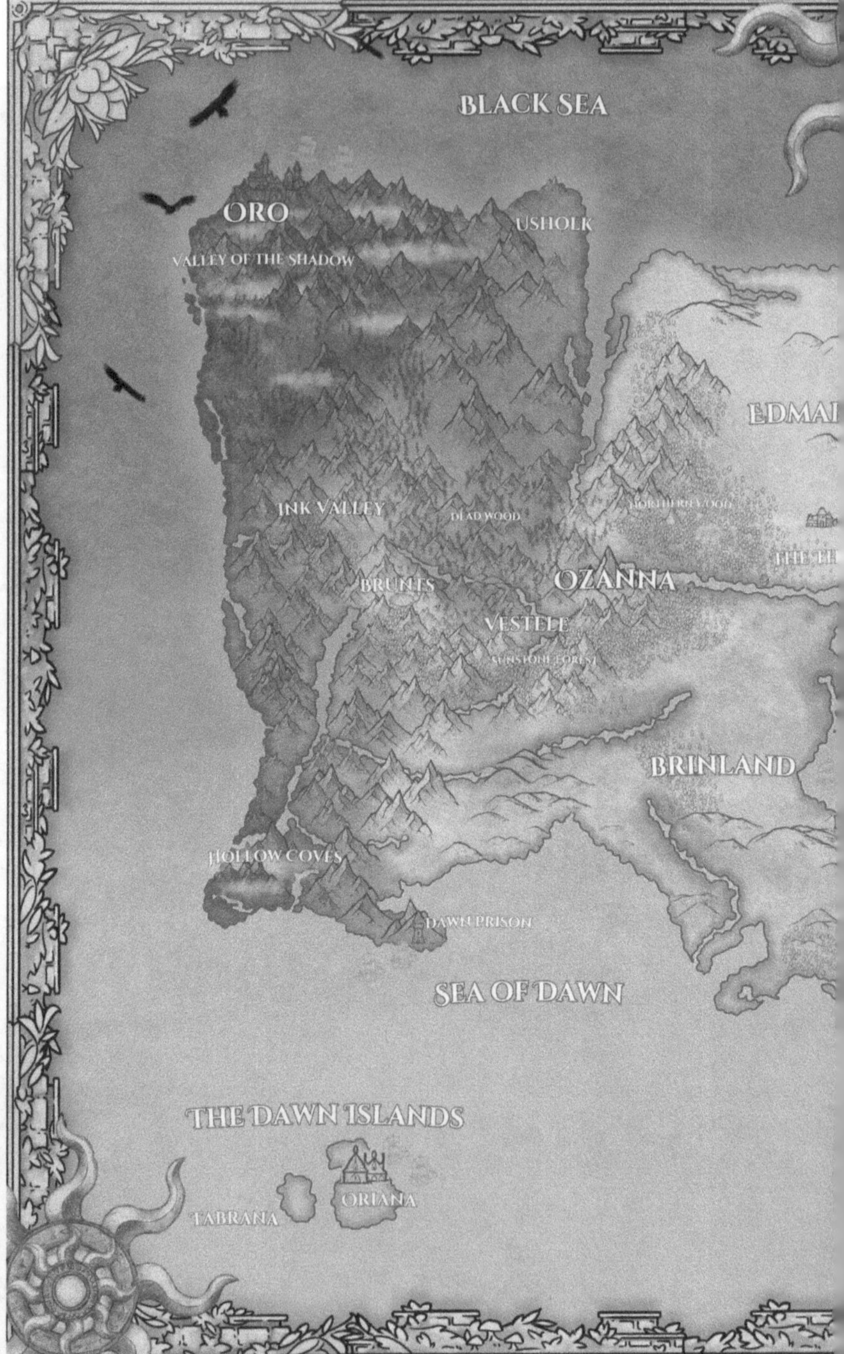

BLACK SEA
ORO
USHOLK
VALLEY OF THE SHADOW
EDMAI
INK VALLEY
DEAD WOOD
NORTHERWOOD
THE TE
BRUNES
OZANNA
VESTELE
SUNSTONE FOREST
BRINLAND
HOLLOW COVES
DAWN PRISON
SEA OF DAWN
THE DAWN ISLANDS
FABRANA
ORIANA

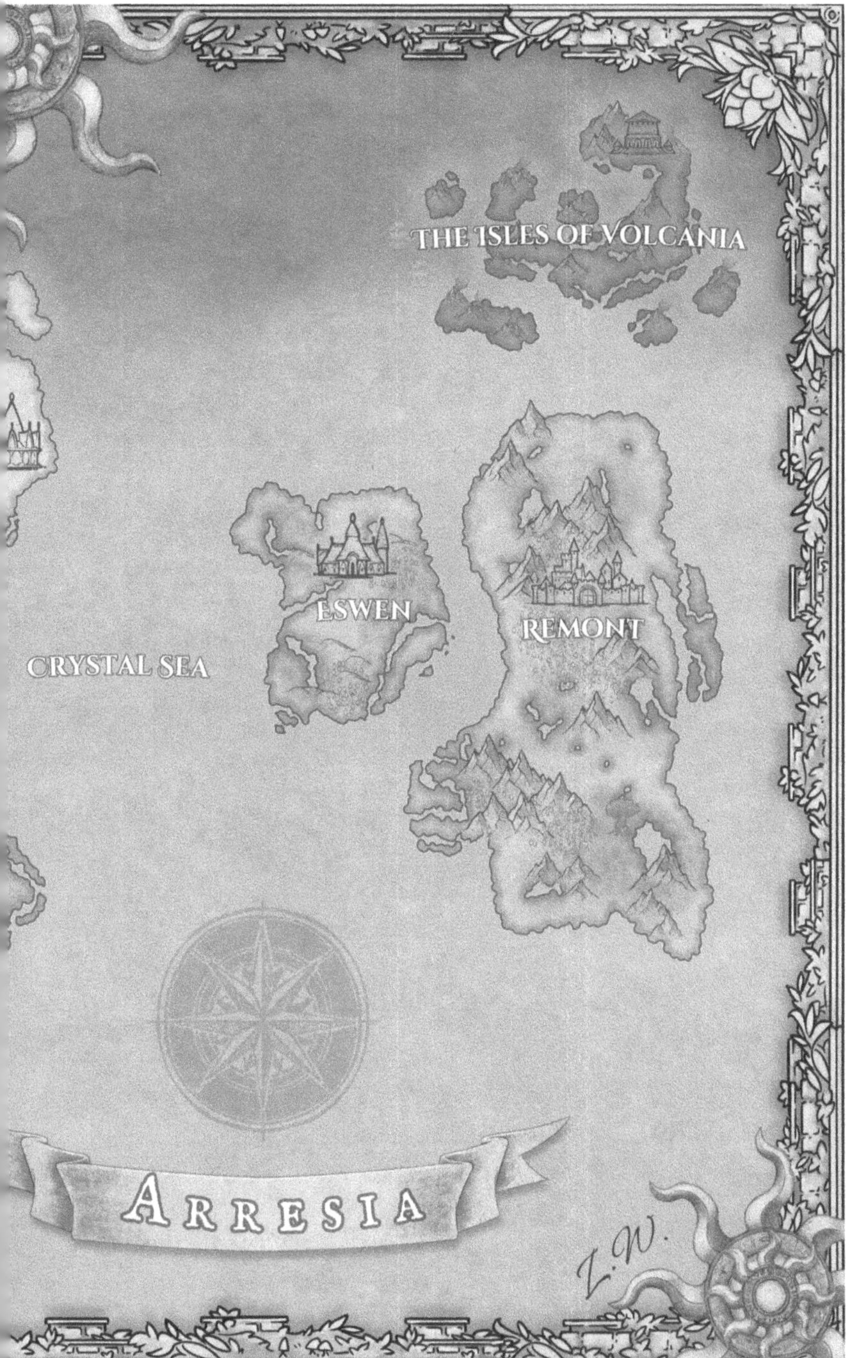

THE ISLES OF VOLCANIA
ESWEN
REMONT
CRYSTAL SEA
ARRESIA

PLAYLIST

For those of you who want the reading experience to be like a
movie in your mind...
Visit WWW.ABIGAILBRIER.COM for the official cinematic
playlist guide.
Find the official "Rush of Ravens" playlist on Spotify.

PRONUNCIATION GUIDE

- Ravenna - Ruh-veh-nuh
- Arresia - Uh-ree-juh
- Ashreya - Ash-ray-uh
- Degare - Deh-gair
- Despiri - Deh-speer-ee
- Edme - Ed-may
- Gerrin - Gair-in
- Jara - Jar-uh
- Leith - Lay-th
- Lume - Loom
- Nilo - Nee-low
- Ozanna - Oh-zan-uh
- Roarke - Roar-k
- Tenille - Teh-neel
- Vestele - Veh-stell
- Willa - Will-uh
- Xan - Zan
- Zephaniah - Zeh-fuh-nigh-uh

RUSH OF RAVENS

ABIGAIL BRIER

PROLOGUE
7 YEARS AGO

"Your Majesty," said the witch in greeting as she stalked into the Black Temple, her heels clicking against the stone floor. "It is time. The weapon is ready."

Degare, King of Oro, bowed to the golden statues of the goddesses before turning to face his lover. "How much of the bloodstone did it take?" he asked.

"Every last bit," Jara said. The few measly pounds of the powerful, dark red fragments, mined out of the earth and gathered over the last two decades, would be put to good use. From them, he would raise the darkness. "We've done it, Degare. We've truly done it."

He took her porcelain face in his hands. "Without you, my love, none of this would be possible." She smiled against his lips for a moment.

"Bring it in," she ordered to someone just out of view. There was a shuffling of feet before the doors swung open, revealing the weapon he had longed for since his village had been burned by the Ozannes thirty years ago. The craftsman pridefully watched as Degare took it into his hands. This weapon would solidify his rule—it would ensure that he was never burned again.

His fingers brushed the gold and the crack that snaked through the shiny metal. Within the crack was the dull red of bloodstone, the mighty power of a hundred original witches living inside. Degare tapped the staff to the ground, testing the sharp point of the blade at the tip.

The craftsman smiled wryly. "The blade is made of the strongest metal I had in stock. Gold plated." Degare examined the blade, then shifted back to observe the hilt. The craftsman pointed at the carvings. "The Raven of Oro and some other handcrafted designs—unique to you, Your Majesty." A raven, its wings open in flight, perched atop the staff, ready to rise to the skies.

Degare smiled. "And does it work?"

"The witches and I have worked very hard, Your Majesty." The craftsman looked nervously to Jara for confirmation that the arduous spell, which had required participation from her entire clan on the darkest night of the year, had been successful.

"Well, I will not just take your word for it, will I? Bring me an Ember," he ordered the guards who stood on either side of the temple entrance.

One stepped forward. "Yes, Your Majesty. Do you have a preference?"

"One that has not been tainted by the mines and still bears the radiance of the Light."

The guards dipped their heads and immediately left the temple to retrieve an Ember.

"Your Majesty," Jara said, voice careful and smooth, as if she were trying to prevent his temper from boiling over.

Degare closed his eyes and breathed deeply.

"Are you to do the killing here...in the presence of the goddesses?"

"Why shouldn't I? Think of it as a sacrifice. It is the darkness the goddesses thrive in—and we are to be the ones to return them to it."

"Why yes," she said. "I suppose you are right." She pecked him on the cheek. He hated public affection—but he needed her, for now. "It is all coming together," she said with a faint smirk. *She* had needed *him* to carry out her plan from the beginning, when she had found her mother's spell book and decided to create the bloodstone weapon that was spoken of within the pages.

After the Ozannes had mined all the bloodstone out of the ground in Arresia, destroying the witches primary power source, Jara's clan had been weak and unable to stand against the Ember armies of thousands, which greatly outnumbered them. Without the bloodstone, the witches were weak—the power of thousands now equal to hundreds. But even if they were successful in the making of the bloodstone staff, only a human with no witch blood could wield it. When Jara came across him twenty odd years ago, seeking vengeance on the Ozannes for his own reasons, she had offered him a partnership in the war they were sowing.

"Soon, the Ozannes will pay," Degare said. If the bloodstone staff worked, he would finally claim their many gifts as his own.

"And my clan will be returned to their territory," Jara added, in reference to Degare's promise to grant the witches their own territory, where they could live separate from Oro's jurisdiction. Now that the witches had completed their mission of creating the bloodstone staff, they wanted to move onto their next—rebuilding their homeland while gathering up as much bloodstone as they could find, restoring the strength of their clan.

"Soon," Degare lied. He would not so readily release the witches from the bargain that held them. Somewhere along the way, the dynamic had shifted. Having the witches here in Oro working for him had proven beneficial.

Screams echoed outside in the streets as his victim was brought forth. A wily man, but strong in spirit. His eyes were a fierce blue, and his lightmarks glowed with a brilliance Degare had not seen of the Embers in the mines.

"What are your gifts?" Degare demanded, as the guards kicked the Ember to his knees before him. The staff craftsman trembled next to him, but the guards' faces remained stoic.

"Fire," the Ember spat.

"Perfect," Degare said. He thrust the staff through the Ember's chest without a thought.

Immediately, Degare fell to his knees. A strange feeling rushed through him—draining, yet empowering. It knocked the breath from his lungs, but then it felt like he could breathe for the first time. A thrill of emotions ran through him as he kept hold of the staff, watching the life and power drain from the Ember's face.

He would be the most powerful in all Arresia. The first Despiri—crafted in darkness. And when he had gained the power of hundreds, maybe thousands, and was unsurpassable by men, he would begin selling the Embers in trades for gain of not only power, but wealth. Arresia would fall. Each kingdom, one by one, would plummet into darkness until they cowered at his feet. Ozanne—now Oro—was the first of the seven to turn from the Light. Now, Degare would make it his mission to bring the others with him, starting with the Ember Trades.

"Degare." He released the staff, catching his breath. "Degare," Jara said again, this time resting a hand on his shoulder. Degare inhaled sharply.

"Did it work?" the craftsman asked nervously. An unfamiliar feeling was now churning in Degare's blood, and he knew it for what it was: pure darkness, forged through death.

Degare wiped the sweat from his brow and rose to stand over top of the fallen Ember before the goddesses and his guards.

"It worked. Did you write everything down as you completed it? All the instructions?" he asked the craftsman, examining his own hands as he tried to summon the flame that had been kindled beneath his skin. With practice, he would wield power like no Ember ever had.

"Yes, Your Majesty."

"And you shared it with no one?"

"No one, Your Majesty. Just as you asked."

Degare nodded, pleased, then looked to his guards.

"Kill him."

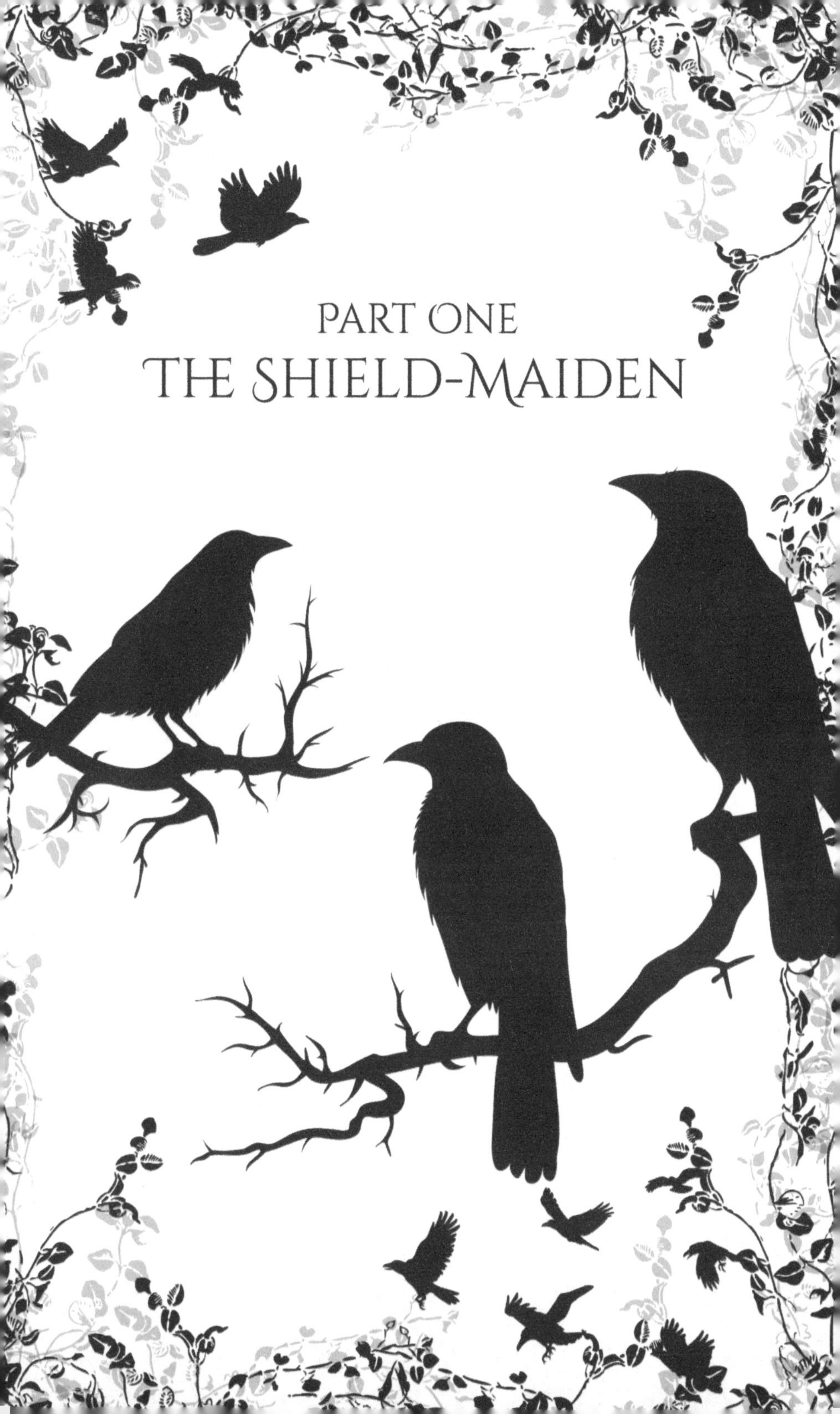
PART ONE
THE SHIELD-MAIDEN

I

FATE

RAVENNA

While her clan slumbered beneath the stars, nestled safely in the depths of the icy mountains, Ravenna would run the Gauntlet.

She smiled as she glanced back at the flickering firelight of Vestele, growing dim amidst the inky backdrop of the night sky. As always, her village's guards had not noticed when she slipped right past them.

The guards were there to keep other clans and travelers from crossing Vestele's borders. Though Ravenna always felt that their main duty was to fulfill an order given by her mother, the Vestelian Clan's shield-maiden—to keep *her* within the boundaries of the village. She was accustomed to sneaking around when it came to doing anything she enjoyed because more than likely, her mother would not approve if it did not involve staying within the security of their quaint village in the valley. In only a matter of months, amid the oncoming spring season and right after her twenty-second birthday, the third moon would rise, and her village's agricultural season would begin. She hoped that by then, the frost would be long gone. Maybe when there was food to eat, her mother would rest and stop worrying so much about Ravenna's harmless endeavors.

Ravenna urged her mare, Fintah, forward into the broadening dale, the snowy valley illuminated by the silver light of the twin moons. Frigid air stung her cheeks as she cut through the late winter winds on horseback. Intricately braided, rust-colored hair whipped at her back, and a newly sharpened blade lay sheathed against her hip.

Ravenna loved the beautiful valley, Vestele and its people, but the adrenaline rush she craved was found in the moments she witnessed the clan's mighty warriors in training. How she longed to be a part of the group that so valiantly protected and watched over her people. Tonight, she would prove herself worthy of belonging.

The Gauntlet was an annual challenge in which one lucky winner would prove himself to be the greatest warrior in all the Kingdom of Oro. It took place in the Brunts, a wretched city buried in the valley five miles west of Vestele, and she would arrive before the two moons had peaked in the night sky. On the horizon, silhouettes of short, stumpy buildings spread a few hundred yards from where she would leave Fintah on the edge of the Sunstone Forest. There, the mare's coat blended against the reflection of moonlight amongst the glistening golden hills of stone.

The tallest structure among the buildings of the Brunts was a Black Temple, which was used for worship of the darkness. Ravenna knew little of what occurred inside, only that those who worshiped the darkness bowed to goddesses and idols and drew their power from the shadows. The ungifted worshipers of darkness were called Shades, and those who had killed to wield darkness: Despiri.

Ravenna's clan worshiped no god. If one were to ask her, she assumed the supernatural legends of Light and its opposing darkness all fabricated for the benefit of those in power—although the existence of the gifted Embers, witches, and the Despiri were otherwise lacking in explanation. She supposed some things of this world could only be explained by the otherworldly.

When she reached the edge of the Sunstone Forest, Ravenna dismounted.

"Stay," she whispered, cradling the ivory horse's chin in her hand, and resting her forehead among the bridge of the mare's nose. Fintah obeyed, as always, watching as Ravenna traipsed through the brown grasses that separated her from the sinful city below.

As she neared, the hair on her arms began to rise, and she pulled her cloak over her head, attempting to keep the brisk wind from her ears. She had fought in the taverns in this city many times before and had never lost. Tonight would be no different. Varieties of blades and daggers were strapped onto her belt, in her boots, and concealed beneath her long, black cloak. She ducked her head as she wove through the darkness beyond the city gates, carefully choosing her route. Entering the Brunts at night always held somewhat of a risk, especially with word of the Despiri becoming more common here, thanks to the king's recent pact with the city.

Across the street in front of the sunstone arena, a crowd of men stammered and hollered, pushing toward what could only be the start of the Gauntlet.

Ravenna cursed under her breath. *I am late.*

She climbed to a nearby rooftop and perched there, observing quietly. The streets were crowded, but she picked up snippets of a few conversations despite the disorder.

"I heard they had more trouble than usual finding the bloodstone this year," a greasy man said to his friend. "The old mines that the Brunt slaves are allowed use of are near dry. The fragment they did find is *far* from pure. Mostly black stone with a few minuscule bits of bloodstone."

Ravenna bit her cheek.

"I bet it will still sell for a few gold ravens. The king is mad for it, and I hear the witches are too," the friend replied.

Ravenna had never laid eyes on a real gold raven—a coin stamped with the emblem of Oro, equal to nearly *four thousand* coppers. In Arresia, the wealthy were untouchable, and the poor were *poor*. Vestele did not deal in coins or even trade with other clans. Though, Ravenna believed that to be a mistake on her mother's part.

Ravenna assumed the Brunts to be a wealthy city, since their mercenaries provided more Embers to Oro than any other territory. The Gauntlet alone brought in outrageous amounts of revenue every year, yet the streets and the buildings still looked like slums.

Where did all the money go? She turned her attention to another set of onlookers, listening to the tail end of their conversation.

"Of course, I'm betting on *him*. He just looks like he could kill every man in that arena," the woman said. Ravenna searched the line-up for any hints of which contestant they may be speaking of, and decided it was probably the largest of the twenty. One by one, they would have their turns, and Ravenna knew the host had purposely placed him last to make the competition last longer and bring in more bets.

She had never witnessed the Gauntlet, had only heard stories of the handful of warriors in Vestele who had attempted it and failed. Her mother had since forbidden her warriors any involvement with the challenge. All but one of the night's contestants would die trying to claim the bloodstone prize, and only after the first chosen twenty had failed, would they open the arena for new contestants. Ravenna was not worried. She would have her turn.

The one who came out triumphant with the stone in hand would be labeled as Oro's best warrior. It was likely no one except Ravenna wished for the title. What it would gain Ravenna, was her mother's recognition of her skill and a place with the Vestelian warriors. It was the valuable bloodstone that had people from all over Oro's territories coming to the dreadful city of the Brunts each year, hoping for a chance to run the course and risking their lives. The winner would either use the bloodstone for himself—drawing from the supposed dark magic within it—or sell it for a large sum of gold.

"The course is more difficult this year. They added more soldiers, and the snakes are venomous." Ravenna's eyes scanned the arena.

Below her, the arena consisted of a great, multi-level wooden structure with many obstacles scattered among it. At the edge of the arena, Embers had been lined up in shackles to watch the competition. Ravenna guessed they would continue north to the Ember Trades in the morning.

She examined the many challenges: hot coals, burning fire, venomous snakes, rolling logs, spikes and metal blades that shot out from the platforms, then paused on the half a dozen massive, sword-wielding men that were scattered about the wooden structure. Broad shouldered and well-trained men, it would appear. Toward the far end was a ladder, which led to the three highest points of the creaky wooden platforms, where the bloodstone awaited her.

A few men in the crowd peered in the direction of the stone, too. They spoke loudly of a popular topic here in this city: the Ember Trades. "The king's spelled staff is made of that very stone, and you should see what he can do with it. I attended the winter trade, and I'll be going back up north for the spring trade in a few weeks. I can't afford a kill, but it sure is something to witness."

Ravenna ground her teeth as she listened. If she were shield-maiden, Vestele would fight for the Embers' freedom, but she was not.

"Now, if I would have gotten a place in the Gauntlet this year, I could have won the stone and sold it for enough to buy an Ember," the man boasted.

She scoffed, nearly tumbling from the roof where she still perched. This man was scrawny, and his build suggested he was an apprentice, not a warrior.

The Embers served the Light, and in return, were said to be blessed with gifts. Opposite, the Despiri were those who had killed an Ember for their gifts. For each Despiri, an Ember had to die. No one in Vestele spoke of the atrocity, but Ravenna had put the pieces together. The Ember Trades that now happened quarterly; at the dawn of each new season in the Kingdom of Oro, were trades of *people*. Like slave trades, but King Degare was selling Embers into their certain deaths.

When Ravenna had the rock in her grasp, she would not be so stupid. She *would* sell it, but would use the gold to purchase food and perhaps a better plot of land with fertile ground for her starving people. Perhaps the marriage alliance her mother often spoke of would then be rendered unnecessary.

At the sudden sound of the cannon, Ravenna's heart beat louder in her chest. Contestant one ran quickly across the coals with his bare feet, failing to leap over the entire width of the flames. His flesh singed against the heat, but he continued through the sand spread on the platform and over top of the log, which started to turn and sway with his weight.

As the man tumbled down into the pit of entangled snakes, he shrieked. "Forfeit! Forfeit!"

Even Ravenna, in her lack of experience with the Gauntlet, knew there would be no forfeits. She winced as one of the Brunt soldiers sliced through the small man with a sword, the sound of cutting flesh echoing into her ears even at her distance a few hundred feet away. The crowd gasped in a mixture of excitement and horror. The soldier turned carelessly as if he had not just slaughtered the man like an animal, and viciously awaited contestant number two's arrival on the stands. When the guards made him remove his shoes as well, Ravenna began unlacing hers and secured her blades elsewhere. The slovenly man made it over the flames and across the log, despite his severe limp. But, when he made it to the first platform, he was promptly shoved backward onto the metal spikes by one of the six fighters who awaited him.

Ravenna looked away.

The Brunt soldiers fought dirty and unfairly, cutting through each contestant, one after the other, before they even had the chance to breathe. One contestant against half a dozen fighters was a nearly impossible challenge, and the spectators were here for the gore of it all.

Ravenna knew it was a gamble. But it was between death and enough wealth to feed her village, while gaining her mother's respect and freeing herself from the bonds of an impending marriage. She had to make sure she was the one who walked out with the bloodstone in tow. Most of the contestants wanted the bloodstone only to be able to afford to place a bid at the upcoming Ember Trade.

In all her endeavors, she had never seen an Ember that was not already enslaved, wasting away to nothing as they worked in the bloodstone mines and awaited death's greeting at the soonest trade. The Ember race had become nearly as rare as the bloodstone they were forced to mine. Still, Ravenna had no desire to be caught between the two rivals, essentially powerless against the legends of mighty magic and power strong enough to move mountains.

Just before leaping down from the roof onto the lower level, she saw contestant seven enter and begin to climb up onto the platform. The crowd silenced, and the awaiting contestants pushed and shoved, arguing for their turn. The man held only one weapon, unlike Ravenna. She would not be caught dead without a backup or three whilst fighting the dishonorable men on those platforms, whether the extra weight slowed her down or not. Just watching him prepare to begin had her palms sweating.

He was quite tall and more broad in the shoulders than the previous men had been, but still not nearly the size of the largest contestant. Beneath his dark cloak, his silhouette showed promise of strength, his body merely a shadow against impending death and the night sky. He was straight postured and seemingly fearless against the certain doom that awaited him. Ravenna looked him up and down, preparing for his inevitable failure. She would bet with the arrogance that filled the air around him, he would make it to the second platform and disable half of the guards, then fall to his death from the narrow beam of wood that was now occupied by two Brunt soldiers.

When the cannon sounded, he ran swiftly. He moved straight across the hot coals, then leapt over the wide berth of dancing flames without a lick of fire touching his bare heels. She leaned forward, intrigued with his celerity. With quick footing and one lengthy and unexpected jump onto the distant platform, he tucked and rolled, yanking a concealed, gemmed dagger from his cloak. He plunged both of his blades into two of the soldiers, leaving four remaining. Ravenna smiled. He had landed the first two Brunt kills of the night.

Would her prediction stand firm? The contestant pulled his blades back and ducked, dodging the two men that now cornered him on the small platform. With serpents behind him and metal spikes on the two remaining open sides, he maneuvered skillfully. To Ravenna's surprise, the contestant was able to shove one soldier off onto the metal that protruded from the ground below. As he advanced toward the ladder that led to the first tower, the remaining soldier at his heels closed the gap. The contestant spun around on the ladder to aim a dagger at his persistent, approaching enemy, and Ravenna saw the flicker of a smile on his lips.

"Send more men!" the crowd hissed, urging more soldiers to replenish the ones the contestant had cut down. The awaiting contestants grew furious as he neared the end of the Gauntlet. In the unfairness of it all, more Brunt soldiers entered the course.

With a flick of his wrist, his dagger rang true, finding its target in the heart of another Brunt soldier.

Ravenna stilled. *No.* He could not win. With only two more soldiers between him and the bloodstone, her chance of cashing it in for her freedom was diminishing. The Gauntlet was rumored to claim *dozens* of lives each year, and contestant *seven* of the night was about to succeed. She could not allow it. She *needed* that bloodstone.

Just as the mysterious man began ascending the next ladder to the towers and more soldiers filled the course, Ravenna wrapped the fabric of her black shawl around her face and jumped from the roof, shoving her way through the crowd.

Her bare feet smacked against the frigid sunstone as she wove in and out of the masses of people. After a few grueling seconds, she found herself at the foot of the platform. The soldiers and the crowd were too occupied with contestant seven to notice her. Her heart thundered in her chest, a fair warning. But the thrill of it all kept her moving forward, and she let the adrenaline in her veins soothe her as she scaled her way to the top of the first platform.

She was like a gust of wind, across the hot coals in the blink of an eye before she could even comprehend what she was doing. Within mere seconds, the crowd's attention gravitated toward her, and some began yelling, some cursing, that a woman had begun the Gauntlet. Women were not permitted to partake in the challenge.

Ravenna smiled.

Dozens of soldiers surrounded the Gauntlet and joined the others, unsure if they should pursue the man who was about to claim the stone, or the audacious woman who was running directly toward them with the promise of death in her gaze. She let out a low laugh as her feet hit the ground just beyond the fire. Sliding slightly on the sand but quickly regaining her footing, she shimmied across the log as it twisted and turned in an attempt to throw her to the snakes that crept below. She did not dare look down.

At the next platform she would face eight men. They all crowded the tight space where she would be forced to enter onto the platform, no doubt ready to kill her or take her back to their commander. She would leap onto the metal prongs below before letting them imprison her in this city.

With no place to safely step onto the crowded platform, she had nowhere to go. She squatted down in one swift movement, making it appear to be a misstep. She let the log roll her until she was upside down beneath it. When the soldiers neared the edge to peer down into the pit, she was already moving, hanging by her arms underneath the platform and clambering up the other side at their backs.

The crowds roared at the soldiers. "Behind you!"

Ravenna used what little time she had to climb the ladder, reaching the top in a matter of seconds. She was so close. Her left hand reached for a dagger. Though her palms were sweaty, she tossed the blade. It found its mark in the leg of contestant number seven, who was preparing to leap to where the bloodstone lay on top of a wooden box on tower three. He winced as the blade sunk into the back of his calf and he fell forward. Ravenna sped toward him, leaping from tower to tower and using her hands to balance each landing. Again, she avoided glancing downward. There was no need for spikes or snakes below, the fall alone would kill her.

She landed next to the man whose leg she had just wounded and debated sending him over the edge. It would be a better death than the one the guards would grant once they reached him. But pesky remorse pinged in her gut, hitting her like a wave of heavy black waters.

His eyes were a raging hazel beneath his dark hair, and she could have sworn she recognized them. In that quick passing glance, despite the inconvenience she had caused him, he threw her a smirk as if he were impressed. She did not let herself fall into the distraction of his mysterious grin, but instead, gave him a smug look and leapt forward onto the top of the third tower where the bloodstone and her freedom awaited her.

Her fingers grasped it, the tiny, cool mineral quickly becoming slick against her palm. Without looking back, Ravenna descended to the ground. Some of the onlookers cheered. Most of them stood silently, mouths forming noiseless gasps as a group of two dozen soldiers barreled toward her.

Oh, no.

She ran, soldiers trailing her like rabid hounds after a fox. The city streets were hard to navigate at night, but she had to get out of the mobs. Men grabbed at her, trying to slow her down, but her legs hurled her through the masses. When she was finally spit out at the edge of the crowd, she did not look back.

"Have you gone mad?" a familiar, exasperated voice called out behind her as she turned a street corner.

She released a breath, spinning around to face her friend and insufferable guardian, Xan. He stood in the shadows of an alley, half concealed by a stack of crates, blond hair blown back and disheveled as if he had run his horse as fast as it could manage. He was visibly angry as he anticipated the fight they were about to indulge in. Judging by the whiteness of his usually sun-kissed face, he saw no way out of this alive.

"Xan? *Why are you here?*" Ravenna plunged toward him, catching up to where he stood waiting with wide eyes. Xan scoffed in disbelief at her ignorant question, and they squatted behind a crate as a group of soldiers rushed by.

"Why am *I* here?" His eyes crinkled at the edges as he looked up to the starry sky, as if searching for patience. "For the love of Light, Ravenna. Your mother will *kill* me."

"You are not in charge of monitoring my every move. I am allowed an evening to myself."

"I *am* in charge of monitoring your every move. It is quite literally my job, Venna. To protect you." When the soldiers were out of sight, he pulled her further into the alley, not hiding the annoyance on his face. "This is what you call an evening to yourself? Running the *Gauntlet*?"

She smirked, holding up the valuable bloodstone. "Running the Gauntlet, *without a scratch*," she corrected him. His eyes grew wide as he grabbed the stone to examine it.

"Well, now you've really ticked some people off. Taking the stone and, may I mention, throwing a dagger at the leader of the Ink Bloods."

What?

He tossed the bloodstone back to her and grasped her arm, maneuvering them further into the depths of the city. "Leith runs the Gauntlet almost every year, and you've just taken his prize and injured his leg. Let's just hope he doesn't find out where you reside, or all Vestele will be in danger."

Ravenna grimaced. How much had the man known of her when he had made his marriage proposal four years ago and was rejected? Had he recognized her this evening?

Xan's grip on her arm tightened, and he continued down the alley. He sighed. "You scared me tonight."

She did not remind him that the excitement of the evening was not over, as they had yet to escape the entire Brunt army. However, she did not and would not apologize. She had just proven all she needed to prove, and he still did not see the capabilities she had.

"Does my mother know?" She demanded. He crouched against the wall, concealed in shadow, and looked down at his hands, running his blade between his thumb and his forefinger.

Then, his muddy brown eyes met hers, barely illuminated under the darkness. "You can tell her yourself, if you wish."

She had planned on it. Oh, yes. She had planned on marching right into their cottage tonight and demanding her mother listen to the story of how she obtained the bloodstone and succeeded in the Gauntlet that so many of Vestele's strongest warriors had failed at.

"I *will* tell her. There is no way she can keep me from training with the warriors now."

"You can think that, but your mother is a stubborn woman," Xan said.

Ravenna knew that Xan would be held accountable and would be punished in some way, for the rules *she* had broken this evening. But to gain her freedom from the confines of her mother's diligent and constant oversight, she was willing to throw her friend to the wolves. She knew he understood, deep down. Though, Xan took his job very seriously and enjoyed it a little too much for Ravenna to see it as a burden on him. She also knew that her mother would initially be angered at her and label her decisions tonight as irresponsibility. But, once the shield-maiden thought it through that Ravenna had emerged from the impossible Gauntlet triumphant and had made

Vestele wealthier in the process, her stubborn mind was bound to be changed.

"She cannot deny that I am better than even she was at her strongest. I am better than you, and you're a warrior," Ravenna said.

Xan scoffed. "If we make it out of this alive, you're on," he challenged, unamused.

But they both knew it was the truth. Ravenna had succeeded him in skill years ago, and completing the Gauntlet tonight unscathed was all the proof she needed that she deserved a position with the warriors.

"Tonight was about more than my place with the warriors, Xan. You know she is pushing me to marry." Xan averted his eyes, and Ravenna watched his throat bob.

"I want to choose my own fate. I want freedom." She kicked the dirt, scattering dust. "I deserve to choose." Xan kept his face turned from her, but she refused to stop. "I do not want to steal her title. But when the day comes, is the position not rightfully mine?"

Xan shifted against the wall, and when he finally looked at her, there was sadness in his gaze—because he knew a shield-maiden could not marry.

"Yes, Venna. You have earned it." To hear him say those words of approval was all the affirmation she needed.

But even if she had not been able to prove to Xan or her mother that she was worthy, she had proven to *herself* that she was worthy of a life full of excitement and freedom, and that she could handle the responsibility of being shield-maiden if she dared.

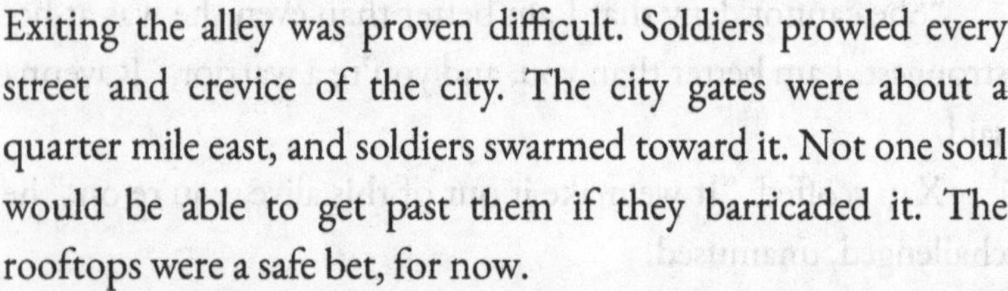

Exiting the alley was proven difficult. Soldiers prowled every street and crevice of the city. The city gates were about a quarter mile east, and soldiers swarmed toward it. Not one soul would be able to get past them if they barricaded it. The rooftops were a safe bet, for now.

Ravenna began climbing, using anything she could to hoist herself and then Xan up onto the roof of an apothecary. Their footsteps were not silent but were quiet enough amidst the chaos below. Xan cursed under his breath behind her as they monitored the growing mass of soldiers at the gate. Their only exit. The soldiers would not let her carry the bloodstone out of the city, though she could argue that she had won it fairly.

Under her bare feet, one of the clay shingles of the roof cracked and slid. She lunged for it, trying to stop the inevitable. It clanked, bouncing off the edge of the gutter and falling to the street, shattering. If they had been lucky, no one would have heard it.

But the dooming sound echoed into the ears of many. Soldiers began pointing to the roof, and Xan immediately yanked her backward, retreating onto the back side of the building.

"If we get a running start, we can make it to the next roof," Xan whispered. "We'll keep going until we reach the temple, near the gate. Then we'll climb down the far side before they can trap us."

"I'm sure they'll have the gate barricaded by the time we get there," she snapped.

"Well, then we have to beat them," he said.

They backed up, jolted forward, and made the leap. The adrenaline she felt now was not exhilarating. Not with Xan involved. She would not let him be killed due to her mistakes.

"Xan, *go*! They didn't see you. *Just go*. Please!" she begged as he pulled her further into the city, leaping from roof to roof. He ignored her pleas, and though the thought of him being killed because of her made her stomach churn, she kept going along with him, secretly thankful for his company.

She was, for once, glad he had come after her. She knew he would have done it whether it was his *job* assigned to him by her mother or not, however official or unofficial that title may be. Her mother was Ashreya of the Valley, shield-maiden to Vestele and all its warriors, and she had asked Xan to watch out for her daughter, so he did. Always.

They ran across the rooftops together until there were no more buildings, until dozens of soldiers mobbed the streets below and yelled slurs at them as they awaited their descent. It was not until soldiers had them cornered on all sides, a few of them beginning the ascent to the rooftops, that Ravenna realized it was over. Despite the cool winter air, sweat beaded on her forehead. Perhaps they would be hung in the streets tomorrow morning, side by side. She squeezed Xan's hand.

Just as a brawny soldier reached them, sword drawn, Ravenna drew hers. She and Xan were trained in fighting. *Well-trained*. In fact, if she was now the best warrior in Vestele, he was second best. He could challenge Ashreya tonight if he pleased and take the position of shield-master.

Though Ravenna's mother did not allow her to train *with* the warriors, Ravenna had trained with Xan *as* a warrior. They trained in every spare moment together by the fork in the river. He had taught her to defend herself and how to kill. He had even taught her how to start a fight, if needed. She had used that skill in the taverns many times.

She recognized the apprehension in his gaze as a fear for her life, not his own. After an exchange of unspoken words, she struck the nearest soldier right as Xan chucked a dagger into the throat of one on the ladder. The two of them moved in a perfect, choreographed dance of blows and swipes. They would not go down without a fight.

"Duck!" Xan yelled as he swung a knife where her head had been. Soldier after soldier piled onto the roof while the legion below grew denser in numbers. Her attention remained focused on the immediate threats of swords swiping at the unprotected parts of her body, where her leathers and the fur from her cloak were thinnest.

Dozens of men surrounded them on the rooftop, gathering like moths to a flame. Locals and witnesses roared on the streets, watching the fight unfold. A soldier grabbed her arm, yanking her sideways, and she looped her leg through his before he could think. They both fell near the edge of the roof, and she kicked him, sending him over the edge without remorse.

"Seize them already!" one of the men yelled. She rose again, this time careful to keep the men at a blade's length. But as hard as she tried, the roof was crowded, and they were surrounded.

There are far too many soldiers. We will never be able to fight them all off.

Right as she crouched to avoid the slice of a sword from the scrawny Brunt soldier in front of her, an arrow from one of his own men came flying by on a strange gust of wind, burying itself in his chest. The soldier's sword clanked against the rooftop, and she smirked, picking it up, the once-gemmed hilt large in her small hand.

Soon, there would not even be enough room to swing a blade. The two of them were doomed, two sparks against a raging sea. Her hand wrapped around the bloodstone. Xan was still at her back, holding his own and keeping the swarm of soldiers at bay. It was only when she was pulled from him in an abrupt motion that he halted, spinning to face her as she stood in the grasp of a soldier with a blade to her throat. The soldier pried the sword from her fingers. A trickle of blood slipped down her neck, and for the first time in her entire life, Ravenna surrendered.

2

LIGHT THE WAY HOME
RAVENNA

With the knife pricking at her throat, Ravenna was doubtful of any chance at escape. Tomorrow morning, her mother would realize neither of them were in Vestele and would send out a search party of Vestelian warriors. The shield-maiden would be at the front of it and would likely be the one to find Fintah near the outskirts of the forest just outside of the Brunts, where the mare would be awaiting Ravenna's improbable return. Only after finding Fintah abandoned, and then entering the city through the gates, would her mother understand the full extent of what had happened. When she saw Xan and her daughters' bodies hanging limp in the city gallows, she would put two and two together. Her reckless daughter had run the Gauntlet.

Ravenna was going to be sick. She could already taste the bitterness of dishonor on her tongue. She had come here to make her mother proud and to gain her respect by saving Vestele from starvation.

I am to be plagued with a dishonorable death, she thought.

Dishonorable or not, the city of the Brunts would pay for hurting her, she was sure of that. Her mother would avenge her death by stringing up every Brunt soldier she could find. Oh, how Ravenna wished she could participate in bringing the city to its knees for the sins its people had committed. Not only had they captured her and ruined her plans, but the misogyny within the walls of this city was endless, and the cruelty to the Ember race here, egregious. The Brunts captured and delivered more Embers to Oro than any other city across Arresia.

"Climb down or we'll cut her!" the Brunt soldier spat at Xan.

The soldiers led Xan down the ladder first, and Ravenna kept her eyes on him the entirety of his descent. The knife continued to prick the skin on her throat, and the trail of blood began to soak into the collar of her tunic beneath her cloak. Ravenna kept track of the sword that was now moving toward her back to force her down the ladder.

It was safe to bet that every single soldier in the city was within a stone's throw of them, marching them toward the keep, where she knew their beloved commander resided. She and Xan would be delivered to him to receive their sentence. Ravenna breathed in deeply as they passed by another group of shackled Embers—headed out of the city to Oro. Ravenna had never seen so many at once, their glowing marks shining against the darkness.

One of the soldiers that she recognized from the Gauntlet ripped the cloth from her face, uncovering her mouth. "You're a fool to think you could outsmart us—a pathetic woman. You have no place in the Gauntlet."

She took the chance to spit at him and did not look away from his dreadful gray eyes that held no color. He stepped forward and raised a hand as if readying to smack her. Ravenna only cocked her head at him with a challenge in her gaze. Xan stiffened beside her at the threat, and the soldier directed his attention to where he stood at Ravenna's right. He then looked back to Ravenna with a smug smile before plummeting the smack meant for her into Xan's temple. She clenched her jaw as she watched Xan waver.

He'll be fine, she assured herself. She had hit him harder many times before.

They continued forward through the icy, sunstone streets between the many buildings of the Brunts. Snow began falling from the sky, flakes finding their homes in her eyelashes. Her breath fogged in front of her like smoke, and she thought for a moment, *if I could breathe fire like some Embers are rumored to, I would smite the soldiers right here*. She had never witnessed such things, but the stories she had heard of the gifted ones sparked her curiosity.

"We have them," one of the soldiers called to the guards that stood outside of the tall walnut doors of Commander Hendrik's keep. Two massive pillars shot up from the top step until they reached the roof. Inside, to Ravenna's surprise, the ceiling was ornately decorated. Carvings and depictions of the many goddesses, witches, and idols of the Shades spread across the surface above, coming together in the center to meet a chandelier of black stone and bronze. The bronze matched the two siren statues on either side of the entrance, and Ravenna marveled at the design. It was decorated how she would imagine the Black Temple to be on the inside.

"I see where all the money goes," Ravenna muttered to Xan. It was as if the commander had kept every cent the city had for himself and used it to fill his beloved keep with decadent and lavish items. The complex architectural design had surely taken years to finish, but with the free labor of his many Ember slaves, it was not surprising.

"Shut up, or I'll knock him out," a soldier said.

"Do your worst," she said, calling the soldiers bluff. Xan gave her an incredulous look.

What? she mouthed innocently, shrugging her shoulders. As Ravenna suspected, the soldier did not bother.

It was not until they were well within the black stone walls of the building that she began to feel doomed, trapped permanently as they tunneled into darkness. The light of the two moons did not seep through the narrow windows, so they walked only by candlelight. Xan's gaze bore into the blade at her back as if he might move it with his mind.

Hands clasped her shoulders as the blade withdrew from her spine. She was jolted forward through a narrow hall that led to an elaborate but considerably small room. Voices echoed from inside.

"We finally received our new shipment of spelled shackles this morning from Oro. The Embers are ready to ship out at dawn."

In response, there was only a grunt, and then a pause— perhaps at the sound of the soldiers' heels clicking against the stone as they brought Ravenna forth.

Only two soldiers remained with her; the space was much too tight for any more men. She heard Xan begin to protest from where he was detained in the hall, then he quieted down at the crack of a fist. Ravenna winced, and tried to look back to make sure he was still upright. But brute force shoved her forward until he was just out of sight. Her legs brushed up against a large table. It filled most of the room that must have been designed for council meetings of some degree.

She stood at the foot of the table, eyes finding the gaze of a cruel looking, middle-aged man who appeared to be high ranking. The soldiers beside him bowed their heads in his presence. Faint, swirly shadowmarks on his forearm marked him as a Despiri. Ravenna guessed this was Commander Hendrik. Why would he not be a Despiri when he was wealthy enough to purchase a kill in the trades?

"You are the woman who completed the Gauntlet?" he asked, unconvinced. He mistook her femininity for weakness as she stood between his two burly men. She said nothing. "*You* are the *woman*," Hendrik spat, "who ruined my games?" Ice formed at his fingertips as his blood boiled.

Ravenna's breath caught in her chest, and she watched him closely, giving no response to his questions. He raised one of his hands, silently instructing his men. Another blade found its way to her throat, and a wry smile crept onto her lips.

"Let's try this again," he breathed deeply. "Where is my bloodstone?" Rage coated his tongue.

"It was lost in the excitement," Ravenna said, cocking her head to the side.

He licked his mouth before continuing. "Who is the man that escorts you?"

"My brother." Not friend. Not husband. No, brother. Because being a husband would surely earn him death, and they would not believe him to be just a friend.

"I do not appreciate being lied to. My *bloodstone*," Hendrik reiterated in growing frustration, opening his frosted palm toward her, awaiting the stone. Ravenna wondered what exactly he used his gift of ice for, and why he had chosen that one out of the whole stock of Embers.

She did not answer him, and the cut on her throat grew slightly with the added pressure of the knife.

"Please." The pressure lessened at Hendrik's spoken command. "At least check her for lightmarks before you kill her. And get my bloodstone back," he added.

Lightmarks? As if I could be one of the gifted Embers? So he can slap shackles on me and sell me into the Ember Trades in the Kingdom of Oro?

The soldiers began robbing Ravenna of her cloak, roughly grabbing her arms and examining her for any glowing mark that would identify her as an Ember.

"If I were an Ember," she said as they searched her empty pockets and her clothes for the bloodstone, "do you not think I would have used my magic against you by now?" Their strong grips bruised her skin. She watched them fuss over her in perplexity as they pulled her collar to the side to examine her upper back and shoulder.

If she were an Ember, they would most definitely sell her into the upcoming Ember Trade. The reminder that they did such things sent her anger swelling.

A faint, winter breeze whispered through the window. The soldiers began to rip at her tunic, and she twisted out of their grasp. They were foolish to underestimate her after she had just finished running their *impossible* Gauntlet.

Her hand found the long sword in the belt of the soldier at her left, and she swung its hilt backward into the other soldier's nose. He was sent staggering against the wall. But before she could strike again, a rumble shook the keep, and her footing suddenly grew clumsy.

What is going on?

A piece of stone crashed down from the ceiling. It landed right atop Commander Hendrik. Ravenna stumbled back as the ground shook with a deep rage. The entire keep began to move, the stone beneath her feet trembling. The two soldiers she had been fighting abandoned her and rushed to Hendrik, trying to free his lifeless body from under the heavy rock. She stared into the hall, lowering her brows and studying the walls to determine if she was seeing correctly.

Yes.

The walls of the keep were beginning to *shake*. As a crack snaked up the stone to her right, she grabbed her cloak, sprinting for the only exit she knew.

Ravenna heard swearing from the four soldiers who still held Xan, and two of them left his side to run past Ravenna and toward the commander who lay dead in his chair. Xan's face was that of pure panic as she rounded the corner and slung the stolen sword across one of the soldier's legs. He buckled, and Xan whirled on the other, knocking him down with a swift elbow to the face.

"Ravenna, run!" Xan yelled. "Don't stop!"

Her bare feet flew forward, one after the other, death at her heels. Her racing heart filled her veins with panic as the beautifully carved stone ceiling began to crash to the floor in pieces. She urged her legs to move faster, and she flew out the doors between the fallen bronze sirens, Xan right behind her.

Chaos had broken out in the street. Ravenna glanced to the side at Xan, then began running toward the gates, sprinting faster and faster as the city fell behind them in a mass of tumbling rock. Her knees gave out from under her as the ground shifted, and Xan hauled her up, dragging her along for a few steps until she regained her footing. Screams of pain and agony carried on the wind as the city residents were crushed under stone and fallen pillars. Even the Black Temple—bragged to be indestructible—went up in a plume of dust.

"Keep going!" Xan said, pushing her through her shock as the temple stones crumbled at their left. Ravenna had never thought she would recognize an earthquake as a blessing, and she did not particularly believe in a higher power, but she took a moment to thank whatever force had sent it and bought them enough time to escape. She only looked back once as the keep crumbled down upon every soldier that had just run inside, searching for their beloved commander. Chunks of stone now laid across bodies, trapping them beneath the wreckage. Ravenna raced through the gates toward Fintah and Xan's horse that had been left beside her. No soldier tried to stop them.

The entire city collapsed, the gates falling last. Clouds of dust and debris rushed past the walls of the Brunts, filling the clear night sky with a haze that could be seen for miles. Flocks of ravens rushed past her, ready to pick the flesh from the bones of the fallen before the ground had even finished quaking. Xan did not allow her time for gawking as he shoved her toward Fintah and tried to hoist her onto the mare's back.

"I've got it!" she snapped, annoyed at the urgency that his hands on her waist displayed. There were no Brunt soldiers left to follow them. They had made it. It was only once they were mounted and racing toward Vestele that Xan looked at her and a smile sprung onto her face.

"Ha!" she bellowed, racing alongside him and plucking the small bloodstone from the hilt of the stolen sword. A hesitant grin spread across his scar-flecked face. Amusement crept into his brown eyes, though he rolled them in a façade of annoyance.

"How did you manage that?" he asked beneath a breathy laugh.

On the rooftop, she had noticed the sword was missing a gem from its hilt as it had clanked to the ground before its fallen wielder. She had seen no way out, not without running and risking the entirety of the Brunt army following them to Vestele. So, she had bent to retrieve it and had exposed herself in the process, while she clicked the bloodstone into place and allowed the men to take her captive. She had known it would be easier to escape once they were taken to the commander and most of the army had been dismissed.

She shrugged. "I won't reveal my secrets."

Xan's gray horse, Alf, was at a full sprint, and though he was a male, Fintah towered over him.

"Life sure would be boring if I stayed in Vestele and only did as I was told." Ravenna grinned, urging Fintah on past Xan. Their laughter carried through the valley. It bounced between the golden oak trees of the Sunstone Forest on their right and absorbed into the blackness of the Dead Wood and the Black Rock Mountains on their left, where only bare trees stood tall, twisted and winding.

The two half-moons were making their way lower and lower into the night sky, and the stars shone bright. It was a winter night clear enough for billions of stars to light the way home, *toward Vestele*. Ravenna looked back only once, at the havoc wreaking the Brunts. She smiled, turning the stone over in her palm and clenching her newfound freedom in her fist. She had always hated that city.

3

THE BLOODSTONE
RAVENNA

Just before dawn, Ravenna slowly pushed open the creaky wooden door to the cottage, careful not to wake her mother. Unfortunately, the shield-maiden had waited up for her.

"You lied to me," her mother said from where she sat on the edge of their bed, eyes flitting to Ravenna's throat, where she had forgotten to conceal the small cut. Her mother's face was tired with worry.

Ravenna clenched her jaw, shutting the door against the frigid wind. The one room cottage was warm, and she was thankful for the fire still raging in the hearth.

"I went to your workshop; you hadn't even thrown one pot. Xan must've noticed your absence before I did because he was already gone by the time I sent for him."

Ravenna laid her cloak over the rocking chair. "Don't blame Xan," she said, warming her hands in front of the fire.

Her mother ignored her statement. "I don't make these rules to ruin your life, Ravenna. They are set in place to keep you safe. You are to stay within the boundaries of the village. I will not tell you again." Her voice was stern and unwavering.

"Or what, Mama? You'll force me to marry?"

Her mother winced. "I'm not speaking with you about this right now."

"No, please do, because I am dying to know what you have planned for my future."

"Ravenna Zenevieva. As shield-maiden, I cannot marry. As shield-maiden's daughter, you can. If for an alliance that can help our people—"

"I *love* our clan, Mama. But I will *not* marry. If you were so worried about an alliance, why did you turn down Leith of the Ink Bloods' proposal before I even caught wind of it four years ago? They are the strongest clan south of Oro—that alliance would have helped us, yet you turned it down. Why?"

Her mother had always been adamant about self-sufficiency and did her best to make sure Vestele never encountered other clans or experienced altercations. Avoidance was key, though the shield-maiden had often explored the idea of marriage alliances that could benefit them. Each had been turned down, though.

"I considered it, Ravenna. I did. But they are dangerous..."

"I am aware. But they proposed an *alliance*. To have them on our side, with their wealth, cattle, crops, strength..." *Why am I even arguing?* she wondered. She was grateful her mother had turned the proposal down. But none of it was adding up.

"Ravenna, not now."

Ravenna pulled the bloodstone from the pocket of her cloak that she had draped over the chair. She sat it on the table.

Her mother's eyes flashed with rage. "Get that out of my house," she hissed.

Ravenna stood her ground. "I ran the *Gauntlet* tonight. This bloodstone could easily be worth a few gold ravens," Ravenna said, repeating what she had heard in the Brunts.

"More," her mother said bluntly. Ravenna glanced down at the speckled red rock on the rickety wooden table they had eaten so many meals at, but her mother held her gaze. "You have no idea, child, what that stone is worth to some."

She knew what her mother referred to, of the matters of life and death that plagued the Ember race.

"You may have proven yourself a great warrior. Maybe you are even the best. But I will have nothing to do with such atrocities, and that stone is to be destroyed. Not sold. Not kept. *Destroyed.*"

"But Mama..." Ravenna reached to grab it from the table, and her mother shot her a look. Her mother was so careful not to get involved in the politics and conflicts of Arresia. Ravenna could not stand it. The words were out before she knew she was thinking them. "If I were in your position—I would do something. I would help our people, and when we were strong enough, we would fight for the Embers."

"Be careful how you speak to me, Ravenna. Our people come first. Fighting for the Embers would endanger our clan. There is a reason you are not in my position," she spat.

"If our people come first, why not purchase a new plot of land—one that we can live off? Why let them starve? Why turn down an alliance with the Ink Bloods?"

Her mother stopped her with another glare. Ravenna dreamed of a lush, green hillside in southern Oro where the crops would grow without difficulty and her people would have plenty of food. Where the land was far enough from the mountains that the towering hills would block out only the first and last hour of light in the day.

"Vestele remains here where we are hidden in the valley. To leave and make our location known to the dark world would be foolish, child."

At that, Ravenna bit her tongue. Vestele had no place on the map she had secretly purchased in the Brunts months ago. Travelers never passed through due to the rocky terrain and the high elevations the valley lay between. She had to admit it to be a safe location, if her mother truly believed the world around them to be so dangerous.

She understood her mother's concern. Especially because the powerful gifts of the Embers and Despiri made them a threat to Vestele, whose people possessed no such things. It was part of the reason her mother had made it her mission to train the warriors to be the strongest in all of Oro's territories. What infuriated her the most was, her mother was aware she could hold her own. She had watched her train with Xan many times. Ravenna may not have been permitted to fight with the warriors, but she had still been allowed, *encouraged*, by her mother to train with her friend daily and learn to defend herself. Those lessons of *self-defense* had escalated more than her mother realized.

Her mother's face softened after a long moment, and she added, "I was forced at a young age to fight, Ravenna. I do not wish you to be forced into this life. Once you enter, there is no going back. I only want you to be safe. *Free*."

Ravenna rolled her eyes at her mother's words. "Free?" she asked incredulously. "But I am to marry? For the sake of an alliance? *Freedom*—but only within the confines of marriage." She scoffed. "Or even marriage with no alliance. Lately you've been speaking of me marrying within our clan. Xan?" Her mother looked away. "I think you just want to marry me off and quell my chances of taking your position as shield-maiden," Ravenna spat.

"Enough!" her mother said through gritted teeth. Her mother rose and smacked a fist onto the table. The bloodstone rattled. Now they were getting somewhere. "Only if a marriage is what it takes to keep you safe. With my life—I will keep you safe." Tears flooded her mother's jade-green eyes. "I will not lose you like I lost your father," she said, her hand drifting to her stomach. "You will not fight. You know the promise I made to him."

The promise that she would start anew with a different clan, Vestele, after the last big war, and do whatever it took to keep Ravenna safe. Her mother had approached that promise with extreme and utter devotion every day since. Her mother was a warrior of stone—never wavering. Shield-maiden, leader, and protector of her clan. But mostly, a shield for Ravenna.

Ravenna reached for her mother's hand. "I'm sorry, Mama." And she was. But Ravenna was certain that her skill level had reached that of her mother's long ago, and she would not take no for an answer. She no longer wished to be shielded. Her place was with the warriors, whether her mother would admit it or not.

4
PAPER BIRDS
XAN

Sweet echoes of a fiddle's melody swept through the morning breeze, whispering amongst the distant caw of a raven. Xan smiled to himself.

"Glad to hear her play again," Roarke grunted, nodding toward the open window above the bakery, where Ravenna's music poured out into the valley. "It's been a while," the burly man said, scratching his coarse red beard.

Ashreya chatted with Asta—the clan baker—at the bakery door for a moment, and a rare smile spread across her face as she beamed with pride at her daughter's talent that echoed down the stairs. Ashreya's hair was black but styled like Ravenna's—and most of the women's in Vestele. Dozens of different sized braids, decadent with beads of brass. Her arms were crossed, and her furs laid over her shoulders, protecting her against the chilly air.

Breakfast would be brought out soon by Asta and her daughter Tenille. Then, the warriors would begin the day's training. The warriors were gathered around the center fire, telling stories of creatures and beasts forged in darkness that roamed the caves and forests of Arresia.

"They are massive. The size of two grown men. With exposed ribs and rotting black flesh," Erik said to the youngest warriors, who stared with wide eyes as he spoke of the witch guardians.

"Have you ever seen one?" Xan asked Erik, raising a brow.

"No, I haven't but..."

"No one has," Xan said, trying to reassure the trembling boys. "And besides, the legends say they only harm you if you kill one. So don't."

The boys nodded quietly, and Xan rolled his eyes at Erik. "Quit trying to scare them." Erik threw his hands up in innocence.

When Xan finished sharpening his knife, he pulled a piece of paper from his cloak. The fire warmed his hands against the late winter air, and he began folding.

"Oh, here he goes again with his paper birds," Nilo said beside him with a wide grin. The warrior's brows shifted beneath his dark hair as he teased Xan. Xan shook his head as his fellow warriors began to laugh, but he continued forming the wings of the dove. The art of paper folding was the only joy he had retained from his childhood, from before his village went up in flames. In the days before the fires, he would often sit and learn to fold with his mother's older sister who had long, copper hair. His aunt, who had been joyous as sunlight before the fires took her.

"Maybe you guys should get hobbies. Perhaps training is not keeping you busy enough?" They all quieted at the underlying threat: that he could make today's training utterly miserable.

The caws of the raven grew closer, and with it, the warriors around the fire stiffened.

"It's a message," Roarke said, rising to his feet to greet the incoming bird. He looked to Ashreya, who was already approaching quickly with Asta not too far behind.

"And so it begins," one of the warriors muttered. "It's probably news that the Ink Bloods are planning to kill us all, because *someone* cannot keep tabs on Ravenna." The warrior nodded to Xan.

Xan rolled his eyes. "I'd like to see *you* try," he said. The raven landed, dropping the small, rolled parchment from its talons. Ashreya grabbed it and unfurled it in her hands.

The warriors had been on high alert for weeks—ever since the incident in the Brunts. Xan had not had to tell anyone of Leith's presence at the Gauntlet. It was a well-known fact that the leader attended every year and won each time he competed. But, when Ashreya had asked Xan about the events of the night the morning after he and Ravenna's return from the Brunts, he had felt it necessary to mention that her rebel daughter had stabbed the man.

"What is it, Ash?" Roarke asked, stepping closer to her. Her green eyes pierced through the words in a mixture of unreadable emotions. She handed him the paper.

"Council meeting, now," she commanded. Every warrior around the fire immediately picked up their belongings and scattered, leaving the discussion to Ashreya and her trusted council, which consisted of Xan, Ashreya's second Roarke, and her best friend Asta.

"Word came from our spy in Oro," Ashreya said. "Gerrin and Willa Ozanne are being transferred." The shield-maiden took the message back from Roarke and handed it to Xan.

Despiri are set to be traveling north with the King and Queen of Ozanna.

Map provided by the navigator sets their path right through the valley.

Be careful, Ash, and don't do anything stupid.

The message was written in red ink and stamped with a feather signum. Xan gritted his teeth. As if the shield-maiden's daughter attacking an Ink Blood were not enough to stress him. "When will they be here?" he asked.

"If they are traveling from the prison, we might have a week to prepare," Roarke said.

Ashreya nodded. "I'll send word to our men in the south. They can update us with a more absolute timeline."

"Send the Vestelian warriors south. We'll reroute them," Xan said.

"*You* won't be going anywhere. Ravenna will not leave your sight," Ashreya snapped.

"Agreed," said Asta.

Xan nodded, breathing tightly and fidgeting with the paper dove. "What does Degare want with the ex-royals, anyway? Why move them now after holding them captive all this time?"

Asta toyed with a graying braid and spoke quietly, "They were once very powerful Embers—known across Arresia. Perhaps this is just a power play to show the remaining kingdoms of Light his dominion over them. Perhaps he plans to kill them and claim their gifts..."

"It doesn't matter," Ashreya interrupted, waving Asta's theories off. "This situation must be monitored carefully. We will intercept them."

"And do what?" Xan said quickly. "What can we do against a group of Despiri?" *Is she out of her mind?*

Ashreya held up a bloodstone—the one Ravenna had just obtained in the Gauntlet.

Yes, she is insane. Now, I know where Ravenna gets it from.

"No way," Asta said.

"I have witch ancestry. I can draw power from the bloodstone, I've done it before," Ashreya said.

Xan grimaced. Ashreya put the small, jagged bloodstone back into her pocket and adjusted her cloak.

"Enough power to fight against an entire squad of Despiri?" Xan asked incredulously.

"How do you know it will work?" Roarke asked, arms crossed.

Asta started again, "Even with the stone, you'll be weak. Especially against a group of Despiri. That bloodstone is not pure."

"Everyone, quiet," Ashreya ordered. The three of them fell silent. "I have a spell. It allows a link to be made between a group of three or more. Once the link is made, and the spell learns the traits of the gifts of the Despiri, I can extend the link to the entire Despiri race."

"Then what?" Xan asked.

"Then," she said, glaring at Xan, "all we have to kill is *one.*"

Roarke narrowed his eyes in disbelief. "It seems too easy."

"And like it would take more power than that bloodstone can provide," Asta said.

"I have witch blood. I don't need to worship the goddesses to draw power from the darkness. Combined with that and the stone—"

Roarke interrupted her. "The moons do not go into shadow for several more weeks."

"Roarke is right," Asta said. "There will not be enough power in the night."

Xan knew little about witches and magic, but this did not sound like a safe plan.

"I don't like it," Xan argued. "It sounds like a death wish."

Ashreya looked to Roarke, whose hazel eyes were swelling with sadness. Asta breathed in deeply, and Xan just awaited confirmation that Ashreya was going to null their votes—that she was going to play diplomat on this one.

"You have to let me try," she said.

The next afternoon at training, Ashreya pulled Xan aside.

"Listen. You are like a son to me," she said with her hand gripping his. Xan bit his cheek.

When he and his parents had lived on the outskirts of Ozanna, and his father had died defending the kingdom those two decades ago—when Xan and his mother had hidden in the cellar of their home as the witch army attacked outside, and their home had been set fire—when Xan had watched his mother take her last breaths in that smoke, and he had been orphaned at five years old, it had been Ashreya that found him two days later under the rubble.

He had lived with Ashreya and Ravenna until he was twelve and could join the other unmarried warriors in the longhouse. Ravenna was only seven when he had left. To Ravenna, he was a friend, maybe even an older brother. But to Xan, Ravenna was the very breath in his lungs.

"I trust you with my daughter's life—you are her sworn protector. But you are also like a son to me. I have no issue keeping you out of the path of imminent danger. You're going to tell Ravenna she may train with the warriors." Xan shifted on his feet; unsure he was hearing correctly.

"When the Despiri are to enter Vestele, I will send you and Ravenna out of their path. On watch as warriors, far from here. She won't suspect a thing, and you'll both be safe until the Despiri are dead."

He tried to imagine it, a world where there was no threat like the Despiri. Where the Embers may reign again, and the Light would return to Arresia. He did not buy it. "I'll protect your daughter with my life. You know that. But I don't want to risk yours."

"I can do this. All warriors have been ordered to stand down. Do not engage," she said sternly. Then, she smiled softly and placed a gentle hand on his cheek. "I'll be fine on my own. Now go tell Ravenna she can join us."

5

WARRIOR

RAVENNA

After breaking through ice to gather clay from the river bottom and hauling it back to her small workroom in the village, Ravenna's eyelids grew heavy. She woke hours before the sun this morning, routine nightmares rendering her unable to find sleep again.

Creating pottery came naturally to her, as she had spent many days since her youth creating pots and basins for any use one could think of. Wash basins, pots for carrying water, pots for cooking, and eating, and gathering berries. She did not care how her pieces were used. She only cared that they were deemed useful in some way since Vestele did not barter with other clans and was always in need of materials. It was one of the few ways she felt she had contributed to her self-sufficient village, though her heart lay with the warriors. Molding pottery day by day in her workroom above the bakery felt insignificant next to their great contribution.

"I've been searching all over for you," Xan said behind her as he ascended the stairs, irritation coating his voice. The scent of fresh baked bread followed him as he stepped into her workroom. She heard him rub his hands together, then blow warm breath into them. She kept her back to him, coating her messy hands in a little more water before adding the moisture to the clay she molded.

The early afternoon sun had begun to peak over the mountains, shining down through the haze and into the window to warm her skin. She did not wish to hear his lectures about how she must be careful. He had been particularly insufferable with his excessive protection since they had barely made it out of the Brunts alive two weeks ago. Miraculously, Vestele had suffered no damage from the earthquake despite being only a few miles east in the valley.

"My mother is aware of my whereabouts," she stated flatly, turning the wheel with her foot. It was true, her mother had woken as she had tried to sneak out of their shared bed this morning.

"Relax." Ravenna had assured her. "I'm just going to the river."

It had been a miracle that her mother had allowed her out without an official escort. But, the river was within Vestele's guarded boundaries, and therefore, deemed safe by the shield-maiden's ridiculous standards. Ravenna was also acutely aware of the guards that had watched her extra diligently lately. She knew that one currently stood just downstairs outside the bakery door, keeping track of her every movement.

Being the shield-maiden's daughter did not make her a princess or royalty, or anything close. It only ensured the entire clan was fearful enough of her mother to guarantee nothing ill happened to Ravenna. Her mother had earned the reverence of the entirety of Vestele, and Ravenna was certain each and every

Vestelian would follow any command their shield-maiden gave, no matter how absurd. So, for the past couple of weeks especially, Ravenna had been followed throughout the village, with eyes always monitoring her. She knew no privacy.

Xan spoke again. "Why so glib? I come bearing great news, Venna."

She smoothed the rounded edges of the stout pot she molded, then tilted her chin, awaiting his next sentence.

He ran his finger through the clay dust that had collected on the table. "Your mother has agreed to allow you to train with the warriors."

Her pot collapsed into itself, and Ravenna stood.

"You're kidding." He shook his head, giving her a tight-lipped smile under raised brows. A grin spread across her face. She wondered what had changed her mother's mind. If she was honest, she did not care. She would not question it.

Leaping onto Xan, she wrapped him in a hug. He smiled against her neck, and his prickly chin scratched her skin.

"You've gotten clay all over me," he said with a tease to his voice as he pulled away and examined the front of his tunic. A quick flick to his nose sent a speck of gray clay flying onto his cheek. Ravenna smiled as his calloused hand wiped it clean. "Be on your best behavior," he warned.

She raised a pinky to indicate she did not anticipate messing up again anytime soon, then wiped her hands clean and pulled her cloak over her shoulders. Winter was coming to an end, and while still cold, the weather was growing warmer each day.

She pulled her hair into a simple, thick braid that snaked down the center of her head. She turned her back on Xan for a moment to grab her new blade—a plain sword from the clan's swordsmith to replace the one she had lost in the Brunts—from behind her pottery wheel. Along with her fiddle, the wheel had been a gift from her mother, a push toward the creative arts and away from the art and danger of fighting. To her own surprise, pottery and music had both become enjoyable hobbies. But hobbies were all they were.

She tensed as Xan began speaking again. "Of course, your mother is probably only allowing this out of fear she may need an extra warrior at the battlefronts when the Ink Bloods come for our heads."

Ravenna stiffened at the reminder of her foolish mistake in the Brunts, at the memory of her dagger finding the flesh of the Ink Blood leader. "Did you tell her?" she blurted, searching his face for any sign that he had spoken of the possible threat. She had not dared mention that tidbit of information to her mother in the heat of their argument those couple weeks ago.

He chuckled. "Relax, Venna. I didn't tell a soul." He opened the door and added over his shoulder, "Though maybe *you* should. It would be best if Vestele was not caught unaware in the case they did attack." She noted the way he leaned against the door frame and cracked his knuckles—as he often did when he was hiding the truth.

Ravenna narrowed her eyes on him and shrugged. "Not going to happen. Besides, Leith is probably long dead, anyway. There is no way he made it out of the city alive."

Xan raised his brows and nodded as if to undermine the hopeful thought, and she pulled the door shut. Downstairs, the bakery smelled like bread. Asta was baking a few loaves—prepping lunch for the clan—though there would not be enough. Her eyes crinkled at the edges as Ravenna came down the stairs behind Xan.

"Oh, just in time. Bread's warm. Have a piece," Asta offered, silver braids swaying as she sliced the end of a loaf. Ravenna's mouth watered as the steam rose into the air, and her stomach grumbled in response.

She shook her head. "No, thanks." Asta extended the piece to Xan. He declined it with a wave of his hand.

"You stubborn kids. You've got to eat. There is plenty," she lied.

"No time," Ravenna said, though time had little to do with her decision to ration what little food Vestele had left for the winter. "First day of training."

Asta raised her brows in surprise as Ravenna turned to follow Xan into the sunny afternoon streets of Vestele. Aside from the main street where the apothecary, bakery, blacksmith, and village kitchen were, Vestele consisted of only a couple dozen cottages and a few huts. Most of the unmarried warriors lived in the long house that was just behind her pottery workroom. She doubted she would be permitted to move into the longhouse with the warriors, but she did not care as long as she could train as one.

Twelve male warriors stood at the river with their broad, muscular backs to Ravenna. They appeared to have been sweating under the late morning and early afternoon skies for at least a couple of hours. Ravenna's mother was at the front of the group, face stoic and painted with the familiar markings she always bore, guiding the warriors through a maneuver while the other groups practiced archery and swordplay.

"I mastered this with you a long time ago," Ravenna said to Xan. "This'll be easy."

He chuckled.

Wooden staffs cut through the air with extreme precision, one after another. Back-to-back with a partner, moving like Ravenna imagined waves in the sea would move. But then, the entire horde of warriors began to move to the left, each one in sync with the movements of the partner adjacent to them. They began to form a circle as if combatting a common enemy in the center, and when they moved, they were fast as lightning. Together as one bolt, they struck, strength spreading between several tendrils of power. They beat the grass-stuffed dummy in the middle of the circle like it was a dance as they ducked below one another's swings and even leapt over strikes to avoid collision. They worked together as a unit, twisting and turning and striking—a team that could not be separated.

Still as stone, Ravenna watched in awe. In all the times she had left her workshop during the day to watch them train, she had never seen this exercise before.

Xan smiled next to her, nudging her with his elbow. "You have much to learn."

"I learn fast," she said, and she increased her speed as she strode toward her mother, eager to begin. She did not let that eagerness show on her face, not in front of the seasoned warriors—and certainly not when she and her mother's last real conversation had ended as it had.

Ashreya motioned for the warriors to halt and beckoned Ravenna forward. Without greeting, her mother handed her a wooden staff and guided her to a position in the circle. "This maneuver is helpful when battling an enemy much stronger than yourself. A Despiri, perhaps, or even an Ember. Move as one with your unit," she said to the warriors, raising a hand and dipping her chin.

The warriors surrounding Ravenna began swinging and ducking. It was no challenge. Her movements were fluid with the maneuvers of those around her. One by one, they each took turns battling the common enemy in a carefully plotted attack. Ravenna ducked and avoided the swipes of her neighbors. Xan's impressed gaze met hers across the circle, and she smirked, raising her brows.

Fast learner.

After a few rounds, her mother ordered the warriors to begin shooting arrows. On the tree line by the river where Ravenna had spent many hours, targets were set up for practice. Each warrior was assigned a target, and Ravenna stood with her bow, awaiting her turn. Xan went first, and then Nilo. Next, Erik and Freya, and the warriors continued down the line until it was Ravenna's turn. Her mother stood with her arms crossed, watching intently. Ravenna gripped the bow and slowly drew the string back. She took no longer than three seconds to aim. The arrow hit her target dead center, and then she moved to the left, aiming again. She heard the warriors begin to whisper behind her. Her second arrow flew, slicing right through the arrow in the target beside hers.

Bullseye.

"Impressive," Freya said behind her. Ravenna's lip tugged upward. She steadily moved down the line, her arrows obliterating those of the other warriors' targets.

"Show off!" Xan yelled as her arrow replaced his on the final target. She proudly turned, only to see her mother moving down the line of targets, doing the same with her own arrows.

"Ravenna," her mother called her from where she now

stood in front of the target to Ravenna's right. "A warrior is as weak as her ego is strong. Today you'll observe." Ravenna opened her mouth to argue, then immediately shut it, dropping her bow to her side. Her mother's voice did not soften. "Tomorrow, you will join again."

Hours went by, and Ravenna kept her eyes on Xan as he successfully completed each exercise. Jealousy writhed in her chest. Of all the days she had been forced to mold clay, fetch water, and pick berries, he fought fiercely among the other skilled fighters of Vestele. His body was that of a warrior, toned and strong, with years of experience.

The grasses whispered behind where Ravenna sat on a thick log, and then a familiar, bubbly voice rang out.

"Isn't he wonderful? Sometimes I come down here just to watch him move. It is like a dance," said Tenille.

Ravenna clenched her jaw. "Yeah, wonderful." Sarcasm laced her words. "Every time I've come to watch them train, my mother runs me off."

"I don't know why you're so insistent on training with them," Tenille said. "I could never do this all day. Keep me in the kitchens," Tenille said, handing Ravenna a mug of herbal tea. The healer was always mixing up concoctions and bringing them for Ravenna to taste. She found her place next to Ravenna on the log, then pondered for a moment. "But I guess it is natural to be drawn to what you're good at." She winked, nodding to Ravenna's sword.

Between exercises, Xan looked to where the two of them sat and waved, taunting Ravenna. Tenille's golden-brown cheeks reddened, and a smile spread wide across her face as she waved back. Ravenna shook her head, taking a sip of the tea.

"Ask him to marry you already," Ravenna said.

Tenille rolled her eyes. "No way, I want a man to *yearn* for me."

Ravenna wiggled her brows, then broke into a giggle. "What are you talking about? Are the three men who have already asked for your hand not enough? What about him?" Ravenna teased, nodding to Nilo, who could not keep his eyes from her. Ravenna knew he had already proposed marriage with no response from Tenille.

"Ravenna!" she whispered, playfully smacking her arm and ducking her head. "I don't want any of these other men. A soulbond is too precious, and I want it with Xan. That is...if you still don't care?"

Are we truly going to have this conversation again?

"Soulbonds are rare, if they even exist at all," Ravenna muttered. "He's all yours. I'm not marrying," Ravenna said for the hundredth time.

Tenille raised her brows, as if to say, *uh huh.*

"In fact," Ravenna said, "If you could hurry up and make him fall in love with you a little faster, I would not have to worry about my mother pawning me off to him."

"Oh, come on. A marriage to him would not be so bad. You two go together like bow and arrow." Tenille smiled, proud of her joke, and Ravenna shook her head. "Besides, Xan would never force you into marriage. I think that is the one thing he would refuse your mother." Tenille was right. If Ravenna did not want it, Xan would not go through with a marriage to her.

"Yeah, he's a good man. You two deserve each other," Ravenna said truthfully.

Tenille was gentle and kind, and possessed a great beauty that any man would be lucky to have. Her golden-brown skin was smooth and held no scars as Ravenna's did, and her thick black hair hung in many neat braids that were always beaded in shiny brass clasps. Her face was marked with the tattoos of the native Vestelians who had dwelled in this valley long before Ravenna's ancestors had immigrated from the eastern lands.

Tenille smiled and reached into the pocket of her apron, then offered Ravenna a handful of not-quite-ripe, light-yellow berries.

"Where did you get these?" Ravenna asked, stomach rumbling. She took a few into her hand. They were the first wild berries she had seen this year—she had not expected to see any for at least another month. The winter had been harsh, once again, and the ground had only been thawed for a couple of weeks.

Fresh fruit was hard to come by in Vestele. Between the lack of sunlight in the depths of the valley, and the harsh winters, her village was accustomed to starving through the colder months. She and Xan sometimes hunted for meat but always within the safety of the Sunstone Forest and always with her mother's permission. Aside from the occasional meat and fish from the river, food was scarce.

"Down by the river." Tenille smiled. "There is a small bush, not enough to share with the village yet." She winked, concealing the remainder of the unripe honeyberries in her pocket.

Vestele was nestled on the should-be fertile ground in the biggest fork of the Edmarian river. Where the wide waterway branched off into two, the ground was said to have once been lush and full of nutrients. But each year the ground seemed to harden, and the harvest seemed to lessen.

"So, the Gauntlet," Tenille said, glancing at the fresh scar on Ravenna's neck. "That's intense. Some people are saying you could be the next shield-maiden."

Ravenna straightened her back.

"That is my mother's worry," Ravenna said. "Probably why she's pushing so hard for marriage." Tenille had no words to give.

To hold the title of shield-maiden or shield-master, one must remain unmarried, dedicating their life to the task of being leader to the clan. Ravenna's mother had never married her father, Reid. He had been killed in the war while Ravenna was still in the womb.

"Your mother works hard at her position. And it is very dangerous...I can see why she would worry for you," Tenille said, trying to reason with Ravenna. "Do you *want* to be shield-maiden?"

Ravenna pondered for a moment. "I do not wish to be. Not yet." The rumors had spread around the village like wildfire. It had been a topic of conversation around every fire pit every night this week. With all the talk, her mother was wary, misunderstanding Ravenna's true reasons for running the Gauntlet. "My intention was to gain a little freedom," she explained, hoping Tenille would use her words to reassure the shield-maiden later. "I just wish to be a warrior. That is all."

"It looks like you've succeeded, then." Tenille gave her a small smile and went back to watching Xan train alongside the other warriors of Vestele.

6

LIKE A PAINTING

RAVENNA

Wind, cool and brisk, swirled through Ravenna's red hair, pulling strands from her braids, and licking at the bare skin on her arms. The early spring air rushed through Fintah's stringy mane and danced at Ravenna's fingertips. The valley was divine, like a painting straight from the art hall in the abandoned palace in the City of Ozanna. Laughter bubbled up from inside her chest, and she smiled boldly, spreading her arms like wings. It had been nearly a month since the Gauntlet, and she finally welcomed the first day of spring and all the vibrant colors it would bring to the valley she called home.

Vestele grew nearer. Outside of its borders, she felt free. She urged her mare to run as fast as she could, racing through the tall grass that was beginning to grow a little greener with the warmth the day's sunshine had bestowed upon the land. Today was a good day because after a week of training and proving herself obedient, it was the day her mother had promised her a night watch. Her accomplishments in the city of the Brunts had initially been recognized only as recklessness, but her mother had begun to see her potential during her training with the warriors. She had even allowed her out of Vestele a few times. Of course, Xan always accompanied her.

"Ravenna!" his gruff voice called from behind. He closed in on his stallion, trying to catch up to the brisk pace Fintah had set. "Slow down. You're going to fall off and I'll have to explain to your mother why our best fighter is out of commission."

She kept her arms spread wide. "What a fool I'd be if I fell off. If that happens, I deserve to lose my newfound title. You're just mad that you can't keep up." She shot him a grin then briefly tugged Fintah's mane and squeezed the horse's sides with her legs. Circling back to meet Xan, she noticed his umber eyes were clouded with annoyance.

"I thought you'd be happier with the promise of warmth returning to Vestele." She knew *she* was happier. After a harsh winter, their clan was in dire need of a bountiful crop, and this sunshine brought hope. As had the valuable bloodstone which she had given to her mother to do with as she saw fit. Ravenna guessed the shield-maiden had destroyed it.

"Warmth? It's freezing," he said as his horse, Alf, caught up to hers. Ravenna had picked the name for his stallion many months ago, after Xan had refused, insisting that horses were mere tools and that he would not be getting too attached.

"Better than yesterday!" she called, taking off again like a bird in flight, laughing. She did not wish to hear his lectures about how she must be careful, or his complaints. She was enjoying the return of the sun after a very cloudy winter. Black ravens flew beside her, feathers slick and shiny. Fintah went faster, leaving them behind in a flock of darkness that fought against the rays of daylight.

As Ravenna neared Vestele with Xan not too far behind, she noticed two young boys fishing in the half-frozen Edmarian River that ran through the village. It flowed through the abandoned City of Ozanna, between the kingdoms of Brinland and Edmaria, and all the way to the Crystal Sea, which was about a hundred miles east.

The smallest boy must have been seven or so and the eldest looking about twelve. He would be starting to train with her and the other warriors soon, if not already. Perhaps he had begun official training before she had even been granted permission to start, but she did not recognize him.

"Catching anything?" she called. The youngest immediately turned his attention to her, looking up in complete wonder. One thing her recent endeavors had gained her were looks of disapproval from the older of the Vestelians and awestruck glances from the younger of her clan. Even envy had worked its way onto the faces of some of her fellow warriors and peers.

The eldest noticed her gaze on the empty basket and quickly offered an explanation. "They aren't biting today."

"Not biting?" From where she sat atop Fintah, she could see schools of fish in the stream beneath the ice. "They're more active than I've seen them in months!" If she had not had her eighth day of official training to get to, she would have stayed and fished for hours if it meant feeding the struggling families that she shared the village with. Climbing down, she took an arrow from her quiver and tied a lengthy piece of twine from her saddle bag to the end of the arrow, knocking it into her wooden bow. She aimed into the opening in the ice.

Xan arrived in time to witness the first kill. She pulled the fish onto shore and shot two more, both boys grinning ear to ear as she threw them into the basket.

"Now you'll have plenty for dinner," Ravenna said with a grin. They would learn soon enough how to be great hunters. For now, she quite enjoyed showing off.

Xan stared at her, eyes crinkling as the corners of his mouth tilted upward, creating dimples on his cheeks. She noticed his skin had grown lighter through the winter like her own.

"And a couple of berries to go with them," Xan said, dumping a handful from his pocket into their outstretched palms.

Ravenna gave him a curious look.

Where did he find those?

She had searched after Tenille's find last week but had come up empty handed. She had figured it was still too early in the season.

He rolled his eyes. "Maybe if you would've listened to me, you wouldn't have raced past four berry bushes unbeknownst."

Ah, so their daily morning joy ride had turned into a gathering of berries. Her favorite pastime.

She led the way to the stables, acutely aware of Xan's attention at her back. The many braids she wore had been tugged loose from the wind, and she pulled them to the side to let the early spring breeze kiss her skin. The many horses in the stables had freshly braided manes, and Ravenna turned to look at Xan, raising her brows. "Tenille's been here. Too bad she couldn't freshen Alfie up." She patted Alf's back, and Xan rolled his eyes.

"Your horse is looking a little rough, too."

"Fintah. Her name is Fintah, and she looks lovely," Ravenna said.

Ravenna noticed her mother coming to meet them in the stables. The shield-maiden's angular face bore a rare smile, but her jade-green eyes had an uneasiness about them. Bracing herself for a lecture, Ravenna leaned back against her mare, the horse's large head turning to nuzzle her cheek.

"You're late. I expected you back an hour ago," her mother said. Ravenna rolled her eyes and gently stroked Fintah's mane before walking her into the stall and closing her inside. Her mother looked to Xan for an explanation, and he floundered for a reasonable excuse.

Ravenna relished in it for a moment before cutting in. "Oh, Mama. We were just out riding, no need to fret," she said with a little tease in her voice. Her mother knew where they had been. "You act as though the hills are crawling with Despiri."

"Despiri may be rare, and the Ember race may be heading for extinction, but they are all still very powerfully gifted. Quit being so foolish," her mother said. "You should fear them."

The shield-maiden took Ravenna's face in her palm and smiled, placing a kiss on the opposite cheek. Ravenna recoiled, studying her through narrowed eyes. Unbound, midnight hair fell around her mother's ears just below her shoulder blades. Xan's posture stiffened to a stance that reflected honor and reverence. When the shield-maiden was around, he was always standing with a confidence that could be recognized from a mile away. He tended to study her actions carefully, as if awaiting orders at any moment and reading her for any sign of distress in the village. It frustrated Ravenna that he could never relax.

"What truly has you so worried?" Ravenna asked. It was not unlike her mother to keep close tabs on her, but usually when she was with Xan, the shield-maiden did not brood as much. She had always trusted him with Ravenna's life.

"Am I not allowed to worry for my daughter's safety?" she said, avoiding the question. Xan still studied the shield-maiden with intensity.

"It is quite infuriating," Ravenna said, "how you hover." Ravenna painted her lips with a soft smile to lighten the mood, and then continued. "I've earned my title as best warrior. That makes me a candidate for shield-maiden, but as I've said, I do not want your title. But it would be proper for me to begin serving as your second in command."

If her mother were to follow tradition, as the best warrior, Ravenna would take Roarke's place and begin serving as her mother's second-in-command. By tradition, Vestele's shield-maiden would never go unprotected and would always have a second. Maybe if she became her mother's, the stubborn woman would quit acting as if Xan could protect Ravenna better than she could protect herself.

"Absolutely not," her mother snapped. "It is too dangerous."

"I know, I know." Ravenna waved a hand. Xan clenched and unclenched his jaw beside her. If Ravenna were to decide to challenge her mother's position as shield-maiden someday, Xan would become *her* second. Xan and Ravenna were a unit, and he would always do everything in his power to protect her, as she would for him.

Fintah huffed a breath. The unspoken words that now ricocheted between Xan and the shield-maiden were making Ravenna uncomfortable. Who knew how many conversations they had about her future without her involvement or knowledge.

They communicated almost silently now, whispering under their breaths and exchanging worried glances as Ravenna tended to her horse. For a moment, Ravenna pretended not to notice and offered Fintah some fresh water. But then, she decided she could not take it any longer. "Are you talking about my love life again?" After the many times her mother had hinted at marriage between Ravenna and Xan, Ravenna had no doubt this conversation was about just that. Xan's eyes grew wide, and Ravenna rolled her head back on her shoulders.

Ashreya spoke words that neither she, nor Xan, wanted to hear at this moment. "You two are the best pair I have seen among the people of our clan." They *were* a unit, he and her. They were best friends, inseparable, and *excellent* in a fight. But Ravenna had no desire to ruin that relationship with the confines of a marriage, where she would be expected to tend to the duties of a wife while he was out enjoying the freedoms and joys of life as a warrior.

"Oh, stop, Mama." Ravenna sighed, and Xan cleared his throat. Her mother pressed for marriage now because she feared Ravenna taking her title. It was the only reason that made sense. Though Xan could challenge the shield-maiden as well and come out victorious, he never would. He *wanted* to marry, and he wanted to marry Ravenna.

Her mother was growing older, and Ravenna thought herself and Xan were both deserving of the title, but maintaining the title of shield-maiden kept her mother in control of Ravenna's life. Ravenna did not expect her to give that up easily. She did not dare say it aloud, but her mother had likely realized that marriage between Ravenna and Xan would eliminate both potential threats to her title.

Her mother had been fortunate, finding Ravenna's father,

someone whom she truly loved. However, after his death, she was grief stricken. Still to this day, she was unable to move on. She still painted the charcoal markings down the bridge of her nose to signify that she was taken in marriage, though she never truly had been. Her mother claimed she loved him, and the marks she bore on her face were in memory of their great love. Ravenna would never let herself fall so deeply for someone when there was the hovering possibility of it ending in such monumental grief.

The cottage was exceptionally warm due to the last few hours of the spring sun beating down on the thatched roof. Her mother sat on their bed and assisted Ravenna in redoing the braids in her hair in preparation for her first night watch. She would leave with Xan straight after dinner for the northern Dead Wood Forest. Ravenna thought it strange that her mother had chosen this particular post for her very first watch, but she had no arguments about it. The Dead Wood had always captivated her, and she would much rather have an exciting first watch than one spent in the safety of the ordinary Sunstone Forest south of Vestele.

The shield-maiden's meticulous fingers wove strands of hair in and out to form a large braid down the center of Ravenna's head from front to back, while Ravenna created skinny braids that hugged her scalp and fell behind her ears, bound with beads and twine.

Turning around to face the shiny looking glass that hung near her bed, she caught a glimpse of the family heirloom hanging from her mother's neck. The small green stones in the brass matched her mother's eyes quite perfectly. Ravenna's reflection peered back at her in the mirror, reminding her that the jade stones matched the color in one of her own eyes quite perfectly as well. Her right eye was green, while her left was as blue as the Crystal Sea. Both eyes were filled with gold splotches and speckles.

A mosaic. Asta, Tenille's mother, had once said to her when she was young. *Little pieces of your mother and your father.*

Ravenna's eyes filled with tears at the thought of her father whom she had never met, nor seen even a painting of. Reid of the Valley. A warrior like her mother and now herself. She knew that her red hair must haunt her mother with memories of him every day.

Her mother finished securing the braid between Ravenna's shoulder blades and then smiled faintly, walking around to face Ravenna. "I love you, my girl."

She finished a thin braid along Ravenna's temple and secured it with brass clasps alongside the thick one, then placed another kiss on Ravenna's cheek. Ravenna stiffened at her mother's repeated and unusual display of physical affection today. Her mother reached behind the table and drew an unfamiliar dagger, revealing a meticulously designed hilt. Ravenna knew of no blade-smith in Vestele with such talents— and Vestele did not trade with outsiders.

Her mother offered it to her, and she took the blade gently in her hands, inspecting it further. It was forged of gold-plated metal, and in the hilt was a red garnet, framed by the body of a dove with wings spread wide. A depiction of seven falling feathers snaked its way from the bottom of the hilt to the sharp point of the short blade, interwoven in golden branches that seemed to gleam in the light.

Beautiful.

She looked up at her mother. The shield-maiden's soft smile settled in her green eyes as she spoke. "A gift. To celebrate you becoming a warrior—and your first watch." Her mother placed a warm hand on her cheek. "I am proud of you."

Ravenna's eyebrows scrunched together at those words, her face growing hot. She looked away, examining the gift further. "Thank you, Mama."

Her mother's face filled with something like sorrow, and she brushed a finger down Ravenna's cheek. "I have some business to attend to with the council this evening, but I'll see you in the morning, after your watch."

Ravenna nodded, sheathing her new blade and pulling her quiver onto her back. "I love you, too, Mama," she whispered, because she realized she had not said it back earlier.

She rarely said those words—but she meant them. She loved her mother, whether she felt that love had been fully reciprocated or not. She offered her mother a grim smile, perturbed about the concern on her face, and the suspicious business with the council.

When a heavy knock sounded at the door, Ravenna cracked it open to see one of her mother's most trusted warriors. He stood stiffly, as if waiting for instruction.

"Roarke, come in," the shield-maiden's voice said from behind Ravenna.

Roarke was her mother's current second-in-command, and though he was a muscular, rugged fighter, Ravenna was quicker. Where he was a vessel of brute force, her speed and acuity were lethal.

Ravenna stepped out of his way and allowed him entry into the small, one room cottage. His massive body all but filled the doorway. When he entered, Ravenna glanced back at her mother, who was nodding for her to continue on her way.

"Shield-maiden," he said, lowering his head slightly in reverence. "Ravenna."

Ravenna offered him a nod and tightened the strips of leather on her new boots, since her old ones had been left in the Brunts. Looking back once more, Ravenna saw her mother staring into the mirror as she began to retrace the charcoal markings across the bridge of her nose and shade the thick shadowy bands below her eyes and along her cheekbones.

She did not wait before Ravenna was gone to say to Roarke, "News, I assume." Her voice was grave, and it sent a wave of unease through Ravenna's chest. It was a statement, not a question.

Ravenna paused only for a moment before she crossed the threshold into the impending night.

7

WATCHING SHADOWS IN THE NIGHT

RAVENNA

Xan sat with Tenille near the fire circle. Though Tenille was always hovering around him, he still did not notice her like Ravenna thought she deserved to be noticed. Her beauty was unmatched in their clan, but Xan paid no mind to the many men that showered her with gifts and flirted with her day by day as she brought them meals and tended to the wounds they had acquired at training. Ravenna thought some of the men got injured on purpose so they would have an excuse to be touched by the beautiful healer. Ravenna was certain that Tenille would have accepted one of the many proposals by now if she had not been so undeniably in love with Xan.

From where her two friends sat, Ravenna noticed Tenille's usual attire, a long brown dress with an apron and a thin fur shawl that hung loose over her narrow shoulders. Her dark hair hung in dozens of intricate braids, and her ears were cuffed with a dozen brass rings. The caramel color of her eyes seemed to glow as she laughed at something Xan said.

"Ravenna!" Tenille noticed her approaching and motioned for her to come sit, stretching her arm across the thick log where she lounged with Xan. She looked uncomfortable, and her cheeks were blushing. It was like she was thankful for the interruption to whatever she and Xan had been talking about. "I made you two some bread and broth before you head out."

Ravenna had eaten *so* much broth this winter. Tenille was a healer, but it helped that she was also a phenomenal cook. The plain soup always went down easily with her fresh baked bread. Ravenna offered her a smile, cupping the warm clay bowl in her hands, grateful for the heat bleeding into her palms as the night grew cooler.

"What would we do without you?" Ravenna nudged Tenille's boney shoulder and sat down on the log next to her, soaking up some warmth from the fire-pit that centered the clan. She looked past Tenille to give Xan a smile, but he was already smiling at her. Glancing back down to the soup in her bowl, she brought a spoonful to her mouth, savoring the salty taste.

"Probably starve," Tenille said sarcastically, her nose wrinkling and the triangular markings on each plane of her bronze face distorting slightly. "Congrats on the first watch, Venna," she said with a genuine smile.

"It's about time," Xan said, grinning. Tenille glanced between the two of them.

"So, what're you two talking about?" Ravenna asked. Tenille shifted on the log.

"Oh, just how Tenille was proposed to for the *fourth* time, and she turned the poor feller down," Xan said, looking to the side at Tenille.

"Heartbreaker," Ravenna teased.

"What are you waiting on, anyway, Tenille? You're not getting any younger," Xan said, nudging her with his elbow. Two children ran around the fire giggling, and Tenille took the opportunity to abandon the conversation. She bent down, offering them each a half of her warm bread.

"Have *you* even eaten today, Tenille?" Ravenna asked with a grimace.

"I had some broth earlier in the afternoon—I'm fine," Tenille said.

Ravenna shook her head, cramming a piece of her own bread into Tenille's hand. As she leaned forward, she noted Xan's overflowing pack and rolled her eyes. "You're more nervous for my first watch than I am," she teased, noting the couple days' worth of bread he had packed along with twice the number of arrows and blades he normally carried. It looked as though he had packed all his food rations—and possibly more.

A worried look passed over Tenille's face, but she remained silent, bringing the bread to her mouth.

"Do you think we are going to get lost, or something?" Ravenna teased. She tilted her bowl up to her lips, slurping down the rest of the broth. The corner of Xan's mouth pulled up into a crooked smile, and he stood up, ruffling the top of Tenille's hair as he did. Tenille blushed, immediately fixing the loose strands. Xan threw his quiver onto his back, picked up his full pack, and motioned for Ravenna to hurry. Dark was falling, and they needed to be at their post soon.

"Wish me luck," she said to Tenille before turning to follow Xan through the misty evening air.

They headed to the northern woods that bordered the village. Walking silently and quickly, they made it to Ravenna's favorite grove of trees before the last of the soft blue light disappeared from the sky. Her mother's protectiveness may be suffocating to her, but it did not keep her from wandering outside of Vestele's bounds when no one was looking. She had been in this forest several times, each in the night when she had been kept from sleep due to night terrors, when she had lied about going to the workroom to busy her mind. Each time, she had snuck her way past the warriors' posts and made it to this very grove of trees.

Typically, this grove was far from any watch posts, and she could venture out here to think clearly about the future she could, or could not have, in Vestele.

"Why are we all the way out here? The last watch post was a half mile back," Ravenna whispered. The air was crisp, whispering by with a drizzle of rain and a hint of smoke from Vestele's fires.

"How would you know?" Xan asked in an accusatory tone. He stepped over the exposed roots of the many dead trees and leaned on a large rock for a moment, awaiting her answer.

"I'm not clueless. But you clearly are," she said with a smile, because he had never caught her out here before.

"You should listen to your mother. For your own safety... and for mine. She'll have my head if anything happens to you while you're out gallivanting across Arresia because you don't like the rules."

"Oh, don't start," she said.

He shrugged and continued through the rocky terrain of the Dead Wood, pulling his hood up to keep the rain from his hair. Ravenna did the same. With the temperatures dropping strangely quick, Ravenna expected snow on the ground by dawn.

In the Sunstone Forest south of Vestele, the stars were

always so much brighter, and the land was filled with sounds of life from the nearby stream. But here in the Dead Wood, there was only quietness. The rain fell in an eerie near-silence, and even the river seemed to hush in the blackness of the woods. Ravenna had always been captivated by the dead, winding trees of this forest. Like a beacon, the tranquility drew her in and allowed her to think clearly about endless ideas and possibilities. The oblivion of the Dead Wood called to her, and like the silhouettes of the dead trees creeping into the night sky, she let the darkness into her veins.

Her mother often reminisced on a time not too long ago when the Dead Wood was filled with noises of creatures and life and the territory was filled with Embers. That was before King Degare of Oro took the throne from the Ozannes and destroyed the old Kingdom of Ozanna. No Vestelian had spotted any unchained Embers within five miles of Vestele in years. Between the Brunt soldiers and Oro's men, it seemed the Embers had been eliminated from the surrounding areas. Her mother and Xan, however, remained unconvinced that Vestele was safe from the gifted ones—even after Degare had begun killing the Embers, in turn scaring them into hiding. Ravenna thought maybe the only thing they truly had to fear in this kingdom was its king and the Despiri he had created.

In this grove, there were two trees diagonal from each other, perfect for climbing. Xan's hand rested on the hilt of his sword, as it always did. He scanned the horizon, though Ravenna already had. *Three times.* He motioned for her to climb the tree that was slightly more hidden by shadows.

She obliged, if only to ensure that she would have the best view to any oncoming danger as her tree had a better vantage point. To her knowledge, the warriors had not encountered any danger for months. The occasional hungry wolf pack passed by, and even rarer, thieves of the night, as Xan had once spoken of. The winter months had been so harsh, thieves would not risk freezing to death or getting lost in a snowstorm trying to steal from their clan. Though with spring, the warriors had learned to watch the borders more intently, specifically the fields and the gardens where the food sources were. They could not afford to lose even one plant.

Hours went by with no sign of movement from either end of the woods. Xan was perched across from her in the tree that overhung the perfect path for horses to take, made by years of foot travel from wolves and deer. They both had a near perfect shot if someone were to trespass into their patch of trees on the edge of the woods, but Ravenna expected an uneventful night. Still, she surveyed the blackness, struggling to see past the thin silhouettes of trees only ten feet in front of them. The darkness of the Dead Wood was unparalleled.

Her eyelids became heavier as the two crescent moons began to align in the sky. The moons now provided more light than they had all evening. With the third moon not due in the sky for several more weeks, the nights had been darker even outside of the Dead Wood, but it was nothing compared to the depthless night that came with the darkening of the moons on Ravenna's birthday. Her birthday marked the start of the week with the darkest nights of the year: The Darkening, which lasted until the third moon's rising. Ravenna knew that many in the Kingdom of Oro celebrated that week, drawing power from the darkness through worship of their goddesses and idols in those strange Black Temples she knew little of.

A light breeze whispered through the leafless trees, creating the first faint sounds she had heard all evening. More noises followed as animals that had been hiding skittered across the cold ground below. Then, the air seemed to weigh down on her with a strange thickness. Noticing the shift, she looked to Xan, who peered west, into a grove of trees where a distant silhouette began to take form. No, not *a* silhouette. *Eight of them.*

Xan drew his blade, and from what she could see, his face drained of color just as it had that night in the Brunts a few weeks ago. He was calculating in his mind just how they could take on this many men.

Why are they here? No one travels through Vestele unless it is on purpose.

Was it another clan coming to take Vestele's women and children? Thieves who did not realize Vestele had no food or valuables worth stealing? Xan turned to look at her, his face grim. He began rapidly climbing down from the tree and Ravenna furrowed her brow, leaning forward on the limb.

You idiot. What are you doing?

When his feet made contact with the wet ground, the imposters were still far enough in the distance that they saw and heard nothing. He looked up at her with a stern glare and mouthed the words, *stay here. I am alerting the clan.* Chucking an extra dagger into the trunk beside her, he grumbled under his breath in a voice barely audible, "Do. Not. Move."

Ravenna plucked the dagger from where it had been embedded into the thick, rotting bark and narrowed her eyes at his back.

Xan moved slowly at first, as if his feet were fixed to the ground. The bone horn he would use to alert the clan bounced against his hip. He would not use it until he was closer to Vestele. He looked back at her, tentatively, until the darkness swallowed him up and she could hear only the sound of his retreating footsteps and the distant voices of the approaching men.

Something on squeaky wheels, a wagon, or a caravan, rolled toward her location. The group of men approached quickly, and she could now make out eight soldiers on horseback, two of them pulling an iron tumbrel. A prison wagon.

She did a mental run-through of her weapons. Three arrows, three daggers, and one sword. In the cover of the dark, she could surely get away with plucking them off one by one with arrows and daggers through the eyes before they pinpointed her location.

Xan's help would have been nice, she thought. *But unnecessary.*

Pulling back the first arrow, she waited. Her guess was, they were coming from the prison in southern Oro that bordered the Sea of Dawn. They must have just missed the guards on the southwest side of the valley—or killed them. No, she would have heard a commotion, a clashing of metal, *something.* There was no reason one would be so deep in the valley that they needed to pass through Vestele's steep, mountainous borders. Travelers almost always passed through the Brunts.

Then, she remembered. *The Brunts are gone.* The city had crumbled and left only destruction in its wake. No survivors had been found in the rubble. Ravenna steadied her breathing as she aimed her arrow at the throat of the man at the rear of the group.

The men moved with carelessness, laughing and joking with each other about some beautiful woman at the castle. The only castle they would be heading to was in the north—in the Kingdom of Oro. It was a castle rumored to be carved into the stone of the cliff that hangs over the Black Sea. Ravenna's breath caught in her throat as she realized they were traveling under Degare's orders. A king who killed Embers only because they possessed a strength that could oppose his own power.

She debated releasing an arrow into the eye of the cocky man leading the group.

No.

She would kill the ones in the back first and the others would be less likely to see the direction from which the arrow flew, if they even noticed at all. Once she was out of daggers and arrows, if she timed it correctly, the last two men—the ones at the front of the group—would be directly below, and she could leap down to end them with her sword before they even registered what was happening. That would only leave the issue of the prisoner, but the prisoner was caged in the tumbrel.

Were these men a threat to her or her clan? Her mother would tell her to remain hidden unless they attacked or entered her lands. If Ravenna were shield-maiden, she too might make that decision. But she was not the shield-maiden, and the shield-maiden was not here. The blood red uniforms of Oro became visible, and she knew she would find ravens with wings spread wide across the men's backs. Oro's men were all Shades —relentless, evil, worshipers of the darkness.

One of the men's voices echoed through the grove, loudly, as if he were invincible to the world around him. Most of Vestele's warriors were skeptical of the Dead Wood, fearful even. The fact that these men did not have the sense to be even a little careful of what attention they attracted in these woods, unnerved her.

"I can't believe we missed the trade."

That's right, Ravenna thought. Today was the Spring Ember Trade.

"Stop your whining," another said. "It's not like you could have afforded a kill, anyway." The other men laughed, and a pale faced man with dark hair and a petite frame spoke up.

"We are out of food, and we need somewhere to rest tonight. I think there is a clan just southeast of us, outside of the woods. I saw the glow of a fire."

Ravenna swallowed at the mention of Vestele, keeping her arrow locked on the stout man in the very back. They pulled the prison cart along in the center of their group, surrounding it on all four sides as they continued forward toward her home. Its wooden wheels splashed through mud as they crept along.

"We'd be backtracking," one argued.

"It's less than a mile," the first one said. "And we need to get out of these creepy woods until dawn. The night is only growing colder, and this rain is going to make us sick."

"It's barely raining," another said. "And the king wants us back in two days."

"Well, Oro is four days' travel from here, and that is without a rickety old wagon. We're behind schedule, anyway."

"Maybe we'll meet some new women," the largest, bearded man said, taking a gulp from his flask. Ravenna rolled her eyes, pulling her bow string taut in the mist of the night.

The leader of the group cut into the conversation. "We go to the village for the night, and we leave at daybreak." His word was final.

Ravenna's thick braids were hot on her neck, though the air was bitterly cold at this elevation in the night. By now, Xan would be warning the warriors, and the untrained women and children would be herded to the center longhouse of the clan, surrounded by every warrior in Vestele. They had been through drills many times in preparation for a moment like this. She thought of Tenille and Asta, helping to lead the children to safety, while Ravenna's mother armed herself and the warriors.

Vestele's horn echoed through the grove just as the blond leader of the group tilted his chin to slowly meet Ravenna's gaze, his breath fogging in front of him. She let the arrow fly.

The arrow took a split second to leave her bow and enter his grasp. He caught it without even blinking or breaking his stare from her own. She took another out of her quiver as quickly as she shot the last. The blond cocked his head to the side, examining her.

"I wouldn't do that again," he said flatly. His cheekbones were sharp as blades and his eyes were shadows under the blanket of darkness that surrounded him. Ravenna revealed no emotion. She did not let even a hint of surprise come across her face, at his unnaturally quick reflexes. "The name is Elam. We travel by orders of your king."

"I have no king," Ravenna spat, and he burst into laughter.

Averting her gaze from him for only a moment, she took in the details of the other seven men and the wagon. Three soldiers had their own arrows pointed at her, one stared coldly as if he did not need one, and the others hid behind raised swords. She inclined her head, smug at the effort they made to intimidate her. Inside the wagon was near black, but for a split second, when the moonlight hit it just right, she saw the silhouettes of *two* prisoners inside.

They had to be Embers. Now she was *sure* they traveled north from the Dawn Prison—the only prison in the King's lands that held Embers before they were escorted to the mines or to the new holding prison near the castle—to be sold or killed in the seasonal trades that had recently become so popular. The Dawn Prison was the furthest possible point in Oro from his castle in the north, and since Degare obviously had a burning hatred for the two Embers, she could imagine he would keep them as far away as possible while keeping them close enough for use when he was ready.

She tilted her chin high to mask her apprehension.

Dropping down from the limb, she landed in front of the blond man—Elam—who still held her arrow in his hand. He looked her up and down, studying her with a smirk on his face. He reached his hand out toward her, setting the arrow gently in her palm. She wrapped her fingers around the smooth wooden shaft, taking note of the shadowmarks that crept over the back of his hand.

"Ungifted," he acknowledged. "Foolish woman."

Ravenna raised her eyebrow, still standing with her shoulders back. "Foolish Despiri, wandering through these woods as if you are the only predators." She tried to search the rest of the men for the shadowmarks that would confirm her suspicions, but the night was too dark. It would only make sense for all of Degare's men to be powerful Despiri.

"Who have we to fear when we are at the top of the chain?" he said, his voice growing louder with each word as he raised his hands in triumph, awaiting the whistles and applause of his men around him.

As Ravenna reached over her shoulder to place the arrow into her quiver, each of the men tensed. She smiled at their unease, continuing to stall them long enough for Vestele to prepare. She expected a dozen Vestelian warriors to join her at any moment.

It was strange that these men traveled with Embers right

now, being that the first day of spring was yesterday—which marked the Spring Ember Trade. *Could they already be preparing for the Summer Ember Trade?* "Perhaps the Embers you imprison and kill will seek revenge some day for the atrocities you committed for your power."

"You think we are undeserving of these gifts?" Elam asked. He shifted slightly on his black stallion, raising one palm to the air. A deep darkness seemed to swirl within his hand and with the flick of his wrist, it spiraled toward her, beginning to tangle around her arm and scale up her neck. The darkness brought with it a sensation of fear and doom that encapsulated her entire body, and then all at once, phantom pain.

Yes, it was phantom pain. The feeling that her arm had been sliced open by a blade was there, but her eyes told her otherwise. There was no mark or wound.

This pain is not real.

She studied him, then felt her arm once more. This time her fingers slipped into a deep gash. She impulsively looked back to her arm. An open wound poured bright, red blood over the stones and black roots of the Dead Wood floor. She blinked.

"I can make you see what I want you to see," a petite, dark haired Despiri man said proudly, nodding to the blond leader. "And he can make you feel what he wants you to feel. Though with the trick of sight, the mind often fills in the blanks, creating pain without Elam's help," he said proudly.

She snapped out of his trance, feeling her arm once again, the skin now complete and smooth. She tried to break free of his mind tricks, and changed the topic of discussion before the fear writhing within her could stake a foothold. She glanced behind him at the caravan once more, and for a moment she could have sworn she felt a tug on her mind as he tried to pull her back.

Behind the barred window, she caught a movement as pale, thin hands grasped onto the bars, and a draft of wind blew a strand of copper hair into the moonlight. A woman, whose face was just barely visible in the night, pressed her forehead as closely to the bars as possible to get a view of the commotion that was beginning to occur around her. She was yanked back into the darkness of the tumbrel by her companion.

Ravenna's hand slowly and secretly moved toward the blade at her side. She leisurely pointed the sword in the direction of the prison wagon. "Who is in the wagon," she said, more a demand than a question.

The soldiers seemed to shift, preparing for a fight as if the question struck a nerve. She smirked, focusing her attention on their leader.

He spoke once more, ignoring her last statement. "We mean you no harm, lady. We are just passing through, transporting prisoners to Oro by orders of King Degare. My men are hungry and could use a good meal. We were rerouted a few miles back and lost daylight."

At the remains of the Brunts, Ravenna thought. To pass through the rubble would be impossible with the wagon.

"Is your clan close by?"

She stiffened, narrowing her eyes on him as he held his palms outward toward her in an attempt to appear less threatening, but she was still wary of the power he held within them.

"I am alone," she lied.

Again came that little tug on her mind, a reminder that he could cause her pain if needed. There was no way she was about to lead Degare's Despiri into the valley where her people resided.

"We heard the horn, you imbecile. Take us." His tone was sharper as he grew impatient.

Just as she was about to do something that would likely get her killed, a voice called out behind her. "I'll take you," Xan called to the men in a gruff voice. All the men shifted their attention.

Ravenna prepared to object, but Xan gave her a look of desperation as he climbed down from her white mare. Why had he come alone? Fintah stomped her front hoof as Xan planted his feet next to her. Ravenna thought maybe Xan was setting a trap for the soldiers, so she played along. Wariness flooded his brown eyes, and he carefully but quickly came to her side, right hand on his blade. He looked not at her, but at the soldiers while his free hand found its place on her elbow, and he guided her a few steps away from them toward Fintah. Ravenna looked to the side at him, but he only stared ahead.

"Do you have a death wish?" he grumbled, his grip tightening on her arm as she tried to shake him off. Xan turned, gently raising his hands up in a slow surrender to the soldiers. "She stays here, on guard. I will take you to our village where you can rest for the night."

What?

They could rest here in the Dead Wood, *dead*, for all she cared. Why would Xan offer Oro's men the luxury of sleeping next to the warm fires and eating the food meant for Vestele's people? She scrunched her brows and tilted her head toward him, perplexed at his stupidity.

"For the love of Light, *Xan*. They are *Despiri*. You need me and I'm going," she whispered. She refused to stay here. The chance of another threat in one night was highly improbable, and if there was one, the entire village was already locked down with warriors posted. She was of much better use where the actual danger lied.

"The girl takes us, you stay!" One soldier called, laughing like a drunken fool. Xan's hand moved toward his blade, and she stepped between him and the men, gripping Xan's forearm to prohibit him from raising his sword like a fool.

"We both go," she gritted her teeth, mounting Fintah and motioning Xan up. Reluctantly, he obeyed, if only because the soldiers were growing impatient. And so, they began leading the men toward Vestele, taking a route that was three times longer than the usual because of the wagon's inability to roll over the rocky terrain.

After an hour of the sounds of roots and rocks crunching under hooves and the squeaking wheels of the cart, Vestele was visible. It was clear to Ravenna now that there was no trap along the way, and that they were in fact, leading them straight into the heart of her clan. They treaded silently, deep into the valley where a new fire awaited them at the narrowest part of the glen by the river. Warriors sat outside of their homes, watching grimly as the Despiri approached closely behind her. Shame overtook her as she and Xan led Oro's deadly soldiers through Vestele, knowing her people saw it as a betrayal.

In front of the center fire, her mother was standing with her arms crossed, fully bedecked in her fighting leathers and her body stocked with weapons. When she noted Ravenna on the horse, her rageful eyes darted to Xan for only a moment before shifting to the men behind him. She had given Xan the order, no doubt, and there had to be good reason for it.

8

WHEN SHADOWS DESCEND
RAVENNA

The prison wagon was parked on the outskirts of the village, and four of Oro's men stood watch over the prisoners while the other half cleaned up with the warm water some of the warriors had carried over for them. Ravenna bit her cheek at the sight of them using pots she had molded. The firelight illuminated their bodies just enough that Ravenna could make out the differing shadowmarks they bore that marked them as Despiri. Some had marks snaking up their necks and some down the backs of their hands. Four had no visible marks, but most of their skin was covered due to the cold night.

They returned to their fire to receive the meals they had demanded from her people. Broth and bread filled their bowls. It was of the same batch that Tenille had served to Ravenna and Xan before they left at dusk. Ravenna watched as Tenille and Asta exited the kitchen trailed by six Vestelian warriors and offered the Despiri each a bowl, somehow maintaining pleasant smiles on their faces. The men did not smile in return or thank them, and instead stared after Tenille. Ravenna's hand tightened on her dagger. Beside Ravenna, Xan leaned against a hut, staring at Oro's men with well-deserved, burning hatred.

"When I was five, and your mother found me orphaned after the fires, I always swore I'd kill any of Oro's men without hesitation."

"So why don't you?" Ravenna asked. "Just say the words, and they're dead."

He scoffed, still staring at the Despiri. "It would help nothing. What is done is done."

It took about an hour for the Despiri to begin resting for the night. Of course, they rotated shifts and took turns sleeping, two always standing guard. The blond leader—Elam—never actually slept. His eyes were always scanning his surroundings, and she waited for that phantom pain to entrap her body once more.

"Why don't you get some rest, Venna?" Xan said from where he stood beside her.

She scoffed. "I won't be sleeping tonight."

She watched the unwelcome men from outside her cottage for three hours, the night growing so cold her breath stayed a cloud of fog in the air for many seconds before dissipating. The fire did little to warm her body. It was as if the harshest day of winter had returned to the valley on the Despiri's heels and settled into the heart of Vestele.

Ravenna did not allow her thoughts to run free, instead she focused solely on one question that needed to be answered. "I need to go speak to my mother," Ravenna said, rising to her feet. Xan stiffened. "Why allow them here? Into our home, after working so hard to protect Vestele from outsiders? Why *feed* them when half of our people did not eat tonight?"

"There was no way of refusing them what they asked," Xan said calmly. He sat down, inviting her to sit again. They both stared straight into the group of Despiri. After all they had done to protect Vestele from the gifted ones tonight—on her very first watch—eight Despiri and two imprisoned Embers slept around the same fire as her loved ones. It was a war they had tried so hard to stay out of.

Her nostrils flared as she watched her mother patrol the invisible line that separated Oro's men from the rest of Vestele. Her mother had given them a fire near the edge of the village, close to the river. If Ravenna were shield-maiden, Oro's men would be dead. But if she had no other choice, she would have placed them in the same spot her mother had chosen. Far enough from most huts and cottages and backed against the river so the men could not easily flee if Vestele decided to defend their territory.

Ravenna was so intently focused on the smallest man of the group—the one who could alter sight—that she did not hear Tenille approaching with two cups of warm tea until she was in her line of sight. Ravenna gave her a quick nod before turning back to the significantly small man.

"I wonder what their gifts are," Ravenna stated, eyes darting to the other soldiers.

Tenille spoke softly as if in worry the Despiri would hear her from where they laid around the fire many yards away. "The little man—I heard some warriors say his name—Jio. Mama says he is one of the king's most valued soldiers. His gift..." She paused on the word gift. "He is rumored to be a reader of the mind." She gave Ravenna a warning glance that seemed to say, *be careful what you are thinking.*

Ravenna scoffed at the thought of him not only altering her sight but reading her mind and seeing just how unwelcome he and his men were in this valley. If he messed with her mind again, she would show him just what she wished to do to them all.

Ravenna held the warm tea in her hands, contemplating what it must be like for the petite man—Jio—to roam freely through other's thoughts. His gift gave him the power to find an enemy's weakness—and the ability to make them see their greatest fear.

Tenille and Xan sat on either side of Ravenna, and she was acutely aware of them exchanging glances over her as she watched Jio search through his saddle bag. She was thankful for the tea and its warmth as it trickled down her throat. She cupped the small mug in her hands, letting the heat thaw her fingers, which had gone numb hours ago. Xan shifted beside her, and Tenille began to move closer just as Ravenna's head began to spin. She blinked, then looked at the mug that she had molded herself. She immediately looked to Tenille with accusation.

"Just a sedative," Tenille said quietly, her face full of remorse.

"Why?" Ravenna blinked rapidly, fighting the urge to close her eyes. "Why," she said again through gritted teeth. Not a question, a command. Xan looped his arm around her, hauling her up with ease as sleep claimed her.

Ravenna awoke in her bed. The fire had been stocked, the cottage was warm, and she was alone.

She rubbed her forehead, trying to rid herself of the pounding headache that must have awoken her. She struggled to sit up against the pain...and the sedative...*what had they done?* Ravenna shifted to the edge of the bed and placed her feet on the wooden floor. Her boots were still on, and she mustered up the strength to stand slowly. Once she was upright, bracing a hand on the chair next to the door, she grabbed her new dagger.

A splitting pain seared through her head once more and shot down her spine, this time bringing her to her knees. A cry beckoned out of her as she fell. She clutched her head as the door flew open and Xan filled the doorway, panic-stricken.

"What's wrong? What is it?" Xan knelt, turning her body from side to side, searching for any physical wounds.

"The sedative?" Xan looked to Tenille, who was now hovering at the threshold, mirroring his panic. The two of them seemed to speak to each other silently for a moment, debating on their next course of action, and Xan's hand shook in fear against Ravenna's hip.

"No. No. It's not the sedative," Tenille said hurriedly. "I use it on patients all the time. With this dose, she should have been out until noon."

Ravenna looked between the two of them.

What have they done? What are they hiding?

Another shot of pain seared through her—a replica of what she had experienced just hours before in the forest.

"The Despiri," she choked out.

This pain was not real, but the man just outside her cottage could trick her body into believing it was. She rocked on the floor, holding her head between her hands, eyes wide against the pain.

Ravenna fought the discomfort and shot to her feet, pushing past Xan with a blade in her other hand. Tenille blocked the exit and, to Ravenna's surprise, she was quite difficult to move aside.

What is going on outside? Why did they sedate me?

Ravenna blinked past the pain that trickled down her spine and the exhaustion that rippled through her body. She shoved forward past Tenille, racing out the door and through the village to the riverside where she had left Oro's men. Xan and Tenille trailed behind her, but not quickly enough to keep her from seeing exactly what she was not meant to.

Ravenna found her mother amid the eight Despiri, hands raised in two fists. She was chanting words Ravenna could not identify, words that she had never heard leave her mother's lips.

A spell?

The shield-maiden's long black braids seemed to blow faintly in a soft wind as she continued her repetitive chorus of words. Then, she opened her eyes, and for a moment, the chanting halted as she set her sight on Ravenna. Fear consumed her mother's angular face.

Ravenna's muscles went rigid, and her vision seemed to blur, whether from the Despiri or the shock of seeing her mother practicing dark magic, she couldn't tell. This was the type of fear that always cradled Ravenna in her sleep, trapping her. She was not seeing clearly. Any moment now, she would wake up. She always woke up. This was just another mind game. This could not be real.

The soldiers were standing in place, immobile. Her mother stared through her and began chanting once more.

My mother is a witch.

It occurred to Ravenna then that the Despiri could not move even if they wanted to. This strange spell was binding them in place. Her mother, Ashreya, leader of the Vestelian warriors, was planning to free the Ember prisoners from the tumbrel.

Is she out of her mind?

After all her mother had done to convince Ravenna that siding with the Embers was a bad idea, her mother was doing a *spell* right in front of her. Her mother, a witch? Vomit tried to make its way up Ravenna's throat.

"Ravenna, no!" A dozen voices called behind her as she made her way toward her mother; to help her or stop her she did not know. In a heartbeat, she was recounting the soldiers.

One, two...seven. Where did Despiri number eight go?

Elam was missing.

She was sprinting in a blind fury now. Her mother seemed so far away. Feet fumbling as they never had before, Ravenna rushed toward her. Warning did not have time to leave her mouth as Elam appeared out of the thick black darkness, smirking at Ravenna. He sent another unforgiving wave of pain through her as he brought his blade high over her mother's head.

Ravenna's steps came to an abrupt halt. It was like the world and everything in it slowed, leisurely spinning around her, pulling her under and stealing the air from her lungs. The blade swiped across her mother's neck, leaving her body collapsing to the ground with a deep red cut drawn across her throat.

9

RED

RAVENNA

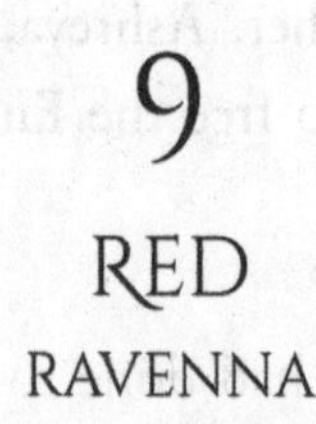

R ed. She loathed the color. The cursed hue of blood and the beginning of every sorrow. Each child came into the world enveloped in it. The sorrows of life and death, already staking its claim on a new body. A bath would wash the skin clean of the color, but it would not change the fact that one was made from it, filled with it, and could not live without it. The body's need for blood was infinite. Blood coursed through the veins. Blood drained from skin at the slightest injury. Blood often poured from a body in death. One could only lose so much blood before they were dying, and her mother had lost too much.

Ravenna knew this before she even set out to kill the Despiri. That terrible, disconsolate thought clouded her mind before she threw the first dagger under the crescent moons. The blade left her hand in an instant. Elam had been caught up in the kill, and he did not catch the weapon in his hand this time. There was no smirk from him, no remark, just blood and a swift death that he did not see coming.

Ravenna's name was being called—shrieked—by voices she did not know. Her eyes did not falter from her enemies. The name *Ashreya* left the lips of dozens of the warriors, echoing across the valley, confirming that this was real, and Ravenna was not trapped in a nightmare. The fear she felt was authentic, *tangible*. The Despiri had caused her *real* pain after all.

Her ears pounded as if underwater. Pressure came from all sides and muffled her hearing. Screaming. From somewhere...from...*her*. She was on her knees beside her mother, grasping, holding, shaking her broken body. No. She was running. She was drawing her sword.

She was going to kill them all.

Her steps moved too quickly for her conscious mind to keep up. Blind rage overcame her, her shell of a body consumed by it. Her name was still being called, as if being yelled from across the three great seas.

Then, at the sound of a newly familiar voice in her mind, she froze.

Ravenna, I've been in their heads, and I know your secret.

As the words were whispered into her mind, her body trembled. Jio, the mind reader, was smiling smugly at her from where he stood on the other side of the roaring fire, in the same spot her mother had just bound him through her mysterious magic. He was baiting her. Ravenna's feet flew forward, and her hand gripped her blade so tightly that it ached.

Only five more seconds and Ravenna would have her sword driven through Jio's spine. The other Despiri would surely kill her before she ended life number three, but she did not care. Her eyes were fixed on the small dark-haired man.

Four seconds.

Three.

Two.

Suddenly, she was yanked backward into a crevice between two cottages. Xan's panicked, blanched face appeared an inch in front of hers. His hand covered her mouth, and his eyes were wider than she had ever seen them. His other hand was on her arm, and she felt the indent of his fingernails in her skin. Morning would come and she would be without a mother. Her body twisted out of his grasp, but he had disarmed her. Her sword fell behind him into the weeds that had grown up along the edge of the stone cottage. Ravenna's head spun wildly.

"Venna, *please*," he begged in a soft voice which seemed to break in two. "Please." A single tear fell down his cheek and his hands were on her shoulders, shaking her aggressively without yielding. "Do not fight me." His forehead was on hers and he pushed just enough that she met his gaze for a split second. His hands cradled her face and his fingers pressed into her skin as he stared down at her in an attempt to hold her attention.

Ravenna squirmed to look back in the direction of the soldiers.

"You're not thinking clearly," he said gently. *Sadly.*

Her eyes darted to him in accusation. "This is your fault!" she spat.

He winced, and she turned from him to see the Despiri exiting Vestele along the river to the Dead Wood with Jio at the front of the group. The wagon shook across the rocks, certainly rattling the prisoners inside. Slowly. It moved so slowly.

She could run and catch up to them. She began to push Xan off her, but he only held her tighter against his statue of a body.

"They will kill you, Ravenna. Do not," he begged, his breath hot against her skin.

"They killed her!" she rasped, the knot in her throat eating her words. A stammer of unrecognizable sounds left her mouth, and she began pushing away from him, struggling to get the footing she needed. She would fight him if she had to.

There was not a sound above the wailing of many. No clashing of swords, of battle, or revenge. The entire clan of Vestele and all its warriors only stood still, gawking as the Despiri left the valley, fearing no retribution for what they had done.

Why did they not stay to kill us all?

Ravenna looked to each warrior, then across the fire where Roarke held her mother's body. She stopped struggling and returned her gaze to Xan's sorrowful face.

This is not real. This cannot be real.

Xan's hands trembled against her shoulders.

"Why aren't they fighting?" Her face was wet. Xan bit down on his lip and his eyes swelled. With a bold, shrill voice that was not her own, she charged, shoving him backward. "Why aren't *you* fighting?" She screamed the words across the hills and valleys, and Xan's hands circled her wrists as she beat against his chest.

"Her order, Venna." He staggered backward, breaking eye contact with her as he looked to her mother's body just yards away. "Ashreya's order. Do not engage." He choked on his words, neck bobbing. "She had to try," he whispered.

"Try *what*?" Her voice was barely an audible breath and her body revolted against the sorrow that wrenched in her gut. She fell to her knees, Xan going with her. "Why aren't they fighting?"

He cradled her head, and they rocked gently. "It would be a bloodbath. Vestele would not win." His voice cracked, and Ravenna tried to focus on anything but the weeping around her.

With the release of Xan's grip on her waist when the Despiri were out of sight, she rushed and pushed through the crowd of Vestelians who gathered around their shield-maiden's body. Across her mother's neck was open flesh, and the sliced leather strip of the necklace she always wore beneath her fighting leathers. It was a family heirloom—a gift passed down for many generations. Ravenna scooped the spherical brass pendant into her hand, and her empty gaze fell to the bloodstone prize that lay in her mother's open palm. She had not destroyed it after all. She had kept it for this...spell, and it was all Ravenna's fault.

The events of the past few weeks replayed in her head. Her choices to disobey her mother's commands to gain her respect. Her foolish acts in the Brunts that had almost gotten her killed. The acts that could have gotten all her people killed if Leith from the Ink Bloods decided he wished for retribution for the hurt she had caused him. If he was alive, and there was a chance that he was, he could still decide that. She should have killed him when she had the chance.

Similarly, Ravenna wished she had taken the shot at the Despiri in the forest. Maybe she could have killed them all from the treetop if she had been quick enough, but it was a foolish thought. Now she knew that there was no world in which she could fight eight Despiri and win. She may have once been prideful enough to think so, but not anymore. She looked to the ground as her heart thumped in her throat. There, in the night, was the fierce motherly face that had always protected her, despite all her foolish decisions.

Collapsing beside her lifeless body, strange sobs exited Ravenna's mouth without warning. Clouded vision and tears with no foreseeable end were all devouring. She drew her mother to her chest, and with utter and immeasurable brokenness, a scream beckoned out of her. She swore that even the mountains quaked with her misery.

Only when the dawn broke did the tears halt, as she gathered herself and gently shut her mother's green eyes. The two of them rocked back and forth, *back, and forth*, her mother's blood staining her hands and clothes.

Red was the color that started and ended it all.

IO

IN DEATH

XAN

That scream. It haunted him. Ravenna's head tilted back, and what left her lips was a scream to be heard across seas. Mountains quaked, and every single soul in Vestele fell to their knees as if the breath was taken from their lungs. No sound came from the creatures in the woods, no crackling from the fires, no noise from the flowing river just yards away from her. It was only *that* scream, penetrating the depths of the seas and the heights of the skies.

Xan watched from his state of oblivion where he had collapsed on his knees as every Vestelian and warrior alike witnessed Ravenna, broken and shattered amongst the muddy ground, unleashing that near endless cry of agony amidst them.

In death, there was either weeping or silence.

Ravenna wept over her mother's body. But slowly, she fell silent.

Xan had never seen her so distraught. So utterly broken. She had never allowed him to hold her before, but when he had hidden her behind the cottage and pulled her from certain death, she had crumpled in his arms. In those moments, she had been so unlike herself. Fearful. Unsure. Unsteady. Knocked astray from the path she had been set on since they were kids.

Until she had come to her senses and blamed her mother's death on *him*.

"This is your fault," she had said.

She's not in her right mind, he told himself.

But seeing her now—in a cage of silent grief—it broke him, too, and he thought maybe it *was* all his fault.

Tonight, the shield-maiden had set out on her most dangerous mission to date, and it had cost her life. Their plan to attack the Despiri was risky. The whole clan knew that it could fail miserably. Ashreya had not practiced magic for years, and though the moons were small crescents, the near complete darkness was still not enough for her to draw from. There would have been more power during the celestial event of the annual Darkening that was approaching in a few weeks, but they were on a time restriction, as it was not every day the Despiri traveled through.

The council should have tried harder. The clan, the warriors, *someone* should have stopped her. They should have just rerouted the Despiri and stayed out of this war as they always had. If Xan would have ignored her order to stand down, maybe she would still be here. But he had not ignored it. And for that, Xan would blame himself the rest of his days.

Oro's path must have changed, sending them backtracking toward Vestele from the Dead Wood. Xan had panicked. It was not part of the plan. He did the best he could, practically begging Ravenna to stay hidden in the treetops. He should have known better. He *did* know better than to expect her to submit to his orders. Ravenna barely obeyed her own mother.

Running faster than he ever had in his life, he had plummeted toward Ashreya in the valley. He wished he and Ravenna had taken their horses out to post, but it was easier to stay hidden on foot. He would never have been able to convince Ravenna to flee on horseback, anyway.

Upon arrival at the southwestern border of Vestele, Ashreya's gaze had met his own with an intense mixture of fear and anger. "Where is my daughter?"

Calm rage rippled from her as he began to explain why he had left Ravenna in the woods. It was either risk the stubborn warrior ignoring his advice to not attack Oro's men, or run like mad and get orders from the only person she *might* take them from before she attacked.

Ashreya had called for the fastest mare, Ravenna's beloved Fintah.

"No slip ups when it comes to the safety of my girl. Leave her in the Dead Wood and lead the Despiri to me."

No slip ups when it comes to the safety of my girl.

Those words had echoed through his mind a hundred times before he had found Ravenna contemplating the murder of every Despiri that had wandered into Vestele's territory. If it would not have meant her life, he would have loved to see her try. But he had promised Ashreya he would keep Ravenna out of this. They had all promised. And so, they would.

"I should have killed the men while the spell immobilized them," he said to Tenille, who stood beside him with swollen eyes. If he had, his shield-maiden would still be alive. "I don't care what Ashreya ordered. I should have done it."

Tenille shook her head. "It would not have worked. Killing

the Despiri before Ashreya had successfully linked them would only put Vestele at risk of an attack from Oro." Tenille squeezed his hand and wiped her cheek. "You did all you could, Xan."

He knew she was right. The dark power the Despiri possessed was too strong, and killing one would sever the link that Ashreya was trying to create among the entire Despiri race.

"And the Despiri race still reigns," he muttered. If only Ashreya had been given a few more minutes, she could have succeeded in killing every Despiri in Arresia—the King of Oro included.

In a perfect world, she would have succeeded. But she had not, and now she was dead. Xan could not have broken Ashreya's trust and risked Ravenna's life. He had taken a blood oath to obey every order from the shield-maiden whether he liked it or not.

"I just don't understand," Xan said. "Ravenna said it was the Despiri that woke her. How was he able to get to her? She was not even within his sight, and I saw him—the blond one— he was bound by the magic too, until Ashreya saw Ravenna." The Despiri were much more powerful than he had imagined, and that scared him.

"I don't know," Tenille said. Witches and magic, Despiri and talk of Embers—it was all so unfamiliar to them here in the hidden valley. "But somehow, he knew to use the shield-maiden's daughter to distract her. He must've still been able to use his mind gifts, even though he was physically bound. His mind was still free."

Xan was going to be sick. "When Ashreya saw Ravenna, she lost focus, and he was able to slip into the shadows. That was his plan all along. How did I not notice he was missing?"

Xan asked. He should have noticed. Now, Vestele was at risk because the Despiri had lived to tell the tale to their precious king.

Rain poured over Vestele now, heavy droplets splashing up around Ravenna as she cradled her mother in the mud. Soon, the rain would turn to ice, or snow, but it seemed Vestele had already frozen over.

Roarke walked toward Xan now, and he climbed to his feet. "You have to help her—this is your—your duty," the warrior choked out. Xan stared at him for a moment.

"And what of your duties to Ashreya?" Xan asked, voice louder than he anticipated. "You should have advised her against this! You should have never let her do it!" Xan shoved him, and the warrior stumbled backward, gaining the attention of a few grieving Vestelians. "You were her second. Her protector!"

Roarke winced at his harsh words and pointed a finger into Xan's chest. "And *you*," he jammed his finger forward, "are hers." He nodded toward Ravenna. As Ashreya's second, Roarke was now acting shield-master, and Xan had no power over him. Tears welled in Roarke's eyes, and he pushed past Xan, toward his fellow warriors.

Xan had spent hours with the warriors of Vestele—both men and women—and had never seen one of them cry. But tonight, there was not one dry eye in the village.

It was Tenille that grasped his hand at dawn and nudged him forward in all her gentleness toward Ravenna's brokenness. She urged him toward his friend. His love. His responsibility.

"It is no one's fault," Tenille said. "Especially not yours."

He slowly began to approach where Ravenna remained

hunched over and trembling, covered in Ashreya's blood. The brass heirloom was nestled into her fist, and she held her mother's head, whispering inaudible words into the shield-maiden's dark, silken braids.

Instead of speaking, because there was nothing he could say, he crouched behind her and pulled her back against his chest. With no resistance, she collapsed against him, and he could have sworn he heard his own heart break in half. He had craved the sort of intimacy with Ravenna for years. He dreamt of more than friendship. A true bond. A relationship in which she loved him back and allowed him to bear her burdens. Unfortunately, the situation was far different than the ones he had dreamt up in his head. But he would be what she needed, whenever she needed, just as he had promised Ashreya years ago when he had been just a boy. More than a friend for her daughter. A protector. A partner.

If Ravenna still wanted the title of shield-maiden, she could challenge Roarke and claim the title. There was not a doubt in his mind that she would win. And when she did, she would lead Vestele's warriors into war on the Despiri that killed her mother. If the Despiri did not come for them first.

Xan breathed deeply and smoothed her hair. "I know it hurts, Ravenna. But remember, even after the darkest of nights, light still dawns in the morning." He said the words not only for her, but for himself, too. Everything had gone wrong today. Soon, Ravenna would have questions that he could not give her answers to. She would ask them—demand answers— and because of his oath to Ashreya, he would not be able to offer them to her. He would keep his word, but he feared losing Ravenna's trust in the process. The entire clan now had an oath to keep, a *secret* to keep, from their future leader.

II
FALLING
RAVENNA

All Ravenna knew was that her mother was dead, and she had been lied to by not only her mother, but by her entire clan. By Xan. Her best friend. For now, she allowed his arms to cradle her into sleep. But with the shutting of her eyes, she entered an unyielding, endless nightmare. The fear closed in on her from above, a dark blanket of trepidation that wholly devoured her.

Ravens flocked above her, flying north with intention as if they had somewhere to be. The sound that echoed through her ears was not of many birds, but of only one. It was a screech that deafened those in its path and traveled across the sky, shaking everything in its wake.

Then, she was in the air above them. Next, falling. Straight down from the sky, she tumbled through thick black air and crashed through the flock of ravens, listening to only the pounding of her heart and the flapping of wings around her. She fell further, deeper into the pit of a valley burned in what must have been a wildfire. The ground was like charcoal and

"

the smell that filled her nose was that of a familiar plant—one that grew in the open valley during spring. Yet somehow, its scent was harsher. It swept through and burned her lungs until she could no longer breathe. She drew her final, shaky breath inward, and her body shattered against the ash-covered ground.

No pain shuddered through her, just those throbbing waves of fear that settled in her chest, as if they were making a nest inside the depths of her soul. She remembered who she was, and that her mother had been taken from her. Perhaps this fear was better than the truth that awaited her once she opened her eyes.

12

BENEATH ICE AND SHADOWS

XAN

"She has nightmares," Xan said as he watched Ravenna sleep.

"We all do," Tenille said. She did not look at him, but instead, distracted herself by examining the folded paper animals Xan had made and displayed on his wall.

Xan and Ravenna were good at keeping things from each other, but he knew the bad dreams haunted her, too. The difference between their night terrors was that Xan knew why they haunted him, and Ravenna did not.

Nearly nine hours had passed, and the sun began its afternoon descent. Soon, it would fall behind the mountaintops. Ravenna would then be waking up to a real nightmare after writhing against them in her sleep all morning and afternoon. Tenille had not left Xan's hut since Xan had brought Ravenna here in the early hours of the morning after she had fallen victim to exhaustion in his arms. Ravenna asleep in his bed as if it was her own, was yet another scene he had dreamt up in his mind over the years, but again, this was not how he had wanted it to happen. He did not think Ravenna would want to wake up in the bed that she once shared with her mother, so he had brought her here.

Her braids were still woven in the style that Ashreya had helped her with the evening before. A thick braid down the center of her head and onto the nape of her neck, and a few tiny braids hugging her scalp along the edges. It was a style he had seen in her hair often. Firelight from the hearth danced across her cheek, illuminating the freckles dispersed among her fair skin. The winter months and the stress of recent events had drained the color from her face.

"You should eat," Tenille suggested gently. She held out a steaming bowl of soup, but he shook his head, his stomach roiling as he leaned forward in his chair and studied Ravenna's face.

At a knock at the door, Tenille huffed and turned to open it. She was greeted by her mother and another woman who were both curious about Ravenna's well-being.

"Hush, Mama. You'll wake her. She needs rest," Tenille said in a tone of annoyance that Xan had never heard her use.

When he heard the door shut, his current, most prominent worry left his lips. "She will ask questions when she wakes," Xan said, attempting to swallow the shakiness in his voice. He took Ravenna's calloused, blood-crusted fingers into his hand.

Tenille seemed to read his thoughts and directed her attention to the bucket of water near the hearth, gathering the supplies to wash Ashreya's blood from Ravenna's skin. She answered him carefully, in a tone that could have been comforting had it not been for the harsh truth her words held.

"We do as we promised. Ravenna stays out of it." She placed a gentle hand on his shoulder. "We tell her none of it." There was a sternness in her gaze as she seemed to remind Xan of what was at stake if either of them were to break the spelled blood oath. Blood oaths reigned even in death.

He released Ravenna's hand and took a paper from the shelf beside him. "She is the rightful shield-maiden now," he said slowly, nervously fidgeting with the paper and folding it until it resembled a mountain. "If she wants the title, it's hers. Ravenna against Roarke in a challenge—she would win by a landslide."

How will Vestele keep the truth from their own leader?

"Surely there is someone—anyone else who could challenge her," Tenille said, looking longingly at Xan. "You?" she suggested.

Xan scoffed, setting the paper mountain on the shelf. "I would never take that from her. It would ruin our trust. And besides, I couldn't if I tried." Ravenna was the best, and everyone knew it. To challenge her would be anarchy.

Ravenna's eyes snapped open. Those beautiful, striking eyes. They did not wander around the home that was not hers. They did not look for clues of where she was. They only stared straight forward, as if seeing nothing at all. Silence radiated from her and consumed the entire room, and the crackling embers in the hearth seemed to quiet. He had never seen her so empty, eyes like a deep well into her soul that may very well be dry forevermore.

As Tenille neared Ravenna with the bucket of water and a rag, Ravenna continued staring straight up to the clay ceiling of the hut. Tenille did not speak anymore, only offered Xan a wet cloth as she took Ravenna's other hand. They began wiping the blood from her skin, but Ravenna yanked her hands back and sat up. The bed creaked with the abrupt movement, and Xan stood upright, backing away from her.

She threw the fur hides to the side and stormed toward the door, gasping for air.

"Ravenna—" Xan started, going after her, only to be stopped by Tenille's surprisingly strong grip on his arm.

"Let her be," Tenille said.

Xan knew Ravenna like the back of his own hand and was also sure that she needed a moment to be alone and process the events of the night, but his instincts—and perhaps the blood oath—begged him not to listen. Though he had only been five years old, he remembered what it was like to lose a mother. He would allow her a few minutes of peace, and then he would be there once more.

It strained him to allow her to walk out the door alone. Tenille gave him an apathetic look. For once, he had listened to her, mostly because he feared what he would say to Ravenna when he caught up to her. What would be the first answer she demanded from him?

"Xan, you need to breathe," Tenille said behind him. He kept his fist tight on the doorknob, with his forehead against the wooden door.

"Tenille, I can't see her like this. I cannot be what she needs. I do not know what to do."

"Let me help you," she said, leading him to the edge of the bed. He did not understand what was happening. His throat constricted, and his voice cracked.

"She's gone," he whispered. Ashreya was gone.

"I know." Tenille stood before him, pulling his head forward and cradling it against her body. An ounce of comfort against a sea of grief. He never wanted to leave that quiet moment, but Tenille turned and scrambled to get Ashreya's blood out of the bed linens before Ravenna returned, and he remembered his duty.

He blinked away the tears in his eyes and stood to pace the length of the small room. Maybe he should not be giving Ravenna space. She did not need time to think up questions they could not give her the answers to. This had all gone so terribly wrong.

He should have broken the oath and disobeyed the order to stand down. He should have intervened. A broken blood oath would have killed him, but maybe he would have been given enough time to ensure Ravenna still had her mother. If only he had given her that—she would not be so broken.

As he turned back to the door to go after her, screams from outside echoed into the hut. Xan rushed out in an instant, taking immediate care to find her. A herd of people ran toward the river where blocks of ice had broken apart to reveal the raging current below, and he followed them. The air stung his face and his heartbeat echoed in his ears. This weather was unforgiving. It was as if winter had returned at full force. All of yesterday's warmth had left the valley, and Vestele was engulfed in the bitter air once more.

Nilo saw Xan searching and yelled, "She's in the water! She's fallen through the ice!"

Xan heard no sound above the rushing of blood in his veins. His legs moved quickly across the frozen ground, passing every warrior, and racing downstream toward the Dead Wood.

The ice had begun to melt and then freeze again over the last couple days of differing temperatures, and on the edge of the forest where the river wound into the first grove of black roots and stumps, red hair floated just below the surface. Her body had snagged a root, and she stayed there, *face down in the water.*

His heart dropped to his stomach. She knew how to swim, and yet she did not tread the water. Instead, she began to sink, her face buried under the rushing current.

"Ravenna!" Xan yelled, pleading.

The root snapped and her body jolted forward as he ran toward her, faster, until he was on the bank a few feet from her. Ahead, the river was still a sheet of ice, and Ravenna was about to be sucked underneath it. He sent his body hurtling toward hers, throwing his cloak behind him into the weeds. He did not give his body time to revolt as he stepped into the frigid waters. Warriors were beginning to arrive at the bank behind him, now watching in dead silence as he trod through the rushing current toward her. The water slammed broken chunks of ice into his body.

He did not understand. She did not fight the current.

Why did I let her out of my sight?

Straining against the current, he pushed through the icy river as quickly as he could, but the strong flow of water pulled her body free and carried her straight under the ice before he could reach her. He climbed on top of the slick sheet, trying to get ahead of her, then prodded and punched the ice with his fists. Blood spilled from his knuckles as they cracked and thrashed unrelentingly against it. He could see her red hair approaching below. He continued to strike harder and harder each time.

Come on.

He could hear Tenille yelling from the shore. Her screams were the only ones that echoed out to him as the other bystanders stood still, completely speechless.

At last, the ice gave way. He threw all of his strength into widening the crack he had made, and his hand went through to the frigid water below, just in time to catch Ravenna's arm as she drifted past. A few warriors snapped out of their shock and hurried onto the ice, scrambling to help him make a hole big enough to haul her body up through.

She was too cold. Her once rosy lips were blue. Her wet hair caked to her neck and arms, immediately hardening with ice upon exposure to the wintry air. Roarke exited the water right behind them, grabbing a hide from the ground and throwing it over Ravenna. He tried to cover Xan with a one as well, but Xan shrugged it off, dragging Ravenna's limp frame further up the bank and lifting her into his arms.

"Is she alive?" Roarke asked breathlessly. The warrior's eyes had grown dark circles beneath them.

Xan stared at him in disgust and drew Ravenna closer to his chest.

Tenille pushed through the crowd and bent down next to him. "Come, Xan. You need to get up." She pulled on his arms as a sob broke from his throat. He glanced up at her and saw the light that somehow still remained behind her eyes, and something shifted in his mind.

There was still hope.

He hauled himself and Ravenna up from the ground and rushed toward her cottage, which was closer to the river than his hut. Tenille was behind him immediately with blankets and her woven basket of herbs and natural medicines, ready to tend to the woman they had sworn to protect. Xan's heart skipped in his chest, and he thought he may vomit as he watched Tenille and Asta strip the wet linens from Ravenna's limp body. He averted his eyes until she had been covered with the fur hides from the bed.

"Please wake up," he choked. Her name spilled from his lips repeatedly on each rasp of breath. He shook violently, unaware that his own body was too cold. With all his weight, he fell back against the wall as he watched Tenille check Ravenna's pulse. He knew there was no heartbeat before Tenille's face confirmed it.

Without looking up from Ravenna, she ordered the onlookers that stood at the open door, "Give us space. Leave us!"

Xan crawled across the floor, pulled the door shut, and crawled over to where Ravenna lay in front of the fire. Tenille's hands worked fast, digging through the basket and placing a few drops of liquid into Ravenna's mouth. Tenille grabbed his hand, stopping his frantic caressing of Ravenna's wet hair.

"You need to get out of these wet clothes," she said, looking him in the eye for only a moment before turning back to Ravenna. Asta urged him up, trying to move him from Ravenna's side.

"Not until I know she is okay," Xan said, planting himself like stone beside her. Asta did not argue.

"Quickly. Do it quickly. There is not much time," she pressed Tenille.

Tenille's small hands started to press against Ravenna's chest, pumping her still heart. She tried to get the blood to flow, and Xan pressed his lips to Ravenna's, forcing air into her lungs. Her chest rose as her lungs filled, but she did not stir.

So cold. She is so cold.

Xan looked to Tenille for some sort of reassurance that Ravenna was going to live, but she offered no such thing. Her concentration remained solely on the patient in front of her. Asta hovered over the three of them, one arm hugging her body and the opposite hand pressed against her mouth.

Xan whispered, each breath a plea to Ravenna. "We need you. *I need you.* Wake up. Wake up. *Wake up.*"

There were tears in his eyes. Over twenty years had passed since the last time he had cried tears of such broken desperation, when he had watched his own mother die. He thought that day had completely broken him, kept him from feeling so deeply ever again. But then Ashreya died. And now this. *This was worse.* Grief was like that. All consuming, all at once.

For what must have been half an hour, Tenille, Asta, and Xan took turns pumping Ravenna's heart and breathing into her cold body. With each of his breaths, Xan urged her to wake up. Her body grew warmer, but she still lay breathless on the floor.

"More blankets!" Tenille yelled to Roarke, who had just burst through the door with more wood for the fire. His face drained of color as he looked upon Ravenna on the floor of Ashreya's cottage, and he turned to leave in a haze of panic, scouring Vestele for more linens.

Finally, after too many minutes of absolute desperation, Ravenna began to heave. All the tension in Xan's body relaxed. He sucked in a sigh of relief and began to cry over top of her. He had not failed yet. He tilted her body upward and water escaped her lungs as she coughed and gasped for breath. Tenille fell to her knees beside her friend and quickly tucked more blankets around her, covering her bare back. Asta tightly clutched her chest, then turned to place a few more logs on top of the fire.

They had gotten Ravenna back, and Xan would not let her out of his sight again.

I3

UNNERVING DARKNESS
RAVENNA

She had not planned it. She was just going to the river to wash the blood—her mother's blood—from her skin. She could not stand to be in Xan's hut with him and Tenille speaking about her as if she was not there any longer. They spoke about secrets and promises that she had no part in, things that had been kept from her for her entire life.

She could not allow those thoughts to take hold right now, not with the death of her mother so fresh in her mind. Her mother—who had died doing some sort of spell, like a witch. The clamorous thoughts had her jumping from the bed and exiting the hut into the crisp air without a cloak, still groggy from whatever Tenille had sedated her with the night before. She had not even bothered looking at Xan or Tenille as they had called out behind her. She owed them nothing—but they owed her an explanation.

She had stalked to the river, determined to scrub every ounce of the dried blood from her body. It was when she bent down at the edge of the river where some of the ice had melted, that she slipped off the bank and slid into the water. She had never planned on submerging herself, but once she was under, the thoughts inside her head began rushing in like the raging river, pulling her deeper. She could not withstand it. She *chose* not to withstand it. Her body begged her to stop immersing herself, but she went deeper until her face was swallowed, and she saw the pink water clouding around her. Her mother's blood left the surface of her skin, but it would always run through her veins. Her mother. She did not deserve the breath in her lungs when she had caused her mother to breathe her last.

She is gone.

Ashreya of the Valley had lived her whole life for their clan, *their family*, and lost so much in return. Ravenna could not live in a world where she did not. Not when she had been so unappreciative and so rebellious toward her mother. In a way, her rebellion had cost her mother's life. So, she let the water take her. She let it pull her downstream to the Dead Wood, let it hurl her into rocks and logs and roots. She let it break her. She welcomed it with each breath until she greeted the darkness with a sigh of relief.

Death was dark. Not the somewhat dreadful darkness she met each night in her nightmares, or the silent darkness of the Dead Wood that would swallow one up, but an all-consuming darkness that grabbed hold of her soul and seemed to wring it out of all life. It was an infinite, unnerving darkness.

Until they brought her back.

It was like crawling out of one nightmare into the next.

Life without her mother—and with guilt—or a dark death. She had planted her heels in death, but her friends had pumped and pumped her chest to exhaustion, cracking her ribs. She had entered back into life against her own will on the floor of her cottage, body naked under those fur hides, with Xan hovering over top of her, begging for her to take a breath.

She now sat in front of the fire in her cottage, wrapped in a hide blanket that Tenille had draped over her shoulders, along with many others Ravenna had tried chucking off, only to be wrapped in again. She was burning up. Tenille kept piling more and more covers over her and Xan persisted to keep the fire stocked and burning as hot as possible. He assumed because he was still thawing out from the water—that she too, was cold.

The sun had set and risen once more, and she had not yet had a chance to be anything *but* warm. Broth had been forced down her throat and a freshly boiled herb mixture refilled in her cup repeatedly to help with the pain of the broken ribs. Ravenna was skeptical of drinking anything from the healer, but hot tea was soothing to her throat. Xan and Tenille had not left her since she had woken, and Asta had been in and out all night and all morning. Occasionally, Roarke peeked through the window with hollow eyes.

Tenille tended to the torn and bruised flesh on Xan's hands, and Ravenna shut her eyes at the sight of it, hugging her knees to her chest. Xan seemed distant. He was caught up in everything he could be doing to help her; stocking the fire, getting more blankets—he never sat down long enough for her to ask him anything. She knew that was intentional. Her head was spinning with all that had occurred. She laid back down and turned on her side, careful not to mess up the covers and the pillow on her mother's side of the bed, preserving what little traces of her that she could.

As she plopped her head back onto the pillow, a slick white feather floated out of it and into the air. Her heart sank in her chest. She remembered the day her mother brought the dove's feather to her from her hunt in the Sunstone Forest. *To protect you while you sleep*, she had said, before placing it inside Ravenna's pillow. Its softness was soothing between her fingers.

"We need to leave tomorrow," she said quietly beneath the covers as she rubbed the feather between her calloused fingertips.

There was a long moment of silence before Xan spoke. "What do you mean, Ravenna?"

"The burial. She needs to be buried as my father was." Ravenna heard Xan shift on his feet. "In the Crystal Sea," she added.

"Ravenna, I don't think you're well enough—"

"I have to bury her as she wished," she said.

"Your mother would be fine with a burial in Vestele—"

"No."

Another long pause. "We'll talk about it later," he said. "Get some rest."

She was weak and exhausted, and when she tried to stand, she grew dizzy. But whether Xan liked it or not, tomorrow, they would start the four-day journey to the clear sea that bordered the eastern coast of Brinland. Her parents would be together at last, and she would be here without them.

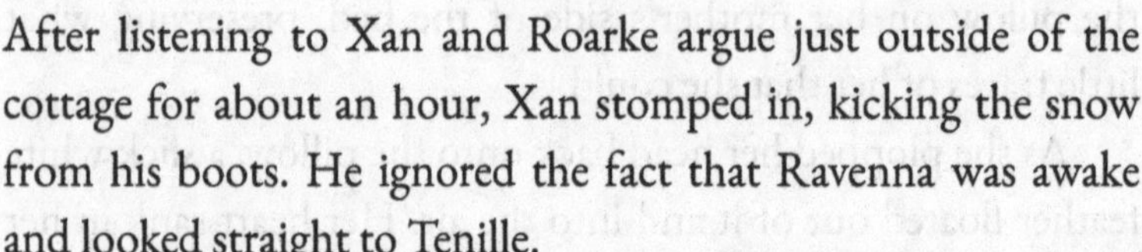

After listening to Xan and Roarke argue just outside of the cottage for about an hour, Xan stomped in, kicking the snow from his boots. He ignored the fact that Ravenna was awake and looked straight to Tenille.

"Is she well enough to handle the journey?"

Ravenna looked between the two of them.

"If she says she is, I think you should go," Tenille said. "I will come with you, too, to make sure she is healthy—"

"Not necessary," Ravenna said. "I'm perfectly healthy."

Xan scoffed, throwing his hands into the air. "Well, it would seem it's four against one here." Ravenna knew that meant that Asta and Roarke had also argued for a burial at the Crystal Sea.

"Make the arrangements, shield-master," Xan muttered to Roarke through the crack in the door, then slammed it in his face.

Ravenna let her head sink back into the pillow and took a deep breath.

Memories of her mother chanting amongst the Despiri entered her mind, but she did not push them aside.

Focus.

The flames in the hearth twisted and curled around the logs, consuming them, and slowly turned them to ash. She blinked. There was no denying it, it was obvious that her mother had been casting a spell. Somehow, her mother was connected to the dark magic said to flow through the remnants of bloodstone in the earth. She had kept this secret from her daughter, and Ravenna would find out why.

Asta entered the cottage. Ravenna did not look in her direction. She stared into the fire from where she now sat at the end of the bed, rolling the pendant of her mother's necklace between her fingers. Asta offered to keep her company for a while, and Ravenna rolled her eyes.

Xan was hesitant to leave at first, but after Tenille's nagging him to take a warm bath and eat a fresh meal in preparation for the long journey tomorrow, he reluctantly agreed, making sure to remind Asta not to let Ravenna out of her sight.

Ravenna began to rise from the bed. Asta said nothing, just held her chin high, bracing for the impending questions and demands. As an elder of the clan, a council member, and someone who had been around longer than Ravenna, Asta was sure to have the answers Ravenna sought. Whether she would give them to Ravenna or not, was the question.

Ravenna stood up and met her gaze. When she was out from under the blankets, she realized that she was indeed, slightly chilled. Making sure to hold eye contact, Ravenna straightened her shoulders and began her spiel.

"As rightful shield-maiden," she paused, letting her words sink in, "I demand answers. My mother was a witch. How?" Asta waited for a moment before lowering her eyes to her lap.

"Your mother was a witch, yes. From a distant lineage." She spoke slowly and carefully.

"Does that make me a witch?" Ravenna knew little about witches and magic, but she assumed that having a mother with witch blood would mean that she too, had witch blood.

Asta smiled softly and shook her head, biting her lip. Ravenna took note of her nervous movements.

"You are not a witch, just as you are not yet acting shield-maiden," she stated. Asta looked Ravenna in the eye once more.

She was right, Ravenna realized. She would not become the official shield-maiden until she challenged Roarke and took an oath in front of the Vestelian Clan.

"If I am not a witch, what is the secret being kept from me by my own people?" she demanded.

"Child, listen to me, and listen carefully. I do not know what you've overheard from Xan and Tenille, but the knowledge we hold is dangerous. Shield-maiden or not, I took an oath. We all did." Asta glanced down to Ravenna's hand, which had found the hilt of a dagger.

Ravenna let out a shaky breath and released it, letting it clink onto the stone ground.

What am I thinking?

Her thoughts were slow, and she was dazed. She felt like she was going out of her mind. Yes, she was sad. But she was also angry, and that anger frightened her.

As the dagger rattled upon the floor, Xan entered through the door carrying two bowls and a loaf of bread. His ashy blond hair was ruffled and wet from his hurried bath. He could not have been gone longer than a couple of minutes. She rolled her eyes at his inability to leave her side for even half an hour.

"What's going on?" he asked, eyes darting to the blade on the ground as he shut the door behind him.

"Ravenna is only excited to get back to training. I think it would do her some good," Asta said. It was not a complete lie. Keeping her cooped up inside the cottage all day had been a bad idea. She needed some way to distract her mind. "Perhaps the two of you could go out—a little bit of normalcy might be nice."

He looked at Ravenna. "There will be plenty of time for that when we return. For now, eat and rest." He sat the bowl next to the bed on the small round table.

The darkness was falling, and on a normal night, the rest of the clan would gather around the fire pit by the longhouse at the center of the village to play music and dance. The joyful sounds of fiddles and flutes often echoed through the valley as the days ended by firelight and under the glow of the moons. Ravenna had always played the fiddle or danced among the others; she had never just sat to listen. Tonight, the music that seeped through the walls of this forsaken cottage was a somber tune she had never heard before. It mourned the passing of Vestele's beloved shield-maiden and crushed Ravenna's soul.

Slowly, she rose from the edge of the bed. She did not pick up her sword or load a quiver onto her back as she always did when leaving the cottage. She sauntered out the door and followed the music, ignoring Xan's questions. He huffed and then attempted to stay quiet as he followed close behind her with her hide cloak in hand.

Her hair was unbound aside from one tiny braid she had refused to unravel. Her mother had woven it together on her last day. The rest of her hair laid in waves as it had dried, falling to the small of her back. Typically, her loose, thick hair would have driven her insane. Tonight, she did not care. The music called to her and twisted in her gut. The man who played her favorite instrument was a warrior by the name of Birger. She had watched him train with the others for many years as she dreamt of joining them. Usually, the strong male had a beaming smile on his face. But not tonight.

With notice of her approaching, he quickly averted his eyes in respect, or out of discomfort, and let her grieve silently. Birger played the mournful notes for hours, the occasional tear sliding down his cheek, while Ravenna sat by the fire surrounded by her people. Though she would not get answers from them due to the mysterious oath, she did find comfort in their company. They were her family. They were all she knew.

They all gathered in sorrow, and when the second moon was at its peak, Ravenna wept. Ingrid, an elderly woman who often spent her days sewing, consoled her with a soft hand on her shoulder. Her face was pleasant and inviting, full of many years of joy and sorrows. The fire was growing weak now and would soon go out for the night as the crowd began to dwindle. Everyone headed to bed, entering the longhouse, cottages, and huts, and Ravenna picked up the wooden instrument that had been laid beside her. Xan was watching from somewhere not too far—she was sure.

Pulling the bow across the far-left string, she created a long, deep sound and began to play. The hair on her arms rose—not from the frigid air—but from the song of many sorrows. Note after note, it was like poetry. Her mother had loved to hear her play, and so she would play for her one last time before they laid her to rest in the Crystal Sea.

One by one, the people who had long since gone to sleep started to gather outside of their homes again to listen. Her audience began to hum and sing an exquisite melody while she played and wept, until her eyes grew heavy. And Ravenna realized then, that there would not be a moment of time that grief did not steal.

14

TO THE SEA
RAVENNA

Morning fog rolled over Vestele, diffusing the light brought by the morning sun. As the first moon, a violet-colored crescent, faded beyond the mountain tops, Ravenna finished packing her saddlebags with enough food and water for the trip. The trek to the Crystal Sea would be a treacherous one. On horseback with adequate weather, it was a four-day ride. One resting point would be Ozanna, but today she could care less about the beauty they would see in the old city of pearls and gold and light. She would not admit it to Xan, but she *was* exhausted and cold. But for her mother, she would endure it.

Draped over her shoulders was a coat of black fur designed for mourning—a gift from Asta. Underneath were two more fur hides and a tunic, which she had hoped would keep her warm enough that Xan would not notice her shivering. Over her head, she wore a black veil, which hid her puffy, tired eyes. Last night, she could not sleep. It was as she expected. She had stayed up late playing that melodious song, and when she had finally returned to the cottage and slipped under the blankets, it was difficult to succumb to the heaviness of her eyes. Especially when she knew what horrors awaited her in the abyss of unconsciousness.

Xan's snoring was enough to keep her awake on its own. It had taken all her strength to resist the urge to smack him upside the head, though she was thankful for the distraction from what the day would bring. All she could focus on was his incessant snoring.

Vestelians bustled around her, packing saddle bags and hugging their family members goodbye. Unable to completely abandon their clan for the burial, most of Vestele's warriors would stay in the valley. They would keep the clan functioning and protect what little resources the winter had left them with until the others returned.

"I still think I should go," Tenille said to Roarke as he passed by. She may have been appointed Ravenna's personal healer by Ashreya, but Roarke agreed with Ravenna and deemed this a trip for only a few warriors in hopes of making the journey quicker. Roarke waved the comment off, and Xan said nothing.

"I promise to be on my best behavior," Ravenna muttered from where she leaned against Fintah. Tenille's gentle and encouraging presence would be needed in Vestele in the coming days. Though, Ravenna now wondered if she had made the right decision in keeping Tenille in Vestele. Her presence could have served as a distraction to Xan and been enough to lessen his hovering. It was wishful thinking. When Ravenna was around, Xan hardly paid Tenille any mind.

Tenille finished shoving herbs and salves into Ravenna's bags on the other side of Fintah. She was rambling. "You'll use this for an open wound, and these herbs will help you sleep. It is expected that one would have trouble sleeping after..."

Ravenna cut her off with a scowl, and the healer's caramel-colored eyes widened as she tightened the leather strap. "Thank you," Ravenna said in the sincerest voice she could manage through her frustration.

Tenille's dark braids swung behind her back as she smiled sadly and spun around to proceed toward the shield-maiden's body. Asta had prepared it with some help from a few other women. In her black hair, they had placed beads of brass and one of jade, and they had laid her upon a bed of strong-smelling cedar. They had packed snow around her, and her pale skin almost matched it perfectly. The deadly wound was covered by her high neck tunic, and the yellow-gold fabric of her clothes seemed to shimmer in the light along with the morning dew. Someone had taken the time to clean and re-paint her face with three specks of kohl down the bridge of her nose; a tribute to her should-have-been marriage with Ravenna's father.

Mindlessly, Ravenna moved toward her. Under the shield-maiden's eyes were thick shadowy lines, with intricate designs beneath—her warrior markings. Between her eyebrows were two swirls, extending from the bridge of her nose. They were new to her mother's skin, but Ravenna knew exactly what they symbolized.

In life, in death, with great respect.

A verse that the clan spoke aloud over their warriors in death. A show of love, great sacrifice, and thanks. An appreciation for her years of service.

Ravenna smiled softly. She pinched one of her mother's small braids between her fingers, and slowly ran them down it, then turned away. Her own braids had taken her twice as long this morning. Without her mother to help her, she had quickly surrendered the task, leaving most of her hair down in waves as it had been last night. The braid her mother had created was woven within the few thick and messy strands Ravenna had added and wrapped across the crown of her head.

Xan had only stared at her with a wrinkled expression as she broke down in front of the looking glass where she had sat with her mother just three days prior...before Roarke had knocked on the door to alert her of news, to which her mother's grave tone suggested she had been expecting. The council meeting that evening, the news Roarke delivered, and Ravenna's post location in the northern Dead Wood...they were all part of a grander scheme that she had been kept utterly unaware of.

If she had known of the plan, perhaps things would have ended differently. If she had listened to Xan and stayed in that tree—*not fired that arrow*. If she had not enticed the leader of the Despiri to use his gifts on her and given him a foothold to use during her mother's spell while she was supposed to be sleeping. If she had stayed in the cottage instead of running out and distracting her mother, creating an opening for the Despiri to break free of the spell which held him. Not to mention the bloodstone which her mother would not have had access to if it were not for her.

I know your secret.

Ravenna stared forward, remembering those words the mind reader had spoken into her head in those dreadful moments. What secret was he referring to?

She clenched her jaw as she observed the small ceremony happening before her. A crowd gathered and people walked by the shield-maiden's body, lowering their heads in reverence. Some placed trinkets and notes upon her still frame. Xan—a paper bird. Tenille—a bead from her own hair. Roarke—a strip of leather, tied into a bracelet. Four warriors gathered around her, their swords meeting in the middle to hover over their fallen shield-maiden.

Together, they declared the words, "In life, in death, with great respect." They raised their swords higher. The rest of the crowd repeated after them.

Though Ravenna's heart had sunken low into her stomach, and her head felt empty, she collected herself enough to mount Fintah. Her horse galloped before all Vestele's people. Ravenna took in a sharp breath and pointed her sword to the sky, announcing the start of the procession to the Crystal Sea.

"For Ashreya of the Valley, shield-maiden, *my mother*." She paused as the knot in her throat tried to cage the words, and then she looked to Xan. "With great respect, we ride."

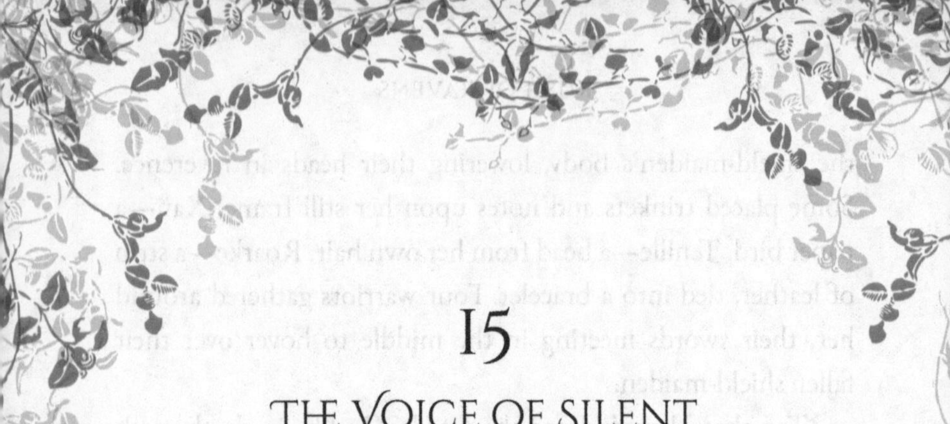

15
THE VOICE OF SILENT DESTRUCTION

XAN

"I don't like it," Xan said to Roarke as he watched Ravenna sway atop her horse. One last time, he would beg the shield-master to cancel the trip and order them to turn around.

"What do you suggest we do? Degare's men will be arriving in Oro tomorrow, if not tonight, and my guess is, the king turns them right back around to come and kill us all." Roarke looked at him for a moment. "I don't think you want Ravenna home when that happens."

He had a point, but Xan still argued. "So, we just leave Vestele without a leader? Defenseless against the Despiri?"

"I've given strict orders. You know the warriors, boy. They are prepared to die for her—as am I."

Xan gritted his teeth. "But the women and children—they're sitting ducks," Xan spat.

"Ravenna comes first. You know that better than anyone. The clan has a better chance in Vestele than traveling in these conditions anyway."

Xan sighed and urged his stallion forward. Ravenna had probably not considered the consequences of killing one of the king's beloved Despiri, but Xan certainly did not judge her for it. Vestele could have reaped consequences anyway for what Ashreya had attempted. It was part of the reason Ashreya had ordered everyone to stand down during the spell: to appear as innocent bystanders in case things went wrong. Even so, Xan doubted that King Degare would show mercy on them. Vestele had committed treason. If the king's men were to return to Vestele in the coming days, Xan supposed he would rather Ravenna be far from the danger, with him.

As Ashreya's second, Roarke should have been leading the procession, but he suggested Ravenna take charge. Xan agreed so that he could keep a constant eye on her. She had become almost catatonic. Never speaking, only staring forward. Roarke believed that Ashreya would have respected the decision to allow her daughter to lead the procession. Xan was not so sure. He was sure of one thing, though. When they returned to Vestele, if they had a clan left, Ravenna would challenge Roarke and take his position.

Allowing Ravenna to claim the title of shield-maiden may be foolish with all the secrets that must be kept from her, but *not* allowing her to be shield-maiden when the title was rightfully hers, well, the consequences would be catastrophic. More suspicion would be raised, and Xan was not so certain Ravenna would willingly stay in Vestele where he could watch over her. She had always strived for more and had never wished to live a quiet life alongside him in their hidden valley. It was in her blood to want more—to wish to make a difference. He knew of the many conversations between her and Ashreya, when Ravenna had tried to convince the shield-maiden to join the war and ally with the Embers. She was enraged at all Degare had gotten away with—killings, village burnings, and that he had left Xan and many others without family in his quest for power. Xan worried that Ravenna would try for vengeance, but as shield-maiden, she could do nothing without first thinking of Vestele's safety. Xan hoped that her love for her people would be enough to keep her out of this war.

He did not blame her for being angry, but he had always hoped she would come around and just be happy to settle where he could keep her safe away from the conflict that would come with getting Vestele involved in the war. When Ashreya had allowed Ravenna to join the warriors, Xan was relieved, in a sense. It meant more danger for her, but it was also an incentive for her to remain in the valley. In joining the warriors, she had been given purpose, and he had known she would stay.

Over the years, he had fallen for Ravenna, and Ashreya had seen it happening. She had given him her blessing, when and if Ravenna was ever ready. He wished for a wife, a family of his own. Xan hung on to what little hope he had left that Ravenna could someday love him as more than a friend.

All day, he and the other four warriors had a view of her back, her red hair falling in long waves, slightly bouncing with each movement of her horse. Xan could not remember the last time he had seen her with her hair unbound aside from the last two days. She had jerked away when Tenille had tried to braid her hair the day before, and today, only a few simple braids wrapped around the crown of her head.

With her hair down, he could not help but notice her unmatched beauty. She was divine. He had fallen in love with the fierceness that radiated from her, but as the ferocity grew over the years, she was becoming harder and harder to tame.

When her hair was pulled from her face, it seemed to illuminate her sharp cheekbones. Surrounded by soft plush waves today, her face seemed softer. The warrior markings on her skin normally contrasted with her eyes, revealing a plethora of vibrant colors. The jade-green eye and the other eye of bright blue, both woven with gold, were like nothing he had ever seen. But today, even against the bright whites of the snow, her eyes were duller than ever. Dark circles burrowed beneath them, and her mouth stayed caged in a tight line.

Her silence was destroying him.

He had been holding his breath for hours, watching her sway back and forth atop Fintah and attempting to stay upright. She refused to stop and rest.

"We will make it to the abandoned palace and then rest until dawn," she had spoken to no one in particular.

Roarke had exchanged glances with Xan, as both noticed her beginning to slump forward.

"Why don't you ride with me?" Xan had suggested, pacing his stallion to match Fintah's speed. Ravenna stared forward and inhaled, her breath leaving her lips in a cloud of fog. "You can lean on me until we make it to Ozanna."

"I'm fine," was all she said in response, urging Fintah forward.

They made it to the palace with little to no altercations or problems. The wind was frigid as expected following along the

Edmarian River in the early spring, and he could see Ravenna visibly shaking during the last hour of their travels. It was all he could do to refrain from asking her to stop so he could build a fire. Sitting upright as she was for hours on end, atop a horse through the mountainous terrain with cracked ribs, was certainly not easy. They were nearly out of the mountains, and midday tomorrow they would cross over into the flatlands of northern Brinland: yet another kingdom ruled by the darkness.

Xan spoke to Roarke under his breath. "Tonight, we'll be safe in the palace, and tomorrow, we'll be under the cover of trees. But the next night, I'm not so sure. Brinland is all plains. Open fields." They would have no cover from the weather and would have no shelter against wandering Despiri or other creatures of darkness that may be lurking by.

Ravenna had never been fond of the King or the Despiri, but now that they had killed her mother, she sought retaliation. Avoiding a fight, if they were to come across another, would be impossible.

She laid there among her mat, the curves of her body stretched out by the fire in the middle of the throne room floor, underneath the ornate, pearly ceiling of the palace. Her eyes were closed, but he knew she did not yet sleep. The bitter cold made it nearly impossible. The throne room had one direct entrance from outside and many available exit routes, hence why Ravenna had chosen it. Xan would be lying if he said he had not hoped for a bed for the night. But the bedroom chambers in the towers would not be a safe bet, and they had been ransacked years ago, anyway. Rodents and animals had likely destroyed the bedding, but that did not stop him from checking.

He snuck away and left Ravenna under Roarke's

supervision for only a moment to find her some blankets. He shot the warrior a warning glare and walked across the throne room tile where he and Ravenna had ridden their horses to take shelter from a storm a few years prior. That day had been burned into his mind like a brand.

It was not ideal to be traveling with a decaying body through the forests. They would have left a day earlier if it had not been for the river incident. Now they would be traveling through a territory of darkness with a body of mouldering flesh, its scent like a beacon to the beasts of dark magic that likely lurked here. Ravenna had little clue what skulked in the world outside of Vestele. He did not care if she was considered the most skilled of the warriors. Against a Despiri or a beast, and with a clouded mind, she stood no chance. At least Xan had previous encounters he had learned from when the warriors had purposely taken to the woods to train against such creatures.

Massive paintings and artworks lined the walls beneath the golden arches of the hallways. Xan's favorite was any painting that depicted the kingdom in all its glory. Sunlight poured over the lands in every painting, and lush greens surrounded the many rivers and waterfalls that cascaded down the flower covered mountains. Doves and butterflies fluttered through the blue skies, and the Sunstone Mountains glittered with gold. The land was once bustling with life, and Xan was taken back to those few years of his childhood spent living right along the river's edge in a village on the outskirts of the kingdom. At the first lick of flame and smothering smoke against his mind, he shook the memories away.

Up the steps and into the closest tower, he came to what must have been the royal chambers. Wind whistled through the colorful, broken glass in the windows, and he held up his torch, scanning the room for any warm linens. The chambers had a view of the eastern mountains, but the war had scorched the villages below the balcony in fire, and Xan averted his eyes, following the sprinkling of glass across the floor to the bed. The linens had been stripped from the feather mattress, but a tapestry hung on the wall. A meticulously woven depiction of a golden tree with seven branches spanned across it, and Xan moved closer, ripping it down with a swift tug. It could serve as a blanket. His torch hit the stone as he backed away from the tunnel that was revealed beyond the tapestry.

Servant passages.

He plucked the torch up from the floor and waved it into the tunnel, revealing an infinite hall of darkness. His forehead wrinkled, and he took only one step in before he remembered why he was here. He needed to get back to Ravenna.

Before he left, a portrait above the bedside table caught his eye. King Gerrin and Willa, The Barren Queen, were depicted in golden crowns, waving from the very balcony that now crumbled above scorched, abandoned villages. The two soulbound lovers held hands, and their faces radiated joy. Upon the queen's cheek was a glowing mark, and its silver hue complemented the silver of the jewelry box on the table below. Xan's eyes were drawn to it. He was surprised it had not been stolen in the years since the kingdom's fall, and he pocketed it for himself, shoving it deep inside his cloak.

When Xan approached the throne room once more, Roarke still stood, staring out into the blackness as he had been when Xan left. Occasionally, he looked over his shoulder at Ravenna, who Xan now covered with the large tapestry, hoping to provide her with a little warmth. Her body still shook, and he was sure she felt pain in her ribs from where he had pumped her heart into rhythm the morning before. He winced as her eyes crinkled in discomfort, then sighed. He had not seen the stubborn woman take any of the medicines Tenille had stocked her saddle bags with this morning, and he doubted she ever would. He lay next to her, a couple feet away, close enough to reach out and touch her—but he did not.

16
WITH ME OR AGAINST ME
RAVENNA

Never straying far from the riverside, their navigation for this trip was quite easy. What made the journey most difficult was the ice that rained from the sky for the first two days. The Edmarian River ran straight through Vestele from the Dead Wood and into the Crystal Sea. They traveled along it mile by mile. Tomorrow evening, they would sleep near the sea after the ceremony, and Ravenna thought she may finally get some rest.

The entire trip was mentally and physically draining. It took a full day to make it out of the worst of the mountains, over steep inclines and rocks. They took many breaks in between for the horses, and because it was difficult traveling with her mother's body. They had slept on the hard, frozen ground of the forest last night after spending the first evening in Ozanna. Fintah was not nearly as exhausted as the other horses, and on a normal day, Ravenna would have boasted her mare's superiority over the others. Today, however, she did not feel like talking.

Each day, she led the group, Xan flanking her right and Roarke on her left. The other three warriors—Nilo, Erik, and Freya—traveled behind them with her mother's snow-covered body. It was late evening now, and they were preparing to stop for the night. Tomorrow, they would make it to the coast.

A few hours after crossing the border into Brinland, the land opened into miles and miles of open plains. The grass was still brown from winter, as spring had not yet grown warm enough to pour life back into the land.

Ravenna knew the kingdom of Brinland to be a kingdom ruled by a King who worshiped the darkness and allied with Degare, but that darkness had not yet spread over the land as she heard it had in Oro. Just across the river was another unfamiliar territory with a dark king. There was forest across the river as far as the eye could see, but beyond that, Ravenna had heard of the vast sandy deserts and hot sun that plagued the north with an eternal summer. Right now, warmth did not sound so horrible.

Ravenna's gut twisted as she glanced back in the direction of her mother. The warriors were all tired and cold, as was she.

Tonight, we will set up camp here.

She held up a fist and motioned for the others to halt before dismounting Fintah and bending down near the edge of the river to fill her canteen. She was too aware of Xan's hovering presence behind her.

"Go start the fire. I'll be fine," she said as the water trickled into the mouth of the small waterskin. Xan did not leave. Instead, he bent down next to her and took her numb, shaking hand, into his own.

Her eyes met his under scrunched brows. "I am here for you," he whispered.

Ravenna shut her eyes for a moment and inhaled. "That is all you are, is *here for me*," she spat, unable to swallow the hurtful words that raged out of her.

He let go of her hand, his eyes crinkling at the edges as he sat back in the brown grass. The weather had grown too warm for snow this close to the coast, though the breeze still held a chill. Ravenna sighed and sat back next to him, overlooking the width of the river and the trees and the sandy soil of Edmaria on the other side. She rubbed a hand over her face.

"I am sorry. This is all too much. I need you to be...*you*. Not my caretaker, not my guardian, *my friend*. As it was. Quit treating me like I am broken." She left her head in her hand for a moment, then took a sip from her canteen. "The mind reader knows my secret, and I do not. Does that not put me at a disadvantage?"

Xan looked to the ground, then his eyes widened as he looked back to her in realization at what she had said. "What did he say to you?" Xan demanded, gripping her hand.

"What is the secret, Xan?" Ravenna challenged, ripping her hand away. Fury radiated from them both, and Xan stood, hands behind his head as he turned a slow circle.

"This is *so* dangerous Ravenna; you have no idea." He paced around her, contemplating, and she rose to meet him where he stood.

"You're either with me on this or against me. Tell me or not, but I *will* get my answers." She stalked off and left him at the river's edge, not caring about the other warriors that watched as she made her bed in the tall grass a few yards from the water. Three large rocks and two lone trees provided the most shelter they would find out here in the plains on this side of the river, and she cozied up against one of the thick trunks, propped up with her blade at her side.

She drifted into a sleep deep enough to rouse some of the terrors out of their hiding places in her conscious mind. Her mistake.

Quietly, in her dream state, she crawled through the Dead Wood. Something was coming, a shadow on the horizon. She moved behind a thick, spindly bush and held her breath, pleading with the wind to blow in her favor and not deliver her scent straight toward the approaching silhouette.

It was as if she had been completely rewritten in her dreams, always fearful and cowering against some approaching darkness that promised to devour.

Out of the shadows came a raven and its handler. The black bird perched on the man's shoulder, and he sent it off with a message. A promise of darkness. At once, she felt a sort of chill run through her body that she had felt before. It was how death had felt in the river.

Ravenna awoke abruptly with a gasp of cold evening air.

Heaving for breath, she lay on her back and stared straight up at the few branches above her. It was past midnight. The first moon was directly overhead, a tad fuller than it had been the night before, and ice had begun to form on the trees. The temperature had dropped since she had fallen asleep, and it would only grow colder until the sun rose. The promise of spring's return seemed to be long gone. That joyride with Xan through the valley seemed like a lifetime ago, and she wondered if warmth would ever return, or if an eternal winter would follow her.

Looking over her shoulder, she saw Xan with his eyes shut, still as stone a few feet from her, though she guessed he was aware of her movement when she slowly rose from the ground. The fire was burning hot, and Roarke leaned against the second tree with his eyes on the horizon.

Her mother's body was surrounded by sleeping warriors, and her frame was still covered in cedar and snow, though some of the snow had begun to melt and refreeze. It was good they would make it to the sea tomorrow. Ravenna turned the bloodstone over in her pocket and walked loudly, ensuring Roarke was aware of her approach.

"I'll take the next watch," she said. Shifting slightly on his feet, he kept his eyes averted. His uneasiness when she was near did not go unnoticed. These last few days, it was as if he had been walking on eggshells, probably trying not to back himself into a corner with her inevitable questions. She had noticed the face of guilt he bore—she understood it all too well.

There was a long pause with only the distant sounds of a wolf pack howling and the breeze whispering through the tall grass of the plains. She had always loved the peace brought by wind, and for a moment, she allowed it to calm her. The sound of rushing water from the river met her ears, the current so strong it would be impossible to cross if they had wished to get to the other side. Just when she thought Roarke was not going to speak at all, he spoke under his breath so the others would not hear.

"She should have told you. She *wanted* to tell you." There was a flatness in the tone of his gruff voice, as he offered her a quick glance. She was not usually one to break eye contact, but his hazel eyes gleamed with a buildup of tears, and she caught herself flinching away from his pain. It was stirring something in her that she did not wish to awaken.

With a gulp, Ravenna quickly looked over her shoulder to

see Xan still sleeping. She brought her gaze back to meet Roarke's. "What should she have told me?" She knew the topic of this discussion was secretive, and that her mother had left her out of it for some reason which she had seen fit. That did not stop her from wanting the truth.

With a shuddering breath, he let a few words leave his lips. "You know by now that Ashreya of the Valley was a witch." His chest rose and fell with a deep breath as if he were about to elaborate.

She nodded.

"And Asta says that I am not. But how?" she asked.

He kept his eyes focused on the darkness that lurked beyond the horizon, and his body tensed further. With the two moons reflecting off the brown grass, the plains were bright enough to see a decent distance. Though she rarely knew Roarke to be a relaxed person, it set her on edge, the way he was standing as if he were ready for war.

She followed his gaze and sure enough, just beyond the horizon, approached a threat. It was something not entirely human—grotesque and large in build. Ravenna sized the creature up. It was *fast*. Her hand was on her sword no longer than a few seconds before the monstrous beast stood tall, towering over them. The distant hoot of an owl silenced, and the wind stopped caressing her cheeks.

Ravenna's breath caught in her lungs, and true fear flowed through her veins. She had led her warriors here to rest for the night, where they were about to be attacked by this monstrous creature of darkness. This beast was likely just one of many threats prowling in these woods. Its ribs were exposed with open flesh, and a black heart was nestled between them, level with Ravenna's eyes. It stood like a man but held its head low, exposing its gnarled teeth. Its eyes were cloudy and seemed to be looking straight over Ravenna's head—at her mother's body. Roarke whispered under his breath as they both stood statuesque beneath the hovering giant, unsure of their next move.

"There are many things you do not know, child. No matter what, do not kill this beast. *Let me*," he uttered in a low voice.

With a strong, swift, and unexpected movement, Roarke pushed her behind his own body and lunged for the beast with his sword. He aimed for the heart, but his blade missed and cracked against the beast's thick ribs. The panic in his eyes sent her leaping forward as she tried to distract the beast to give Roarke time to make a killing swipe.

Its enormous arm flew toward her, landing a blow right in the center of her chest. Her heart pounded against her already cracked ribs, and she gasped for air as she was sent back far enough to land with a thud on the ground next to Xan. He jolted awake, and shoved her behind him, his sword already in his other hand. Ravenna coughed, but quickly rose to her feet, racing toward the monster. Xan yelled behind her, and the creature made a hideous, low growl. With that, she heard every sleeping warrior begin to stir.

In the faint light of the moons, she could make out a shimmer of something forming at the middle of the beast's arm. A shard of bone peeled through its skin to form a makeshift blade. With a motion quicker than man could move, the monster maneuvered to the left, and pierced the bone straight through Roarke's abdomen. Ravenna screamed, and she forced herself forward, past the pain of moving and toward the creature with her sword in hand.

She fought like mad, ducking and dodging the creature's

blows, drowning out the sound of Xan yelling incomprehensible words and orders. The beast's movements were fast, but she moved faster. She sliced with her sword and stabbed with her dagger, contacting whatever soft tissue she could reach.

Xan joined her and tried to take over, to force her away from the beast, but she pushed back. One of her warriors—Freya—screamed in a panic behind her. "Ravenna, stop!"

Erik yelled, "Don't kill it!"

But when that black heart hovered in front of her face, with a robust swing, she plunged her favorite dagger through the meaty, rotten flesh. Black blood sprayed onto her face and her cloak, and she could have sworn the blade warmed in her hand against the icy winter. Slowly, the monster collapsed to the ground with one loud crash. It belted a low snarl that seemed to reverberate through the ground beneath her feet before drawing its last wavering breath.

There was silence all around her. Roarke lay on his side, curling into his open wound. His breathing was ragged, and she ran to him, placing her hands on his abdomen in an attempt to halt the bleeding. She heard the other warriors gather behind her.

"A witch guardian. You *killed* a witch guardian..." Xan whispered in disbelief. "They'll never stop coming for you."

A witch guardian.

The words were heavy, unclear as the adrenaline swept through her. Ravenna had been warned of the witch guardians. But in the heat of the moment...

Xan stared straight forward; his face grim as his gaze rested on the dead beast. Ravenna looked between her friend and Roarke, who was dying before her.

Roarke's face grew paler by the second, and she grasped his hand, begging him to stay with her. "Please. Just hang on."

The warriors stood still, staring down at her. Nilo's sword hung at his side in defeat, and Erik paced in a circle.

"Why is no one tending to Roarke? Help him!" she demanded as her knees sank into the dewy grass. They should have brought Tenille. With her hands, she put pressure on the gaping wound, Roarke's blood pouring out around her fingers.

Red.

Freya and Nilo stirred from their shock and bent down to help. With a quick and panicked sweep of sight, Ravenna noticed Xan had not even moved one muscle. He only stared straight forward at the dead beast with a distant expression. Her hands were covered in bright red blood, once again.

How long had Roarke known this beast was following us? Why was I so quick to kill it, so careless? She knew the stories.

Roarke took in one shaky breath and the grip he had on Ravenna's wrist began to loosen. Why had he tried to keep her from helping him?

Roarke turned his head to the side where the witch guardian lay dead, and then slowly turned it back to Ravenna. He shook his head at her. "Child, *what have you done?*"

A sound of defeat choked out around the knot in her throat as Roarke took his last breath. His worried, crumpled gaze remained on his face even in death.

17

THE WEEPING

XAN

Xan watched Ravenna weep over yet another body, and all he could think about was how she would be hunted for the rest of her days by the entire race of witch guardians. She would not survive this curse.

How is this happening?

The argument had angered him, and foolishly, he had fallen asleep. From what Xan could gather, Roarke was going to sacrifice himself and kill the witch guardian which had come to retrieve Ashreya's body. Perhaps the warrior had redeeming qualities—but his efforts had failed once again. Without failure, Roarke would have lived a life of solitude, on the run— hunted unto death. Now, Ravenna faced that same sentence.

Where the guardians came from, Xan did not know. He assumed the witches to have control over them in some way, but Ashreya had never mentioned their origin. If she did not mention it, it was probably because she had not known. There was a reason that the Ozannes had done their best to mine the bloodstone from the grounds of Arresia. It was through the bloodstone that the system of dark magic thrived. Through those minuscule, tiny particles and veins of bloodstone, the dark power reverberated through the ground.

Now, with the lack of bloodstone, it was even more important for the guardians to maintain what dark power was left. None of it could be wasted. The dark magic was limited, as opposed to the Light that Embers possessed, which seemed to be infinite. Legend had it that the guardians would stop at nothing to avenge their own.

"Xan, what are we going to do?" Freya said beside him, brushing her blonde hair away from her face. Nilo leaned against a tree nearby, and Erik still paced nervously.

All the warriors knew what it meant, to see the beast lying dead next to Roarke, black blood and red blood alike staining the front of Ravenna's cloak.

He shook his head. "She is cursed. I don't know how to get her out of this one."

"Roarke is dead. Ravenna is now the rightful shield-maiden if she still wants it. But she is cursed, so she cannot be our new leader, right? The witch guardians will never stop coming for her. The Despiri are sure to attack—Vestele will be gone when we return, and let's not mention that the Ink Bloods are probably also seeking revenge—"

"Enough," Xan said to Freya, who was rambling out of fear. "You don't have to say every thought aloud."

Tomorrow they would bury two bodies, and soon, they would bury yet another shield-maiden, the one they had all given their lives to protect. Who would take Ravenna's place? Vestele would have to settle for him as shield-master. He had never wanted this, and without Ravenna—without Ashreya—he was not sure he could bring himself to stay.

Nilo spoke up. "I've never seen one."

"Me either," Freya said, staring at the dead guardian.

"That is because they only come out when there is a dead witch. I should have known. I should have remembered the stories. I should have been prepared." He had heard the stories as a child. Stories of their black hearts and their large, monstrous frames that embodied the strength of a dozen men. The monster had thrown Ravenna twenty feet as if she was weightless.

How had I been so careless, overlooking the possibility of a guardian coming for Ashreya?

Ravenna had grown up sheltered from many things, but she too, had heard the stories of the witch guardians. Like Xan, she had probably never seen it as a possibility that she would ever have to kill one. Witch guardians did not attack unless one prohibited them from retrieving a witch's body—which Roarke had done for Ravenna, so that she may see her mother laid to rest. In the moment, Ravenna did what anyone under attack would do.

"They'll never stop coming for her," he whispered again.

"What do you mean, they'll never stop coming for me?" Ravenna asked as she approached him in her state of shock.

He stared at the black blood on her dagger. "You're marked," was all he could say in response. "You're marked." He was going to vomit.

Ravenna would be hunted, and she would not be safe until every witch guardian in Arresia was killed. Hundreds, or maybe thousands—he did not know. He only knew that killing that many witch guardians was impossible. Once you killed one, you were hunted until death. But the more you killed, the more guardians would come for vengeance. Xan knew Ravenna would keep killing until it was too much to keep up with, until the entire race was in their valley, and she had no choice but to fight to her literal death.

Ravenna was unquestionably the fastest warrior in Vestele—the best. But she was arrogant, and reckless at times, and because of this mistake, death quickly dawned upon her. He would do everything in his power to teach the warriors of Vestele how to defend Ravenna and disable a witch guardian in the event of an attack until she could make the kill. He would even take the fall for her—he would kill witch guardians until it was only his life they cared about.

18

MARKED
RAVENNA

arked. She was marked.

"What do you mean, marked, Xan?" he stared at the black blood on her dagger, and she threw it into the snow. "What do you mean?" She could not help but raise her voice at him, though she already knew the answer. She had killed a witch guardian, and for that, there were repercussions. She did not want to believe it.

"I won't let them kill you," he said, eyes still on the bloody dagger. She shook her head.

"Roarke was going to let himself be marked. For me," she realized. Xan nodded. Roarke should have never done such a thing. She was not deserving of the sacrifice. "Vestele is now without a leader, and likely to be attacked by Oro, because of me. And now the witch guardians," she said.

Nilo added, "And probably the Ink Bloods, too, if Leith survived the earthquake after you stabbed him." Xan shot the warrior a glare.

"We'll figure it out. We'll keep you safe," Xan said.

"This isn't about me. This is about the clan. I've put all of Vestele in danger." Freya's eyebrows raised, and her head nodded in agreement.

"And we'll figure it out, but not now. Right now, we need to keep moving. All we need are more of those beasts finding us without cover." Ravenna looked to the dead guardian, and then to Roarke. Her throat tightened.

"Erik, stop pacing and help Nilo load Roarke. Freya, pack the saddlebags. I'll ready the horses." Ravenna looked around as the four of them shuffled through the darkness, each completing their own task.

Ravenna led Fintah to the river alongside Xan. "I can't go back to Vestele." Xan's brown eyes shot toward her as he began to object, but she cut him off. "You *know* I can't. The guardians will follow me wherever I go."

"You'll be safe in Vestele," he said, as if it were the end of the discussion.

"And what about the others? I heard you arguing with Roarke before we left. You think I don't know your concerns, that the Despiri will return for me while we're gone? The Ink Bloods? And now the witch guardians if I go back. I've cursed our clan beyond measure. *I* am a curse to my own people. I've made us more enemies than we can count."

"It doesn't matter. We can protect you."

"No, you can't. Just like you couldn't protect my mother." Xan flinched, and the hurt that swelled in his eyes softened her voice. "You cannot protect me from this, and I won't let you try." He grabbed her by the arms, forehead creasing.

"Where you go, I go, Venna. So come back to Vestele or

stay out here in these wretched plains where the guardians will kill you. But just know that I will be right there with you. Dead, or alive." She wriggled out of his grasp.

"You're insufferable," she huffed. "If I am to go back to Vestele, it is because I am shield-maiden." She watched his jaw clench and unclench as he tried to decide if he was going to object or not.

He started, "I don't think you're entirely in the right mind to make decisions involving the survival of our clan."

She laughed in disbelief as the river rushed behind them, and the other warriors hauled Roarke's limp body over top of a horse in the distant shadows of the night. She pinched the bridge of her nose and breathed deeply. "But *you* are? You, Xan, are too concerned with *my* safety. I can't trust you. You've kept so much from me. My mother was a witch. What more are you keeping from me? The only thing I can trust you with is my life. You would put me above our *entire* clan. That is not right. So maybe I *will* go back to Vestele. Because as shield-maiden, at least the decisions involving me are mine to make." Roarke had died for her, and so she would become a shield-maiden worth dying for. She would get her clan out of this mess. They would be safe again. Somehow.

"Well, you're not shield-maiden yet, and I am the only one here on the council. So that puts me in charge."

"Whatever, Xan. This time next week, it'll be me. And you won't be able to risk your own neck for my life any longer because I won't *let* you. I am tired of people dying because of me." She fought the tears that welled in her eyes, and angrily swiped a hand across her cheek as she stomped back toward the warriors who waited beside the bodies of her fallen mother and friend. Xan did not call after her, and she did not look at him for the rest of the night.

They had been traveling nonstop for over sixteen hours. The horses were growing tired and though Ravenna would have stopped to give the warriors and herself some rest, Xan kept pushing.

"We'll make it to the Crystal Sea within the hour if we just keep going," Xan grunted.

He was right; she could smell the salt in the air, heavy with humidity. But her ribs ached, and she struggled to stay upright any longer. Roarke's horse carried his body, and Ravenna refused to look back and acknowledge the grief that trailed her.

The late afternoon sun beamed down on them. The grass was slightly greener in the fields they now trudged through, and just over the horizon she caught sight of the blue sea with skies of pink and orange spreading above, swirling like paint on a canvas as the sun set in the west behind them. The ocean was more massive than she had imagined. Waves crashed into distant rocks, spraying white foam.

Xan was tense as he led the group east, straight into the wind, and Ravenna pulled a scarf across her face, shielding her sore throat against the cold front.

"What happened to spring?" Freya muttered.

"We're only a few days in. It's always cool until the middle of the season," Nilo said.

"Not this cold," Freya said under her breath. Erik and Xan stayed silent, and so did Ravenna. Within the hour, they would start the ceremony to bury her mother and Roarke at sea. She could think of nothing else. But soon, Ravenna would begin her journey to healing from the brokenness and grief that had consumed her wholly.

Just as the sun was setting, they made it to the Crystal Sea. Crouching next to her mother just off the shore, Ravenna held her cold hands one last time and brushed a finger down her face as a tear slipped down her own.

The warriors gathered around, carrying the wooden rafts they had built for her and Roarke to the sand where the waves licked the rocky beach. The two bodies laid upon the rafts, covered in cedar. They had prepared Roarke as well as they could in the short time they had between arriving at the beach and sunset. In the distance, a raven perched atop a rock, watching her intently as its feathers swayed with the wind. Ravenna watched it back for a moment, and then she led the four warriors and the two fallen into the clear waters of the Crystal Sea. Wading to her knees brought her mind back to the icy river. Her pulse began to rise, and she breathed deeply, trying to ground herself in remembering who she was and what she owed to her people. She owed them the promise of safety.

Within a few minutes, she had placated her breaths. Shivering, with one body on each side of her, she turned from her mother for a moment to pay her respects to Roarke.

Placing a hand on his chest, she whispered, "Your death will not be in vain."

He had died trying to protect her, and she would not let it be for nothing. As shield-maiden, she would protect every soul in Vestele. She would save them from the enemies she had summoned.

At her lead, the warriors solemnly said together, her own raspy voice cracking, "In life, in death, with great respect."

The others gave her space as she pulled her mother further out to sea and prepared to let her go. She knew they all watched her like hawks from the shallow water, except Xan, who was a mere few feet away, light waves rippling around him as they walked deeper. When the water had come up just over her hips, she looked upon her mother's face. Her markings and her tattoos were beautiful; intricate. The shield-maiden had never let the kohl fade too much before darkening it, but over the four-day journey, the markings had lost their pigment. Ravenna wished she had the kohl or ink to trace over them one last time.

Ravenna's finger traced the circular designs down her mother's thin nose and hovered over the band of thick kohl across her beautiful eyes. They were closed, but she could almost envision their staggering green color that always delivered her to the pines of the eastern Sunstone Forest. Without a thought, Ravenna's hand trailed up to her own neck to meet the brass necklace that now rested there. A knot built inside her heart. It worked its way up her throat and slowly choked her until she started to shake with sorrow.

She slowly reached into the breast pocket of her tunic and pinched a soft, white feather between her fingers. She folded it beneath her mother's hands.

"To protect you while you sleep, Mama."

A tear trailed down Ravenna's cheek, dropping onto her mother's face. Ravenna pushed her further into the water, and as she let go of her mother's hand and watched her drift away into peace, she whispered, "I love you."

In that moment, the ocean breeze wrapped around her and swirled through her hair, kissing her with the comfort of her mother one last time.

19

THE CURSE THAT KNOWS NO END

RAVENNA

Across the river, the sands faded into moss as they traveled west. A few miles west of a coastal town called the Thickets was a forest. As they rode along the riverside, Ravenna peered across the roaring waters, eyes monitoring the trees for any movement. With each rustle of wind, Xan's grip tightened on his blade. Ravenna remembered seeing the forest on her map once. The grove would be a nice place to hide out if needed. It was close to town, yet enough of an uphill trek out of the way that no one would bother to look there or travel through. A little cabin was nestled there just beyond the trees, as if someone else had the same idea as her. Probably many years ago by the looks of the rotting wood and the thin layer of moss that had begun to spread across every surface. She wondered if the cabin was abandoned as it appeared, or if someone currently lived under its leaky roof. She looked to Xan and the way his knuckles stayed white with fear, tension bleeding from his shoulders— then she looked to the other warriors whose eyes did not grow lazy for one moment. Each one watched their surroundings as hawks scouting for prey. But Ravenna knew that in this case, she was the prey—and the guardians, the hawks.

It is foolish for me to think I can protect Vestele on my own.

Perhaps she should stay here and hide herself within the walls of that cabin, far from her people. There was no guarantee that the Despiri or the Ink Bloods would attack, but one thing was certain, and that was that the witch guardians would not relent until they had her head.

Xan was badgering her, as was expected, to get back to Vestele as soon as possible. They were able to travel quicker on the way home with less cargo and an extra horse to alternate between. Thankfully, the air grew warmer each day, and Ravenna held onto hope that true spring was near.

She had plenty of time to think over the last few days spent constantly riding, with nothing but the sounds of rain and hooves and wind to cloud her mind. Roarke had never planned on returning to Vestele, and she should not either.

Xan rode silently ahead of her, and she groaned, nudging Fintah to catch up.

"If this curse is as severe as you all are acting, perhaps I *should* just stay here. I don't want to lead the guardians straight into Vestele," she said. Even as shield-maiden, she feared she would not be able to salvage her home, especially not with the witch guardians trailing her.

Xan kept his eyes forward, back straight. "You're not staying here. And yes—it is severe." He looked at her. "You know the legends as well as I do. It is a curse that knows no end."

"Except death," she said.

"Except death," he repeated. She paused for a moment, allowing the sounds of their horses' hooves on the rocky forest floor to encompass them.

"So, they'll stop at nothing. I can't let Vestele be caught in the middle. I won't be able to live with myself—"

He cut her off. "And I can't let you die, Ravenna. Which you will, if you stay here." He looked at her again. "You are coming back to the valley, where we can protect you. End of discussion."

"How can you protect me?" she asked.

"The same way I always have!" he said, growing frustrated.

"By keeping things from me?" she shot back.

"No. By putting your safety above my own."

"Xan, no." She pulled Fintah to a halt. "You're not killing any witch guardians for me."

He stopped his own horse, the company of warriors halting behind them. He looked around, then said, "We'll talk. But for now, all this loud arguing is just a beacon for them to find you. Keep moving."

With that, she gritted her teeth, and they continued their way west toward Vestele.

A few hours after the sun had reached its highest, when they were nearing the valley and she was growing uneasy, Xan shifted on his stallion to face her.

"We'll explain what happened to the rest of the council and

make a decision—a plan on how to protect you," he said quietly, but his eyes dipped to the ground as he spoke, and she did not believe him.

"The council is now only you and Asta," she said.

"We'll have to re-establish a council with the new shield-maiden. Or master," he said, scanning his surroundings once again for the return of the guardians.

She rolled her eyes. He was forcing her to return to Vestele, and she would see to it that *she* was the new shield-maiden. Xan would not be making any more decisions regarding her life or the clan's survival for that matter. It would be her making all the decisions because her trust extended to no one else. Xan's grip on the reins of his horse did not loosen, and Ravenna eyed his white knuckles in frustration. Each whisper of a breeze and every chirp or caw of a bird earned his hand a place on the hilt of his sword.

Ravenna said in annoyance, "If a guardian *does* jump from the weeds, please, for the love of Light, let me kill it."

Xan grimaced. "Sure, you can make the killing blow," was all he said.

Hours passed, and he had hardly spoken to her aside from their arguments. Though she had yearned for the quietness on the journey *to* the sea, she craved normalcy now more than ever. She would do anything to have her friend back, even if he would not tell her the answers she wanted to hear. She had decided that she could look past the secrecy, for now. But that did not mean she would trust him.

What is he thinking about?

"Xan." His jaw clenched in response to his name, and he continued staring ahead. "I want..." *to talk like we used to.*

He cut her off. "I cannot give you what you want, Ravenna. I will never be able to give you whatever it is that you want." His tone was sharp, and his words cut through her. It sounded as though he was speaking of something completely different than she was.

"I will not apologize for not wanting the same things as you," she said. He still did not look at her. "I need you. You are my best friend. You are keeping things from me, and I just need answers. I need us to be *us* again." He was the only family she had left.

He sighed deeply, contemplating his answer. "Every day, I am burdened with the blood oath that I took to protect you —," she scrunched her brow as he continued. "It kills me. The oath itself is not what you think. I physically *cannot* tell you. Even in death, the blood oath still reins, Ravenna. It was spelled. If I tell you, *I die*. Then who will protect you?"

Ravenna carefully watched his expression. *A spelled oath? Why would my mother go as far as to make Vestele trade their lives for these secrets? What were they hiding?* "Protect me from what? From who?" she pried.

Asta had claimed that all the people in Vestele had taken this oath, and Roarke had been about to tell her something about it before the witch guardian attack because he had known he would die anyway. He had wanted her to know the truth.

"It is better if you do not know," Xan said to her. "And besides, as I have just said, I physically cannot tell you, unless you value such secrets above my life."

Ravenna bit her cheek. No more would die. Not Xan, not

anyone. Especially not because of her or these secrets. She did not say one word as her mind continued spinning and spiraling through the last several days and all that had happened since the night of the Despiri.

She swallowed hard, wishing she could release him of his burden to protect her. Her fingers curled around the reins and her nails dug into her palms as she remembered those four words whispered into her subconscious just over a week ago.

I know your secret.

Promise of revenge trickled through her veins, warming her until she was as a white-hot branding iron. Ravenna knew where to find her answers: in the heart of Oro with the Despiri that had likely read every mind and learned every secret in Vestele. She would track Jio down before *he* could get to *her*, and revenge would find the king for what his Despiri had done to her mother. Vestele would know no enemies, and Degare and his men would pay before she let the witch guardians steal the breath from her lungs.

20

SHIELD-MAIDEN

RAVENNA

"Are you sure you want to go through with this? Shield-maiden is a big responsibility," Asta said as she wove her hands over and under, strands of Ravenna's rust-colored hair coiling around her fingers.

"I know the commitment I am making," Ravenna said. "And if someone wants to challenge me for the position, let them. We all know it is where I am meant to be."

Asta exchanged a glance with Tenille, who mashed some charcoal in a small bowl at the wooden table of the bakery.

Thankfully, the last three weeks since her return to Vestele had been silent. Her clan remained unharmed, no word had come from Vestele's spy in Oro on the Despiri's probable attack, and nothing had been heard of the Ink Bloods. But, Xan was still on edge, and Ravenna awaited the imminent return of the witch guardians. "I've gotten us into this mess, and I will get us out."

"And just what are your plans?" Asta said as she secured the last of the numerous braids to Ravenna's head.

"I have many. But I've already started with prepping the warriors for war. We've grown too accustomed to the safety of our valley that may not remain without conflict much longer."

Tenille made a racket at the table as she powdered the charcoal. "You can't just volunteer us for war because you are vengeful," the healer said. Asta shot Tenille a look of warning, and Ravenna rolled her head back on her shoulders.

"What is it with you and Xan? You both assume that as shield-maiden, I am planning to take our clan to war. I'm trying to protect Vestele because *I've* attracted enemies, and I am the only one I can trust to get us out of this mess. Who else can do it? Not Xan. He *only* cares about me. My life. Not anyone else's. He has made that clear."

Tenille's cheeks reddened and her teary eyes shifted to the table.

"Speaking of Xan, I think he is coming by soon. He has something for you," Tenille said. Sunlight flashed into the kitchen as she opened the door and waltzed out into the streets of Vestele, her long, beaded hair swaying behind her.

"You'll have to forgive her. She is growing impatient with Xan. It's hard for her to see how he cares for you."

"It is not like it's genuine. He took a blood oath. He is required to care," Ravenna muttered, rising from the stool to buckle herself into her leather tunic.

"You know that is not true. He did take an oath; everyone did. But not every man in Vestele is in love with you." Ravenna flinched at the four-letter word and tightened up the straps of her boots.

With impeccable timing, Xan stepped through the door.

"You look like you haven't slept in ages," Ravenna said. He shut the door and rolled his eyes, kicking the dirt from his boots before he walked further. The harsh breeze that swept through the valley today had reddened his cheeks and ruffled his hair, and she smiled as he tried to tame it with his fingers.

He nodded his greeting to Asta. "I'll give you two some privacy," she said before shuffling up the stairs to the pottery workshop. Ravenna and Xan had not spoken much on the topic of her becoming shield-maiden, or of anything else for that matter, but she was aware that he was not keen on the idea. Since she had already set her mind to it, he had probably realized it was not worth arguing about.

"Everything is ready for the ceremony. Are you sure you're ready for this?"

"Born ready," she said, forcing a smile. There was an odd silence, and then, only the patter of his knuckles drumming on the table. The bowl of charcoal rattled.

"Tenille mixed it up," Ravenna said as Xan reached for it.

"For your face?" he asked.

"Do me the honor?"

He smiled, skin around his eyes crinkling. "You're going to trust *me* to paint your face?"

"Just do it before I change my mind," she said, shoving him with a fist to his chest. He pulled the stool in front of him and motioned for her to sit facing the window where the light was bright. "Do it like Mama used to wear hers."

He dipped his thumbs into the shadowy powder and cupped her face in his hands. He brushed his fingers over her skin, forming a dark band across her eyes. When he was done, he tilted her chin up with a soft touch and examined his work.

"Beautiful, Venna," he said.

Her hands fidgeted in her lap. "Tenille said you had something for me?"

"Oh, yeah." He reached into his pocket and pulled out a small silver box. "I got this for you to keep your necklace in. I know it is one of the last things you have of your mother, so I figured you might like a safe place for it."

"Xan, this must have cost a fortune. Where did you get this? Where did you get the money?" she asked. Vestele did not participate in buying or selling and had no need for currency.

"I didn't buy it," he said.

"You stole it?"

"*Found* is a better term."

She examined the intricate designs, the small, hand painted doves that graced each flat surface and the brushed gold vines that seemed to hold the birds captive.

"It is beautiful. Thank you," she said, allowing him to wrap her in a hug.

"Try it out," he suggested as he pulled away, brown eyes flitting to the necklace at her chest. But she had not removed the necklace since the night she had put it on, and the thought of doing so quickened her heart rate.

"I will later," she assured him. "But I think we need to head out. It's almost noon."

"Don't want to keep them waiting, shield-maiden," he said, wrapping his arm over her shoulders and escorting her toward the door. Things were beginning to feel natural between the two of them again, but those secrets were always at the back of her mind. Despite it, she leaned into him, soaking in each moment of normalcy she could get.

The green grass of the valley—brown only a few weeks ago—now flourished with life, and the sun was shining overhead amid the bright blues of the sky. The sunstone mountains glistened golden in the light, and the trees began to sprout new leaves. But behind her, the shadows of the Dead Wood loomed. Four warriors stood guard around the ceremony, each watching fixedly into the trees of both forests. Xan's arms were crossed, and his eyes were on her, but every few moments they darted from side to side, monitoring for witch guardians. Ravenna stood before Vestele on a small platform in front of the wooden longhouse where the warriors were now exiting to witness her vow to Vestele.

Small children ran through the crowd handing out honeyberries and little pieces of bread that Asta and Tenille had baked especially for this occasion. The feast would come later, and for once, there was to be enough food for everyone. Ravenna could not help but smile as she watched the little ones running freely without care. They knew nothing of the threats that lay outside of Vestele. Not too long ago, Ravenna had been ignorant as well, but not anymore.

Xan stepped up onto the platform beside her, and the entire clan fell silent as they awaited his speech. He cleared his throat.

"After the death of our beloved Ashreya, the Vestelians are without a leader. The position of shield-maiden is to be won by a warrior whose skills are unmatched. The shield-maiden is to lead and protect our clan with her life, and Ravenna has sworn to do so."

Her people stayed silent, each set of eyes peering up at her.

"If anyone wishes to challenge Ravenna, to claim this position as their own, and to vow their life to the safety and survival of the clan, speak now." Utter silence remained, but a few eyes zipped between him and Ravenna. Ravenna found Tenille peering expectantly at Xan from the crowd.

Xan continued, and Tenille sighed as if disappointed. "If there is no one to challenge her, we all know Ravenna to be a great warrior—"

"The best!" A young boy proclaimed, raising his sword. Ravenna hid her smile.

"She will make a great shield-maiden," Xan said. His lips tightened, and he gestured for Ravenna to make her vow.

She swallowed and stepped forward, watching her clans' proud, beaming faces.

"As a child, I was childish. Unaware. Not privy to the information my mother—and you all—keep from me. Because of these things, I was reckless. I have been prideful. But it is in my pride that I have been made to bow before you. You have all given something for me. For some reason, you have all risked your lives so that my mother could be sure of my safety. She was always so scared of losing me after the death of my father, and now, we have lost her. The survival of the Vestelian Clan— my people—*our* people—is definite. Because I vow to uphold Vestele, to protect this clan against all darkness, to separate us from the enemies which I have made. As your shield-maiden, I will allow no harm to come to you. Once protected by Vestele, now protector *of* Vestele. I am the shield in which our home stands behind."

As she lifted her sword to the air, the clan cheered. As she prepared for the selection of her council, she scanned her people one last time.

"Nilo, a warrior," Ravenna said, calling her friend up to the platform. "Xan, my second in command." Because it was always going to be him. "Asta, my elder." Asta dipped her head in reverence as she joined them. "And Tenille," Ravenna said, motioning for her friend. "My healer." Tenille looked surprised but fell into place next to her mother.

Ravenna smiled. "This, is my council," she announced. Her council, chosen because when she was gone, killed by the Despiri or the guardians, these four would protect Vestele with their lives, just as she had. As second, the position of shield-master would fall right into Xan's lap, and he was too honorable to walk away. The five of them held hands as the clan cheered, and Xan leaned in to speak words only she could hear. "Protect your clan, but do not kill yourself trying."

She let go of his hand and said aloud to everyone, "Let's eat!"

As she released her clan to feast, she pulled Nilo to the side. His shoulder-length hair was messy, and his smile was wide with pride in his new position.

"Yes, shield-maiden?"

"I need you to do something for me," she said quietly. His brown eyes flashed with curiosity. "I need you to ride west. See if anyone in surrounding towns have heard of Leith's survival... or death. We need to know if the Ink Bloods are a threat."

His eyebrows scrunched together in the center. "When do I leave?"

"Tomorrow morning," she said. Nilo nodded, and she knew she could trust him.

Xan watched carefully as they spoke, and she turned toward her people as they swarmed her with hugs and cups of rum. They feasted on fish and venison and drank until dusk. Dancing men and women circled the fire, joyfully carrying on beneath the twinkling stars while the quick melody of Ravenna's fiddle echoed through the valley.

Even when the lavender skies faded into black, her people still celebrated, and the night was almost as it was before the darkness had touched her.

21

THE RETURN OF HAPPINESS
RAVENNA

She is dead.

When Ravenna woke, her mother's death was the first memory that came to her. Ravenna turned to the side, letting her head sink into the feather pillow. Her eyes went straight to the dagger on the table—the one she had used to kill the Despiri, and then they fell to the bloodstone beside it. It was the stone that Ravenna had claimed in the Brunts and given to her mother, who had drawn from it to do the spell that had led to her death. Uncontrolled and reckless anger overcame Ravenna.

Her feet hit the floor and her hands found the covers. She ripped the furs and pillows from her mother's side of the bed, gathered the clothing out of the wooden chest, and threw it all into the fireplace. She turned to the mug that still sat on the table where her mother had left it a month ago. It had been the first piece Ravenna had ever made on the pottery wheel her mother had gifted her, and it was lopsided and had since been chipped at the top. But each night, her mother drank her tea from it while she sharpened her blades or carved arrows from stone. Ravenna shattered it against the rocky wall of the cottage. Furious shouting spewed from her mouth, and she bent to collect them, throwing each tiny piece into the flames. She continued in her fury until Xan threw the door to the cottage open.

"Venna," he said, crouching next to her, taking her hand in his. "Let me help you."

"I do not need your help!"

"Ravenna, quiet down," he said.

"Why? Are you worried our people will think I am insane? Because my mother is dead, and I am in here yelling at no one and burning all her things, and there are secrets being kept from me? My mother was a witch, she was trying to kill those Despiri—an *attack* on Oro, and was she trying to save the prisoners in that wagon? And what is the blood oath she made you all take? I am drowning—"

Xan pulled her to him and rested his chin on top of her head. She knew he peered at the black smoke now rolling up the chimney as her mother's belongings burned.

"I cannot stand it," she said, gesturing toward the clothes. "I cannot stand to be reminded. Not when those men still breathe."

He pulled her closer, rubbing her back.

Ravenna would do as her mother would have and protect her people at all costs. But once she knew Vestele was safe and taken care of, she would avenge her mother's death. Starting with the man named Jio. She would pry those secrets from him, and then she would kill them all, including the king. She did not care that Oro was a four-day ride, or that she would have to sneak out without plans of ever returning to the valley. Xan would be fine. They would *all* be just fine without her.

"Rav—shield-maiden," Tenille addressed her.

For the love of Light, she was tired of this, and it had only been a week since the ceremony.

"Ravenna is fine." The motivation to be a great leader that had bloomed after Roarke's death was still there beneath her skin—beneath the guilt. But today, she did not wish to be reminded of her new position. Not after she had woken this morning and destroyed all her mother's belongings. Death and duty had been the only things on her mind, day, and night.

"Sorry. I brought lunch." Tenille motioned to the five young women behind her, who all carried soup in the clay pots that Ravenna had made in her workroom several weeks ago.

Thank the Light, her warriors were starving. Tension between the two of them remained. Tenille was apologetic, and Ravenna was trying to forget how Tenille, and everyone in Vestele, was keeping something from her. Ravenna had not forgotten, but answers would come soon enough, when she deemed Vestele safe and left for Oro.

She and Xan had been training the warriors incessantly all day. The weather was finally warm enough to train without a cloak but chilly enough in the night that a fire had to be kept in the cottage hearth. The warm weather would not stay until after The Darkening—the darkest week of the year—which was to happen in a few days. That week, the temperatures would fall once more, and only after would they peak with the summer season. Tenille's gaze was fixed behind Ravenna on Xan's bare back as he went through repeated motions with his sword, his muscles shifting with every movement. Four dozen warriors mirrored him. It made her proud to see so many new men and women training to protect their home in the valley.

"Cease," she ordered them. Every single warrior, in a unified motion, placed their swords at rest.

Beyond them, a few men tilled up the dirt in the plot near the river, harvesting the winter crops and readying to plant for spring. Life seemed to be good, aside from the fact that her mother was gone, and she was not sleeping at night. The nightmares had never left, only grown worse with time. They were mind altering. Sleeping had become like growing cold from the inside out. Death had its inviolable grip on her, and she could not break free. The witch guardian's mark on her soul felt that way, too. Like darkness and death growing around her, swelling with each passing night.

She had not asked any more questions of Tenille, Asta, or Xan. They still tiptoed around her occasionally, and she could tell they were always waiting for those words to leave her lips. *Why did my mother hide that she was a witch from me? Why did she try to take down Degare's men? What is the blood oath you all took?*

Her people would be of no help in finding the answers she searched for, and she did not expect them to be. Not when they had taken blood oaths and would die if they told her. Ravenna had concluded that her mother kept these things from her for good reason, but that did not stop her from wanting to know them. So many questions jostled in her mind in a cloud of confusion and anger and sadness, and though she just wanted to move past all of it, her curiosity was growing each day. She could not help but think up a plan of revenge which also provided her with answers.

The next afternoon, Ravenna sat at the fire circle while she and the other warriors ate lunch.

"Didn't sleep much?" Xan tried to make small talk with her, obnoxiously chewing his bread. Eager to get back out and train, he eyed the warriors who already clashed swords to their right.

She had been tired today, exhausted. She scoffed at his ridiculous question and ate quickly while Tenille asked Xan about the jeweled pommel of his sword.

He mumbled a quick response to her about the topaz being the only relic he had from his childhood before he was orphaned during the war, and then turned back to Ravenna. "I get them too, you know." Something told her he was talking about nightmares, but he did not, in fact, get them too. Not like she did. She was sure of it.

"They're nothing," she lied, focusing her attention on the two empty seats across the fire in front of her.

Warriors laughed and carried on around them as they ate, and she was once again reminded of how life was before her mother was killed. Ravenna was tired of moping. She wanted to have *fun*. Though she had not received her mother's blessing to officially train with the warriors until the week of her death, she had always been one at heart, laughing and sitting around this very circle. It *had* been enjoyable in the valley, though she had not thought much of it at the time. She had always wanted to be free of this place, as she felt it like a prison since she had been forbidden to go beyond its borders. But, before the Despiri came to Vestele, she had laughed freely with her friends. She loved her people. They ate and told stories, and they danced and played music nearly every night around the fire circles. Yes, she had known joy. Without finishing her meal and looking back only once at the two vacant seats between warriors, she rose to her feet and headed toward the river.

Xan grabbed his sword and scarfed his food down to follow close behind her, leaving Tenille alone on the bench. The leaves were growing bigger on the trees with each day, and the forest canopy grew denser. With each day further into the spring season, Ravenna was reminded how long her mother had been gone.

"Where are you going?" he called as he chased her.

She sped up, racing toward the river. A distraction was just what she needed. The water was calm, and its coolness would be refreshing to the men and women that had been training all day.

"Last two in take watch tonight!" she yelled to her warriors.

Like a herd of cattle, they paraded toward the river, pushing and shoving. A few of them tripped and stumbled as they stampeded in laughter and hurled after her. These people were her own, her family. At least she still had them.

She turned to watch them all barrel toward her and caught Xan running at her, grinning from ear to ear. His dimples were visible as he plowed into her and threw her over his shoulder.

She laughed. Really laughed, for the first time in several weeks.

Together they went into the river, kicking and splashing.

"We sure as shadows aren't taking watch tonight!" he said. Xan's handsome smile only grew wider as he saw the one reciprocated upon her own face and wrapped her in a hug, sweeping her through the cold water.

22

VICTORY

XAN

Xan knew the legends, and while Ravenna had seemed to relax on the subject of witch guardians, he had not. He enjoyed seeing her laughter light up the valley, the creases at the edges of her eyes, and the way her freckles danced in the firelight as she played her fiddle. Ravenna's joy had returned, and tonight was a victory.

The center fire was crowded this evening, as clan members gathered all around to witness Ravenna playing. Three others joined in on their instruments, and Xan listened proudly, but his eyes stayed fixed on the tree line. He shifted on his feet as the silhouette of a horse formed in the distance. It was Nilo, returning home from his mission.

Nilo locked eyes with Xan, seemingly eager to share the information he had learned.

"Well?" Xan said. "Do we have to worry, or not?"

"There are rumors that Leith lives," Nilo said. "But if he hasn't attacked yet, I doubt he will."

Xan's eyes darted to Ravenna for a moment, and then

shifted back to the woods at the base of the mountains. "I still don't know if I trust it. If he's alive, he's a threat."

Nilo bobbed his head as if weighing the possibilities, then switched topics. "So, what did I miss?" Nilo asked. "How are you doing?"

Xan chuckled. "I'm in over my head here." All the secrets, the threats on Vestele...it was all too much.

"No, not with that," Nilo said. "Now that she is shield-maiden...marriage is off the table. How are you *doing*?"

Xan gritted his teeth at the painful reminder. *Was it so obvious that he was in love with her?*

Nilo added, "But those rules were just created by Ashreya for the system to have structure. Do they really matter? I doubt she would have made such a rule if Reid had not already been dead." Xan kept staring ahead.

"Ash had her reasons. It was a safety measure, in case she was ever to pass, that the shield-maiden, or master, would be fully dedicated to the clan's purpose and not put their soulbound lover over Vestele." Soulbonds were not common these days, but once, when the Light ruled Arresia, they had been.

Nilo shrugged. "Yeah, but Ash had a daughter." He motioned to Ravenna. "Is that not the same, if not more hindering, than a husband would be?"

"Soulbonds are different, and you know it. They're all-consuming. And I think you're forgetting why Vestele was established in the first place." To protect Ravenna.

"All I'm saying is, I think you could still ask her to marry you. Who would object?"

Xan scoffed. "Ravenna. She would object."

"Yeah, yeah. You never know until you try."

Somewhere during the conversation, Ravenna had stopped playing music, and now approached the two of them with two cups of rum in her hands. Her eyes were on Nilo, and she offered them each a drink, but Xan declined.

"Such a stick in the mud. Always too cautious." Her breath fogged in front of her. Her cheeks had been kissed by the chill of the night and her hair hung loose, with a few braids sprinkled throughout.

"Sorry, Ravenna. Someone must be sober in the event that we fall under attack."

"We're safe, Xan. It's been a month since the guardian," she argued, though she too, sounded unconvinced. "Lighten up." She nudged him with the cup, a small smile on her face, and he shook his head. She turned to Nilo. "Leith's dead, isn't he?"

"Alive, probably," Nilo said. "But I don't think he's a threat." He winked at Ravenna, and she beamed, handing him the cup. Seeing her smile at Nilo in such a way twisted Xan's gut, and he abandoned his post to drag her near the fire for a dance.

Xan's hands held her tightly, and the warmth from the fire caressed his skin.

"You worry too much," she said in his ear above the music.

"You don't worry enough, Venna. This is serious." He spun her, and their feet moved quickly to the tempo of the stringed instruments.

"I worry. But tonight, I just want normal. How it used to be. Maybe you should try it," she suggested, breathing heavily as she moved. He could not relax with the knowledge he had. There was still so much she lacked, so many things she did not know about the world around them, and so many things he was bound to secrecy over. If she only knew, he doubted she would be dancing right now. He forced a smile.

"For you, I'll try."

She knew little more than surface knowledge about the world of Embers and Despiri and witches and beasts. Though they were only five years apart, Xan had lived through and seen things she could not even imagine. Ravenna had been shielded. Though Ravenna killing the guardian had stricken a fear in his heart that had not left him since that night, today at the river he was *almost* able to forget the door into darkness that had been swung wide open.

Each minute of every day felt like an eternity, waiting for the guardians to return for his friend, and waiting for the consequences of the blood oath he had taken at twelve years old to catch up with him.

Why the Despiri had not returned the week of Ashreya's funeral to wreak havoc on his village, he did not know. Though the Despiri had already successfully murdered Ashreya, Xan feared they would be back for revenge. Not only because of the murder Ravenna had committed, but also because of the one simple piece of knowledge the mind reader had gained on his travels.

Unfortunately, the secret Vestele kept from Ravenna had not been safe against a reader of minds. He had come into their village and searched through the web of many thoughts that night, no doubt curious about the woman who had so foolishly challenged them in the forest. What he had learned of her could change the course of history in the worst way possible.

They were lucky the mind reader had not discovered that all of Vestele had been aware of Ashreya's plans and were in on them. Or had he? If he had, the Despiri would surely return for them *all*. If the mind reader knew anything—it was Ravenna's secret as he had told her. But with each passing day, Xan grew a little more confident that they remained safe in their haven in the valley.

The Ravenna he knew was back. Returning, little by little, day by day. Today, though she had not been sleeping much and had been training excessively, she was smiling, carefree, and laughing. He could finally breathe again. At the sight of her beaming, beautiful face before him, he felt a release of tension as his lungs filled with delight. He could not help but free the laughter from his chest and be present with her in this precious, rare, moment as they danced around the center fire with their clan under the night sky. Happiness had finally returned to the valley after the harshest winter yet.

23
THE START OF THE WAR
RAVENNA

Exhaustion hit her and did not relent. Her soul felt heavy, and she knew she had to get some sleep, but even with the rum coursing through her veins, she could not find the courage to go beyond the threshold of her lonely cottage and close her eyes. Instead, she stayed next to Xan by the fire, fighting the strange feeling that was settling inside her. The dancing had turned to fireside stories until the two moons were at their peaks and the children had collapsed, sleeping peacefully near the warmth of the fire or in their mothers' arms.

Right as Ravenna considered heading inside for the night, the familiar screech of a guardian and a horn sounded from the Sunstone Forest. Three bursts of sound. One for each threat. They had finally come for her.

It was the start of the war.

Her heart dropped into her stomach, and she jumped to her feet, preparing to order her soldiers. Tenille rushed to grab the horn that hung on the outer wall of the center longhouse, where many warriors slept. With one swift, long breath, the healer sounded the horn in a return call, and immense chaos broke out in the valley.

Ravenna motioned the warriors and called for the horses. Fintah arrived in seconds, and Ravenna mounted her while Xan climbed atop his stallion. He shot her a worried glance, and she nodded, urging Fintah toward the alarms. A unit of ten men joined her while the others stayed back, forming a barrier of protection around the women and children as they shuttled into the longhouse. Ravenna led the warriors south to where two of their own were on guard. The warriors had been instructed not to interfere with the witch guardians until Ravenna was present to make the kill. None of her warriors would suffer the mark. She would not allow it.

With the edge of the woods covered in shadow, she was unsure of what she was looking at. She kept her eyes on the movement ahead, and as she grew closer, her suspicions were verified. The witch guardians, just as she had feared, had tracked her here. Three of them gathered on the edge of the Sunstone Forest within plain view of Vestele. Her heart thumped in her chest as she watched the last of the children enter the longhouse. This was all her fault.

Xan said low under his breath, "Remember the plan, *please.*"

Let the warriors fight and hold the guardians off until I can jump in for the killing blow. She had to save her energy, since she was the only one permitted to kill them. She refused to let Xan fall to the curse. Vestele would need him when she was gone. Though it saddened her to think that in leading Vestele, he may never marry as he wished, she knew he would readily make that sacrifice for their people. For her—if she asked him. He would keep Vestele alive.

An awful, deafening growl hurtled toward them, and the horses staggered back. Ravenna nudged Fintah and they continued to race toward the monsters that barreled out of the tree line. If Xan was right, they were here only for her. She would not have any more of her men die by the hand of the beasts that hunted her. Just as she leapt from Fintah and was about to dash toward the three creatures, two more emerged from the woods. A total of five witch guardians stormed toward her. It was like she was the beacon, and they noticed none of the other threats around them. She looked to Xan for a split second, who was instructing the warriors to form a circle around her, their shield-maiden. She readied herself, examining each of the ruthless beast's quick, careless movements. They had no rhythm or tactic to the way they moved, and they were unpredictable with that dangerous, brute strength that had thrown her several yards at the last encounter. She now faced *five* of them.

"Strike to maim, not to kill," she said to the group of warriors that surrounded her, ready to face the guardians. Each of the guardians had their eyes fixed on her and only her, their teeth thrashing against the night.

In a clash of swords and battle cries, she and her men left their horses behind and sprinted into the tree line, maintaining the circular formation they had trained in. They each staked a torch into the ground beside them, offering some light to see by. Two men to one beast should have been an easy win, but these monsters were unfathomably swift and strong, and towered over even the biggest of her warriors.

The beasts momentarily halted at the sight of the torches,

and Ravenna watched as they quickly averted their eyes from the light. They did not fear the flame; the light was impairing their vision.

"Keep the torches lit!" Ravenna yelled.

They would need every advantage they could get.

"Xan," Ravenna said, as thoughts of doubt began to crowd her mind. His face reflected her own fearful expression.

"I won't let them hurt you," he said.

"Vestele. You won't let them hurt Vestele," she corrected. The distance closed between the beasts and the warriors, and at first contact between beast and man, a warrior was thrown to the side with a quick swipe of the beast's arm. Her men did not cower but took note of the supernatural strength that the beasts embodied and quickly altered their approach. Two men fought each guardian, doing their best to disable the creatures enough for Ravenna to kill them. Her breath caught in her throat at each swift movement of a warrior, and when she felt Xan's back press further against her own, she tightened her grip on her blade as the circle opened and a witch guardian was shoved to the ground before her.

With the quick throw of a dagger to its exposed black heart, she took yet another of the witch guardians' lives. She felt its last breath like a mark on her soul, the curse that had already dwelt within her blackening and spreading wider. The other four beasts seemed to turn toward her in unison, almost forgetting the men they fought. It was enough for six of the warriors to bring down their beasts, allowing Ravenna to land three killing blows. With each fatality, her soul fell deeper into the curse.

The remaining guardian let out a roar that plummeted into her ears, momentarily deafening her. She spun around, Xan still at her back, where the last creature had made its way into the circle in a fit of rage. It twisted and turned, swiping its monstrous arms into her warriors and launching them yards away until only she and Xan remained within reach. Her injured warriors climbed to their feet to return to her aid. Some of her men had been impaled with the bone shards that stuck out from the creature's flesh, some had broken bones from the impact of being thrown, and most, if not all, had been wounded in some way. She held up a hand toward her warriors.

Her jaw tightened. The guardian was *angry*. It was *too* angry and moving too quickly for her to reach its black heart with a dagger. It tossed another one of her men.

Enough of this.

The tree line was just beyond the beast, and she took off in a sprint, baiting the creature into the woods. Xan followed closely behind in a panic.

"What are you doing?"

"The circle formation is not working!" she said over her shoulder as the beast turned toward her and ran.

"Run faster!" he said. Together, they were able to back the monstrous creature between two trees, where Xan fought it off and barely dodged its swipes as Ravenna climbed to gain leverage. A sturdy limb swept down just over the beast's head, and she quickly raced across it, leaping onto the shoulders of the witch guardian.

It bucked and tried to throw her off, but she held tight, clenching her thighs tightly. With her longest dagger, she struck and stabbed a few times just to get through the guardian's crusted, hard skin. Finally, the thick skin on its neck gave way, and she cut through to an artery that spewed black blood across the forest floor.

Its clawed hands came up to meet the gaping wound on its neck, and it made a roaring, chilling sound as it tumbled to the ground, throwing Ravenna off in a fit of panic and rage. She was pelted against the trunk of a tree hard enough to stun her. She reached around for her blade, unable to see clearly enough against the blow she had just taken to her head and the darkness of the night. It was nowhere to be found, and neither was the sword that had been sheathed at her back. She heard a few warriors rushing toward her, and she climbed to her feet, using the trunk to hoist her body up.

She squinted in the direction of where she had been thrown from. Xan's eyes bulged as the guardian she had maimed crawled toward him quickly. Another approached from the side. There was no escaping the predicament, and Ravenna stumbled toward him without a blade. Nilo reached under her arms to help her balance. "You're hurt?"

"I'm fine. Help Xan," she choked out, and Nilo rushed away, leaving her to search for her lost blade.

Where did my sword land?

She searched for the long silver blade as she dodged each new witch guardian that came from the forest and led them to the group of warriors that awaited them.

When each warrior was busy fighting their own guardian, she knew she had no choice but to begin fighting them herself. The circular formation had been broken with the first set of guardians, and the warriors had never reestablished it. They were all fighting for their lives now, and the guardians were coming for Ravenna with a vengeance.

This is my fault.

She looked around as her men were slashed open and thrown about, and then she ran right into the heart of chaos.

She had given them orders not to kill the things, and because they could not kill them, they were losing. She grabbed an arrow from her quiver and shot the beast Xan had just downed.

"There has to be another way!" she yelled as she approached him.

Xan looked at her with hopelessness and shook his head. How would they survive this?

His eyes darted to the blackness behind her, and she spun, but not quickly enough. A witch guardian was racing toward her with shards on display, ready for her head. She tried to duck out of the way for Xan to strike with his sword, but she was thrown to the ground once more, and the beast hovered over her. Xan's sword clanked against its tough skin, and she watched as the guardian's exposed arm bone scraped right across his abdomen. A scream hurdled from her throat as Xan collapsed, and the guardian turned its gnashing teeth back toward her, pinning her to the ground by her neck.

Her strength was no match for the beast's. Its breath was hot on her face as it stared into her eyes and prepared to stake its revenge. She looked to Xan, who was crawling toward her, holding his waist. Her face crinkled at the sight of him. She did her best to wriggle free of the creature's grip, but it did not budge, and she was left with only one option. She jammed her hand up between its ribs and squeezed its heart, ripping and tearing until the organ broke free from the chest cavity. The creature's grip loosened from her neck, and she coughed, rolling to one side as it collapsed.

"Are you okay?" Xan made it over to where she lay coughing, and glanced at the bruises she was sure were already forming at her throat. She coughed again, choking down a scoff.

"Are *you?*" She nodded to where his hand held his stomach, and he removed it just enough for her to see the blood that trickled down between his fingers.

"It's shallow. I'll be okay." He looked around at the chaos and muttered, "If we survive the night."

A few of the warriors had fallen their beasts, and she rose to her feet to start her killing spree with the sword that gleamed in the torchlight a few feet from her, but was stopped dead in her tracks at the sight of the largest guardian yet, hovering over her and Xan. As it stalked closer, she racked her brain, knowing she could not outrun it. Neither of them had a blade, and her quiver was empty. But when the beast closed the last little distance between them and they took their final breaths, a silver blade protruded from its black heart. The beast fell forward.

Ravenna thought her eyes deceived her as she saw Tenille with Xan's topaz pommeled sword in her trembling hands, its long blade covered in black blood. Tenille had come to meet them on the battlefield. Sweet, innocent, gentle Tenille. Her caramel eyes were wide as they examined Xan and Ravenna's injuries. Tenille looked over her shoulder at the other warriors who still fought, and Ravenna noticed her friend's brown mare nearing with her medical supplies loaded into the saddlebags. Xan and Ravenna only stared at her in shock.

Xan was the first to speak. "Do you know what you've done?"

Tenille stared down at the dead witch guardian, breathing heavily.

"It was going to kill her," she whimpered. "And you."

Xan's gaze looked left to right, repeatedly skimming the woods for more threats. Ravenna climbed to her feet and took the sword from Tenille. She headed toward the fight, where her men had thankfully fallen most of the beasts. She went rushing, plunging Xan's sword through the heart of every remaining, barely breathing witch guardian, and hoped she was not too late. When she was sure they were all dead, and the mark on her soul had increased in size, she took a torch to the pile of deceased guardians, willing them to burn up and disappear from her sight. But their thick skin was resistant to the flame.

"Why won't they burn?" she asked in frustration, adding more and more torches to the pile. Nilo looked at the mass of beasts with an empty stare as he held a wound shut on his arm. Ravenna turned to count her men. Three fallen warriors, the others all injured. She threw the last torch with no luck, then leaned up against a tree and sunk to the ground, absentmindedly rubbing the bruises on her neck.

Light footsteps approached behind her. "Xan, what are we going to do?" she asked distantly. They had barely survived tonight, and she was certain more guardians would return to avenge the deaths of a dozen of their own. She felt it within her —a promise. They would now come not only for her, but for *Tenille*. Xan stood slowly and offered her a hand, calling for the horses.

"Tonight, we'll rest. Tomorrow, we make a plan," he said grimly as the horses trotted over.

Back in her cottage, guilt engulfed her and kept her from sleep. They had lost three warriors tonight because of her. Three warriors who had families and children.

The soreness and swelling of her neck had her tossing, turning, and gasping for air.

How am I going to get us out of this?

Her clan was strong, but it did not have the numbers for war. The witch guardians had come at full force. She had not expected there to be so many, and she knew that they would keep returning until they had their revenge. And now that Tenille was cursed, even if Ravenna left, the guardians would still come to Vestele.

How do I protect them?

She stayed awake pondering until the sun began to climb over the mountains and paint the valley with its rich, golden light. It was not until sunrise that she knew what she had to do to protect Vestele, and neither the council nor her people were going to approve.

24

THE PLAN

RAVENNA

Collecting wildflowers from along the riverbank was a past-time she did enjoy, however trivial it may be. These flowers served little to no purpose, other than to be beautiful and distract her from the decisions she had just made and refused to go back on. It was not something she ever thought she would do, nor something she wished to. But she would move forward with this decision for her people whether they approved or not. They were in this predicament because of her, and she would get them out.

She could hear Xan approaching on his stallion with Fintah trailing behind.

"Why are you out here so early?" he asked, motioning for her to join him.

"Just thinking," she said as she pulled herself onto Fintah's back and caressed her white mane.

"Dangerous," Xan said, leaning over last night's injury.

He began to lead, letting his horse leisurely trot along the riverside. They had planned this morning hunt before the events of last night, and though Xan wanted to cancel, Ravenna had nagged him until he agreed to meet her. She knew he would not let her go into the woods alone after the attacks, and she needed to talk to him privately, anyway. She would not be taking this plan to the council. A morning hunt in the Sunstone Forest was the perfect escape, and no one would suspect a thing.

"Maybe we should stay in the village," Xan said. "With the other warriors." Though her mind was still running with images and the events of the night, she was confident they would be safe during the day.

"The sun is our shield. The guardians are obviously nocturnal." Both times the witch guardians had attacked during the deep hours of the night, and Ravenna would bet her life that the woods would be safe until dusk.

"If they do come for me during the day, at least we'll be away from Vestele."

"And once they kill you, they'll go straight into the valley for Tenille," he said. Ravenna breathed tightly.

When an hour had passed, and she was sure the two of them were far enough from Vestele, she stopped Fintah. Xan's gray stallion—Alf—halted as well. Tension seemed to roll through Xan's shoulders as he turned to her.

"So, what is your big idea, and why did we have to come all the way out here to discuss it?"

She took one deep breath and fed him the plan.

"I'm going to the Ink Bloods."

25

A FOOL'S ERRAND

XAN

Ravenna has lost her ever-loving mind.

26

RIVER OF INK
RAVENNA

"Absolutely not! How could you be so stupid?" Xan yelled.

"I'm going. With, or without you. It is our only hope, and you know it," she said.

"It is not your decision alone," he countered through gritted teeth.

"The council cannot stop me. They are there to advise—but I've made up my mind on this."

His cheeks reddened, and his voice echoed through the trees. "No, Ravenna! I will not stand by and watch this. I cannot!" He waited only a moment for a response from her before he pointed his horse back toward Vestele.

Ravenna had expected refutation from him, but not a full-blown tantrum. His negative response would not stop her from doing what she had to do. Xan was her best friend, and her second-in-command, but *she was shield-maiden*.

"I am shield-maiden, Xan. The decision is mine," she

reminded him as he began to race back toward the valley without her. He did not turn back, and he did not falter.

Wasting no time, she began her ride west through the valley. Xan would be telling the council she had gone rogue, and they would be on their way to ruin her plans soon. It had been a while since she had taken this route, and it would be a long day of traveling. She had prepared to go alone but had not anticipated it. Likely, if she ran Fintah as fast as she could, she would make it back to Vestele just before dusk. She only hoped Xan did not come with a group of warriors to try and stop her.

About an hour into her ride, after weaving in and out of forests and valleys, she came upon the Brunts. She had not seen the city since the night she had run the Gauntlet and claimed the bloodstone. Since the night she had set it all to motion, unaware of the consequences she would reap. Her stomach twisted. Ravens and buzzards still flocked above the remains of the fallen city. Ravenna urged Fintah around the outskirts, along the crumbled stone walls, and she took in the sight of the strange, thick cracks that crept across the ground from one common point where the arena had been.

As she bypassed the Brunts, the valley slowly transitioned into an alluring, luscious green. After two hours of running, Fintah was beginning to slow. Ravenna would allow her to rest for a few minutes. At the nearby stream, Ravenna found some small round fruits on a young sapling. They were not completely ripe yet, but they tasted sweet enough and would briefly satisfy her raging hunger.

Fintah fed on some tall grass, and Ravenna bent down near the stream to splash some cool water on her face. The last time she had come *this* far west, her mother had accompanied her on the joyride. They had sat somewhere along this small brook and laughed, just happy to simply *be.* She smiled at the faint memory.

As the valley began to widen, she knew her destination was growing near. She had once purchased a map in a shop in the Brunts with the bet money she had won in the taverns, and she had studied it time and time again, learning every hill and valley in the entire world of Arresia. She had learned each of its kingdoms, whether ruled by the Light or ruled by the darkness.

She remembered how the depiction of the valley spread and then funneled into a skinny crevice between two mountains, one of black stone, and one of golden. On the black stone side, there was little sign of life, like the Dead Wood that bordered Vestele. Opposite, the Sunstone Mountains carried life and lush green plants. Like Vestele, the clan she was approaching was not labeled on the map, partly because it was established under five years ago and her map was at least eight years old. The Ink Blood Clan's name had become well-known in recent years, as it made its way to the top of the chain. It was the largest, strongest clan south of Oro, and Ravenna did not expect them to be welcoming of her presence. They would consider her an enemy, as one would any outsider.

Ravenna took in one last glance of the lively greens of the valley as they readied to turn north and re-enter the Dead Wood, which spanned from Vestele to a mile east of Ink Valley. Fintah walked slowly and carefully as they wove between the trees. Ravenna listened to only the sound of twigs snapping under Fintah's hooves. When they came to more open land, they strode along the edge of a hill for over an hour before the base of the tall black stone mountain was visible. Fintah grew nervous as they proceeded to where Ravenna suspected the Ink Blood's guards would be posted. A siren sounded from one of the two watchtowers, which were situated on either side of the gates at the edge of the mountains—at the entrance into Ink Valley.

The inky black stone of the mountain on the left bled into the bright golds and yellows of the mountain on the right, meeting in the center of the valley and blending into a river of spilled ink, where huts and village shops spanned as far as the eye could see. At the base of the mountains were homes and many people out working for the day, but at the sound of the watchtower's warning, they began gathering in small groups, preparing for her arrival. Despite it being only the start of spring, in the distance, she could see fields and gardens flourishing with lush green plants and vegetables, and her mouth began to water. She continued forward slowly, trying to appear feeble and weak. Today, she was presenting as an ally—not a threat.

She heard the whispers of the guards and could see the gleaming of their drawn swords as the afternoon sun reflected on the shiny metal. Six guards—three on each side of the valley —awaited her arrival.

In front of her stood the only solution to the problem that faced Vestele. Most of the guards' faces were grim and impertinent, as she expected. Xan had been right. This clan was dangerous.

"What brings a young woman like yourself to our valley unaccompanied?" The guard closest to her left called out. His hands did not rest on his blades and along with the others, he wore all black with chained iron armor that covered every inch of skin aside from his face. He was arrogant to assume she would not kill him for the tone of voice that suggested she was weak.

By the way they spoke, they did not expect her to know how or to try to defend herself in the event of a threat. The man stepped forward and she fought the urge to draw her blade as her body tensed. She had prepared herself with hidden blades and weapons. They were concealed in her hair, her boots, and under her cloak. She would be safe, if she got in and out of the valley before Xan could return with the warriors and declare war between clans that had no reason to fight. She knew her people would do anything Xan ordered without her presence, as he *was* second in command. But she had commanded him this morning to stand down. Would he listen?

"I need to speak to your leader." Her voice did not waver. The bloodstone was heavy as lead in her pocket, and she held her head high and did not bow. Leith could provide her the help she needed to protect Vestele if he had made it out of the Brunts alive. She scanned the guards for his familiar hazel eyes. They studied her, observing her clothing and her intricately braided hair.

"Vestelian," one of the men muttered.

"Dismount and remove your cloak," the tall guard on the right said. She looked among the others, some stone faced, some watching curiously. She slowly climbed down from Fintah, careful not to put too much pressure on her injured leg and she dropped the cloak from her shoulders. The guards tumbled into laughter as four of her hidden blades were exposed.

"Does she even know how to use those?"

She hardly refrained from rolling her eyes. *This is part of the plan*, she reminded herself.

"Hand over your bow and remove the blades," the stone-faced man ordered. Fist clenching, she tossed her bow to his feet. Then, she slowly pulled each blade from its sheath, adding them to the pile but never breaking eye contact. Rage heated her cheeks in response to their haughtiness. "Turn." She tilted her chin up slightly and spun, no visible weapon left on her body. The guard nodded. "Take her to Leith."

So, he *was* alive after all, and Ravenna had successfully tricked the guards into thinking those four blades were all she had. She held back a smile. If she were to need weapons today, she would have plenty.

Another low-pitched horn sounded, and she allowed the men to lead her through the tall gates. They surrounded her on all sides, and she whistled for Fintah, who closely followed. Having her here slightly eased Ravenna's mind.

Through the gates, the village was beautiful. A stream of clear water ran right down the center of the valley and the trees that grew from the golden mountain produced so much fruit, and were so prosperous, it made up for the lack of life on the opposite mountain. At the river bottom were rounded stones of black and golden minerals. A tall tree spread its branches and towered above her, dropping bright red fruits onto the ground below. Children wandered around, collecting the fruits in baskets. There were enough fruits for everyone in Vestele to have one every day for a month, and she could not help but stare in awe. She had heard of the wealth of the Ink Bloods—but to see the abundance of their land was enthralling.

Flocks of black birds flew overhead, sending her chest tightening. The sounds of the flapping wings and the caws took her back to her night terrors, and it was all she could do to keep moving forward with the guards. She felt as though she had seen this all before, and an unnerving fear began to swallow her whole.

For Vestele, she reminded herself.

Passing huts, little bakeries, clothing shops and smokehouses, she admired how luxuriously these people lived. Even their early spring crops appeared successful enough for them to be able to put back food for winter while remaining well-nourished in the warmer months. The fighters she passed on the road were not of the typical build, they were a range of all different sizes. Most of the Ink Bloods were marked with two leather bands around their upper arms, if their arms were not covered by a cloak or armor. Ravenna observed all she possibly could about the valley, the village, and its people—who seemed to be of all different languages and ethnicities. She had never seen nor heard of a clan like it. Her interest peaked. If this were truly the strongest clan south of Oro, she would find out what gave them their strength.

They came upon a sizable hut. The wooden door frame was decorated with tiny stones and gems, and leading up to it was a skinny wooden bridge that crossed the quiet stream running below. This hut was quite far from the others and contained two windows of glass on either side of the door. Beyond the wooden door, someone whistled a tune. The whistler hit every note perfectly and sounded a lovely melody. It would have blended beautifully with the music they played in Vestele around the fires at night. She smiled faintly at the memory of last night's celebration but was quickly reminded of what had occurred next. She swallowed and held back a wince as soreness radiated through her bruised neck. She adjusted her tunic.

The tallest guard moved ahead to knock on the door, using the ornate brass door knocker. "There is a Vestelian woman here to see you."

The whistling stopped. From inside, a guttural voice invited them in, laced with a heavy accent that Ravenna had never heard in Oro. The guard who knocked entered first, and behind her, another placed his hand on her back, ushering her forward. *Just breathe,* she reminded herself. She gritted her teeth as a push directed her through the door.

A few feet in front of her sat Leith just as she remembered him. Cocky and arrogant. A young woman about Ravenna's age sat in a chair across from him, wrapped in a blanket, her blonde hair loose and tangled, her piercing blue eyes tired. Though it was plenty warm outside, a fire was raging in the hearth. Leith cocked his head to the side and smirked as he noticed Ravenna, just as he had that night on the platform during the Gauntlet.

Dismissing what must have been a lover, he looked Ravenna up and down with a trivial and predatory, yet handsome face. His hair was a rich brown, so dark it was almost black. It was chopped to a couple inches in length and laid in a mess atop his head. His face was chiseled with the sharp structure of his jawline and his cheeks had begun to grow stubble where they had been clean shaven on the night of the Gauntlet.

"To what do I owe the pleasure, beautiful Ravenna of the Valley?" he said, a heavy accent buzzing in his deep and inviting voice. It was of a land she did not know, and it seemed to tip toe over her skin, leaving eerie chills, as if her body itself were trying to evade the strange sound. Leith's smirk did not waver as he motioned for her to sit down across from him on the meticulously beaded cushion.

She remained standing, and without a shake in her voice she said, "I am here about a past proposal for a marriage alliance between our clans."

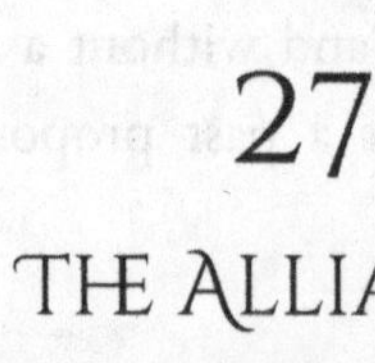

27
THE ALLIANCE
RAVENNA

If he was surprised, he did not show it. Dismissing the guards with a wave of his hand, he proceeded to inspect his nails. He motioned one more time for her to sit, and she did, taking note of the two windows behind him and a long fire iron directly next to her seat.

Four years ago, Leith had proposed an alliance between their clans, and in return, had promised her mother protection for Ravenna and all of Vestele. Well, now the clan needed protection from the witch guardians and the Despiri, and as shield-maiden, Ravenna could offer him the alliance he once sought.

She was head of the council, leader of Vestele, and they were out of options. If Leith were to accept and she were to marry him, Vestele would be offered protection and new leadership in the process. She would be giving up her title as shield-maiden. She bit her cheek. None of it mattered anyway. She did not plan on staying, not with vengeance still calling out to her, and the witch guardians on her tail. They would marry, and then she would leave him and her people to embark on her journey of revenge.

"The nerve you must have to come here to my valley and propose an alliance after you've injured my leg." He blinked at her with his hazel eyes, and she could not tell if he was being serious. His leg appeared unharmed, propped on the table with his other, ankles crossed. She tried to hide the annoyance that crept onto her face.

"Your leg is fine. It was a flesh wound."

"I am aware." He tilted his chin. "Still wasn't nice." Her eyes flitted to the wall of daggers behind him where *hers* hung dead center. His smirk grew as he noticed where her attention had gone.

"What do you want from me?" she asked, eyes shifting back to him as she pushed for his cooperation in the matter at hand.

"What can you offer besides yourself as my wife?" he asked. He studied her under furrowed brows for a moment.

She said nothing. *Had he already married? Was she too late?*

Her eyes wandered over the plethora of rings that graced his fingers—not one where a wedding band would be. Her sight then traveled up his arm to the leather band that hugged his bicep, where two ivory feathers hung, dipped in ink. She slammed the bloodstone down on the table in front of him. An offering.

His eyes did not move from hers as he took it in his hand and rolled it between his fingers, keeping his eyes on hers.

"It is not this bloodstone that I want."

Her eyes narrowed in response, and she straightened her shoulders. His gaze flitted to her bruised neck, and he flicked the stone into the air. She caught it without hesitation, pocketing the valuable fragment immediately. There was nothing else of value she could give him as her part in the alliance.

She awaited further explanation. Sitting with her back to the door, she crossed her legs to appear more lady-like, and perhaps less on edge. Though, their recent meeting at the Gauntlet likely told him all he needed to know about her. She was sure about this alliance. It would work. The question of the matter relied solely on whether or not Leith of the Ink Bloods still wanted her as his bride. Why he had wanted her in the first place, before he had ever laid eyes on her, was a mystery, and quite frankly, one she did not have time for.

She had washed her face in the stream on the journey here and attempted to clean up the mess that was left of her braids after the events of last night. She had managed to save the tiny one that she had come to hold dear. His gaze hovered on her hair, and she knew he noticed it was unkempt. He smiled faintly in amusement, and his hazel eyes traveled from her shoulders to her boots as he analyzed the rest of her appearance. Her face grew hot.

Finally breaking the unbearable silence, he asked her, "So, has Ashreya of the Valley changed her mind about my proposal?"

She swallowed. "My mother is dead."

His eyes flashed with something like surprise, and he briefly looked her over for any sign of emotion. His curious gaze seemed to land on her bruised neck once more.

"So, what brings you to my valley, Little Dove?" He leaned back in his seat, placing his hands behind his head, interlacing his fingers. She narrowed her eyes at the nickname he had given her. "What makes you think my offer still stands?"

Her back stayed straight, and she nonchalantly ran her finger over the fine wood of the small, hand carved dining table. It was next to a large window that faced east—which could serve as an exit if needed.

"You have not yet taken a bride, and I know you wanted something from my mother that she was not willing to give. I am the shield-maiden now, and I can give you whatever it is that you want." She paused as he tilted his head to the right, waiting for explanation. "But I *need* an alliance."

He lowered his brows and studied her, his eyes still hovering on her neck. She had no idea what he wanted from her or Vestele, and while it may have been completely and utterly ignorant, this was her only option.

"And what trouble have you gotten yourself into, that you would risk an alliance with *me*?"

He was right to wonder. Every clan south of Oro trembled at the feet of the Ink Bloods, and it was strange for her to be here, especially alone. It either made her very brave, or very stupid. Probably both. Brushing some dirt from her thigh, she effectively removed his gaze from her neck. She had been foolish to leave the bruises exposed.

Making eye contact once more, she stood. "There is no trouble. My people are suffering through the harsh winters. We grieve the loss of my mother, and as the new shield-maiden, I desire to strengthen my clan."

He seemed to tense as she stood, and his gaze surveyed her once more.

She caught herself favoring her left side and quickly balanced her weight on both legs, so as not to draw attention to the injuries she had obtained in last night's grapple with the guardians. Pain shuddered through her right knee, which had been smashed against the tree when she was thrown.

"And how do you expect this *agreement* to work?" he inquired, raising one dark brow. Redness bloomed on her cheeks.

"I need men—well trained warriors, and food." She swallowed and added, "and cattle."

He smiled, leaning back in his seat slightly and landing his gaze on the wooden slats of the ceiling, not bothering to look at her any longer. The chuckle that escaped his lips was almost offensive.

"Half of my best warriors to Vestele, and half of yours to Ink Valley," Leith said. He did not look at her. "Fifty head of cattle, and half of each harvest from here on out."

She tried to hide her shock at the generous offer. *Maybe this will actually work.*

"But—" he continued, holding up one finger. She held her breath. "In my homeland, it is customary for a bride to join her husband in his home. You will leave Vestele and live with me here in Ink Valley."

"And *where* exactly is your homeland?" She probed, pushing her luck. They were not in his homeland, and she would not join him in Ink Valley without *all* her people.

He smiled, glancing off to the side where his drink sat on the oak desk. "I have no doubt you have never heard of my land, nor should it be of your concern. I will not be returning anytime soon."

She pictured the map she had purchased and wondered which of the seven kingdoms he had come from—one of darkness, no doubt.

He kept his gaze locked with hers. "Do we have a deal, Little Dove, or not?" He took a sip of his drink, its strong aroma burning her nose. The glass clinked on the table.

After a deep breath, she spoke. "We will unite our clans in one location." It was what she had hoped for, anyway. She thought of the tall iron gates and the protection of the steeper mountains they had here, and the fact that the Despiri of Oro could easily return to Vestele and kill her people. "Here, in Ink Valley."

His eyebrows rose. It was better for her people. They would be safer with the protection of the Ink Blood warriors and all their defenses. They would never have to worry about food again. When the witch guardians came for Tenille, she would be well guarded, and if the Despiri ever came for her people, they would have the protection of the Ink Bloods.

"You favor your left side," he said. "How have you injured your leg? Not a dagger to the flesh, I assume?"

Ravenna went rigid.

"Riding incident," she lied. He looked toward Fintah, who was visible just outside the window.

"Mmm," he hummed, and slowly sat up in his chair, his gaze flitting from Ravenna's leg to her bruised neck. His eyebrow ticked in curiosity. "Undo the collar of your tunic."

Her cheeks burned. She studied his face, waiting for him to speak again. He only urged her on with a wave of his hand.

She took a deep breath and began to undo the button. She knew the bruising on her throat spread to the top of her chest, and she slowly pulled the fabric apart from the buttoned middle to expose the top of her purpling collarbone. She allowed him to see the glint of the dagger she had hidden beneath her tabard, successfully fooling his guards.

The room was drafty, and a shiver snaked down her spine. His eyes wavered from hers for a split second and traveled down to halt on the bruising exposed at her collar bones. Something like satisfaction flickered upon his face, but he quickly composed himself.

He spoke clearly and firmly, "Now button it back up, and remove that blade along with the two knives from your boots, the one in your hair, and the blade against your thigh."

She swallowed. Thinking she had fooled the guards had given her a sense of pride, and he had just plundered it down to nothing. Slowly bending at the waist, she pulled the blades from her boots.

"Hand them to me," he ordered. She obeyed, if only for the sake of the alliance. "No more trickery," he stated tightly, examining the weapons he had just taken from her. All but one —the one her mother had given her—were much less valuable than the bejeweled ones that he displayed on the walls around them, her other dagger of bone in the center. She ground her teeth as he inspected the red garnet in the golden hilt of her most cherished blade. "I know who you are and what you are capable of," he said, running his thumb and index finger along the sharp blade.

She stiffened.

She was sure he had heard the rumors of how she had become the best warrior in Vestele after the night she was triumphant over him in the Gauntlet, and he now knew that she was sworn shield-maiden. Had he truly been surprised at the news of her mother's death? It was hard to tell.

He rose from his chair, setting her dagger on the desk and came to stand only inches before her. His gaze moved to the bruises one last time. She tilted her chin up to meet his stare.

"From now on, you will treat me with respect, Little Dove. Go to your people and return in seven days with three witnesses. We will be married in one week's time at the third moon's rising."

She nodded, ignoring the thrum of her heart in her chest as she turned to exit the room.

"And Ravenna," he spoke again, his breath warm on the back of her neck. She spun to face his hazel eyes once more as they gave her a wink. "*Happy birthday.*"

28

THE TROUBLE

RAVENNA

Knowing good and well that her journey home would be long, and Xan had likely brought reinforcements deep into the valley and the forests to retrieve her, she opted for a different route home than she had taken on the way to Ink Valley. Distant groans and cries sounded through caves under the mountains as the witch guardians awaited sundown, but Ravenna did not care if she would be in the woods past dark, as long as her people were nowhere near her when the beasts attacked.

She was thankful *most* of her weapons had been returned to her upon her exit through the gates. Leith had chosen to keep her favorite dagger, and though her mother had given it to her as a gift the night she was killed, Ravenna could not risk the alliance by requesting he return it. She would soon be his wife, anyway. She could retrieve it then, before she snuck off to Oro.

She would travel tonight with a torch of oil ready to be engulfed by bright fire. She hoped the flames would give her enough leverage against the malicious beasts that hated the light.

Leith had accepted her proposal with no further questions asked about what particular *trouble* she had gotten into, and in just seven days, Vestele would have an alliance with the strongest clan south of Oro. In one week's time, she would have a husband whom she did not love nor like. He was hardly tolerable, but she would manage the few days she would have to be in his presence, if only for the sake of her clan. Alone, she knew the guardians would destroy her people. Their chance of survival through this raging war was much higher if they were united with the Ink Bloods, and she was far, far away.

Ravenna would forfeit her freedom to unite Vestele with the clan she knew could offer them the best protection. Now, she just needed to choose her three witnesses. She doubted Xan would be one of them, considering his reaction when she had told him the plan this morning. She would deliver the news to her people when the ceremony was complete, when she returned to lead them in the transfer to Ink Valley. They would need to be escorted by the Ink Bloods through the mountainous forests and the valleys. Ravenna would insist on it. Vestele needed a shield against the guardians as they journeyed. She did not even want to think about the possibility of the *Despiri* returning for her people.

This is the only way out, she reminded herself. The safety of her people was in her hands.

Ravenna was certain her mother never would have stood for this decision, being that she had already turned down an alliance with the Ink Bloods. But her mother had never endangered the entire clan by making one stupid mistake, *until the day of her death*. Now Ravenna had to fix both of their mistakes and discover what secrets her mother had hidden from her.

She sucked in a breath, tightening her grip on Fintah's mane. The horse galloped through the tall weeds as the sun began to set behind the mountains, and Ravenna knew it would not be long until the guardians came out to greet them.

She so badly wanted to rest. Her body was sore with exhaustion from the injuries she had obtained last night. She had some of the crushed, dried herbs left in her saddle bag that Tenille had given her for her broken ribs last month, and she made sure to chew some before what would likely be a long night. The witch guardians' low snarls echoed through the woods, and she tensed as the sun fell behind the mountains.

She avoided the cave systems as best she could, though in these mountainous territories, caves were prominent. The guardians moved with a speed that was unmatched, anyway. Not even Fintah could outrun them all. The guardians' cries for vengeance resounded through the hills and valleys, but she kept pushing forward, torch in hand, awaiting the first strike.

About two hours into running Fintah as fast and far as she could go, the golden light that had once poured through the trees and painted the water in the stream beside them, withered away into complete blackness. Tonight marked the start of the darkest week of the year. The moons would not be visible again until her wedding night, when the three of them rose together and returned a sliver of light to the nights of Arresia.

Thankfully, she was still far from home and the witch guardians would come nowhere near Vestele. But she had little chance of making it out of this forest alive if she did not find high ground.

Ravenna slowed Fintah to a halt and dismounted her,

resting her chilled cheek against the mare's. Fintah focused on the blackness ahead, her hooves dancing with nervousness. Even the animal could feel the strange presence that had seemed to follow them since the moment they left Ink Valley, and Ravenna just hoped she survived the night and made it home to Vestele to collect her three witnesses and return to Leith. She only needed to survive six more nights, and then she would be on her way to seal the alliance.

Leading Fintah to drink from the stream, she pulled a couple of unripe fruits from her sack and let the mare eat from her palm, trying to calm her unease.

She collected the last of the fruits from the saddle bag that draped over Fintah's side and with a hand on her neck she whispered, "Home, Fintah." The gentle giant stared at Ravenna, knowing exactly what she was asking of her. Fintah's unwillingness to leave Ravenna would get her killed, and Ravenna would not allow it. "Home! Go on!" she yelled.

The horse turned quickly, and began to head east, toward Vestele, where she would find safety. Pausing to look at Ravenna one last time, she huffed and continued her retreat to the heart of the valley, where Vestele's people would find her and assume Ravenna dead until she returned on foot.

I will return, and the alliance will work.

A tall oak towered over the stream, and she began her ascent. At the first hint of a guardian, she would strike her flint and flash the fire torch in defense while she obtained a good point of leverage.

Somewhere in the treetops around her, branches jostled, and she backed against the thick trunk of the oak to remain obscured from view. Ravenna would wait out the remainder of the night here in the canopy of the Dead Wood. She felt a presence around her, something unfamiliar. It seemed different than the darkness that called to the mark the witch guardians had made on her soul.

Soon after, the pit in her stomach seemed to warn her of the guardians' presence. The first attack came quickly, following the sound of twigs snapping under heavy feet. She sat up straight, looking down at the ground around her in search of the culprit. Sure enough, a guardian stood below. She was nearly fifteen feet high, and its height reached halfway to her. It wandered aimlessly in circles, searching the ground and the forest around it, as if it had an exact location on her, but she was not there. Could the minuscule bits of bloodstone left in the ground tell the guardians exactly where to find her? An underground system of magic, weakened or not, seemed probable.

Ravenna's body went rigid, and she tried not to breathe. She saw no evidence of any others, but she knew they would be arriving soon. The trees swayed in a gust of wind and the guardian's empty stare shot straight up to where she clung to the limb. She moved fast, striking the flint she had found by the stream and igniting her oil-soaked torch mere feet from the beast's cloudy eyes. It staggered back, startled in sudden blindness.

With a swift throw, her bone dagger made perfect contact with the black heart that drooped between those nasty, exposed ribs. As a deafening roar sounded from the giant, Ravenna knew it was a call made to the others with its dying breath.

Scurrying further up the tree, she struggled to put out the beacon of fire that still glowed from her torch. Behind her, something splashed through the stream. The tree top next to her swayed once more. In the black of night, she could not decipher where the threats came from.

She counted at least four guardians below, and within seconds, more gathered until all she could see beyond the limb where she perched were snarling faces and giant, clawed hands reaching for her. With a swing of the torch of flame across their faces, they winced, but did not stagger like the first one had. Their anger was too strong.

They continuously scratched the trunk of the tree as they tried to reach her where she climbed higher. All her nightmares bled into reality. She threw all her daggers, most of them finding their marks in the black hearts of the beasts—two of them missing and dropping to the ground. Her arrows flew next, and when her quiver was empty, she tossed the bow to the ground. There were too many guardians, and she had only her sword left.

Some of them had started to climb up as others shook the trunk with a great force from where they stood on the ground. One reached her and crawled across the limb in a rough manner, its large size prohibiting it from swift movements in the crowded tree limbs. It was ready to claim her life. Ravenna shimmied backward, attempting to put as much distance between her and the beast as possible. The limb shook and a growl echoed among the entire forest, deafening her.

She kicked and tried to maintain her balance, finally reaching a point where she could reach the limb above her to climb up a little higher, though she was unhopeful it would be her saving grace. As she reached above to hoist her body up onto the next limb, an object—the exposed bone from the guardian's arm—pierced her side. It left a puncture, one that was deep enough to carry her whole body forward as the sharp bone was ripped from inside her. She screamed out in pain and lurched forward on the limb, nearly plummeting into the sea of guardians below.

The beast seemed to smile beneath its wretched face, and as it crawled toward where she now hung onto the shaking limb, she prepared for all the consuming darkness she had met in her nightmares.

29

A HORSE WITH NO RIDER

XAN

It was early morning, and the squad of warriors Xan had gathered were returning to the village after searching for Ravenna all night. He had been prepared to fight the guardians, or even the Ink Bloods, but neither had approached his men. With no sign of Ravenna by an hour before sunrise, his company of warriors had collectively decided to turn back.

Maybe she returned while we were searching, Xan told himself.

If Ravenna had not yet returned, they would eat, rest, and march straight into the heart of Ink Valley to retrieve her. If she was not there, well, that meant the witch guardians had succeeded in their mission. Xan had heard their bellows within the forest as he searched last night, and though he had tried to track them, he had been unsuccessful in pinpointing their location. So many echoes had sounded from all sides of the woods, as if they came from every direction in Arresia.

Tenille met Xan at the brink of the forest as they entered

Vestele. Her eyes were tired but alert as she searched among the returning men for any sign of the shield-maiden.

"Where is she?" Tenille's panicked voice demanded from him. The morning sun had begun its ascent into the soft pink skies, illuminating the specks of honey in her golden-brown eyes and giving them stunning dimension. He shook his head at her, unable to form words past the knot in his throat. He knew he had just confirmed her deepest worries when her face sagged in sheer desperation. Running her dainty, jeweled hands through her dark hair, she breathed a shaky breath that left her lips in a fog with the chill of the morning air.

"Do you think they're holding her in Ink Valley? Do you think they've already gone through with the alliance?" Nilo whispered beside him.

Xan had only made the council members aware of Ravenna's plan. The clueless warriors gathered outside of the longhouse and awaited his orders as they scarfed down their meals.

"How should I know?" Xan asked, pacing in a circle. Calming his temper was difficult when he was failing at his sworn duty to protect Ravenna. Xan's men had suffered his wrath through the night, as if they were not already dealing with enough. Xan clenched his fists. After everything he and Ravenna had been through together, he thought that he would have been a bigger part in her decision to unite Vestele with Ink Valley—especially through *marriage*. He gritted his teeth. She did not have the knowledge of the Ink Bloods and their leader that Xan did, and unfortunately, it was just another thing he could not share with her. If she had somehow survived the night with the whole species of witch guardians out for her throat, she would be home any time now.

Unless she is being held by the Ink Bloods for being foolish enough to go to Leith for aid after wounding and stealing from him. He could have killed her. Or married her.

Both thoughts made Xan's stomach twist to the point of pain.

He rubbed a palm over his heavy eyelids. "If she has married him, we have bigger issues than we did already. Oro will obliterate us in the war." Ink Valley had not yet chosen a side in the war, but Xan knew that Leith's ego was big enough for him to try placing himself at the top of the chain. Ink Valley was the strongest clan south of Oro, but Xan knew that Leith would not settle there. He would challenge Oro if given the chance.

"How could she be so stupid?" Xan said. "Why did I let her go?"

"It's not easy when the woman you love tells you she is on her way to marry another man," Nilo muttered. Tenille quickly ducked her head and went to retrieve more food for the warriors. Xan slumped onto one of the logs by the fire.

I forgot Ravenna's birthday.

Amidst the stress of the attack, and then her ridiculous plan, he had forgotten her birthday.

He rubbed the palms of his hands over his eyes and sucked in a deep breath, filling his lungs with shards of guilt. He should have gone with her. At least then, he would know of her fate.

Why did I ever let her out of my sight?

If Ravenna had made it to Ink Valley, she would have been met with an army of guards at the iron gates. Likely, they would have taken all her weapons and left her defenseless. He swallowed. Painting the picture in his mind was torture, but he could not stop himself. Ravenna would have gone in with somewhat of a plan, but he knew she had not had much time to think, and he had not helped. He had left her when she needed him.

He had no doubts the gate rats would have been intrigued by a beautiful woman like Ravenna traveling alone all the way from Vestele to speak to their leader. When Leith had proposed the alliance just after Ravenna's eighteenth birthday, Xan had been infuriated. Leith had wanted something from Ashreya, and what that *something* was, the shield-maiden had never disclosed to Xan, but he could guess. On top of that, Leith had claimed the alliance needed to be bound through a marriage— preferably a soulbond. Xan had told himself it was likely just a marriage of power Leith searched for, being that Ravenna was the shield-maiden's daughter, and Vestele, though small, was a strong clan. Something had always made Xan question the truth of that, though, and he worried that Leith knew more about Ravenna than he thought.

It had enraged him, more than he thought humanly possible, that Leith would demand marriage with his shield-maiden's daughter. That it was Ravenna he wanted, of all the women in Vestele. He had spent the next few days training and throwing dagger after dagger into a thick trunk, until the tree had leaned to one side.

Lights. How could she be so stupid to go to him after the Gauntlet? To try and trick him into an alliance? If he did not have her head already, he will when he finds out she used him.

Vestele had lost some of their strength in warriors and their shield-maiden since Leith's proposal. Surely, he would not accept Ravenna's offer. Though if Ravenna presented herself to him as the new shield-maiden, and he was sure she had, Leith would realize a marriage alliance would gain him a whole lot more than what Ravenna was aware of.

Vestele kept to itself whenever possible. They had been able to stay off the maps and stay out of the War of Light and Darkness that raged between the two kingdoms still ruled by the Light—Eswen and Remont—and the rest of Arresia. Oro was at the head of this war, leading every other dark king and their kingdoms into it so that with the strength of their armies together, the Light may be drained from Arresia. Xan knew that soon, Remont and Eswen would fall, too. Vestele was not foolish enough to expose their throats to the realm of evil. They lay low and drew no attention to themselves. It was one of many reasons why they had not joined with another clan, even if it had meant nearly starving through the winters. He knew Ravenna could not entirely understand why they kept Vestele as hidden as possible, and why they must stay in this infertile valley, where crops did not grow, and where the land was cursed.

Though, *it would be nice to have another food source to rely on throughout the winters,* Xan had to admit. Vestele had grown barren throughout the years, and they continued to struggle more each year as time went on. He had suggested relocation to Ashreya many times, but the shield-maiden would not even consider it. She claimed it was a curse that followed.

He took a deep breath. Maybe the alliance *would* benefit them in some ways such as protection, but picturing Ravenna married to someone else—he could not stomach it. There had to be another way.

Ravenna had the guardians to deal with, which had been the start of this problem. They would continue to come for her, and the attack on their village a couple of nights ago was enough for her to see that. He knew what she was thinking and understood that she was putting their people first, but it killed him.

"Xan," Tenille whispered from beside him, her usually glowing skin drabber than he had seen it before. The exhaustion they were all feeling was utterly draining. He released a breath as Tenille's gentle hand touched his knee.

"Xan." Tenille's voice grew more panicked, and he looked up at her again, vision spotty from rubbing his eyes so hard. She pointed to the tree line and said, "Fintah."

At the sound of the name, he jumped up from his seat and looked to the edge of the forest, where a white mare returned home *with no rider*.

His stomach flipped as his heart dropped from his chest. Erik dropped his bowl and Nilo cursed. Hysteria broke out in the village as everyone realized all at once what the horse's lone return must mean. Without orders, the warriors raced to the forest in mass chaos. Some of the villagers cried and ran toward the woods as well. Tenille was gathering her medicines and herbs, and Xan left her, already beyond the tree line and racing toward the unknown in a blind panic. Alf came to him amid his sprint.

Ravenna would not have strayed far from the stream, and Xan ran his horse along the edge for miles while his warriors fell behind. His eyes scanned the trees and the ground for any hint of that lovely red hair that always seemed to catch the light so beautifully.

At no sign of her still, after the sun had reached its highest, he started to feel a wetness on his cheeks. Tears streamed from his eyes, and he kept moving forward until he reached the fork in the stream halfway between Vestele and Ink Valley. The warriors were nowhere to be seen, and Xan had run Alf for so long they could not continue at the pace he had set. Black birds were swarming above the tree limbs. The sounds of flapping wings and uncanny caws infiltrated the entire forest, seeming to grow louder the closer he got to Ink Valley.

He left his horse to rest at the fork of the river and continued on foot, following the flock of ravens above the tree line. After running a half mile, he could see what the birds were circling and feeding on. He stopped dead in his tracks, realizing the pile of charred, smoking ash consisted of the remains of at least three dozen witch guardians. Here, there had been some sort of powerful fire.

The scent was overwhelming. Watery eyes, he fell to his knees, frantically looking among the bones for any sign of his beloved Ravenna. Minutes felt like hours as he searched, and the world seemed to spin in slow motion. His head was dizzy, and his limbs seemed to move too slow. He could not search fast enough as he scoured the nearby surroundings for any sign of her; that vibrant rust-colored hair he adored, the soft sound of her boots amongst the forest floor...anything that would hint to him that she was still alive, for what had happened here was a massacre. Whatever powerful force this fire had come from was of the Light or of the darkness—of supernatural strength.

There.

Under the pile of flesh were the remains of a bone dagger, its metal hilt melted by flames. It was one of Ravenna's, and it was still warm.

A desperate noise left Xan's throat as he turned it over in his hands. If the fire had been hot enough to destroy the metal, Xan was sure it could obliterate human flesh at the close distance Ravenna must have been at to throw the dagger. Only the bone blade remained intact.

What had happened here, he did not know. But the scene was near confirmation that Ravenna was dead, and he would be returning without her. Vestele had failed its mission. They had failed Ashreya.

I have failed Ashreya.

He could not move nor stand. Alf had caught up to him and was now nudging his shoulder, urging him up, the stallion's soft nuzzle a small bit of comfort on the forest floor.

When Xan finally climbed to his feet, it felt like he had pounds of mud weighing down inside him. He had never felt such a burden before, like his shoulders physically could not straighten with the grief that had made its perch on top of them.

Alf slowly carried him back toward Vestele with no command, and Xan realized the horse could feel his grief.

Solemnly, he rode beside the calm river waters with his head drooping low, and he stared at the bone dagger for miles.

She is dead.

30

SOME WILD MIRACLE

RAVENNA

There had been far too many guardians, and she knew she had no chance of fighting her way out of the attack. She had known she would die as that guardian approached her on the limb. She had positioned her sword in front of her, waiting for the opportunity to plunge it into the beast's heart. But she had seen in its eyes that it was ready to throw her into the mass of guardians below, and it would stop at nothing to be sure her life ended there. Oh, sweet vengeance. How it must have felt for them to have been so close.

Being that near to death, her final thoughts were of her village. She had known that without her, the guardians would come for Tenille, there would be no alliance, and more of her people would die.

She was about to take her last breath as she clung to the limb, when an unworldly gust of wind came upon the trees, blowing her hair across her face and ripping the breath from her lungs. The limb bounced as the guardian was knocked sideways in the wind and fell to the ground. It landed with a thud that seemed to shake the forest grounds and trail up to the highest mountain tops.

The hefty breeze ripped the torch from her hand and sent it spiraling down on the guardians. As the fire fell among them, something strange seemed to whistle through the air in another, smaller rush of wind. The torch hit the shoulder of one of the guardians below, and suddenly, white flames burst across the bodies of every beast.

Ravenna watched from above as every guardian was overtaken with the inferno. Behind her, another rustle in the treetops sounded, and she turned to find nothing there but the mysterious wind rushing toward her. The heat from below quickly became unbearable on her skin, and she climbed higher into the brittle branches of the treetop until the bare skin on her arms stopped welting.

It took mere minutes for the flames to devour every inch of them, their bodies turned to ash and dust. It did not make sense; the way the fire spread so easily over the guardians' skin. She had attempted to burn the deceased guardians the night they attacked Vestele, but their skin had refused to catch fire. Now, only their lifeless, charred bodies lay below.

The tree she took refuge in caught fire, and the bottom of the trunk turned to ash before her eyes. She staggered upright and shimmied across a limb, barely able to move as pain rippled through her burns and the deep wound in her side. She braced for the tree to fall.

I just need to make sure I end up on the top side and not trapped between the tree and the ground, she thought.

The tree swayed to the right as the trunk began to break

off, and she shifted left as best as she could. She tried to hold her eyes open against death, but she had lost too much blood, and she was beginning to grow faint. She fell in and out of consciousness as the tree finally collapsed.

Somewhere during the fall, she must have hit her head, because when she awoke entangled in branches, pain traveled from the back of her skull to the front. The fire had gone out, and the forest was near black. There were no more witch guardians in sight, but no daylight to save her either. Her hand found its way to the wound just below her right rib cage. Despite the depth and fatal location of the stab wound, it had stopped bleeding.

Light blue tones began to paint the skies above before she dared move from the cover of the fallen tree. Smoke was still rising from the charred bodies and the burnt wood. Against all odds, and with the help of some wild miracle, she had survived the night.

The river was calm this morning, as the fog hovered above its clear waters and clouded the forest. Birds chirped overhead, and the tranquility around her soothed her anxious soul. Her tattered boots were more of a hassle than they were help, and she kicked them off as she walked, leaving them on the forest floor. Blisters and calluses covered her feet from the heat of the fire last night, but the coolness of the mud between her toes momentarily subdued the discomfort. Her skin was red, as if it had been burned by the sun during a long day of training in the open valley.

Her headache was still present, and though the wound in

her side had stopped gushing blood, an incessant pain was rooted there, making it nearly impossible to drag her feet more than fifteen steps without a break. She would stop here at the river to drink and tend to her wounds, then continue her way to Vestele.

Her people would have questions that she had no answers for. But they should understand since they kept secrets from her, their shield-maiden.

How did I manage to survive the night?

She welcomed the cold water against the burns that now plagued her skin. What little was left of her singed, wet clothing, clung to her frame, effectively cooling the heat that seeped across her wounds.

She had not understood what had happened last night with the wind and the fire, but she was sure it had not solely been nature's doing. It was something different, an *unnatural* occurrence. She suspected a Despiri, perhaps, but it made no sense why one would save her life from the witch guardians that drew from the same dark magic as them. She had done nothing to deserve the aid of one, and she doubted they would be very kind toward her if they knew what she planned to do to the Despiri who had killed her mother.

"Ravenna." A voice sounded from behind her. She stiffened and huffed a breath, dreading the chastisement that was sure to follow. "Venna." Again, Xan called her name softly, barely audible over the sounds of the river.

"Oh, if you could just stop your incessant brooding!" she called in annoyance, dropping her arms to her sides in a motion aimed to draw less attention to her wounds. Preparing to explain herself and undermine the severity of her injuries, she turned to face him, then had the mind to cross her arms over her chest to cover her mangled, torn tabard. Pain recoiled through her at the movement, and she winced.

Xan nearly fell off his horse, and he approached her, slowly, as if she were a wild animal that may dart at sudden movement.

He looked like death. His usual confident, protective demeanor was completely altered and he had shrunken into the shell of a man who appeared to have seen the likes of war. Ravenna was sure she looked no better. His dirty blond hair lay in disheveled waves atop his head, and his shoulders seemed to slink further south with each step closer to her. Her suspicions rang true. It did appear he had been searching for her in the forest all day and night with no sleep in between.

He stepped closer to her, the sound of her name leaving his lips once more. It was then that she noticed a shake in his voice and heard the sighs of relief he blew out with each breath.

I did this to him.

The water rushed around her, concealing the severity of her wounds from his sight. Xan came into the cold spring water without hesitation, and his hand met hers, gently. Ever so softly, he traced a finger over her palm—a comforting touch. Or a touch meant to reassure him that she was tangible and alive. Those muddy brown eyes stayed locked with hers for a moment before he scanned her body for injury.

Burns had blistered upon her skin, and he examined them without a word. Under furrowed brows, he slowly cradled the back of her head in his palm and placed a kiss into her matted hair. She could have sworn she saw a tear fall from his cheek into the river below.

He led her to the bank of the river where a mossy log lay in the tall reeds. Xan had *never* been gentle or calm in these kinds of situations. Anytime she had a scratch in the past, he had scolded her for being so careless. She awaited the reprimands that were sure to come.

Face still grim, he called for his horse. Alf listened well, trotting over to where Xan knelt before her where she sat on the log. Though she had been gone for just over a day, Xan had surely believed her to be dead. Guilt bloomed in her gut, rooting down deep inside her. While she was certain the nausea was from the physical trauma her body had endured, she wondered if it was possible to throw up from remorse. Xan was silent for a long while, and he held tension in his jaw as he wordlessly inspected her wounds.

"Xan—"

His gaze left the burns on her leg and shot straight up to meet her face. Her eyes widened at the intensity of his movements, and she stuttered out, "I... I just didn't want anyone else to get hurt."

He scoffed at that, and her temper began rising at the return of his insufferable attitude. "You're lucky you're alive, Ravenna!" he yelled, the silence of the Dead Wood swallowing up his words. "What happened to you? Did you make it to Ink Valley?"

She scrunched her brows and scooted away from him, then winced at the pain in her side and doubled over. "Yes, I made it to Ink Valley."

Realization crept onto his face as he noticed the blood beginning to soak her singed tunic, and he was at her side again in an instant. Grabbing onto her shoulder and pulling her tunic up from the bottom to expose the mangled skin just under her rib cage, he cursed. He looked closer, trying to clot the blood that was now pouring out with a torn piece of fabric from his own shirt. She grew more faint by the second and slouched back on her arm to keep steady.

"Who cauterized this?" he said.

She took a deep breath and tried to hold her eyes open. "What are you talking about?"

Her own confusion reflected onto his face. When he noticed her leaning to the side, he looped his body under her shoulder, hauling her up. Alf knelt on his front knees, lowering his body for them as Xan tried to lift her onto the horse's back. Ravenna caressed Alf's side softly before grabbing his mane and dragging her body weight up onto the saddle. It seemed her adrenaline had worn off when Xan arrived.

"Tenille is out here somewhere with her supplies." The usual responsibility in Xan's voice returned, and he now hauled his own body up onto the horse behind her. As they rode toward Vestele, he did not speak or ask any further questions. "Focus on breathing. Stay awake," he said.

The bumpy ride jostled her and sent pain through her bones at every step. Xan held her tightly and was able to keep her upright against his chest as they tried to find help in the forest.

It was not long before she heard the other warriors, searching the trees and the grounds for any sign of her. She pulled back on Alf's reins.

"What are you–" Xan clutched her waist tighter, trying but failing to stop her from climbing down.

She shoved him off. "I'm fine to walk."

He scoffed at that, eyeing her burns, and noticing her recoil as her bare, blistered feet hit the ground. He tossed her a cloak from his saddle bag, and she pulled it over her shoulders, using it to cover her injuries.

"Unbelievable," he sneered, shifting his gaze to the distance between them and the men sent out to find her. "You cannot hide this from them, too, *Ravenna*. Sooner or later, you will have to be honest with your people, *our people*," he hissed, "about what it *is* you were doing in Ink Valley."

Angry then. He was angry.

"Sooner or later, Xan, *you* will have to be honest with *me* about the secrets *you* keep," she snarled.

His jaw tensed, and she knew she should not have used such things against him. She did not value those secrets over his life, which would be taken if he told them. But right now, she did not care if her words hurt him. She would not cower, and she would not allow her people to see her as feeble and weak. That would only plant doubts in their minds about her plan to unite the Vestelians and the Ink Bloods. This was all for them, and as much as she hated it, she needed Xan's support on this.

She stood as tall as was possible with the gaping gash in her side and spoke to him once more with a deadly calm.

"As my second-in-command, you will support me in my decisions whether you like them or not. Or you will no longer be my second."

He climbed down from the horse to stand next to her and said nothing, tense as ever, as a few warriors appeared in the distance.

Faraway cries echoed through the foggy, morning-lit forest. "She's alive! Over here!"

Ravenna limped forward one step, Xan catching her elbow.

"I thought you were *dead,*" he spat under his breath against the back of her head as he held her against him.

She ripped her burnt arm from his grip and continued to move forward, correcting her limp before her people could notice.

31
SIX NIGHTS OF SECRETS
RAVENNA

Tenille fret over Ravenna's injuries the entire journey home. They were two hours deep into the Dead Wood, and Ravenna had foolishly chosen to ride with Tenille over Xan, unable to deal with his attitude much longer.

About an hour into the trip, Ravenna was struggling to not rip Tenille's head off, and she suggested Tenille and Xan ride together so she could have more room on the horse's back. She complained that her burns were pressing and rubbing against Tenille's back.

Tenille blushed, and she took it as an order, dismounting her brown mare to climb up behind Xan, who was giving Ravenna the silent treatment. That did not stop his eyes from boring into her back at her every movement, making sure she was not about to collapse. It *was* difficult to stay upright. She was weary and dizzy, but thankfully, Tenille had been able to stop the bleeding. She had confirmed that the wound had previously been poorly cauterized, probably a coincidental burn from the heat of the fire that had scorched the rest of her skin. She should be thankful for the burns that saved her life, she supposed. If they did not become infected.

Tenille paced Ravenna's cottage and spoke in the language of her ancestors, no doubt about Ravenna's stupidity. Her friend's frustration filled the room. The pacing was driving Ravenna to madness. It was impossible to rest in her own bed with Tenille's continual clacking of footsteps across the wooden floors. From where Ravenna laid in the bed, she could see Xan with his arms crossed just outside the window. He only glanced inside every few minutes before redirecting his glare.

Her mother would have been proud of her for taking charge and doing something for the good of her people—she hoped. Yet everyone around her was either furious or still clueless as to what she had been doing in the Dead Wood on her way home from Ink Valley without the support or company of her second.

"Mave root, mave root..." Tenille repeated as she rummaged through her bag, tossing dozens of herbs and medicines aside. Ravenna's injuries had left her feeling foggy, and she watched Tenille continue to search for the mave root, her olive toned dress swaying as she moved. A sigh of relief came from her friend, and Ravenna heard the mortar and pestle begin grinding herbs.

"Ah!" Ravenna winced as Tenille hastily spread a cool mixture across her skin. Her friend's tattooed face showed no reaction to her pain.

"You think you can just unite Vestele with another clan to get us out of this mess?" Tenille hissed.

Shock at her usually reserved friend's words blossomed on Ravenna's cheeks.

"You think I have a *choice*? You killed a guardian, Tenille. They'll come to kill you, too. It's only a matter of time."

Tenille added pressure to her touch upon Ravenna's skin. "I killed the guardian to protect you," she spat. "And I'd do it again." Her eyes met Ravenna's for a split second before she began bandaging her puncture wound. "Let them kill me. It is you we cannot afford to lose." Tenille swallowed, and Ravenna slowly shimmied against the wall to sit up.

Before Ravenna could speak, Tenille's words cut her off once more.

"You know, Xan lost a mother, too. And he lost another one when Ashreya died. You should listen to him; he cares for you. You're lucky the alliance didn't work out."

Ravenna swallowed, ignoring the last bit of her statement that was laced with a hint of question. Guilt rippled through her. She had not yet discussed her journey with anyone. Of course they wanted to know what had happened in Ink Valley, but Ravenna was beginning to think she could not risk telling them until after the ceremony, until after the alliance was complete. She hoped she could trick a few warriors into witnessing it.

Xan thinks he knows what is best for me, she wanted to say. *He thinks he understands, but he does not.* But there he was, hovering just over the threshold outside the door. She pinched the skin between her eyebrows, scrunching her eyes shut in pain. Her head had been throbbing since she awoke in the Dead Wood.

It was obvious the blow to her head in the fall had caused some sort of concussion, as she swayed with dizziness upon standing and greatly preferred thick darkness over any amount of light. But the latter fact did not stop Xan and Tenille from bursting in and out of her cottage all throughout the afternoon, letting ample amounts of sunlight in, enraging the pain in her head. She thought maybe it was a form of punishment.

Tenille's footsteps finally stopped sounding across the wooden floor. Ravenna opened her eyes slightly to see her friend standing directly in front of her, handing her a small clay pot. "For the headache," she said in a sharp tone. She had never seen Tenille so irate. "Take a nap. I'll be in and out to check on you." And with that, Tenille strutted out the door, beaded braids swaying behind her.

Xan and Tenille, both angered at her decisions, would come around. And if they did not, well, at least they would be safe. Ravenna could not live with herself if the guardians raided her village and harmed Tenille or anyone that would get in the way to protect her or Ravenna. They needed reinforcements and Ravenna would deliver them.

Six more nights.

She had a little under one week to convince Xan that the alliance had not worked out and that she would be staying in Vestele to fight the witch guardians alongside their warriors as planned. It was the only plan he would accept.

Xan waltzed into the cottage, ducking his head as he came through the doorway. He only stared at the fire and the tea Tenille had made, steam still rising from the small painted pot. His arms were crossed over his chest, and he kept his back to her as he stood. She knew he awaited an explanation, but she said nothing.

Her head felt so foggy, just as it had been the moment her mother had been killed in front of her. That day was strange. She could relive it over and over in her head, every detail as precise as the night it had happened—and she did. Often.

The world and their lands as she knew them had changed that night. Everything she thought she knew had turned to doubt and uncertainty. Her closest friends—and her *best friend* —were hiding things from her. They had known that her mother was a witch when Ravenna had somehow been clueless to that fact her whole life. Xan and Tenille had been in on her mother's plans while Ravenna had been purposely kept in the dark.

Soon, she reminded herself. Soon, she would bring it all to light.

I know your secret.

No, she would not explain herself to Xan. Vestele would unite with the Ink Bloods, and her people would follow her lead because she was their shield-maiden. She owed no explanation to anyone, so she shut her mouth and pretended to sleep until Xan left, still brooding in his frustration.

32

THE PINING
XAN

It had been four days since Ravenna returned from her visit with Leith of the Ink Bloods, and Xan had not spoken to her since they had arrived back in Vestele after her night alone in the Dead Wood. It was driving him mad that he did not know all the details and events of the journey and what exactly had happened between her and Leith.

On their search, he could not tell the warriors what Ravenna was doing in Ink Valley, so he told them to search the forests and valleys while he sat outside of the gates for hours, fighting the temptation to storm the Ink Blood guards. But Ravenna had already left or taken another route. Xan did not know what he would do if she had married Leith.

He knocked on the door of Asta and Tenille's cottage. Sounds of clinking jars and utensils echoed beyond the stone walls, and Xan backed up a step as he awaited Asta's invitation inside. But it was not Asta who opened the door. Tenille stood before him, braids a disheveled mess, olive skin glowing in the golden hue of the sunset.

"Xan, what is it?" she said, wiping her hands on the front of her cream-colored apron.

"Is your mother here?" he asked.

"No. Won't be in until late. I think she's trying to keep her mind off...everything."

"Can't say I blame her," he muttered. Tenille's thick brows lowered over her sparkling eyes, and she motioned him in.

As she moved to the side, Xan caught a glimpse of his defeated reflection in the mirror beside the table. He resembled his late father in both appearance and temper, and he had spent most of the last two days proving that by chucking daggers into a log, and swinging his sword until he could not move his arms. When he was not training, he was standing watch outside of Ravenna's cottage, making sure she did not try to leave.

"I do not know what to do, Tenille. I'm going mad," he said as he walked through the door. It slammed behind him.

"There is nothing more we can do. We are doing our best. She is the shield-maiden now." She placed her hands on her hips and added, "I told you to challenge her position. I knew it would lead to something out of our control. But you wouldn't do it." Xan breathed tightly as Tenille took a swig from a flask and offered him a drink.

"It would have ruined what we have," he said, guzzling some of the burning liquid down.

"You and Ravenna? You mean, you pining after her, and her rejecting you time and time again? When are you going to move on, Xan?" He was taken back by her abrupt tone, and he pulled a wooden stool out from the table to sit.

"I don't know," he said under his breath.

"She loves you, but not the way you love her."

"I know." It was the harsh truth, but he needed to hear it.

They sat in silence as they finished the rest of the flask, and Tenille's face stayed turned to the side. He watched her throat bob.

Finally, she turned to him with reddened eyes. His gaze met hers, and she scoffed, wiping a quick hand across her cheek, then rose from the table to busy her hands with her jars and herbs.

Xan wanted to ask her what was wrong, but he knew. He understood, all too well, the rejection she was feeling. Everyone knew she was in love with him, just like everyone knew he was in love with Ravenna. *Why did I come here?*

He was rising from the stool before he realized it. "I'm sorry I came," he said, before he walked out the door.

The next morning, Ravenna still refused to speak to him, so he spent most of his time outside of her cottage instead of within its walls while she rested. Because of The Darkening, the week's sun had been hazy and dim. According to Tenille, who now met him with apprehension after their conversation last night, Ravenna's burns were healing exceptionally quick, and her headache had subsided. They were the only words the healer had spoken to him all day.

When Xan was not outside of the cottage, he continued his training with the warriors, and as second-in-command, he acted as leader while their shield-maiden recovered. He led each training session. The council had held a secret meeting without Ravenna just that morning, where they collectively agreed upon allowing a handful of the warriors to kill the guardians that came for Ravenna or Tenille in the future. He volunteered, and Tenille had only opened her mouth in objection for a moment before deciding otherwise. The agreement he had with Ravenna no longer stood. He would break her trust if he had to. He could not bear to lose her. *This* was how he could protect her.

Luckily, no witch guardians had returned to the valley yet, and he wondered if whatever had happened in the Dead Wood that night had momentarily made them reconsider their vengeance. Or, maybe it was just taking some time for more of the vicious beasts to find their way to Vestele from wherever they had lurked before. It was likely, he pondered, that with the death of so many guardians recently, their numbers in Oro had dwindled so low that they must travel from other kingdoms now. Whatever the reason, he was thankful for the hiatus.

More women and young men had begun training in the last week. Xan had encouraged that everyone young or old, man or woman, had some sort of knowledge on how to protect themselves in a fight against the witch guardians or any threat that may appear. He had even hosted a small training session for the children, though most were so small they could never stand an actual chance against one of the creatures. It kept his racing mind busy though, and prevented him from hurdling through the cottage door demanding answers from Ravenna.

He kept a closer tab on her now, more than ever. He had assigned three warriors to watch her every move. If Ravenna tried to leave the cottage, she would discover she was being held captive in her own home, but he did not care. The council had agreed on it with little disapproval.

I don't think she is going to appreciate that, Nilo had said.

I don't care. She is making rash and foolish decisions, Xan had responded.

Until Ravenna was better, both physically and mentally, she needed to be contained. They had tried to keep her in Vestele, and that was not enough. Now, she would be kept in her cottage where they could make sure she remained safe. She would hate him for it, but at least she would be alive.

"Are you going to talk to me?" Xan asked her. He recoiled as the words left his mouth in a fit of unexpected rage.

"Not with that tone," she snapped from where she sat in the chair sharpening her blades.

"I am your second. I need to know these things."

She looked at him for a long moment and then spoke. "Leith was not interested in my proposal."

"He just *wasn't interested* in an alliance? I don't buy it." Leith had been *too interested* four years ago. Ravenna shrugged, and his eyes fell to the necklace at her throat, then to the vacant jewelry box that sat next to her bed.

"Did you offer him the bloodstone?" he asked.

She took it out of her pocket. "He didn't want it."

He narrowed his eyes on her. Perhaps Leith truly was holding a grudge over the injury he had sustained at the Gauntlet by Ravenna's own hand. Xan could not say that he would trust her, either.

"I've told you my secrets. There must be *something* you can share with me. Something to share that won't strike you dead?"

Xan scoffed and closed his eyes. "If there was, Venna, I would tell you." He turned from her, and his hand found the doorknob. With his back to her, he said, "There is nothing I hate more than keeping secrets from you. All secrets do is tear us apart."

33
LIES
RAVENNA

Two mornings from now, Ravenna would depart on her four-hour journey to Ink Valley. She would bring three young warriors for what she would claim was a day of special training. The newest warriors were blind followers, and she knew she could count on them to follow her orders—*if* she could sneak them away from Xan. They would attend the wedding ceremony as the witnesses required by Leith to complete the alliance. Once the ceremony was complete, and their clans were united, the four of them would return to Vestele with some of the Ink Bloods and Leith to tell her people of the news. They would be met with disputes—the worst of them from Xan—but he would be rendered helpless against the finalized alliance.

Ravenna's belongings were packed and hidden beneath the bed linens. All the extra food she could gather, a blanket, and every single one of her weapons, aside from the ones she had yet to sharpen.

"Xan said you told him Leith turned down the alliance. I

guess I don't blame you for lying to him," Tenille said by way of greeting.

Ravenna stopped sharpening her blade as the healer walked into her cottage. Outside, the night was falling, and the firelight was a warm glow against the blue and purple hues of the valley. She looked at Tenille with an expression that seemed to say, *I do not know what you are talking about.*

"I am no idiot," Tenille said, closing the door behind her and blocking the chill of the night air. "There is not one reason Leith would turn down an alliance with you—especially when you offered him a bloodstone which he so diligently seeks. You are to marry him, aren't you?"

Ravenna bit her cheek. "Three nights from now, as the third moon rises," Ravenna said.

Tenille nodded, biting her thumbnail as she processed the information.

"You can't tell him," Ravenna said.

"I'm not going to tell him. I don't think I can handle that. Besides, he'll try to stop you, and I do not think you should be stopped."

Ravenna shifted at the table, her side lightly aching with the movement. "You're agreeing with my decision?"

"I think you've weighed your options, and this is our best chance at survival. You want to ensure that Vestele is safe before you leave us."

Ravenna's brows pinched together. "I'm not leaving you, I'm—"

"Yes, you are," Tenille said. "You're going to settle Vestele in the safety of Ink Valley, and then you're going to Oro. I know you better than you think, Ravenna. You're loyal to your people, but you're also vengeful. I knew the moment the

Despiri killed your mother, that you would not let them live."
Tenille's eyes fell to the many blades and knives Ravenna
sharpened and to the collection of new arrows gathering in her
quiver.

Ravenna swallowed. "I cannot rest until I know they are
dead."

"I know," Tenille said. There was a long pause, and then a
flow of unexpected words from her friend's mouth. "There are
many things we cannot tell you without the promise of certain
death. I wish I could tell you everything, but I have traded my
life to make sure you keep yours. Do what you need to do,
Ravenna. Discover the secrets that have been kept from you.
But for Light's sake, stay alive long enough to make something
of all this."

With that, Tenille exited the cottage with her chin held
high. It was all the push Ravenna needed. A minuscule bit of
hope had been restored within her that she *was* doing the right
thing—that she deserved to know the truth. With certainty, she
would set foot in the castle of the Kingdom of Oro, and Degare
and his Despiri would pay.

34
THROUGH THE SMOKE
RAVENNA

A few hours into the night, after being lost in thought, Ravenna finally dozed off. Ravens circled above her in her dream, cawing and swooping down toward where she lay on her back on the charred ground. Black wings and beaks filled the sky, casting a shadow on the land below. It was suffocating. They were taking all her air. They ransacked the sky, the forest, the cottage, and she could not breathe.

The cottage.

She sat up, vision spotty from sleep, and her eyes darted around the room as she realized she truly could not breathe.

The air in her cottage was hazy and dark like the ravens in her dream. Smoke filled her lungs and with each gasp, no oxygen nourished her body. A pound sounded at the door. Coughing, she grabbed the sword from her bedside and pulled her cloak over her nose. Undoing the chain and yanking the door open, ready to strike, she found Xan in a panic.

"What is it? The witch guardians?" she asked hastily. He shook his head and stood there, stunned.

A waft of smoke shot through her and entered the cottage, bringing water to her eyes.

Where is the smoke coming from?

She quickly scanned the village. Chaos broke loose behind him. He motioned for her to come, to *flee*.

What is happening?

She looked beyond the dozens of cottages and huts placed throughout the valley to see fire and smoke surrounding them all. Smoke plumed into the air, growing in giant puffs and spreading through their nook in the mountains.

"*Rastweed,*" she said aloud, choking on the poison in her lungs. A deliberately lit fire burned in a circle around her village. Somehow, someone had placed piles of the poisonous plant all around them, entrapping Vestele within a pit of deadly smoke.

Xan grabbed her arm, ushering her out of her home and into the thick, toxic haze. She spotted Tenille with a cloth over her face, attempting to pull two young children—the boys Ravenna and Xan had taught to fish at the river—from their *dead* mother. Women were carrying their little ones as quickly as they could beyond the flames and smoke, fleeing toward the only opening in the raging fire.

"It is a trap," she choked out. Her people were being baited to the only exit. Ravenna ripped her arm from Xan's grasp and stumbled back into the heart of the valley.

"Please!" he begged as he followed behind her, coughing.

She would not leave her people. She went to the home where she knew two elderly women slept, and she quickly ushered them from their beds, urging them south behind her. "Go! Quickly! Bring everyone south!" Her voice was a raspy plea. She needed to make another point for her people to exit by. With the only water she could find—three buckets left out by a hut—she headed toward the fires near the Sunstone Forest. Her people could find refuge there. They knew the forest well. It was where they hunted and gathered, and they could find shelter in the caves.

Xan rushed behind her, both struggling to stay upright while carrying the water. She needed to put the fire out in this spot, so the clan could safely cross. They poured the buckets at the base of the flames, but the fire raged on, barely dwindling.

No.

The two elderly women grew weary behind her, and she saw the disappointment on their faces as she struggled to put out the flames. One fell to her knees, taking the other with her. Ravenna rushed forward, placing her hands on their shoulders, searching, looking for any other way out.

"Ravenna," Xan tugged on her. "Ravenna," he said, his tone growing more anxious.

"I'm not leaving them," she said through gritted teeth.

Ravenna tried to haul them up from the ground, but weakness had overcome her. Xan was behind her in an instant pulling her up, though he himself was overtly struggling to breathe, or even move. He left the elderly behind, and Ravenna screamed. As he dragged her toward the only opening in the circle of flames, she squinted through the smoke, looking for any clue of who had initiated this attack on them.

Her suspicions were correct. As they set foot beyond the two walls of flame, out of the haze of yellow smoke, the bright red uniforms of Oro came into view. The Despiri had returned. Ravenna stood no chance against them. She and Xan both wielded weapons, but their limbs had grown too stiff with the toxin, and they could not move quickly or with enough force to fight efficiently against even one man, let alone six. The Despiri were able to easily slaughter her weakened people as they exited Vestele, and she watched as one by one, the Vestelians were led into the trap the Despiri had set. Though she was certain Xan used every last ounce of his strength to hold onto her, she was easily ripped from his grasp as the Despiri took her hostage.

She tried to breathe, tried to fill her lungs with any smokeless air that she could to gain some of her strength back, but it was too late.

The damage was done.

She was paralyzed with the effects of the poison and was thrown over a horse's back, and Xan...*oh, Xan.* Xan was on his knees, begging for her life with every ounce of his that he had left.

What have I done?

She could not move. She could only watch as her village burned, her family, and her people with it, dying slow and horrible deaths. She cried out, trying to reach for Xan, but she was unsure if her hand even moved an inch.

The soldiers spoke loudly, yelling over the crackle of the fires and the deafening, agonizing pleas of her suffering people.

Why, why, why?

"This is the one from Jio's memory. Check her!"

Jio? He must have shown these men an image of me in their minds.

The men yanked her body upright and she could not fight as they tore her clothes from side to side, searching for something across the length of her body, just as the men in the

Brunts had done. Xan's eyebrows knitted together tightly as he watched, helpless.

One of the men pulled the bloodstone from her cloak's pocket and held it up.

"Ha! Look what I found. This will be valuable to the king."

How were these men not suffering effects from the poison? It occurred to her they must have been using dark magic in some way, to protect themselves. Perhaps they were being shielded by a spell. Ravenna knew Oro often worked closely with the witches.

"Degare said she was an Ember. She is ungifted. We have the wrong woman," one spat. "There is no way this is the same woman who was able to kill Elam."

Had she heard him correctly? She tried to argue, but no words left her lips as she fought unconsciousness. She held no lightmarks, no gifts. One of the soldiers brushed the hair from her ear, and she felt a warm breath on her cheek as the blurry shape of a man's face examined her closely.

"The hair, the *eyes*, it's her," he confirmed in a low voice that snaked through her veins. *Had the king suspected her to be an Ember because she was able to kill a Despiri?*

"Just get her out of here before she dies. He wants her alive. I'll finish up here," one of the soldiers said plainly, as if torturing and maiming entire villages were just a typical part of his day.

The king wants me alive. He has murdered my clan for what I have done. This is my fault. She fought the poison with all her strength, and she willed her body to move toward Xan, but nothing happened.

"Sympathizers. All of them," another Despiri said in

disgust as he looked upon her people. Xan crawled toward her so slowly, still pleading with them to let her go.

"Please," he said in a whisper. "Please, let her be." With each word, his voice became softer, and Ravenna saw the reflection of smoke and fire haunting his gaze.

One of the younger Despiri who looked to be her age, knelt before Xan, hand on his blade. Ravenna watched helplessly, but then, he rose to his feet and called out, "Leave them, they'll die soon anyway." His voice was softer than she had imagined, less guttural than the others.

"Fine, but you get to share a horse with the prisoner," one said in response.

With that, the young Despiri mounted the black mare, sitting in front of her, and they began the journey toward the castle in the north, her people's screams and pleas fading into certain death.

When Ravenna woke, still gasping for air from where she lay on her belly across the horse's back, she could see her wrists had been shackled. With the current darkening of the two moons, she was unable to estimate how long she had been unconscious. Her head was pounding once more, and though the wound in her side had been stitched and was healing, this position had enraged it.

Fire light blended into the blues of the night sky just south, where her village burned. She coughed, gaining the attention of the soldier whose body was in front of hers.

His horse came to a halt.

"She's awake," he said plainly, alerting the others. Ravenna heard the crinkle of a map as the man in front of her shifted to place it into his saddlebag. *He must be the navigator.*

Sounds of flowing water echoed nearby. No, directly below her. They stood in the stream and the soldiers were arguing around her in the glow of the torchlight, still on the same topic of whether they had taken the correct prisoner or not.

"How do we know it was even the right village? *Vestele* was not even on the map," one of the men sneered at the navigator.

The navigator responded calmly. "It was the right village. I received directions from Jio—and I mapped his route the first time. Navigation is my job, but if you'd rather lead the way, be my guest."

The navigator winced as another Despiri gripped Ravenna's sides, pulling her body from his horse and letting her splash right down into the water. Her shoulder crashed into the bed of rocks below and she groaned, immediately pushing up onto her elbow with all her strength to keep her face from the water.

Being separated from the smoke had allowed her to regain a little movement, but her throat shrunk and constricted with each gasp for air, and she was thrown into a coughing fit that ended in her vomiting. "She's clearly not an Ember, you fools! I told you. The poison is killing her," the Despiri with the deep voice sputtered. "If she were an Ember, she could have healed herself!"

The navigator spoke up, "Not all Embers have the gift of healing. Don't you fools know this by now? And if she bears no lightmark, she is not an Ember." Ravenna's head was spinning.

"Well, we haven't checked everywhere," one of the Despiri said. "She could be marked beneath her clothes."

"She'll be searched in Oro," the navigator said. "But finding a lightmark is not likely. Embers are usually marked at pulse points on the limbs or neck."

Another grunted, "Whatever. Wash the poison from her skin, and let's get to the castle quickly before she dies, or it will be our heads on the stake!"

She was dying, as were her people. She had failed them. She had broken her vow. She leaned forward, involuntarily falling face first into the water. A Despiri brute with shadowmarks beneath his cropped, dusty-colored hair and a long beard pulled her up by a fistful of braids.

She forced water out of her burning, aching lungs. He dunked her again, this time holding her under for a few seconds. Was he attempting to kill her or cleanse her skin of the poison? Either way, she knew she would die. The damage had already been done.

Drowning. She had thought about it the day after the prison wagon had taken her old life from her. The day Oro had stolen everything and set her on a path of destruction. Drowning would be preferred over ever entering the heart of the kingdom of darkness while unable to defend herself.

She inhaled, letting the water cool the burning in her lungs. She let it enter through her nose and into her chest.

He pulled her up in an instant like she was weightless. "She's trying to drown herself!" he exclaimed in disbelief. Her body retched and forced the water from her lungs. The Despiri hauled her up, supporting her full weight and squeezing her face in the grip of his hand. "You fool!"

When he peered into her eyes, a look of realization overcame him, but it disappeared as quickly as it had come. "She *does* fit the description the witch and Jio gave." Ravenna's mind spun at the mention of a witch. Her teeth gritted. "She *is* the one who killed Elam."

Perhaps Ravenna was the woman the king searched for, but why had His Majesty believed she was one of the legendary Embers?

35

WHEN DEATH DRAWS NEAR

RAVENNA

The Despiri had repositioned her, and she now leaned against the navigator's back, her hands shackled around his waist to keep her from toppling over. As far as she knew, they had not stopped to rest through the night, but she had been in a heavy sleep brought on by the poison that ravaged her body.

How has it not killed me yet?

It had been over half a night and a full day of travel. They were traveling quickly, and at this pace, they were sure to enter the king's lands by dawn tomorrow. She heard another flock of ravens above her, and she wriggled her aching body, trying to view more of her surroundings. Her head was pounding, but through her spotty vision, she could make out the rocky, mountainous landscape as they traveled deeper into the Dead Wood Forest toward the Kingdom of Oro. Stones slipped under hooves, and curled branches framed her view into the foggy skies beyond the bare forest canopy. The day was dim due to The Darkening, like those few minutes of diffused light before the sun rises in the morning, but the sun was high, trying to shine through the thick, gray clouds above. It was afternoon, and if she was right, tonight was night number six since the two moons had first entered shadow. Tomorrow, the three moons would rise together as three slim crescents.

The third moon's rising. Tomorrow was the night she was supposed to be wed.

The next night, in the blackest hour, death loomed overhead, closer than before. She could feel its presence waiting to stake its claim on her. It was a similar feeling to the one she had encountered while surrounded by dozens of witch guardians last week, though different in the way she now wished to accept her fate.

Today, she had nothing left to fight for. Her actions had caused the painful deaths of everyone she loved, and now she pleaded with death to take her, too. But it would be a mercy, and one she was not quite sure she deserved.

As the feeling in her chest burrowed deep inside, and the sound of a witch guardian's cry echoed through the mountains, she breathed a sigh of relief. The navigator tensed, and the other men stopped their horses.

"What was that?" one asked nervously.

"Witch guardian. They only bother you if you're cursed. Keep moving forward, we're safe," another responded. Ravenna smiled faintly, but her eyes remained closed in exhaustion.

It was only a moment before the guardians appeared, trickling out of the caves and trailing them through the Black

Rock Mountains. Ravenna watched as they stalked her slowly, in a different manner than they ever had before, as if they could not decide their point of action.

The navigator was the only one who seemed to be aware of their presence. "You're cursed," he said under his breath. Not a question, a statement.

She remained silent as the terrain jostled her against his back.

Why aren't they coming for me?

She used her strength to turn her neck and peer into the night behind where she could see over a dozen snarling teeth. The movement caught the attention of one of the Despiri, and he yelled so loudly he spooked his horse. "There! In the shadows!" he warned as he noticed the guardians.

All the others—except the navigator—halted. He and Ravenna kept moving forward as the rest of the Despiri dismounted their horses and prepared for a fight.

"Just release me to them and they won't harm you," Ravenna said, hoping for a swift death.

"They won't harm you either way," he said. She wanted to ask him what he meant, but then she saw one of the Despiri sending flames straight from the palms of his hands and into the witch guardians. She had never seen anything like it and tried to get a better look as the navigator's horse took her further north, away from the scene. The guardians did not catch fire as the ones in the forest had—instead, the attack only enraged them.

"He really shouldn't have done that," she muttered. Ravenna lost sight of them, but she heard the swipes and clanks of blades against bone. Her escort stared forward, but his hand gripped her forearm as he tried to steady her against the jostling of the uneven ground.

As the horse carried them closer to the castle, Ravenna tried to maintain consciousness. She focused on the sounds of the Despiri catching up with them. None had perished in the fight. All four returned relatively unscathed, aside from the curse they now bore on their souls.

There was the clinking of metal as they rode—someone's blade on armor. The navigator was at the front of the group and two Despiri flanked them on each side, one more following closely behind. Ahead, was a sliver of light returning to Arresia. The third moon's rising.

The Vestelians used to travel up the Sunstone Mountains to witness the rising, which painted the lush valley and the rivers below in faint, glittering light. This year, she was supposed to be securing an alliance—saving their lives. But she had been too late.

She could not help but imagine Leith's anger when he realized she was not coming. But whatever it was that he had wanted from her—whatever the reason for him accepting the alliance—it was not worth the curse that an alliance with her would have brought. Not just in her trickery with the witch guardians, but because it seemed that every single person Ravenna had ever been close to had suffered for it.

As they came upon a place she had only heard of in stories, every man seemed to tremble with fear. She slumped against the back of the soft-spoken navigator who had convinced the others to leave what was left of her people alive. They likely suffered for hours after she had departed with the Despiri, or perhaps they *still* suffered, like her. Whether it was a kindness to leave them alive or not, she did not know. Ravenna tilted her chin up as much as she could to view their journey ahead.

A crevice between two black rock mountains that must have reached a mile high panned out in front of them. The narrow way through the rocks was jagged and the slim crevice allowed no room to turn a horse around if one were to change their mind about the route. Single file, they headed into the blackness of the narrow canyon with just three finicky torches. The dim light illuminated only a few feet ahead before it was completely swallowed by the gloom between the rocks.

"I'm going in first. Zeph, you follow close behind," one of the Despiri whispered to the navigator.

No one spoke for a few minutes, until the man she leaned on, the navigator with golden brown hair—Zeph, as they had called him—quickly and covertly slipped his hand into hers and whispered under his breath so low she could barely hear, "Valley of the Shadow." He released her hand and went on to hold the reins once more, back still stiff as she sagged against it. She shifted slightly. No light penetrated the depth and the darkness that seemed to swallow them whole with each step forward. The name was fitting indeed.

Ravenna had heard her mother speak of this place once around the center fire. She had thought it was just a scary story to tell the children, but by the fear that rippled from the soldiers around her, she began to believe what her mother had said.

Within the valley, there was no light. No life. Only shadows. But the shadows took breaths and breathed fear into those who dared walk through it.

Ravenna knew it was the only route to the castle, other than by sea.

The Valley of the Shadow was a place wrecked with fear. Trepidation bled from the black stone walls and from the pores of the soldiers around her. She could feel it too—the unease that struck her to her core the second they set foot into this nook in the mountains.

The horses began to whicker. The animals had nearly refused to enter the valley in the first place, but now that they had successfully traveled into its depths, they protested the black water that was puddled ahead of them, surrounded by jutting rocks. With no room to turn around, forward it would have to be. The Despiri did not yell or curse as she expected of them. They only tried to quiet the horses as if they were scared to draw attention to themselves and let the shadows know of their presence. Ravenna's eyes tried to stay open as some minuscule part of her fought the poison, though a bigger part of her willed it to steal her breath.

Why am I not dead yet?

The bulkiest Despiri, who had insisted on entering ahead of the navigator, slowly approached the water on his mare, and she could have sworn he was quivering. She turned her head slightly to catch sight of the murky liquid. He dipped a wooden rod in to check the depths and leaned forward, hovering the torch above the water as he inspected it. The water spanned as far as she could see, but that was not far at all. Visibility was low. The new light of the three crescent moons did not reach these depths. The bulky Despiri motioned the rest of the men forward toward the water, and the horse that carried her went second.

Just as the first hoof hit the water, a shadow shot across the surface where the flame illuminated the darkness, and the horse reared, throwing her to the rocky wall and then the ground beneath. Blood dripped from a fresh cut upon her cheekbone, and she ripped the flesh of her thigh from a rock, leaving a coin sized hole. A mass of a thousand black shadows swooped in from above—ravens. They nosedived from the mountain tops and swarmed the Despiri, cawing and flocking, and frightening the horses. Ravenna leaned on the cool stone, propped against the canyon wall, and watched, completely still and unsure if this was real or another nightmare. The soldiers fought the birds off and cursed, flailing their arms above their heads. Perhaps she was hallucinating.

The navigator—Zeph—was climbing down from his horse, gripping something white in his fist—a small tear of paper. No ravens swarmed him as he approached her calmly. He did not tremble as the others did. He slowly scooped her up and placed her back onto the horse—this time in front—as he mumbled under his breath words she could not understand. He did not wait for the others to follow, nor look back as they struggled and screamed against the now hundreds of ravens that swarmed them and attacked as they were thrown from their horses. It was as if the ravens were feeding on the living instead of the dead.

Zeph's mare trudged through the water, and the ravens seemed to steer out of the way as the two of them neared the end of the canyon.

Ravenna fell in and out of consciousness, gasping for air, and sinking further into his chest with each step. She did not bother to put pressure on the fresh wound on her thigh.

The pain was unbearable. The king wanted her alive, but with his method of retrieval, he had unknowingly harmed her, *an ungifted,* in the process. It was absurd for him to think she was an Ember simply because she had successfully killed one of his beloved Despiri.

With each rattling breath, she wondered how great the king's disappointment would be if she did not make it through the gates of Oro alive.

She had survived *yet another* night, but three of the Despiri had not exited the Valley of the Shadow. Ravenna found it strange that the company did not mention the death of three of their own—did not even seem surprised by it. Almost as if they had expected it.

She noticed her thigh had been wrapped with a torn piece of fabric, and the bleeding had slowed. They now traveled through the northside of the Dead Wood, and according to the map that Zeph held before her, would be under the cover of the barren trees until they hit the black sands of the coast.

It only took a few hours outside of the Valley of the Shadow for the rocky soil to fade into sand, and she knew they were close. She could smell the salt in the air, but it was different from that of the Crystal Sea. Here, the air was not as dense. It felt empty.

The weather grew colder the closer to Oro they got, even with the rising of the sun, which painted a vague glimmer of light on the dark waters of the Black Sea that bordered the kingdom. She had never been this far north. Though The Darkening was over, heavy fog still loomed, and Ravenna guessed it to be prominent in this unfamiliar, sinister territory. They traveled silently along the tree line on the beach for miles.

Suddenly, the horses came to a stop. She doubled over at the rash movement and nearly fell off the horse. Zeph stabilized her with a quick arm as she was thrown into a coughing fit and vomited blood all over the boots of the grim-faced Despiri that had come to stand next to her.

"She's not going to make it. Blood's a bad sign."

Between heaves, she smirked faintly at him, amused at the fear that took root around him when he realized he would not fulfill the orders of his precious king. She was aware of her body's inability to regulate her temperature, and she knew that death drew nearer.

The lanky soldier suggested resting for a few minutes, but the other soldier countered. "It's only a few more miles. She'll make it." They shoved her back into an upright position behind Zeph, who had been mysteriously quiet this journey aside from the mumblings that she could not understand, and the one bit of information he had fed her as they passed through that wretched canyon.

Valley of the Shadow, he had stated grimly over his shoulder.

Had he offered her his hand *for comfort?* It was strange considering he had come through the valleys and depths of the forest to deliver her to Degare.

But Ravenna considered that maybe he was just a man trying to make a living for his family. Or maybe he believed in all the king stood for and was just a quiet person. Either way, she hated him for it. She slumped forward, blood from her chin staining the embroidered crest of Oro on his cloak. The deep red stitching depicted a raven in flight, wings spread across his back.

Salty air struggled to find its way down her swollen throat

and into her lungs. Breathing came with pain, but didn't it always? She had tried holding her breath until she passed out, and she had considered throwing herself from the back of the horse onto the jagged stones of the beach to rouse death, but something was stopping her. And though she fought that force as hard as she could, she regrettably, kept breathing.

Roaring sea waves crashed directly to the left of them, and they headed north toward the castle, which sat upon a cliff of jagged black stone. No, the castle *was* the cliff. As they grew closer, she noticed the entire kingdom had been carved *out of* the stone. Hundred-foot-tall towers were chiseled out of the rock. Every window—every inch of the kingdom's stone walls that towered up from the black sand—were molded from the cliff itself. Steps climbed from where the sea struck the rocks to the base of the towers, and she shivered. There were no signs of life, other than the hundreds of ravens that flocked overhead, aiming straight for the castle. She wondered if they would soon feed on her flesh, too. They seemed to follow her here as they did in her dreams, increasing in number the closer they got to the castle. An omen, as they awaited her imminent death. Her vacant stare aimlessly followed their eerie dance through the fog, until a few perched atop of the tallest tower where Ravenna saw the faintest flicker of a candle in the window.

It was the only light within the entire city of Oro.

PART TWO
ORO

36

THE SUN IS NO MATCH
RAVENNA

The kingdom inside the black stone walls was luxurious, but there was a somewhat familiar darkness that loomed there, and it ignited a fear that rooted deep within her. The prominent silence of the kingdom was chilling. It was as if every living thing held its breath upon her arrival through the gates.

There was only one point of entry by land, and it was through the Valley of the Shadow and along the black sand beach that led straight through the iron gates and into the heart of the kingdom, where a dozen guards awaited her with stiff expressions upon their pale faces. There was no reason they would have taken the route they had if it were not the only way. It was not only a fireside story, then. Her mother had, for once, spoken the truth.

No one in their right mind would voluntarily enter that narrow path between mountains that offered no light and was home to shadows that could kill. Ravenna had seen the fear that nearly paralyzed the soldiers as they had come upon the

Valley of the Shadow, and that fear was proven appropriate when only three of the six had come out the other side.

The sun was no match for the thick blanket of mist that covered the kingdom. No sympathy was evident on the gate guards' faces when they saw her on the verge of death. She did not know why she expected anything different.

Zeph was the first to speak. "Get her a healer, now," he ordered with a stern voice, only to be met with snarls and an exchange of glances between the many guards.

"On whose order?" the oldest one asked.

Zeph did not cower at his remark. "On *my* order, one of the lowly ungifted in the king's guard, whom the king chose to send to Vestele over all of you."

Every guard stiffened but held their tongues. So, Zeph was *not* a Despiri. Ravenna had just assumed that all the king's soldiers were Despiri, and that the ones who appeared unmarked had shadowmarks under their clothes. These men suspected the same of her with her supposed lightmarks, and she did not know if she was thankful or disappointed that they had not examined her further. Perhaps if they had, they would have left her in Vestele to die with her people.

A young guard scrambled up the stone steps and into the square where carts and shops were set up for the townsfolk to buy fabrics and foods. He moved quickly through the crowd, his blood red uniform standing out against the plethora of drab colors.

Ravenna observed her surroundings as best as she could through her fading vision. A ripped banner hung in the streets, evidence of the recent festivities that surrounded The Darkening, when the moons were black. It was not something her village had ever celebrated. Instead, they had always focused their rare feasting and fun games around her birthday and the third moon's rising at the end of the week, which had looked entirely different this year. She wondered what Oro's celebrations had looked like.

There was no music and barely any movement in the square. It was much different than Vestele or Ink Valley. This land was somber; darker than even the Brunts—as if it were the very source of darkness in all of Arresia. The movements she did see in the streets and the square were slow. The people that were out and about walked heedlessly and slowly, with no expression on their faces. That is, until they walked by the soldiers posted at each corner, to which they picked up their pace and hurried along. Ravenna took a mental note, that even the people amid the kingdom seemed to fear its authorities.

The bearded Despiri they traveled with stepped forward and began to argue with Zeph. "King's orders. She goes straight to the throne room upon arrival."

Zeph spat and she slouched against his back a little further, eyes closing. "She won't make it to the throne room," he said in response. She nearly breathed a sigh of relief.

Soon.

She could rest soon.

She needed water, but if she were to drink, she had a feeling she would not be able to swallow. Her mouth was like cotton aside from the tang of blood that still lingered in her throat and coated her tongue. Her breathing was more like gasping now, and Zeph grew more tense every minute they were delayed. She wondered what his punishment would be if she died before the king could do whatever it was that he wanted with her.

Would it be death? Death to his family?

Ravenna's heart sank deeper into her stomach at the thought of more people dying because of her, Vestelian or not.

He nudged the horse and bypassed the guards, leaving them behind in a fury. They yelled after him, but he kept going, the sound of the horse's gallop across the stones pounding through her head. He quickly freed her wrists with a rough jingle of a key. It was not long before he dismounted the horse, and she slumped over into his arms as he carried her flaccid body through the streets. Her hands, finally freed of the shackles, found the brass pendant at her neck.

Soon, she thought. She would join her mother soon.

Her body swayed in Zeph's arms, and she could not help but fixate on the heels of his boots thudding against the stone, one after the other. The sound grated against her sensitive ears.

Click. Click. Click.

They came upon a little house that was built into the black stone among a row of others just alike. The wooden door creaked as they entered through without a knock. The inside of the house was small, and it felt like her cottage in a way—her cottage that had likely been burnt to ash.

The one room living space had a bed in the center next to a small metal fireplace. A large tapestry separated the bed from the remainder of the home, and dozens of herbs and plants hung from the rafters in baskets woven from reeds that Ravenna had often seen down by the river in her village.

My village. My clan. All dead.

She vomited blood again, all over the beige linen sheets on the bed as Zeph sat her down gently. She saw him wince before she collapsed back onto the ruined fabrics and closed her eyes.

"Galen! You're needed. *Now*."

"Zephaniah?" A woman's concerned voice rang out from

behind the tapestry. Hurried footsteps immediately followed. Ravenna fought to open her eyes enough to reveal a kind faced and stocky middle-aged woman in an apron. Her hair was a light coppery brown, and probably long, though it was braided on top of her head. She rushed toward Ravenna and placed a cold hand on her face, feeling for fever. "Oh, *dear*."

Ravenna listened to their voices, trying not to fade away just yet. She *so badly* wanted to rest. What was stopping her?

Zeph's voice sounded again. "Rastweed smoke inhalation. Please tell me there is something, *anything,* you can do," he pleaded. The woman's—Galen's—voice heightened in sudden realization.

"Is she...?"

An Ember? No. She wanted to argue. *I am not.*

"Apparently, Galen. And if the king doesn't get her alive, none of us are going to have a good day."

Ravenna's eyelids fluttered, watching as Galen's eyes widened at the motivation Zeph had given her. She rummaged through her bag, searching for anything that could counteract the poison in Ravenna's veins. Zeph turned Ravenna to her side as she retched once again, more blood spilling out, this time onto the rug on the floor.

Galen spoke again. "Does he not have enough Embers in the prison? Why her? Why must he continue this way?"

Zeph was silent for a moment. "I don't know. He gave us no further information. But I do know I've never gone through this much trouble to deliver an Ember before."

Galen sighed, and Ravenna heard water being poured. "He must think her to be very powerful. I'd bet he is saving her for the big celebration of the anniversary of the Ember Trade." The anniversary of the trade was not for four more months, in the autumn season. Ravenna shuddered as warm, strong hands reached beneath her body.

The pain was excruciating, but she had no energy to object. She was sure the end was nearing, and she so badly wanted to give into it, to rest.

Just let me die, she wanted to say.

It was better than what was in store for her in this kingdom. But still, something within would not allow surrender, and Galen and Zeph certainly wouldn't.

Suddenly, she was being sat down into a tub of lukewarm water mixed with herbs that smelled sour. Galen was forcing liquids down her throat, one after the other, and she struggled to swallow them. She heaved over the side of the tub. The woman was rambling too many words for her to comprehend in her current state.

"For the internal bleeding, to counteract the poison, uh..." she was reaching into a basket of freshly picked herbs as she listed off Ravenna's ailments. "And for the pain."

Ravenna groaned, wishing for that medicine to kick in the quickest. Closing her eyes and beginning to relax at the little bit of instant relief, she began to slouch down into the tub. Zeph lunged for her, holding her head above the water. He was horrified he would lose her, his precious trophy, before the king had the chance to reward him. She watched curiously as Galen squeezed his hand.

"Relax, it's just the sedative so she can rest," Galen said.

Ravenna heard a sigh of relief before she was out cold, and today, she was thankful for the sedative.

37

KEEPING HIS FAVOR
ZEPHANIAH

By the time Zephaniah stepped out of the cottage for some air, word had reached the king that the young red-haired woman had arrived in Oro. Rumors had already begun spreading like wildfires, as they always did in this kingdom. Some called her a witch, while others had heard of her supposed lightmarks. It was more likely, people figured, that she was an Ember. The king did not typically take witches captive, but instead, allied with them. His Majesty had his own witch who did most of his dirty work for him and who had made the creation of Despiri possible. No one guessed that Ravenna was ungifted. Zeph knew well enough, being ungifted himself, that the king would likely want nothing to do with her if she had no power for him to steal. Though, Zeph's story had played out a little differently than most peoples' did in Oro.

By the spice cart in the busy square, a young girl with deep brown hair gossiped about his captive. "I heard she was being shipped in for the Ember Trade and escaped. The mongrel deserves a bit of discomfort before her death."

His cheeks heated. This kingdom was filled with shallow, evil people who were entertained by the suffering of others. The Spring Ember Trade had taken place just over six weeks ago, but with the Summer Trade approaching in another six, the red-haired woman may very well be one of the new stock. He would not put it past the king if she *were* an Ember. But as far as he could tell, she was not, and he figured Degare had much more in store for her. After all, Zeph had never gone through this much work to deliver one sorry soul to the trade before. He was just as curious as everyone else as to what she was doing here.

Jio claimed that this woman had killed one of Degare's best men...a *Despiri* by the name of Elam. Zeph would not be lying if he said Elam had deserved it. But, saying something like that in this kingdom would get him killed.

His guess was, Degare needed to see who it was that killed one of his best and punish her how he wished, whether that was burning her at the stake or hanging her in the kingdom square for all to see. Degare had likely just assumed her to be an Ember—since she was able to successfully kill a Despiri. Personally, Zephaniah thought she had gone through enough pain and suffering already, but if it meant keeping the king's favor, he would do what the king had asked and deliver her alive.

Zephaniah *had* to keep the king's favor.

It had been a few hours, and Ravenna was still sleeping, passed out on the bed. Zephaniah wished that he too, could be sedated. Utter exhaustion riddled his bones. Because of

Ravenna's declining health and the curse of the witch guardians, he had urged the other men on through the nights, leaving little time for rest. The journey home had taken half the time as the journey to Vestele, but it had felt just as long.

He rubbed his eyes. Galen had done her best to clean up the blood that stained the sheets and the rug on the floor. The healer briefly looked over a shoulder before continuing to tend to his prisoner. Galen had brushed her red hair and pulled it out of her face, leaving one small braid. The woman was strangely beautiful, with fair, lightly freckled skin, and prominent cheekbones. After the lengthy journey and her medicinal bath, her face was no longer stained with kohl.

"She bears no lightmark," Galen said. "She is ungifted. What has she done to deserve this fate?"

"Completely unmarked?" Zephaniah asked, pondering for only a second before moving on. "Whatever, it's not my business," he said plainly, choosing to ignore Galen's jab at the king they were bound to serve, and the crime she had just committed in her questioning of his orders. "When can I take her to him? He is growing tired of waiting."

Galen shot him a glance of disapproval and sighed, rubbing ointment on all the recent cuts and wounds upon Ravenna's pale, nearly purple skin. "You did not even tell me you were traveling. I was worried sick."

Zephaniah had been gone for nine days without warning. "I'm sorry. There was no time to tell you. The king ordered me to his throne room late in the night. I was given shoddy verbal directions from Jio, and by dawn, I was guiding a group of soldiers to some measly, unmapped village called Vestele." Galen's dull blue eyes shot up to him.

"Vestele?" she said.

"You know it?"

"Never heard of it," she said. He watched as her gaze quickly shifted to the faint bruising on Ravenna's neck.

"Looks like an old injury," he said. "Probably from a witch guardian."

"She's cursed?" Galen asked, strangely stunned.

"Yeah, the guardians came for her before we passed through the Valley of the Shadow. They wouldn't have attacked," he assured her, "but Killian's fear got the best of him, and he struck first." Galen mixed a salve at the small table beside a heap of dried plants, biting her lip in nervousness. She did not respond, so he filled the silence. "Three of the Despiri didn't make it through the Valley."

"Oh?" Galen looked at him. "The shadows were hungry, were they?" She turned, slipping some gauze and the fresh salve into the pocket of her apron.

"Hungry for sin," Zephaniah muttered. The shadows fed on sin, but the ravens had fed on the fleshy remains of Killian, Edmund, and Silvio: the three Despiri who had been the guiltiest of the atrocities committed in Vestele.

"What happened there, in Vestele?" Galen pried.

Zephaniah fidgeted with a wooden stamp—which depicted a feather signum—from Galen's cluttered table as he recalled the events of that night. "We gathered rastweed for a day. Edmund concealed us, and we placed it around the village in mounds. Killian lit the fires in the night." Galen's haunted face sunk, and his stomach churned with guilt. "I tried to stall them. I wanted to warn the people, but Edmund would not let any of us go far, so he could keep us concealed. When the entire circle had caught flame, Edmund released the hold he had on the visibility, and the village went mad with chaos. The Despiri herded the Vestelians through one exit and killed them as they fled." He heard Galen sniffle, and his eyes fell to his lap while she continued care of his prisoner.

Ravenna.

The blond warrior had called her *Ravenna* as he had reached for her in his final moments. The name was familiar; Zeph had heard it before. The man had reached for her like a lover would, and Zeph doubted a woman like her to be without a husband. His heart ached, knowing he had played a part in ripping them from one another.

He knew the pain of being separated from family all too well.

He peeked to the side, to where Galen now tended to the open gash on Ravenna's thigh. It was deep, and he cringed as she packed the flesh with a wad of cotton.

"Is it infected?" Zeph asked, setting the wooden stamp down and trying to get a closer look. She had received it in the Valley of the Shadow when she had been thrown from his horse into the jutting rocks of the canyon walls. He had not noticed till daylight had returned and had ripped his cloak to wrap it as best as he could.

Galen shook her head. "Not yet, but it will be if I don't pack it. It's too deep. Don't want the skin closing before the inside heals," she explained, placing a few drops of an amber liquid inside of the gash, then shoving the rest of the gauze inside. She spread some salve over it and then placed a thin bandage over top before tugging the skirts of Ravenna's new dress back down over her legs. "She has lost a lot of blood."

Zeph grunted in agreeance as he looked to the floor at her crumpled, bloodstained trousers. The fresh wound across her cheekbone had been stitched, and her breathing had slowed from her previous, desperate gasps for air. He placed the back of his hand on her cheek. Her fever had broken.

He noted the scars on Ravenna's skin. Scars of a warrior—as the face paint she had borne in the valley would allude. After all, she had exited the fire circle with a death grip on her sword as if she had fought a thousand wars.

Dusk fell, and the clocktower sounded, and Oro's people retreated indoors for the night. Zeph rose and lifted her fractured body from the bed.

"She is still unconscious! You cannot take her yet, she needs to heal—she needs to wake up first, I need—"

"King's orders," he cut in with a grimace. "I can't hide out here all night. He'll have my head." Her mouth clamped shut.

"Fine. But I will have to see her again. The tincture will help to fight infection, but I'll need to change the gauze in a week or so." Zeph nodded, and she continued. "These will help with the pain," she said, hastily shoving a few herbs into a pouch, then strapping it beneath Ravenna's skirt.

She then placed one finger to her lips, entreating him to keep her secret.

Zeph had already dreaded delivering Ravenna to the throne room, but when she woke while he was carrying her to her certain death, he dreaded it even more. She did not fight or even say one word to him. She was a warrior. She could try to fight him off if she wanted, but he knew she had accepted her fate. It was clear she had chosen death, though somehow, it never came. He did not know the depths of her story, or the darkness that she had faced before his company had wrecked her village, but he had a feeling she had already been a shell of who she once was upon their arrival in Vestele.

Zephaniah took the alleys, the least popular way of travel from Galen's, to the center of the city where the king's black stone castle began its ascent into the foggy night sky. The guards opened the tall wooden doors before him, and just beyond, he was met by four of the king's soldiers—two who he knew to be Despiri, the other two, probably ungifted, but Shades nonetheless. They took Ravenna from his grasp and restrained him by his arms.

"What are you doing?" he snapped. One of the Despiri that Zeph had been traveling with this past week, Faxon, smirked under his dark beard as he forcefully held Zeph's arm.

"King's orders, Zeph. I told you to deliver her immediately."

"He wanted her alive," Zeph argued, glancing hopelessly to where Ravenna hung limp in Callan's arms as he carried her toward the throne room. Zeph was escorted behind.

The enormous room panned out before him, its towering, black stone ceilings caked with stalactites, an impending doom ready to crumble upon him. This room doubled as the ball room, and Zeph could not help but recount the party in celebration of the Spring Ember Trade that had occurred within its walls six weeks ago, and the two hundred Ember lives that had been sold and taken in the newly constructed coliseum on the eastern side of Oro.

The four men escorted Zephaniah and carried Ravenna amongst the vast stretch of smooth stone floors to the foot of the dais where the king sat, his throne positioned upon mirrored tile. Around the edges of the tile, where the floors turned back to stone, stalagmites protruded all around, forming a backdrop of pointed rocks.

Degare awaited them on his dark velvet throne, stormy eyes full of disdain and shadowmarks covering much of the exposed skin on his neck and hands. Zeph kept his own eyes down and tried to salvage what little respect the king had left for him. Zeph had served him well for seven years as a soldier and navigator, ever since the king had killed his family. Surely this one mistake would not ruin all the work he had done to maintain his position here, close to his enemy.

Callan threw Ravenna onto the hard floor, and Zeph flinched as her bones collided with the stone. She stirred but did not open her eyes.

"Zephaniah, come forward." The king's gruff voice sounded, and Zeph stepped out of the grasp of the soldiers that held him, keeping his face tight. He bowed and then looked to Degare, whose expression was unimpressed. The King of Oro was flanked by one of his most beloved Despiri, Jio, and by Jara, his witch—who Zephaniah knew did not work well with Jio.

The bloodstone staff was never absent from the king's hand, and tonight was no exception. Zephaniah swallowed, praying Degare would not use it on Ravenna. The only time the king did not wield the staff was during the seasonal Ember Trades, when the spelled bloodstone weapon was in use by a buyer. But even then, Degare was always close by, monitoring his dearest possession.

His hair seemed grayer than it had been when Zeph had left just ten days ago, and his wrinkles trapped his face in a permanent grimace. Power radiated from him, and as he began to speak again, Zeph stiffened.

"This girl is not gifted," the king realized as he looked upon Ravenna's weak, broken body. "Because if she was as powerful as she was said to be," the king shot Jio a look, and the mind-reader nervously shifted on his feet, "she would not be lying here on the verge of death." The king grew hostile, but Zeph did not so much as blink. A perfect soldier.

"Correct, Your Majesty," Zeph agreed, careful with his choice of words. Jio and Jara exchanged a look behind the king. Ravenna was, indeed, an average human with no gifts of Light or even darkness running through her veins. She was neither Ember, nor Despiri, nor witch. "She has no lightmarks."

"Why have you brought me an average girl when the woman I sent for is destined to be gifted beyond measure?" the king questioned. "She killed my strongest Despiri, for pity's sake!" His rage echoed until it bounced from the ceilings in the throne room, and a few stones crumbled down, shattering the mirrored tile without harming the king.

Jara, the castle witch, stepped out of the shadows from behind the king, and whispered something into his left ear. She wore a black dress that drifted across the floors and hugged her figure. It was an outfit that was very unlike any Zeph had seen before. Her dark hair was pulled tightly back and spiraled into an updo that was lined with a fanning of lustrous black feathers. Degare motioned her forward.

She walked with a preternatural stillness that made Zeph's skin crawl, and kept her narrow neck straight with her pointed chin tilted up. Her face was thin and her features delicate. Her skin was like porcelain, surrounding her fiery orange eyes. She approached Ravenna, who still lay sleeping upon the throne room floor. Jara reached a dainty hand toward Ravenna's cheek, and her gaze seemed to shift into the open air in front of her as if seeing a vision that no one else could see.

That was exactly what she was doing, he was made aware, when she turned to the king and announced, "This *is* the woman I saw in my vision." Her voice was smooth like silk. It was a deceptive voice of numerous evils, and Zeph had witnessed many of them.

"Jio, explain," the king said. Degare's fury filled the room as he waved an impatient hand to Jio, who stepped forward on command.

"I witnessed her speed, her skill," Jio said. "She did not cower in our presence. And when I returned with the Ozannes and Jara showed me her vision, I realized this woman matched the description Jara gave perfectly. I've never seen a woman with those eyes, the hair—"

"You're rambling," Degare said.

Jio took a shaky breath. "I looked into the minds of her people. I told you they were hiding something, and that something was *her*. That's all I could get. Their minds were so unexpectedly...guarded."

Zephaniah looked amongst the three of them, trying to piece it all together. Degare looked to his witch for further explanation.

"This is inarguably the woman from my vision," Jara said, "which means she is of a highly gifted heritage. The entire lineage of her family were Embers with gifts beyond what we have seen before. Their gifts would have gone for ten times more in the Ember Trades than our current stock. Their gifts could have crumbled your empire." The king balled his fist.

Zeph tried to focus on his posture, though his mind was spinning. So, they thought because Jara had some strange vision of Ravenna coming from a gifted lineage, it guaranteed *her* to be gifted? Had they not learned with him that not all who come from gifted parents are gifted themselves?

If one was not lightmarked, they had not accepted the Light and, therefore, were not gifted. It was that simple. It was common for a person with Ember parents to accept the Light and come into their gifts in their teen years—when they could choose for themselves: Light or the darkness. If they chose to trust in the Light's power over the darkness and to walk in the ways of the Light, they *usually* came into their gifts.

Now was the time in which he would expect them to rob Ravenna of her clothes and check her for lightmarks. Gifted or not, she would die.

"There is no reason that would explain her lack of *Light*," Jara said. "If she is who we think she is." She snarled at the word Light, and as Degare began to speak again, the witch cut him off. It was a risky move that would have landed anyone else in the gallows. Frustration crept upon his red, aging face. Jara pondered for a moment.

"In her mind, I saw a witch. A witch whose face I could not place until now."

Ravenna stirred on the ground now, struggling to sit up.

Jara looked at Ravenna and smirked, cocking her head. "*Ashreya*." She stated the name loud and clear, and Jio's eyes widened as if in realization of something. Jara turned to the king. "The witch who attacked your Despiri was Ashreya Ozanne."

38

YOU ARE NO WITCH

RAVENNA

The mention of her mother woke her in an instant, and her blade was in the witch's side before any of the soldiers or Despiri could move.

The king's witch was a beautiful woman, and there was a familiarity about her that Ravenna could not quite place. She had towered over Ravenna, searching the memories in the depths of her mind. Ravenna knew she was about to reveal her mother's name, and an anger had bloomed inside her like never before.

Vengeance.

She knew that the healer—Galen—had hidden a blade in her bodice. It was when she felt the cold metal of the weapon prodding her sore chest, that she remembered her original plan. The Despiri, first. Then Degare. She now had an entire village to avenge. What had become of them all? What of Fintah? Her vision blurred at the memories of the flames and the face of her best friend. *And her mother.*

The witch's hand immediately grabbed for the blade in

her side and turned her body to see Ravenna, who was on the verge of collapsing from where she now sat up on the stone floor. Ravenna practically begged the witch to kill her as she mustered up a smirk. The witch pulled the blade from her side, and Ravenna watched as the wound knitted itself shut.

She blinked.

The bloody blade was turned toward her and pointed at the base of her neck. Ravenna heard a shuffle of feet behind her as someone stepped forward once and then halted. She leaned into the blade until its tip pressed into her skin. The witch's flaming eyes darkened, and before she could swipe the blade across Ravenna's throat, the king spoke loudly.

"Jara, enough!" With the speed of a bolt of lightning, the witch's other hand gripped Ravenna's unbound hair, and by it, she held Ravenna's full weight. Ravenna only laughed in her face, exposing the teeth that she was sure were still stained with blood.

Jara's features were strange and delicate. She was so thin in every place on her tall figure, Ravenna thought she could have snapped the witch in half with one hand. Yet when Jara held Ravenna up by her hair, the grip she had on her was a grip of unrelenting strength. The witch was stronger than even Roarke had been—a broad man of brute strength and pure muscle. Jara dropped her then, sending Ravenna collapsing onto the stone floor.

Degare now stormed toward her, his wrinkled face the picture of pure rage. Jara stood to his left, still scowling down at her. "How did we miss this? That Ashreya still lived?" He turned to Jio, pointing an angry finger. "That it was her who attacked you on your journey? You fool!"

Jio spoke quietly. "I had never seen the woman. But Jara —"

"Years, Jio! It has been years since I laid eyes on her—and even then, it was only for a moment. And in the memories you showed me of the attack, her face was covered in paint. How was I to recognize her? Especially when I believed her to be *twenty-two years dead*!" Jara spat.

"Enough!" The king yelled as he pounded his staff into the floor, cleaving one of the mirrored tiles in two. He stepped onto the stone and eagerly, Jara awaited instruction from the king on how to torture or kill Ravenna. "We thought Ashreya to be dead, but perhaps she was just hiding, concealing this *girl*."

The king crouched down. From the scarred skin that was exposed on his hands and arms, Ravenna could tell he had once suffered severe burns. A calloused hand brushed the damp hair from her face in an abrupt motion, and he jerked her chin up forcefully. She allowed her eyes to meet his, and she glared, refusing to break his stare as she spit blood onto his face. He staggered back. His eyes widened; his gaze transfixed by hers. He wiped the blood from his cheek and said, "It is she."

Whoever they thought *she* was, it had sparked her curiosity. He turned to Jara and reached out his hand. She placed her thin fingers into his palm, her skin white against his pink toned flesh. Ravenna guessed the witch was sharing the memory she had taken from her.

After a moment, the king spoke. "Ah. Ashreya, counselor to the Ozannes—your *mother*." The wrinkles around his eyes deepened as he chuckled. "But *not* your mother."

Counselor to the Ozannes? Not my mother? What is he saying?

"Witches do not give birth to mere humans or to children with gifts of Light." He smiled at her, a dark, looming grin, and looked her over from head to toe, as if he had just found his most prized possession. "And you, child, are *no witch*."

She mustered up the strength to speak, her words coming out softer than she planned. "I am not gifted, either."

What did he want with her, and why was he convinced she carried gifts within her? She was not lightmarked, she did not follow the Light or the darkness. She simply survived, hiding within the world where the two powers clashed. Jara tensed and stepped forward as Ravenna tried to sit up, and he raised a hand to stop her from intervening. The soldiers stood still around them.

"But why?" He inquired, stepping closer to her, the staff tapping her chest. "Did Ashreya raise you in the darkness?"

Zephaniah shifted beside her. "Your Majesty." The king stiffened in annoyance and turned to face the navigator.

"What, soldier?"

"May I ask why you believe her to be gifted?" Zeph said.

"You're out of line, and you're snooping out of your ranks. But if you must know, since you have brought her to me safely, her true parents are Embers." Zephaniah scrunched his brow.

"What are you talking about? Why did you kill my entire village?" Ravenna spat the words. Her voice was still raspy from the poisoned smoke, and her head spun from being upright for only a few seconds.

"The rastweed worked, then. I see it nearly killed *you* in the process." He furrowed his brow, shadowmarked hand still on the staff he had been holding since she arrived in the throne room.

"Jara, explain this." He ordered the witch without breaking

his gaze from Ravenna. Jara did not look at the king, only spoke to him while keeping her eyes on Ravenna as well.

"A gifted one would have had the ability to heal herself and the girl did not." Ravenna saw Zephaniah shake his head in disagreement behind the witch.

"Perhaps she wanted to die?" Degare suggested plainly.

Not a lie, Ravenna thought.

"She is not gifted. She did not follow in the footsteps of her parents," Jara said.

Who are they talking about?

"We've been through this before, witch. We know her parents were gifted, and yet they present no gifts. Ashreya hid those gifts somewhere, just as she hid this girl from us," he spat. "Who is to say she was not gifted before, and is trying to fool us?"

"You're right, Your Majesty," Jara agreed. "If she was gifted, Ashreya could have placed the gifts elsewhere. Hidden her gifts somehow...masked them with a spell."

What are they talking about?

Degare looked her in the eye once more and grabbed her chin. "Where did she hide your gifts, *Ravenna*?"

She winced at the pain that was sent through her jaw at the slight touch of his hand. It was like a shock being sent through her head. Screams she did not recognize escaped her.

"Your Majesty," Zephaniah's voice rang out into the air again, and he spoke quickly. "I do not believe this woman even knows what the Light is, let alone is she gifted by it."

Ravenna studied Zephaniah as Degare released her and she fell from her knees to her side, barely catching herself on her elbow. She remembered that Degare was the most powerful of all the Despiri, though his body looked ill, as if he was fading quickly despite him only being her mother's age. She looked him over from top to bottom, piecing together the little bits of information she had gathered over the years. He had armed himself and his kingdom with immense power that could never be matched before he had ever begun to sell to other kingdoms in the Ember Trades.

Degare must have been taking the gifts from Embers and creating Despiri for his own kingdom for *years* before starting the trades just under a year ago. Money. Wealth. Power. Because of the lives he had taken, he had all three.

Degare ignored Zephaniah's claim and started again. "Where are you hiding your gifts?"

Another shot of pain rippled through her head and traveled down her spine, leaving her writhing on the floor. Her eyes found Zeph's again, the man who had delivered her here and made sure she was alive for this.

Something like sorrow flashed in his eyes, and she could have sworn he winced as she retched forward in pain once more.

Does he feel guilt, or is he indifferent to the pain he has caused me?

She screamed. "I did not know she was not my mother. I know nothing of the Light you speak of!"

The king looked to Jara and she nodded. Then, the whips of darkness halted, and Ravenna fell unconscious across the throne room floor.

39

GUILTY CONSCIENCE
ZEPHANIAH

What is it the king wants from her? Who do they think she is?

"Zephaniah Wilmore." King Degare said his name slowly.

Zeph stood square, peeling his eyes from the frail body that lay just mere feet from him. He awaited his punishment. He was just a lowly soldier who was fairly talented in the art of navigation, and he was expendable.

"See that she stays alive until I get more answers. She is still of use to me, Ember or not—though I am not convinced she is telling the truth. Deliver her to her cell in the tower. You're on watch, to be posted outside her cell until I relieve you." Zeph's shoulders sagged ever so slightly.

"Your Majesty, he is just a navigator," Faxon said beside him.

"Do you question me?" the king said.

"No, Your Majesty," Faxon responded quickly.

"Zephaniah has kept my prisoner alive when otherwise, she

would have died. I think he can guard her cell. He has trained just as the rest of my Shade Soldiers have." Zeph tried to hide his disgust as the king grouped him in with the Shades—ungifted ones who worshiped the dark goddesses in the Black Temples. Zephaniah did no such thing. "Can I trust you to do this, Zephaniah?" the king asked.

Zeph bowed his head. "Yes, Your Majesty."

"Take her, then."

He was thankful for the permission to leave the king's presence, and he promptly lifted Ravenna's body from the ground.

"Jara." The king addressed the witch. "Find out if Ashreya could have hidden the gifts we search for. She was a gifted witch, after all."

So, they had originally thought she was an Ember, hidden by her witch mother all these years. *They thought she was an Ember who surrendered her gifts in some sort of spell?* Zeph thought it unlikely, though with someone like Degare after you, it would be wise to hide.

Maybe it had been Degare's plan to sell Ravenna at the next Ember Trade. Perhaps Degare had planned to wait until the fall. The Autumn Ember Trade would be a greater celebration, bringing in lords and noblemen from across Arresia. There would be yet another ball, but the audience would be larger than it was at the usual Ember Trades, being that the autumn season would mark one year since the first trade. Maybe if Ravenna were gifted, she would be solely for the *king* to drain the life from. Or, perhaps Degare intended to flaunt his power over Arresia as he killed her. Zephaniah shook the horrid thoughts from his mind.

The hundreds of winding stairs were the hardest part of

delivering her to her cell, where someone had at least done the kindness of raking the waste to one corner. He had done his fair share of unforgivable things under the reign of this king. But somehow, leaving this broken woman in this cold and dirty cell seemed to top them all. A voice seemed to reach out to him and beg him not to do it, not to leave her here unconscious on the stone floor in the cell that reeked so badly his eyes watered.

But he sat her down gently and closed the door behind him, unable to look back as he sank to the floor and ran his hand through his messy hair. He could not bear the sight of her suffering any longer. He was at his wits end serving this king.

He had obeyed and delivered this woman to Oro, just as Degare had commanded. She was not gifted by the Light, and she was innocent as far as he could tell. He hoped that for her sake, she was telling the truth: that she had no gifts at all. The only crime she had committed against the king's law was killing Elam—the king's beloved Despiri general. Perhaps she truly was just a skilled warrior.

It did not make sense for Degare to want her left alive, to go through all this trouble to *maybe* find some long-lost gifts that had been masked by the woman who raised her. *Ashreya*—he had heard the name before, but where? Ravenna's true ancestors—the ones Jara had spoken of—were said to have been immensely gifted. Gifted beyond measure.

Ravenna lay amongst the stone, wounded, ill, and still unconscious. Shivers made their way through her body. Whether from the shock or from the cool temperature, it was hard to tell. But Zeph opened the door and placed his cloak over her anyway, if only to follow orders and keep her alive.

Footsteps scuttled up the tower and quickly made their

way toward him. Within a few minutes, the same four soldiers that had been with him in the throne room appeared on the winding, stone steps and stopped in their tracks when they saw him sitting on the ground outside of Ravenna's cell.

One spat through the bars, and Zeph rose to his feet, unsure of what he could even do against the Despiri without tampering his reputation amongst the king's men. He snarled at him, and the man chuckled. The other three soldiers bantered loudly about the king's plans and how Faxon had been promised a kill in the upcoming Ember Trade in exchange for aiding in Ravenna's capture. Zeph was thankful the king had not offered him such a heinous reward.

"Maybe the girl's life will be mine to take," one exclaimed, laughing and claiming he had aided in training Faxon, so was deserving of a kill too.

Another countered, "The king wants her for a reason. He abhors her; that is clear. I bet he'll be the one to finish her, even if she has no gifts."

Zeph cringed, imagining the king, as he had seen so many times, pressing the sharp end of the bloodstone staff into Ravenna's chest, her imagined gifts of Light running through the staff like a river into Degare's body, leaving her lifeless on the other end. Death by the bloodstone staff was always slow and painful from what he had seen. Zeph had lost count of how many followers of the Light the king had killed and stolen from.

The soldiers continued down the hall, still speaking loudly. "I thought we were retrieving her for murdering Elam." Zeph did not think *murder* was the right word.

Another spoke up, "If that were all she was here for, she'd

be strung up in the gallows by now. There's something more. That witch was hiding her for a reason." Zeph turned his face and monitored Ravenna's movements through his peripheral vision as the men disappeared down the dark hall and ascended further into the top cells of the tower.

The next Ember Trade would be taking place in just under two months. *The Summer Ember Trade.* Amid the summer season, ships from all over Arresia would dock in Oro's harbors as the royals and people of high status made their way to the kingdom to bid on the Embers that Degare had been collecting in his prison. The black waters surrounding Oro were considered dangerous to sail in, so some ships would likely dock in Brinland. Its passengers would travel the rest on foot, through the plains of Brinland, the old kingdom of Ozanna, and then through the mountains, entering the south side of Oro through the Valley of the Shadow.

Zephaniah could not help but hope that many of the bidders did not make it through. Though, what would it help? Degare was sure to bring death to each Ember whether it was by his own hand or by someone who had paid him for the Ember's life. The highest bidder would get the kill and therefore, the power. With the Ember Trades, Degare was profiting both power and *money* from the followers of the Light. He had become the most powerful ruler in all of Arresia.

When the king's men found any Embers, they would stop at nothing to deliver the poor souls to the king for a reward in return. The king normally allowed his men one kill for every ten gifted delivered. He always made sure to divvy out the weaker of the Embers to the soldiers and keep the best for himself. The Embers worth selling were held in Oro's new prison on the east side of the kingdom or put to work in the mines where they awaited their deaths. Men, women, or children, they would be knocked to their knees and pierced with the staff in the kingdom square under the dark skies of Oro.

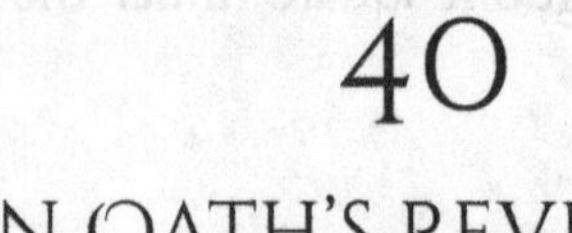

40

AN OATH'S REVELATION
RAVENNA

Ravenna awoke when she heard the group of soldiers walk by. Sitting next to her cell, Zeph continued to guard her and assure she did not escape. Ravenna mustered up the strength to sit back against the stone wall, scooting away from the grime and human waste that lay on the other end of the cell. She mindlessly rubbed her thumb over the calluses on the tips of her fingers from the years spent playing her fiddle in Vestele. Zeph turned to face her, his eyes examining her body, then falling to the cloak that had dropped from her shoulders and now draped across her lap. His bloodstained, torn cloak, with the royal raven emblem embroidered on the back. She pushed it aside and remained upright against the wall, breathing through the pain.

Zeph seemed like he was about to speak, but said nothing.

"Your king is quite lovely," she said to fill the silence. "And you serve him so faithfully." Zeph winced, and she could not help the faint smile that tugged at her lips as her words crept under his skin.

"He is my king," he said too proudly. "I must."

"Mmm," she hummed. The vibration tickled her throat, and she coughed up more blood.

Footsteps sounded in the hall once more, and she turned her attention toward where they neared on the winding steps of the tower. She fought to stay awake and tried to distract herself from the throbbing pain that pulsated through every inch of her body. The dress Galen had put her in was a couple sizes too big, but she was grateful for the extra fabric in this cold tower. No light made its way down from the window above her, as it was still night, but she could see enough by the flamelight of the sconce.

The soldiers were making their way back down the spiraling staircase and into the short, curved walkway that stretched just past her cell. As they grew nearer, Ravenna noticed a familiar, red-haired woman being dragged between the two soldiers in the front. The soldiers who held her were the ones who had just had their hands on *her* in the same manner, throwing her across the throne room floor.

The ragged woman spoke to herself, whispering nonsense under her breath. Her eyes were crazed as she stared forward, but she did not fight the men. Her unkempt hair resembled Ravenna's on a day she had trained for hours in the sweltering heat of summer. No shoes covered her feet, and her skin was as pale as the fog that loomed above this wretched castle, suggesting she had not seen the sun in years.

The soldiers each had an arm looped through hers, hauling her backward down the stone steps. The skin of her bare heels dragged upon the stone behind her, no doubt inflicting pain. Her head lobbed to the side and in an instant, her eyes, *blue as the crystal sea*, met Ravenna's. The prisoner did not breathe while she stared back and then threw herself into an outburst of deranged panic.

The soldiers had not expected the eruption of emotion from her. Zephaniah rose to his feet slowly, readying himself to help contain her if needed. A tall soldier gripped the woman's hair in his hand and pulled her backward, sending her body slamming into the floor. Ravenna's cheeks heated as she sat, unable to move or do anything to help the woman against the Despiri of Oro.

The prisoner stilled when her frail body landed just outside Ravenna's cell. Her cheek pressed to the ground as she looked through the bars at Ravenna. The woman was muttering something. Her arm extended outward toward Ravenna as she tried to reach for her. Blood trickled down Ravenna's cheek from a wound that must have reopened in the throne room. She furrowed her brows at the woman and tried to scoot forward to hear her better. Her body did not obey her. The woman spoke louder as the men lifted her to carry her away. "*My baby*," she choked out in a fit of sobs, clutching her stomach.

Ravenna stilled, directing her gaze to the woman's womb.

Is she pregnant?

The woman was middle-aged, and likely too old to be with child. On top of that, she looked extremely ill, and Ravenna doubted she was healthy enough to conceive. But, if she was pregnant, and these men were treating her this way...well, this kingdom was more evil than she thought.

The soldiers pulled her up between them once more and she spoke to Ravenna on a whisper of a breath. "In this kingdom, you wear a noose around your neck. When the boards are kicked from beneath your feet, be sure to tear the darkness down with you as you fall."

A chill rushed down Ravenna's spine as she tried to decipher what the woman had said, as she was dragged out of her sight. The remaining two soldiers pulled a man from the shadows and as they passed, his face entered the dim light. Suddenly, she was in Vestele, looking into her mother's green eyes again. Time seemed to slow as the man's sad eyes pierced through her. But then, he too, was out of sight, being tugged down the stairwell.

"Who was that?" she asked with a mere whisper that cracked out of her throat.

Zeph turned slowly, crouching on the other side of the bars. He stared down the now empty stairwell, staring into the darkness after them. "The former king and queen of Ozanna." He did not look at her, but she could tell his mind was turning. "Why has the king ordered you here, Ravenna, if you truly have no gifts?"

At his question, her eyes shifted to the darkest corner of the cell. She hugged her knees, running through every new bit of information she had received since arriving here just hours ago. The king brought her here not just because she had killed one of his men, but because he believed her to be an Ember. A being gifted by the Light, though she had lived in the shadows her entire life—*hidden* in that valley by a woman he had claimed was not truly her mother. Ashreya *Ozanne,* the king had called her.

Ravenna's body went rigid.

There was a third and more important reason the king had wanted her.

The king was looking for gifts that were so great and powerful, he had sent men to retrieve her from her home over four days' travel away. She had seen how it had angered him when he learned she had nothing to offer, nothing more for him to take. If Ravenna knew anything, it was that the king's reaction was that of a man who had spent his entire life searching, only to be disappointed once more. She wondered what a power like that which he spoke of would look like in his hands...or if it would look any different in her own.

What would she do with such power like that which he searched for? Would she kill him slowly and painfully, as he had done to so many innocent people? Would she kill *all* the king's men to avenge her own? Would she kill the man in front of her, who served the king but had a certain glow about him that suggested he did not want to be in this kingdom any more than she did? Would she return to Vestele to see if there were any survivors left to help and use her gifts to give them a better life than she could have offered before? With a power like that, would she have been able to stop those soldiers from ever hurting her mother? But Ashreya of the Valley was not truly her mother. It all clicked into place perfectly. The secrets, the blood oath, Vestele's unwavering protection.

Ravenna was not sure how much time had passed since Zeph had asked the question, but she answered as if he had just spoken, as she finally connected the dots.

"I am Ravenna Zenevieva," she paused for a moment before the next words left her lips. "Daughter of Gerrin and Willa Ozanne."

41
WHEN LITTLE DOVES GO FLYING
LEITH

"I told you not to trust her," Edme said from where she frowned at him across the room, arms crossed over her chest. Despite the chill in the air, she wore a sleeveless, tawny, chiffon gown that flowed to her ankles. Her fierce gaze was forever unwavering beneath her unruly, black curls as she awaited his apology for not taking her advice, and for not allowing her to kill Ravenna when she had the chance. "I told you she would bring nothing but sin upon the world, yet you agreed to marry her."

Edme's accusations were mostly true. He had agreed to marry Ravenna without a second thought, and he had trusted the young shield-maiden, foolishly. She had not caused him any grievances aside from the witch guardians that now wreaked most of their havoc on the angry Volcanian woman who sat across from him.

He had trusted Ravenna of the Valley and she had betrayed him. The red-haired maiden had come unexpectedly on the day of the Gauntlet, like a storm. When she had thrown that dagger into his leg and looked upon his face with those vibrant eyes, a new plan had begun weaving itself together in his mind. Then, weeks later as if it were fate, she strutted into his valley and laid it all out before him. She had set a trap and he had walked right into it, unaware. It was too good to be true, that she had delivered to him exactly what he was searching for on a silver platter. At least he had still had his wits about him and was not so foolish to assume there was not some catch to her promise.

After noting the marks on Ravenna's neck made from beasts that he was far too familiar with, he and Edme had followed her back to Vestele under the cover of darkness. He had given Edme strict orders not to harm her, and though Edme had a mind of her own and was accustomed to the role of *queen*, she had reluctantly obeyed.

Just as Leith had suspected when he had followed the shield-maiden into the Dead Wood, the *catch* to their marriage alliance was that the pretty little dove was being tracked by the witch guardians. She had only been searching for a way out from under the claws of the curse, and in sealing an alliance with him, she *would* have gained his unwavering protection. It was not a problem, he had thought. He and Edme had returned unscathed, aside from the new marks that Edme bore on her soul for killing dozens of guardians with her wildfire. The Ink Blood Clan was strong enough to take down the entire race of guardians if they had to, and he would have made sure Ravenna was protected, if it meant she upheld her end of the deal: marriage. It truly was that simple.

Ravenna had been honorable in her dedication to protecting her village with an alliance, and a part of him admired her for it. What he did not expect was that she would stand him up on the night they were to be married. Perhaps she had found another way out of her mess, or perhaps the guardians had already succeeded in killing her. He bristled at the latter thought, though he knew Edme had obliterated so many guardians that evening weeks ago, that the vengeful species would have likely forgotten about Ravenna for the time being, as they yearned for revenge on the woman of wildfire across from him.

He had been so close to all the answers he sought, and they had been torn away right before they met his grasp. He should have demanded the pendant from around Ravenna's neck that day as a ledger. Surely, she would have returned if he had kept not only the dagger with the red gemmed hilt, but both remnants she had of her late mother. Then, all his problems would be well on their way to being solved. He ran the shield-maiden's valuable blade between his fingers, admiring the pure stone.

He turned to Edme. "I do not think you understand what is at stake, *princess*." Her face hardened as she fought the urge to correct him. He knew things she did not know that he knew about her recent endeavors. He knew exactly what had led her here to his valley, to aid him in *his* endeavors.

"I understand *fully*. And because you refused to end her when you had the chance, the King of Oro now holds her in his grasp, " she spat. At those words, Leith leaned forward in his chair.

"What do you speak of?" he asked.

Edme's dark brown skin seemed to burn with rage as she prepared to speak. He placed his hands on the edge of the table and rose, awaiting the response that rolled from her sharp tongue.

"When Ravenna had not arrived by yesterday at dusk, I sent a dove to Vestele."

Leith studied her carefully.

"The bird returned with nothing but a piece of rastweed in its talons. Its feathers were stained black with *ash*."

Leith looked at Edme under lowered brows. The royal kept her chin up, awaiting his reaction. Degare's signature destruction was with rastweed smoke and fires that engulfed whole villages. Leith was certain the king had come for Ravenna, and for the same reasons that *he* had wanted her first. It was for those reasons that Leith knew Degare would not kill her. Not yet.

Leith envisioned her in the wretched, colorless kingdom, her vibrant beauty standing out like a red rose in a thicket. When he remembered her wit, he smiled softly to himself. Ravenna would give Degare a run for his money. Though she had come to Leith's valley and tried to appear submissive and desirable, she was obviously persistent in getting what she wanted; just as the Volcanian Queen was that stood before him. Ravenna was strong and capable. He had seen proof of that in the Brunts and in the way she had sought to betray him to protect her own.

She was fearless, but in the grip of the shadows, he doubted she could see her way out. Perhaps she could still use an alliance. Perhaps he could still get what he needed from her. In the process of retrieving it, he would make sure the King of Darkness regretted stealing his betrothed. He would make all of Oro pay for it.

Leith's jaw clenched harder, and it was all he could do to remain collected as his mind twisted around her name and combed through all the ways he could reclaim her from Oro.

Ravenna.

That name held the solution to all his problems. Ravenna was *his.*

"I sent some of my men to Vestele this morning at dawn," Edme continued. Her voice was rough and wild like untamed fire. Behind it was the promise of retribution on Degare for what he had done to the *mostly* innocent people of Vestele, and the room seemed to heat around them. "They sent word back."

"Any survivors?" Leith asked.

"Yes."

42
A MOSAIC
RAVENNA

Ravenna Zenevieva Ozanne. Unknown heir to the throne of Ozanna. Daughter of The Barren Queen.

The name echoed in her hollow mind. It was the only thought that plagued her for a few moments while Zeph stared at her in disbelief. It all made sense now. It did, but it did not. It explained so many of her questions and brought about so many more.

"Daughter?" he said, as if he did not quite believe it. "Of Gerrin and Willa Ozanne?"

"My clan was hiding something from me. Said they were protecting me from something...*this* would make sense."

"So...you jump to the conclusion that you are a princess? That The Barren Queen had a daughter...and hid her away in a little valley for how many years?"

"Twenty-two," she said. Zephaniah paused.

"It has been twenty-two years since Degare took the throne."

"Twenty-two years last week?" she asked. He nodded. "I was born on the darkest night of the year."

Zeph's eyebrows pinched together. "The night Degare took the throne."

Ravenna rubbed her forehead. A part of her hoped this was all some crazy coincidence, that her clan had not committed treason in hiding some secret princess of Light. But it did not matter anyway, because they were already dead. Ravenna grew up learning little to nothing about the territory before Degare had started his reign. Her mother told her stories here and there, but Ravenna could now understand why she never went into much detail.

Her mother had tried to stop the Despiri when they had the Ozannes in that wagon in Vestele, but until that point, the shield-maiden had never taken a stand against the evils of the darkness—because she was trying not to draw attention to Vestele. To Ravenna.

"You do resemble them," Zephaniah said. "The resemblance is uncanny. Red hair like yours and Willa's is rare, and you have a little of each of them in your eyes."

A mosaic. Little pieces of your mother and your father.

Ravenna recalled these words from Asta, and her head rolled back against the wall as she chuckled through bloody teeth. Ravenna had seen the portraits in the Palace of Ozanna many times. She had admired the beauty of the kingdom and the young barren queen, forever frozen in time in that golden frame. She had even noticed the king's handsome features, and the way his hand laid atop the delicate fingers of his soulbound—his wife. But until now, none of it had provoked any further thought.

Gerrin's eyes were somehow the same eyes Ravenna had

grown up peering into as she was tucked into bed each night as a young girl. They held the same ferocity as her mother's had when she fought and trained with her warriors each day. And somehow, they also held the same love for Ravenna when they looked at her.

They were the same shade of green with golden flecks throughout—the same pigment that swirled in Ravenna's right eye. Willa's eyes of crystal blue were an exact match for her other eye. She had never seen eyes so bright on another person. They were the same eyes she had always been complimented on. They were unusual, and she knew it was not a coincidence. Asta had not been speaking of Reid and Ashreya.

My baby, Willa had said to her. One hand had tried to find its way through the bars—her other holding her once barren womb. *In this kingdom, you wear a noose around your neck. When the boards are kicked from beneath your feet, be sure to tear the darkness down with you as you fall.*

Ravenna looked to Zeph, who was sitting against the wall, still looking at her broken body through the bars. She shook with the shock and trauma of the last few days, and the pain was agonizing. The cold air did not help to calm the shivering. She shifted her gaze down to the skirt of her dress, where blood was seeping through the fabric. She forced her arms to move, hitching the fabric up above her boots and stockings to reveal her bare legs. Her kneecaps were bruised purple, and the deep gash in her thigh had been packed with gauze.

"Galen said the gauze would help it heal. She'll come when it is time to remove it." His face wrinkled in disgust. Ravenna examined it further. Tenille had never used such a procedure on her. Just under her skirt was a pouch that had been strategically placed so no one would find it.

"She put some herbs in there. For the pain," Zeph said.

Ravenna breathed a sigh of relief. She opened the pouch, peering inside. Herbs...and a flash of something white. She looked up to Zeph, assuring he did not see. While he took out a piece of flint and turned his back to light another sconce on the wall adjacent to her cell, she felt inside the pouch. When he turned again, she was chewing on a few of the dried leaves, hoping they could work miracles for her broken body.

"Is she family?" Ravenna asked.

"Galen?" He smiled softly. "May as well be. She is one of my only friends in this kingdom—if you can believe that."

Ravenna raised her brows. "Surely not one of your *only* friends. You've treated me so kindly," she said sarcastically, feebly gesturing around the dirty cell. His mouth tightened and he looked to the side, chewing on his lip.

"She is the closest thing I have to a mother."

Ravenna looked up from her leg to meet his sad eyes. They were gray like the Edmarian River in the winter, when the sun was hiding far above the clouds and the snow reflected off the water.

"Tell me about her later," she said weakly as she leaned against the wall, closing her eyes and trying to rest. The cold and the shock sent her body into a fit of tremors. Her mind wandered as she drifted in and out of nightmares and descended into the abyss of darkness that she was growing too familiar with. She kept seeing those eyes and that long, vibrant hair.

In this kingdom, you wear a noose around your neck. When the boards are kicked from beneath your feet, be sure to tear the darkness down with you as you fall.

Willa's words repeated over and over in her head and

confirmed what Ravenna already knew. The king would kill her, sooner or later. A quick death by hanging would be better than whatever darkness she might endure in this kingdom.

What darkness has Willa endured in her own captivity? How long has she been imprisoned? Since the fall of the kingdom over two decades ago? What is the story of my birth, and how had it undoubtedly caused Willa unimaginable pain over her lifetime?

Ravenna shuffled through a thousand memories, trying to make sense of it all. She heard Zeph moving but did not open her eyes. Exhaustion consumed her every pore. Her face was cold in the crisp air of the tower that contained her, and she tried her best to ignore every hint of discomfort. She focused on the sounds around her and on the memories of her life in Vestele. She let them hover and distract her from the pain she felt.

The cell door creaked open, and if she were stronger, maybe she would have taken her chance at escape. The shield-maiden was gone...the new woman she had become was just ready to die.

No.

A voice seemed to call to her from the back of her mind, correcting her thoughts. She *had* wanted the pain to end. She *had* chosen death...until the woman who carried her in her womb told her it was coming. Until she had been reminded of the king's evil heart.

Before, she would have let death pull her under its sheet of darkness, but now, she at least needed to know the story of what exactly had happened the night of her birth, and she needed to repay the king.

So, it was decided. She would avenge the death of her

mother, whether she was her biological mother or not. She would find out about the gifts that the king so desperately searched for, and she would retaliate against Oro in the process. Degare would not stop until those gifts were in his hands, she was certain. But with or without the help of gifts, when her body was strong again, she would be a warrior once more.

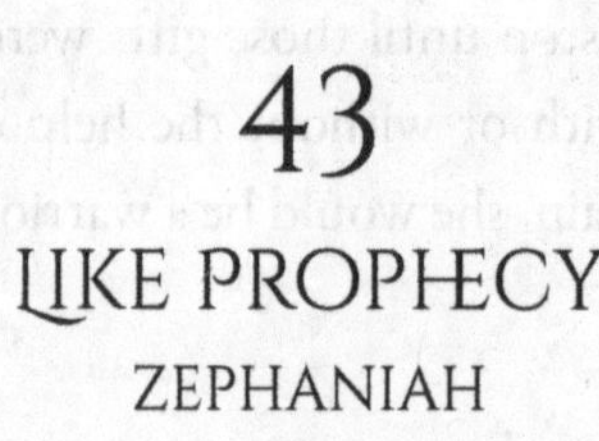

43

LIKE PROPHECY

ZEPHANIAH

When Ravenna had slumped over, asleep against the mucky wall of her cell, another soldier arrived to relieve Zephaniah of his duties. Zeph reluctantly headed to the throne room, where he knew Gerrin and Willa would be in question. He had witnessed Degare's outrage the night the two of them had arrived from the Dawn Prison with no gifts or power for him to take. He thought the king would kill them then, with a wave of his hand and a ripple of pain too powerful to breathe through. Zeph had seen him do it before.

But the Ozannes were different for the king, somehow. Degare's hatred ran too deep. It took root in his soul and bled darkness all around him. Degare lived and ruled to hurt the Ozannes, and he made it his mission to destroy the Light in any way he could. That hatred for the Light and all who stood for it was what had led to the murder of Zeph's family.

Zeph's jaw clenched as he reeled in his anger, preparing to open the wooden doors to the throne room and report to the king. He and his own lightmarked family had once been dragged through these very doors, and he watched the three of them fall victim to Degare's bloodstone staff as it pierced through their chests. Being only fifteen at the time and coming from a village whose grounds and crops had been cursed by the dark magic, he had been scrawny and malnourished. He had fought and twisted in the arms of the guards who held him back, but he was not strong enough to help his family, and he was not special enough to die with them.

Over the last seven years, he had been trapped, gaining the trust of the soldiers in this kingdom. Most importantly, the trust of Degare and Jara. If the two of them trusted anyone, it was each other. The fact that Degare trusted Zeph with his prized Ravenna was a good sign, and he felt he had gotten about as far as he could in proving his loyalty to them.

If only Ravenna did not have to be caught in the middle of this. He took a deep breath and pushed open the wooden doors of the throne room.

Straight ahead, Gerrin and Willa were on their knees, facing the king on his black throne. Jio, the mind reading Despiri, stood beside Degare, and Jara stood between them and the Ozannes, glancing up to watch Zeph as he entered. He kept his face cool as he sauntered in, averting his eyes from Jio and the king, and pushing inconspicuous thoughts into the front of his mind as a safeguard. He went left of Gerrin and Willa and bowed his head slightly before speaking.

He cleared his throat. "Your Majesty." He willed his eyes to maintain their focus, and not to look at Gerrin or Willa.

The king only grunted an order. "Stand to the side." Zeph stood at attention and turned to face the king and queen. Keeping his breath steady during torture was never easy. With

Galen's help, he had trained his mind over the years to be nearly impenetrable—unreadable to the witch and the mind-reading Despiri before him. In this kingdom, he never knew who could be meddling in his mind.

Though Zeph was just the navigator of the journey and had not been given any further information about why they went through the trouble of retrieving her, he did not know how he had not connected Ravenna to the Ozannes at first sight of her. She truly was a perfect mixture of the two.

Degare began questioning them, just as he had every night since they had been in the kingdom.

Zeph realized then that he *had* heard Ravenna's name before. It had flowed from the lips of the former queen when he had placed her into her cell that very first night, after she and Gerrin's arrival in the kingdom. She had whispered it over and over and over.

"I have your beloved daughter. The one you *hid* from me in *my own kingdom*," Degare spat. Willa let out a sob, and Gerrin hung his head at the sound of his wife breaking. Jio furrowed his brow in concentration as he tuned into their most prominent thoughts. "*Ravenna.* I applaud your name choice. Clever, and dark. One would never guess her to be the Dove of Ozanna. But it did not deter me as I am sure you'd hoped." Zeph swallowed. The king clicked his tongue before he continued.

"She has no gifts! *You* have no gifts! What of the prophecy?" Degare's voice rumbled through the throne room and the walls quaked. Zeph held his breath as the king lost control of his rage.

Prophecy?

"Gifts do not just disappear!" The ceilings shook, and the

soldiers around Zephaniah bristled. "I had hoped you had surrendered them to your daughter, or at the least, that she would bear the same strength you once did as your *scrolls* say. Where have you hidden them from me?"

Zephaniah's mind was spinning, shuffling through every prophecy from the Light Scrolls that he could remember until he pinpointed the one he was looking for. The Ozannes are supposed to be of the most gifted line of Embers to ever walk the face of Arresia, and before him, was The Barren Queen.

A once barren queen shall birth a daughter, and she shall become a bright light, a crackling flame. Burning brighter than any Ember before her.

Even those who worshiped the darkness knew this prophecy, and Zephaniah knew it like the back of his hand. It was hope for the Embers, for the Light in this dark kingdom, but when the Ozannes were overthrown and imprisoned, this hope had died. Zephaniah now understood why Degare was so angry that Ravenna had been hidden from him.

Gerrin and Willa would have known of the prophecy, too, and feared for their daughter's life. He guessed that this *Ashreya Ozanne* had something to do with the disappearance of the Ozanne's gifts, and the absence of Ravenna's—to spare her from Degare's wrath. The witch had hidden her in the shadows so that she would never come to the Light in a world where darkness ruled and would try to kill her—a backward form of protection that had negatively impacted the lives of thousands of Embers.

"Where are your gifts? The power you possessed in the war?" the king yelled. The ex-royals had once possessed great power, and they had been able to share that power with each other through their soulbond. From Degare's hands twisted shadows of pure power, and they were sent out in a burst of fury, weaving through the stalagmites around the throne. Then, the shadows sank between the rocks, peeking out and stalking their prey.

Gerrin and Willa would die before they spoke. They were strong. For the last two decades, they had been tortured in the Dawn Prison, kept on the brink of death and locked in spelled shackles to ensure they were too weak to use their gifts of Light. They were kept alive for the sole purpose that Degare could take their gifts one day before the entire world.

Zeph knew Degare had planned to do it on the anniversary of the first Ember Trade, when autumn arrived. Little did Degare know, they were no longer gifted at all. When they had arrived here over a month ago, it was discovered that their lightmarks had faded completely, and Degare had ordered death to the guards at the Dawn Prison for never reporting it. Zeph doubted that after enduring so much pain to protect Ravenna, Gerrin and Willa would give up now.

With the placement of Jara's thin fingers upon the Ozannes' heads, the two of them began to cry out in agony. Gerrin had already been wounded before Zeph's arrival; a fresh bruise was spreading across his cheekbone.

"How did you hide your gifts from me?" As he hovered behind the witch, the king repeated the question over and over.

Jara spoke slowly. "With Ashreya on their side, she *could* have hidden the gifts in a talisman of some sort. But to hold this much power, it would have had to be bloodstone. Nearly pure, I'd say, to be able to withstand the power of their gifts."

"A bloodstone talisman? So, find it!" The king ordered her, and the hair on Zephaniah's arms rose.

A bloodstone talisman?

After a few grueling moments, Willa collapsed on the floor and Gerrin still swayed upright, maintaining his position on his knees. Jara cursed under her breath. They had been mind-searched every day since their arrival in the kingdom, by Jio *and* Jara, and still, they gave no indication of how Ashreya had hidden the gifts—and Ravenna had not been the solution to any problems.

Jara raised her hands and sucked in a breath, her thin lips tightening in annoyance. Gerrin fell onto his stomach and crawled toward Willa. She opened her eyes to look at him as he stroked her face and her unkempt hair. Willa whispered to Gerrin, words Zeph could read on her lips perfectly.

I cannot hide it much longer. I am growing too weak.

Gerrin whispered back to her too softly for Zeph to hear and with little movement of his mouth. He pressed his forehead to his wife's face, and then cupped her brittle hands in his own, rapidly kissing each of her fingers.

Luckily, Jara heard none of their conversation. She was too busy speaking to Degare as if he worked for her. "Bring the girl," she ordered the king. Zeph tensed at the command, and Degare rose from his throne.

Gerrin sat up at those words too, and placed his body between Willa, and Jara and Degare. The king descended the few steps just below his throne and approached Jara on the mirrored tile, his shadowmarked face like stone. Jara stood stiff and tall, her petite frame confident in the orders she had just given, like she was too arrogant to see the punishment that was coming.

Zeph took a deep breath right as Degare's writhing shadows lunged forward from the rocks, seeming to suck all the air from the room, leaving every person hot and breathless as the witch crumbled to her knees. Her hands scrambled up to her throat as she gasped for air. Even her power was no match for the king's. He reigned his darkness back in and pulled her up by her arm.

"Do not make demands of me, *witch*. You almost killed her last time. Remember what is at stake for you." The king taunted the witch with the land he had promised her clan but had never given. Though Zephaniah often thought Degare and Jara more of a team than enemies, sometimes maybe even lovers, this seemed like a threat.

Jara's face tensed as she rose to her feet and bowed her head to the king, despite his broken promise hanging in the air between them.

With a wave of his hand, Degare ordered Gerrin and Willa back to their cells in the tower for the night, and Zeph was ordered to sleep and return to Ravenna in the morning.

44

EVEN THE STARS

RAVENNA

When morning struck, Ravenna's cell door creaked open. The faraway sounds of furious witch guardians traveled up the tower, but her eyes remained shut for a moment because she was too weak to move. When they did open, her sight revealed little more than pitch darkness coming from the high windows above, and Ravenna realized that even the stars fought constant darkness.

"What time is it?" she grumbled to Zephaniah as he tiptoed out of her cell, leaving a plate of food behind. He had laid his cloak upon her once more. This time, she did not push it off.

She could make out his dimly lit silhouette against the candlelight. "It's just before noon," he said, pausing on her side of the door.

She laid her head back and closed her eyes again, humming. "Hmm. This kingdom *is* dark."

He was silent for a moment. "This kingdom is dark, physically and metaphorically. But it's darker than usual today. Degare is out of his mind with this...predicament. He has lost control of his shadows. They seem to swirl above the clouds—I can't even walk the streets without a torch."

The cries of the witch guardians sounded again, followed by the screams of Oro's guards in the streets below. Ravenna smiled softly with her head against the wall. "Wreaking havoc, are they?" she asked.

Zephaniah ran his fingers through his brown hair. "They had to place more guards at the edge of the kingdom to keep them out. General Cleidsdell was hoping that daylight would bring a hiatus, but alas, the king's fury reins darkness."

"Does your king not have the gifts of a hundred Embers? Can he not shoot flames into the sky or something?" Ravenna muttered sarcastically.

Zeph scoffed under his breath. "I'll have to suggest that."

She peeked through a heavy eyelid to watch as he pressed his forehead to the cell door with his back to her, and then stepped out slowly and quietly. With one flicker of candlelight across his face, she saw an expression of remorse as he placed the key in the hole and locked her inside once more before descending the winding tower.

Four days had passed since she had been thrown into the cell. Zeph was there every morning when she woke and left every night after he thought she had fallen asleep. There were other guards on duty at night, but they did not hover outside her cell for long. They walked past once every few minutes, patrolling her cell along with the others in the tower. They paid her little attention as they strolled by, and she preferred it that way.

Perhaps when she gained her strength back, the night patrol would be easily outwitted.

The king's shadows must have subsided, because daylight now crept through the high windows. The first thing she did when she opened her eyes was reach for the necklace that she had fallen asleep holding nearly every night since her mother had passed. But she remembered the necklace was no longer there, as they had taken all her belongings upon her arrival in Oro. She had missed the faint reminder of her mother these past few nights, as the witch guardians' cries echoed into the tower, into this cell where she felt so alone. Instead, as the beasts beckoned for vengeance each night, she held tightly to the braid her mother had woven so many weeks ago.

She was stiff and sore from her injuries and the remaining effects of the poison, but today she felt somewhat stronger. It was the first day in over a week that she was confident she would not succumb to her injuries and would survive until evening.

Unless Degare has other plans.

She examined the cloak from where she was propped up against the wall as she huddled under it for warmth. Zeph was not yet here. She pulled the pouch out of her skirt and dumped its contents into her blood crusted palm, hoping to gather enough herbs to alleviate the pain in her head. She had nearly used them all up, but was able to muster a little pinch of the dried greens to chew. All that remained in the fabric sack was a small piece of paper, folded up to resemble a bird. The art of paper folding, one Ravenna was familiar with. Xan had enjoyed the craft since he was a child. *Oh, Xan.*

Ravenna examined the paper closely day by day, in the

dimness of this tower, wondering why Galen had hidden it where no one else would see it. Now that she had a few minutes alone before the next guard walked by, she quickly unfolded it. It was a shame to ruin something so delicately made.

She squinted her eyes, attempting to read the string of letters in the dimness of the cell.

I know who you are. I can help you.

Ravenna's heart began to thrum in her chest at the tiny words scratched onto the note. Leaning her head back against the wall, she clenched the small piece of paper inside her palm. A small bit of hope rooted within her, but she hated herself for it. It was impossible for her to contact Galen, anyway, and she would not be involving Zephaniah. She did not trust him. She would have to wait until Galen came to tend to her wound.

Her thigh throbbed, and she so badly wanted to pull the gauze from it. Aside from the pain the wound caused her, she could now move her legs more than the previous limit of a few inches. Her arms had increased range of motion as well, and while standing was still difficult, each day, she rose a little higher. Today was the day she would succeed in standing upright and taking a few steps around her cell.

Guessing that Zeph would be there any moment, she folded the note and tucked it back into the pouch, concealing it within the fabric of her dress once more. Ravenna was far too familiar with guilt to not recognize the holds it had on Zeph, and he *had* given her his cloak for warmth, but likely only to keep her from freezing to death. He had orders to follow, orders that involved keeping her alive.

As did everyone else that has been placed in my life, she realized, thinking back to Xan's burden of protecting her, Tenille's duty as her healer, the secrets her mother kept, the blood oath that her entire clan took…it was all some grand scheme that she had lived blissfully unaware of for her entire life.

Ravenna Ozanne.

She braced her hand on the wall and slowly moved forward, step by step. Behind her, Zeph arrived with a hot meal.

"Galen insisted," he said, and Ravenna's heart leapt at the mention of the healer's name.

Maybe Galen had hidden another note for her to find. As Zeph noticed her standing, his eyes rose in surprise.

"Oh, you're walking. Good."

She struggled to move forward to take the platter from him. He held tension in his shoulders as he glanced around the hall and entered her cell, closing the distance between them faster than she could have. "Eat it quickly," he said nervously.

There was no secret message, no paper holding the key to her salvation. But, her appetite had returned, and she was able to eat in haste. She had not consumed a *hot* meal since she last ate in Vestele. Most of her recent sustenance had been the few bites of unleavened bread and berries Zeph had forced down her throat on their recent travels. Between that and the poorly made slop that was delivered for all the prisoners, this meal tasted phenomenal. Once the warm soup and freshly baked bread was gone from the bowl, she looked up at Zeph through the bars, handing the bowl back through.

"I also brought you this," He pulled a small red fruit from his pocket, and his hand stretched through the bars once more.

"Thank you," she said hesitantly, biting into the fruit. A sweet taste spread across her tongue. She wondered where he had gotten it. This kingdom was far too dark and cold for such luxuries.

"The king ordered that you be taken to Jara this morning," he stated flatly. Ravenna paused her chewing to look up at him. If only she were stronger, this would be the perfect chance to kill the witch.

Zephaniah must have read her expression because he added, "Jara cannot be easily killed, just so you are aware. Don't try anything."

She stiffened.

Ravenna was a warrior. The shield-maiden. But since her mother had been killed that night nearly two months ago, she had endured things that had humbled her. She had been broken and ready to die by her own two hands. The night the witch guardians had attacked her on her journey home from Ink Valley, something unexplainable, something far greater than her, had stepped in and saved her life, giving her a second chance.

But why?

She was puzzled at the memory of the great winds and the fire so white and so hot that it had seared her skin from a hundred feet away.

"Can you walk?" Zeph asked, staring at the hand that she had propped against the wall for balance. He reached forward as if to steady her, and she shot him a glare.

"Don't touch me." His hands recoiled and he backed up, allowing her space.

Gritting her teeth, she moved forward through the barred door. She would take in all her surroundings, as she was most certain she would be returning to this cell later. There were no exits until the bottom of the tower. It was precisely what she had expected. The windows were too high to climb to, and the ones that were not were barred to contain the prisoners, used solely for the purpose of light, though they did a poor job in this clouded kingdom.

The stairwell wound down nearly four hundred steps from where her cell was. She guessed that she was near the top, as kingdoms seemed to place their most valued prisoners in the highest cells, so they had less chance of escape. There was a guard visible around every curve, and escape would be more difficult than she had suspected. She would be better off trying to make her move directly in front of the king and the witch and all their gruesome darkness.

Not today, she reminded herself. Today, she could barely walk.

Stopping to rest nearly every twenty steps had Zeph offering to carry her, to which she answered with a scoff and kept pushing downward into the pit of witches and darkness that awaited her below. She assumed he had carried her up all the steps the first night. He was stronger than she had initially noticed. She admired his back, seeing how the muscles seemed to move beneath the fabric of his tunic as he shifted his shoulders back and forth, descending the steps. Though he was shorter than Xan, he would have made a good warrior in Vestele.

She already dreaded the ascent that would come later, but getting out of that dreadful, nasty cell, whether it meant torture or not, was a blessing.

Zeph sat down at the bottom of the steps, inviting her to sit next to him and rest for a moment. She stood behind him and leaned against the rugged wall, awaiting an explanation for why he was not headed directly for Jara, as she knew he had been ordered.

"What are you doing?" she demanded, impatience coating her tongue.

He directed his attention forward when he spoke. "I don't know what I am doing."

She took a breath and leaned down next to him, grimacing at the pain that radiated from her legs as she crouched. "I am cursed, Zeph. Not only by the witch guardians, but by the shadows that trail me. Do not get too close, or they will consume you, too." She took a deep breath, and just as he opened his mouth to object, she continued. "Forget," she gritted, "about helping me. I can see that you want to, and I do not understand why. It will only get you killed."

She could not handle another death on her shoulders. She would not survive anymore guilt. The mixture of guilt and grief that consumed her was far worse than death. Zeph may want to help her, but she would not allow him to.

She stood straight and tall, sharpening her voice. "So, get up and take me to the witch as you have been ordered." Being strong was something she had to do. If she wanted to survive this castle long enough to avenge the deaths of her people—her family—then she would push past the grief and not allow it to crumble her spirit any longer.

Zephaniah climbed to his feet, surprised at the words that shot from her lips like darts. Upon his face was an expression of sadness and confusion as he fought with himself about something.

"When the witch looks through your mind, think of thoughts you know she does not care about. Push as many of them to the surface as you can. It makes her job harder and will wear her out quickly."

Something in her heart poked at her, prodding her to say something kind, to thank him for the generous tip. But she had told him not to help her, and her lips remained sealed as the two of them journeyed down the arched hallways of the castle. It was clear he had been instructed to take the longest route possible to disrupt the map she was making in her mind as she noted every turn and every guard.

They did not speak until they reached a heavy wooden door in the south wing of the castle. Zeph's hand hovered above the knocker, hesitating to alert the tenant of their arrival. He looked over his shoulder at her.

"I am sorry," he said as he knocked on the door. Her face tightened in response to the dread that radiated from him.

Within seconds, the door crept open, and Zeph's grip was on her arm motioning her forward. Jara's thin, pale face floated just beyond the door frame, looking out at them through the crack. Her eyes were the orange of fire, unlike any Ravenna had seen before. They roved over her body in disgust.

Ravenna's clothes were not her own, and therefore did not fit nor flatter her body. The dress was like a sheet on her, and it swallowed her up, making it impossible to fight in, if she were ever to get the chance. But Ravenna knew it was not the clothes she wore that had Jara turning her nose up in disgust. It was the dirt and grime that was plastered over the fabric. It was the blood and the waste that reeked and made her own eyes water. Ravenna glowered at the witch and her judgment, then found it in her to give the witch a smile.

Jara did not return it. "Order my maids in," Jara demanded to Zeph.

He slightly bowed his head in reverence.

Ravenna pursed her lips, and a whip of power seemed to leash around her throat, drawing her forward until she was face-to-face with the witch herself.

"I have some games to play with you today," Jara sneered. The invisible collar of darkness tightened. Ravenna gasped, still trying to remain unbothered. "But first, you'll need cleaned up. I cannot bear to be in the same hundred miles of you looking and *smelling* like you do," she spat. "Do not mistake it for kindness." The witch released her power from Ravenna's throat.

Zeph disappeared down the hall, and Ravenna was now inside what she assumed were Jara's chambers. Luxurious, ornate furniture lined every wall. Tall, unbarred windows offered plenty of light, diffused by the thick cloud coverage outside. The expanse of Jara's chambers was great.

In the west corner was a lounging set and bookshelves lined with hundreds of books. Ravenna had never enjoyed reading much, but her mother had ensured she knew how. As she walked further into the room, she realized the books were all books of magic and spells. She examined the titles closely. In the center of the expansive room was a little table and an open tome. The small title displayed at the top of the page read: *Spells of Delle: The Delle Witches*. Ravenna turned her gaze away from the book when she noticed Jara's attention on her.

The curtains were a deep black, and the room contained three hearths. Only one was lit in the lounge area. It was much warmer than her cell in the chambers, and she enjoyed the heat on her skin. Jara tapped her lengthy nails along the wood of the round table that took up a large portion of the room they stood in. Through an archway behind her was a fancy bed, layered with linens and fine fabrics of deep purples. Ravenna had never slept in such an extravagant manner. She bet Jara slept soundly despite her sins, with the comfort of her feather mattress, fluffed pillows, and clean sheets each day.

But Ravenna would have given anything to be back on the lumpy, thin, feathered mattress in Vestele, next to her mother in front of the fire. She imagined her mother's fingertips brushing the hair from her face one last time, or her mother laughing while speaking of something that happened at training that day. Ravenna had never cherished the shield-maiden's criticism before. She had hated how she would pick apart her fighting style each day when she would check in on her and Xan and tell Ravenna of all the ways she could improve. Though she had kept Ravenna from fighting with them, she had ensured that Ravenna's skill exceeded that of the Vestelian Warriors. Ravenna thought maybe she was getting closer to learning the exact reason. She hoped to uncover the truth about her history, and how she had ended up in Vestele all those years ago.

She directed her eyes to the door as two servants arrived, scurrying in like mice and trying to remain unseen. Both ladies ducked their heads, curtseying before Jara, as if she were their queen. Ravenna bit her cheek, running her fingers across the soft tapestry that hung on the south wall. It depicted a land she had not seen in person, but knew by the stories she had heard.

The Hollow Coves.

Black rock, much like the black rock in this kingdom, spiked out of the black sand in many formations, causing little pools of dark water and shadows to form. It was a coastal territory and appeared to contain very little life. It was said to have once been a land ruled by witches and filled with dark magic—it was the origin of bloodstone and was located about fifty miles southwest of Ink Valley. Some small human clans had lived there, too, but the witch clans had been dominant in the territory.

A sharp voice cut the air, "Do not," Jara said through gritted teeth, "touch that." Ravenna rolled her eyes, stepping to the side to get a better view of the book of spells in the center of the room. Jara must have been studying it recently. Ravenna could make out a depiction of a bloodstone on the page with fingers wrapped around it, but she could only decipher a few sentences.

The top of the page was titled: *How to Retrieve Magic from a Bloodstone Talisman*. Beneath was a broken stone, shattered into pieces of red. *When a bloodstone talisman is broken, the power within is released into the body of the breaker*. Ravenna narrowed her eyes, trying to read the next page titled: *How to Place Power into a Bloodstone Talisman*, but the spell was in an unfamiliar language.

Her legs began to wobble as standing grew difficult, but she did not dare sit without permission. Jara turned toward her servants, and Ravenna saw a flash of surprise in Jara's expression as she noticed the blonde.

"Oh, a new one," the witch said casually before continuing to order them. "Clean her up and get her a clean set of clothes. Make her not *reek*."

The witch's room was pristine. To have Ravenna in her chambers in all her grime must have been driving her to madness. As the servants led her past Jara's bed and into the bathing room, she made sure to drag her dirty skirt across the fresh sheets. It was worth the lash of pain that surged through her spine.

Ravenna stood against the wall as the two women filled the tub with water. The brunette seemed confident and content in playing servant to Jara. She appeared to be around forty years of age, and Ravenna guessed she had probably been a servant her entire life. She followed Jara's orders precisely, and insisted they move quickly with the bath. There was a familiarity about the new servant that Ravenna could not place. She was a petite blonde with thick braids that swirled around at the nape of her neck. She seemed to disdain being here. Ravenna could understand.

The brunette worked to undo the corset of Ravenna's dress, though she could have slipped out of it without it being loosened. Galen had not tightened the thing one bit when she had put it on her. Maybe the healer had assumed Ravenna would like to be able to breathe. She glanced at the doorway and noted that Jara was nowhere in sight. She could try to escape now, but she would not make it far. The kingdom would be locked down before she made it out of these chambers and down the hall on her shaky legs.

The blonde collected Ravenna's clothes and piled them onto the floor. While the brunette was dropping lavender or something fragrant into the water, the blonde waited with a pleasant smile, ready to help Ravenna into the deep tub.

They stirred the water around, adding salts and herbs. Ravenna stepped into the bath, using all her strength to lift her very unstable, injured leg over the steep ledge. The inviting warmth of the water made the second step much easier. Her body seemed to rejoice with every inch deeper into the water, and she sank right in, but she kept her wounded leg elevated above the water to avoid infection. She did not care that she was naked in front of these strangers or that the water was turning black with mud and grime and blood. The heat brought so much relief to her aching body. Before the water could darken too much, she dunked her head under. With the warm embrace, she felt the tension release from every muscle.

She was allowed not even three seconds of relief before the two servants began their mission of making her presentable and worthy of being in Jara's presence. The blonde gave Ravenna a sympathetic smile as rough stones were rubbed against her back to loosen the dirt. She winced in pain as they rubbed her skin raw, as if every bit of her past must be scrubbed from her. She had felt like that once, when the blood of her mother stained her hands and she had gone to the river, hoping to rid herself of the guilt. She breathed. She would not let herself go there, into the depths of her mind that were still ridden with guilt.

She wanted to be present for whatever Jara had in store for her today, whether it was torture or a nice cup of tea to try and sway her to give answers to the things Ravenna did not even know. Ravenna could surely pilfer some answers from *her*, too.

Scrape. Scrape. Scrape.

She leaned further forward with each aggressive movement. The two women spread her arms, each taking one in their grasp and beginning to scrub away with a mixture of clean water and soap from a bucket that sat next to the bath.

A knock sounded at the door and Ravenna did not bother to look over her shoulder, but she could not stop her body from going rigid. The blonde woman—who must have been a year or two younger than Ravenna—placed her hand on Ravenna's wet shoulder, offering consolation as she tensed.

Into the room came four more servants, each carrying two buckets of clean water.

Thoughts wandered through her mind. Had these women chosen this life or had they been forced into it, into servanthood to a witch who could kill them with a raise of her hand? Ravenna watched as they each scurried in and out of the room, leaving their buckets of water on the stone floor behind them. The black water drained around her, and a chill took her body as the air kissed her previously submerged skin. She watched as the last bit of water swirled down the drain, and she wondered where it went after it was out of sight.

The buckets of fresh, clear water splashed into the tub around her and filled it until it reached her stomach. When the dark-haired servant began to untie the braid in Ravenna's hair, Ravenna caught her hand in a death grip with strength she did not know she had.

"Leave it," she said. The braid served as a reminder of why she still lived. *Vengeance.* They would not take that from her.

The brunette tilted her head in surprise, and then let go of the braid. She then gently guided her head down until her hair was submerged, and she began scrubbing Ravenna's scalp. The ache in her head was a dull throb and grew harsher with every motion of the servant's hands.

"Beautiful hair, girl," she said with a grumble. "Blessed with beauty, I'd say. We aren't *all* that lucky." The woman nodded to the blonde, rolling her eyes. The blonde was, indeed, beautiful. Ravenna had never seen such smooth, unblemished skin. No imperfections could be found on her body, unlike Ravenna's scar-flecked arms and legs.

Water spilled over her head and down her shoulders. The giant window that expanded just over the tub let in glowing light—more light than she had beheld in days. She relished in it. Though it was a soft light, and no sun rays beamed upon her skin, just being out of the dark enabled her to breathe deeply again. When her body was clean, she dreaded stepping out of the comfort of the tub and onto the cold, stone floor.

"My name is Cove," the blonde servant said as she handed Ravenna a towel. Even her voice was beautiful, like a song. Ravenna did not look up, but instead, examined the thin, silver band on her ring finger.

"I'm sure you have been told my name by now," Ravenna said flatly. She was not interested in making friends, nor playing nice. She would likely never see these women again, let alone be catered to by them. She was here to get vengeance and then to die, nothing more. A voice in her conscience seemed to speak to her.

Perhaps making friends might be beneficial.

Ravenna wrapped her wet, malnourished body in the towel and looked to Cove while tucking it at her chest and turning from the brunette servant for only a moment. She did not trust the woman to be at her back.

"My name is Ravenna. The king ordered me here for reasons I do not wholly understand." She needed answers. Maybe these women had them. Servants were known to be sneaky. They had access to many different parts of the castle and worked events where information was traded. Surely one of the two women had eavesdropped before.

The brunette was pulling up a small wooden stool, a grimace openly displayed on her face.

"And your name is...?" Ravenna demanded, a sort of shield-maiden's authority bleeding from her voice that she had not realized still existed.

The brunette averted her eyes, fixing the grimace on her face, though she still answered in a tone that angered Ravenna. "Mirren."

Her face was cold and showed no generosity, opposite of Cove's kind, ocean blue eyes. Ravenna would have an easier time gaining Cove's trust, no doubt. It was hard telling the secrets the blonde had discovered within these black walls.

Cove already possessed trustworthy characteristics and eyes that seemed saddened by Ravenna's pain. She was sympathetic, and therefore, would be easy to manipulate. Ravenna would feed off that empathy and use it to her advantage. Mirren drained the bath and started toward Ravenna where she now sat on the stool. Both servants brushed through her tangled hair, Mirren's rash movements more careless than Cove's gentle touch.

They were just starting on a few braided strands when the door burst open, and Jara's annoyance radiated from the connecting chambers. Jara was nowhere near the door, but had slammed her darkness into the barrier with a wave of her hand, sending it forward and exposing Ravenna. Ravenna sat half naked on the stool, body bruised and broken, but healing, nonetheless. Jara raised her brows at Ravenna, taking in the scars and the bruising that snaked over her body.

"She does not need to look like royalty," Jara scolded, seeming to cool the air with her presence as she stalked into the room.

Apparently, I am royalty, though.

The wait was an inconvenience to the witch, and she shifted on her feet as Mirren and Cove hurriedly finished the thin strands they worked on, tying the ends and leaving the majority of Ravenna's hair down to her waist. When she returned to that grimy cell, it would have been nice to have a fully braided head of hair. It would have been much easier to keep clean, but that was wishful thinking. She would have to do it herself, later. If she could find the energy.

On a small wooden table next to the doorway, lay a stack of clean clothes, folded neatly. A dress, she noticed, but one that appeared to be closer to her size. Mirren exited and murmured to Jara in the adjoining room. Ravenna did her best to eavesdrop on the conversation, but Cove began speaking in her melodious voice.

"A new dress," she smiled. "Well, it is one of mine. I thought perhaps it would keep you a little warmer in the tower."

The blonde winked as she offered Ravenna a feel at the dress of thick wool. For someone who acted annoyed to be in the castle, she was chipper when she spoke to Ravenna. It was annoying.

"Thank you," was all Ravenna said as she stepped into the underclothes and stockings. Cove looked like she belonged anywhere but in this kingdom. Her skin had been kissed by the sun, likely over a period of many years, and her bright blue eyes, though tired, had not yet had the light completely drained out of them like many of the others Ravenna had seen in Oro.

Cove must have noticed her staring, because she spoke in a relaxed voice. "My family is not from here. We come from the Dawn Islands." Ravenna had seen the islands on the map she purchased in the Brunts. They were two pieces of land situated in the center of the Sea of Dawn, a thousand miles off the southern tip of Ozanne.

Ravenna observed Cove for a second longer before asking, "Which island?"

"Tabrana," she said as she began lacing the intricate back of the dress. Not the island of the royals, then, though Cove's delicate movements and proper mannerisms could have fooled Ravenna. Oriana was the piece of land in which the royal family of the Dawn Islands resided. She had done little research on the royals of Arresia's seven kingdoms, but she knew enough. The tropical Kingdom of the Dawn Islands, despite its name, had recently swayed from the Light to a kingdom that followed the darkness. Ravenna would say that the kingdom had officially turned to the darkness with the recent engagement of the Prince of Edmaria and Princess Mina of Oriana. Now, it was obvious only two remaining kingdoms of Light remained. Remont and Eswen, which were across the Crystal Sea from Oro, Edmaria, and Brinland.

"Why have you come here?" Ravenna asked Cove. She wondered if the girl had worked as a servant before, in her homeland. Her etiquette would suggest so.

"To serve, why else?" she asked, as if appalled Ravenna would ask such a vain question.

Cove began humming as she wove the ribbon, pulling it tighter and tighter as she went. Ravenna could not place the familiar tune. The string of notes was a beautiful, soft melody. A collection of around seven similar notes that started out low and repeated once. Then at the last note, they began excelling into a divine melody of higher notes, drawing them out in a way that brought chills upon her skin.

As the servant tightened the corset around Ravenna's ribs, limiting her breaths to small, shallow ones, Ravenna had to remind herself that she was safe—for the moment. The air she breathed was not racked with poison or smoke, and her body was healing. She would grow stronger every day until she could claim vengeance upon this kingdom of darkness.

Directly outside of the bathing chambers, Zeph waited with shackles in hand and a face that showed no emotion. Jara stared over his shoulder from across the room, her fiery eyes peering into Ravenna's soul. Mirren had disappeared, and Ravenna's eyes trailed Cove as she too, left in a hurry.

As the shackles clasped around her wrists once more, and the weight of them hung from her, the witch ordered Zeph to remain where he stood.

Jara showed no signs of relief or satisfaction at Ravenna's newly pampered body or clean clothes. The scent of flowers and something like saffron was overwhelming. She had not seen flowers blooming in this kingdom; she would bet the ground of hard stone did not aid in the agricultural industry. It made sense to her now, why the king had resorted to taking half of the crops from each village in Oro, and why her mother had fiercely fought to keep Vestele off the maps. It was not only to hide her. Degare's immediate territory had no fertile ground. By her mother's account, Vestele had once been a bountiful land, in the years Ravenna was young. The health of the soil had plummeted every year since, and being forced to give half of their crop to Oro would have been devastating to the survival of their clan.

Jara stood next to a golden velvet chaise with a predatory stillness, motioning for Ravenna to have a seat. In Jara's eyes, Ravenna saw nothing but coldness. No warmth. She did her best to keep her head high and walk with a confident stride to the piece of ornate furniture that was designed for a queen. The bright color of the chaise did not flow well with the dark design of the room. It was out of place, as if it had been brought in as an afterthought.

Ravenna matched Jara's confidence, striding toward the chaise and throwing a wink at the witch before sitting. She had witnessed this strategy being used by Leith in Ink Valley, when she strode into his home with confidence in what she was about to ask him. The winks and the grins he had shot at her had burned through her skin, seeming to steal some of her sense of control. She had needed the alliance, and just when she was sure he would say yes, her confidence had spiraled against his mockeries. Sadly, in the end, she had only scored the promise of an alliance that would never come to be.

It had benefited her in some way, though. She would play his game with the witch.

Jara ordered Ravenna to sit. "The king ordered me to get the information we need at any cost, so I hope you don't mind my prying."

Ravenna raised her brows, forcing a taunt into her voice as she glanced at Zeph. "If you are to retrieve it at any cost, why is my bodyguard still present?" She knew very well that Zeph was not *just* her keeper. Yes, he had been placed at her cell each day to ensure she did not escape, but also to keep her alive.

The witch scowled at Zeph, who had surely been placed in this room to guarantee Ravenna prevailed against Jara's temper. Ravenna leaned back in the chair and added, "I have told you. I am ungifted. What is it the king needs from me, *witch*?"

Jara stiffened, raising her hand to the air in a gesture that suggested she was squeezing something. Ravenna felt the pressure upon her neck immediately. Just as her windpipe closed and her hands roved to her neck, the pressure was released.

"You are not to speak any further," Jara spat as she circled Ravenna.

With Jara now at her back, it was all Ravenna could do not to turn and face her. She preferred to keep her enemies within sight.

With both hands at Ravenna's temples, the witch began. She began combing through memories, uprooting even the smallest moments in time that Ravenna herself did not remember had even happened. She and Xan, laughing by the center fire about something Roarke had said two winters ago, her watching Fintah graze in the meadow all those days before she claimed her as her mare. Her mother...oh her beautiful mother.

Pain rippled through Ravenna's skull as the memories were ripped from her.

She was sent gasping for breath between lashes of power that surged through her mind as she fought to keep her memories to herself. Whatever it was the king wanted to know, she would not give it to him. All the people in her memories were likely dead by now, and she struggled against the overwhelming grief that came with remembering them alive and well. She squinted her eyes shut, willing the witch out. Out of her mind. Away from all she had left of her family.

She would give Jara no satisfaction, no success in finding what it was the king had resorted to killing Ravenna's entire village for. Ravenna pushed the witch from her subconscious and the witch's power shoved back in determination, wrecking the walls Ravenna attempted to build.

Ravenna writhed in her seat, breathing ragged. A scream pierced the air around her as Jara's black shadows continued through her mind, burning everything in their path.

Sounds of frustration left Jara's mouth, and Ravenna reached for any foothold she could find, but her body was frozen aside from the involuntary muscle tremors in response to the pain that wrecked her.

Still weak from the poison and from days in the tower, she did not possess the strength it would take to completely eradicate her mind of the witch's magic.

"*Ravenna of the Valley*, so they call you." Jara mused. Ravenna met those fingers of dark magic with resistance, doing her best to contain them to a single corner of her mind. If only she knew what Jara was searching for, then she could focus on keeping that memory out of the witch's talons.

Her gaze met Zeph's stoic face for a moment, then she remembered the advice he had given her on the stairs. She began to feed the magic little pieces of information here and there. Pieces that she was sure meant nothing. She pushed the unimportant memories to the surface of her mind, so Jara would have to burn through them before going deeper. She could withstand it. Yes, she would have to withstand it. Jara's magic had to have an end and she would outlast it by feeding her useless nonsense.

She pulled a memory from just two weeks ago, when the entire village had jumped into the river, drunk and joyful. A memory of her picking berries, filling the basket to the brim down by that same river one rare spring morning.

Tendrils of that dark power crept further. Pried harder. She cried out, focusing on the memories she could offer the witch. She showed the witch the moment she taught the two young boys to bow-fish at the river. Pain seared through her, causing her breath to catch in her throat. A memory surfaced, of the day she had arrived in Ink Valley and seen the abundance of red fruits hanging on and dropping from the trees, and the children collecting them from the ground. Then, she flashed a memory of the river there. Then, of the ornate door knocker. The tune that was whistled behind the door. The witch paused for a moment.

"You know what I want, girl. Let me retrieve it, and I'll be sure the king grants you a swift death." Ravenna boiled in anger at that remark. To think she feared death, after all that had been done to her. She gritted a laugh between spurts of pain, sending a special memory just for the witch into the grasps of that greedy magic.

She felt the magic recoil just as it took the memory. The moment when Ravenna had killed Degare's Despiri general. Another: a memory of Ravenna killing not one, but *many* witch guardians. And then for good measure, she concocted a new thought, a vision of herself using the shackles and the chain from her wrists to collapse Jara's throat, her body slumping over the velvet chaise above the expensive rug.

The witch drew back, staggering before catching her balance. Something wet—blood—dripped from Ravenna's nose. Ravenna lay back against the pillow on the chaise and let out a gasp of laughter.

"Find what you were looking for?" she asked.

The witch only ordered Zeph to remove her and return her to her cell.

45

A LIGHT IN THE DARKNESS

ZEPHANIAH

Watching Jara torture Ravenna proved a difficult task. He had been assigned the task of overseeing the torture to be sure Jara did not lose her temper. Degare had finally been convinced to let her poke around in Ravenna's mind again, though she had almost pushed too far the first time in the throne room. Degare wanted Ravenna left alive and was worried Jara may accidentally go too far out of anger. The witch's hatred for her seemed to run even deeper than Degare's. Unless Ravenna was a master manipulator— and she might be—Zephaniah believed her when she said she knew little of the Light or of her ancestry. Why the witch and the king still bothered with her was clear: they were desperate.

Zephaniah doubted Ravenna knew anything of the bloodstone talisman Jara searched for, and he had been afraid to warn her before the mind search. He feared a warning might jumble those thoughts to the top of her mind, if she did know. He would ask her about it soon, when he was sure it was safe.

Aside from subtle reminders for the witch to be gentle with Ravenna, Zeph was unauthorized to do anything about the torture, and he stood like a coward watching it happen. He watched as blood spilled from her nose, and as her body writhed in pain.

Not that he could have done anything that would not have resulted in his own death anyway. Then, who would take his place as Ravenna's guard? Perhaps someone not so merciful.

Zeph grimaced at his own inability to fight back as he led Ravenna out of Jara's chambers in chains, as if she were an animal. Her fragile body that had just been clean, was now shaking and covered in sweat. Once out of Jara's sight and earshot, he offered Ravenna a handkerchief for the blood that now slid down her chin.

She wiped it on the sleeve of her new dress instead. "Don't bother caring. We both know how this ends," she said.

Nausea trailed up his throat. He did in fact, know how this would end. If it wasn't her body taken by the bloodstone staff, it would be her head on a pike or her limp body hanging in the gallows, as he had seen happen to so many others. Every day he spent with her, he wondered if he would be there, hanging next to her for the acts of treason he had committed—even if they were only within the walls of his mind.

He pocketed his handkerchief and led Ravenna through the halls toward the tower to which she had been condemned. Her eyes had a little more fierceness behind them today despite the morning she had. The bath seemed to have heightened her spirits. She certainly looked healthier with the dried blood scrubbed from her skin. The bruises across her collar bone and face had faded to a faint yellow, but her limp had worsened, and he could tell she was growing tired on the ascent to her cell. He did not dare offer to help her this time.

The servants—the blonde of whom had given him the piece of red fruit this morning—had dressed Ravenna in an olive toned, wool gown that better fit her curves.

Zeph had noticed her fairness in days prior, but today, she seemed to glow. Her fiery hair made her stand out against all the black stone of the castle, and *her eyes*. Against the green shade of her dress, and despite the horrors she had faced in Oro, her eyes of two different colors were exuberant.

She had a new will to live, and he guessed it had come from the realization that her parents were alive. Though she had not spoken more than a few words to him in the days they had spent in the tower, he knew that she searched for answers. She *had* given up, but somewhere in the last few days, hope had blossomed.

Zeph knew the cost of the title she had claimed. Daughter of the Ozannes and heir to the throne...if the throne of Ozanna had still existed. Degare would not allow her to live, knowing the family she had come from and the prophecy that could only be speaking of her.

A once barren queen shall birth a daughter, and she shall become a bright light, a crackling flame. Burning brighter than any Ember before her.

The king's hatred for the Ozannes had grown too much over the many years it had spent swelling within him. This was a life Ravenna had not chosen but had been born into. It seemed Ashreya had tried to keep her from the destiny that awaited her.

But what is the whole story? How did the Ozannes do it? Where did they hide their gifts?

The king had brought Gerrin and Willa here to the kingdom in the first place to make a spectacle out of them, during a big celebration in the kingdom square. At the Autumn Ember Trade, he was to begin the event by plunging the staff through their hearts and taking from them what he had already taken from so many others. Zeph winced as he remembered the night those Despiri arrived with the Ozannes in tow, no gifts of Light to be found. Even their lightmarks had faded. Degare had nearly killed them then out of anger and had only decided to let them live these last several weeks because they were his only hope at finding the gifts he sought.

The Father of Lights gives and takes away. Lightmarks can fade—but once gifted, unless one stifles the Light within—the Light shines through them and they will never know true darkness again. Zeph wanted to think he could not blame the Ozannes or any of Vestele for doing all they could to ensure Ravenna's safety. But if they had turned from the Light to do so...

Ridding Arresia of the Light was pertinent to the king's mission of becoming invincible. He wanted to take every bit of power for himself, turning it to darkness. Zeph could see that it drove him mad, that so much of the power he sought to take was out of his reach. Degare had spent hours worshiping in the Black Temple since Ravenna had arrived, and Zephaniah could only assume that he was begging for guidance from the goddesses in his search for more power. Zeph even noticed that Degare had not eaten so much as one bite of his meals for the last three days, and his face had grown thinner and his countenance had aged since Ravenna had entered the kingdom. Even without gifts, she had power over the king, and she did not even realize it.

Thoughts shuffled and flew through Zephaniah's head, and he paused on one long enough to feel a little bit of long-lost hope. Maybe, just maybe, this woman was to be the hope his kingdom needed. A light in the darkness. And he would help her find the Light before the darkness swallowed her whole.

46

LOYALTY LIES
RAVENNA

Something had shifted in Zeph's demeanor after she had come out of the bathing chambers. He had placed the shackles on her wrists with no expression or hint of remorse, as he had shown before. His gray eyes had only looked past her at the wall, his body stiff as a board as her mind was searched by Jara. The excursion which showed Jara Ravenna's many kills had only ended in an angry witch and demands for more restraints on her, effective immediately.

Ravenna's lip tugged upward at the thought as Zeph entered the cell behind her and clasped new shackles around her ankles.

"Sorry," he muttered. "Whatever you showed her must've scared her." His head was still lowered as he locked the shackles, but she could have sworn she saw the hint of a smile pulling on his cheek.

"Has she always grown queasy at the sight of blood?"

Then, she was sure he smiled.

Ravenna looked around, noticing that her cell had been

cleaned. No more waste lay in the corner, and she had been given two clean buckets of water.

A small note lay next to one of the buckets. She plucked it from the ground and backed up to sit against the wall, stretching her arms across her bent knees.

Enjoy the new dress.

- Cove

Ravenna folded the note, thankful for the blonde servant who had provided her with a clean space and new clothing. This dress was indeed warmer, and she felt slightly rejuvenated after the bath. A piece of her had finally returned, and it was the piece that wished to repay the wrongs that had been done to her.

Without any knowledge of this kingdom beside the fact that they worshiped the darkness, Ravenna knew she would need to get more information on her enemies somehow or another. She spoke aloud to the golden-brown haired man that she now spent every day and some nights with. He sat on the other side of the bars, as always.

"So, what's the truth about why you're here?" The guard stiffened at her question. She had barely spoken to him since she had arrived. She had only given him scoffs and eye rolls, and for the other times she had mostly been unconscious or in too much pain to bother with the façade. "I can tell you do not wish to be."

He ran a hand through his hair and his jaw clenched at the question. Keeping his back against the bars and turning only his head, he said, "And how do I know I can trust you, *princess*?" He paused on the word, a light taunt in his voice that sounded like he was not so sure he should have called her by that title. Her body straightened, but she moved past the initial shock of hearing the word aloud.

"I do not believe you should. But if I have been here for less than a week and can tell that you are not loyal to your king, he will find out eventually." Zephaniah did not so much as breathe.

"I am loyal to my king," he stated bluntly, and a little too proudly.

"Are you?" Ravenna mused, prodding further. He had been hiding something from her this whole time, and yet she could not read him. Wishing to know what someone else knew about her seemed to be a common theme in her life these days. She had met traitors before, noted their lack of confidence in the leadership they served, felt the guilt that poured from their bodies as they bowed to the authority of evil.

Zeph was a traitor to the crown he served, and she was sure of that. So, she started on her long tangent of her life story of how she knew not where she came from or how she came to be.

"The woman who raised me in the valley was Ashreya Barrett. I only ever knew her as my mother." Her voice grew shaky at the mention, but she continued. "My biological parents, as you know, are Gerrin and Willa Ozanne." Zeph stared straight at her, the tower's emptiness swallowing the both of them whole. "My people in Vestele were keeping something from me. I especially noticed it in the weeks after my mother's death—after I had been declared shield-maiden." She breathed in, recalling the ceremony her people had given her. "I was their shield-maiden, but I was being kept in the dark about so many things, despite being their leader. I know now that the blood oath they took was to keep my heritage a secret so that your king would not find me."

Zeph spoke softly and quietly. "They were protecting you." Ravenna nodded, and Zeph considered his next words. She breathed in a deep breath as he turned to face her. "Your mother—Ashreya—took you away from the palace and hid you in the valley all these years...because of a prophecy."

"A prophecy? My mother did not believe in such things."

"Are you sure? She would have seen many come true in her lifetime. I think the prophecy is about you, Ravenna. And so does Degare." Ravenna arched her brow.

"And what does this prophecy say?"

"A once barren queen shall birth a daughter, and she shall become a bright light, a crackling flame. Burning brighter than any Ember before her."

Ravenna rolled her eyes. "I think it is a little late for that," she said. "Where does this prophecy even come from? By what authority?"

"You truly don't know anything about the Light, do you?"

"How could I?" Ravenna asked, growing impatient.

"The Light Scrolls," Zephaniah explained. "The prophecy comes from the Light Scrolls. Degare has since tried to destroy them all. They were written by ancient prophets foretelling the promised return of the Light to Arresia, when the darkness will be defeated for good."

Ravenna looked around her shadowy cell, and the mangled state of her body. "And you believe this?"

"I haven't lost all hope, yet," he said. "Even the king fears the return of the Father of Lights."

"The Father of Lights?" Ravenna asked. Zephaniah looked down the stairs of the tower, making sure they were still alone.

"Of course you haven't heard of him."

She knew nothing of him. She pulled the cloak from where

it lay wadded in the corner of her cell, used as a makeshift blanket all these nights. From the pocket of that generous gift of warmth, she pulled a slim piece of paper. With a shuttering intake of breath, Zeph reached for the paper through the bars, willing her to return it to him.

"He is who you whispered to in the Valley of the Shadow." Ravenna stated slowly, beginning to understand. "He is who you pray to."

She had never thought of the Light as a being who could hear, but as an object, a ward against the darkness that plagued their world—if she even believed it to exist at all. Where was the all-powerful Light now when its Embers were fading? She had never paid the ways of the darkness or the Light much attention at all. "He is who you worship, even though it will get you killed."

"Yes." Zeph nodded his head, still willing her to return the piece of paper that contained those forbidden words from the Light Scrolls. His hand reached further, until it grazed her fingertips. She stilled, and obliged his request, handing that tiny torn page that she had read so many times, back to him.

"I have made you a light in the darkness, that you may bring salvation to the ends of the earth," she recited under her breath. "What does it mean?"

Zeph smiled softly, *kindly*. It was a smile she had not seen on him before. It displayed no fear or uncertainty, just peace. "The Embers are his people, who are filled with his Light. They are called to be lights in a dark world. Called to spread his truth like wildfire, that hope will return to the world, that all will come to the faith that out of the Father of Lights' love, he has defeated death and darkness for them." Ravenna pondered on those words, wondering where these people got such faith, after enduring the horrors they had.

"Death *and* darkness?" Ravenna asked.

"Go hand in hand," he explained. "To choose the darkness is just to separate oneself from the Light. And the Father is the Light of life. Those in darkness may live here for a time, but those in the Light will never perish. They will have the eternal Light." Ravenna tried to keep up, tried to understand all that he was telling her.

"I don't understand. Why worship a god who has left you here in darkness? He is allowing you to suffer. He has not defeated death or darkness, just look around!" She was growing angry, and Zeph's worried expression reminded her to quiet her voice. Where was this god now, as she sat in a cell with her suffocating grief?

"Death and darkness may endure for a time, but joy comes in the morning," he said calmly. Ravenna really wished he would stop speaking metaphorically, so she could grasp what he was trying to share. "Look," he said. "This world is dark. That is of its peoples' doing. The Father of Lights never promised us that we would not endure suffering while in Arresia. But in him, we will one day live in eternal Light. That is the promise he has given. And soon, even the darkness as we know it in Arresia will be brought to the Light."

"I do not believe it," Ravenna said. "Especially not if this prophecy is reliant on me."

"I believe the Father can make a way," Zeph said. "You'd be surprised." He spoke again. "What did you know of the Embers before you came here?" She stretched her legs out in front of her, focusing on fixing her wool dress to flow to the sides. The wound on her thigh still ached, and she adjusted slightly.

She sat still for a moment, picking dirt from her clothing. "My clan spoke poorly of them and the Despiri alike, but typically avoided the subject entirely. My mother—Ashreya— would not allow Vestele to fight for the Embers."

"She was trying to keep you hidden," Zeph reminded her.

"Yes, but at what cost?" Ravenna said. Was he implying that by hiding her and keeping her from this fate she knew nothing about, Ashreya had caused Arresia to swell in darkness? She shook off the thought. Zeph said nothing, so she added, "I guess if I did not know better, I would assume the Embers to be violent as Degare claims, and that the Despiri were created to counteract their magic." He winced at the word *magic*.

"The Embers are not people of magic. They have been gifted by the Light, by the *Father of Lights*, to serve his cause and spread his Light across the world," he reiterated. He twisted the piece of paper in his hands. "Degare worships the darkness and therefore hates the Light. He hates it because it will destroy him. It threatens to steal the very breath in his lungs. The Embers have been persecuted since the darkness was able to gain its foothold in Arresia, when the Kingdom of Ozanna was overthrown."

Ravenna hated herself for playing both sides, but she had to ask. "And how do you know you are correct in choosing the Light?"

Zeph spoke to her gently. "The Father of Lights created all of us. He created Arresia. He gave each one of us a purpose, but because he loves us, he also gave us free will."

He speaks of a god who loves and does not just demand respect? Ravenna thought.

"We can choose who to follow and how to live, but in him is the *Light of life*. To live in the darkness is just to choose death—to separate oneself from the Light. Before the creation of Arresia, some of the Father's helpers turned from him out of greed and selfish desires. They turned to the darkness and separated themselves from the Light—and so the witches were born. The Father wanted to share his Light with his creation, and wanted a relationship with us. So he created Arresia, and his people walked with him, freely and by choice. He loved his creation. The witches were jealous, and they wanted to rule their own lands. But they did not have the power to create as the Father did, so when he created Arresia, they invaded and tried to take it as their own. Darkness entered Arresia through them, and it has been a battle ever since."

"So my mother—Ashreya—is of a line of witches who turned from the Light to worship the darkness?"

"Yes. Ancient witches were gifted by the power of darkness. The original witches were very powerful, more powerful than any witch today. They are the goddesses of the Black Temple."

"The goddesses are ancient witches?" Ravenna asked.

"Yes, it is why witches do not have to worship in the temples for their power. It already runs through their blood. But their bloodlines have weakened. Along with that and the depletion of bloodstone, today's witches hold little power compared to the ancient witch goddesses."

Ravenna considered all he had said. "And how exactly was my mother involved in all of this?"

"I am not sure how she was involved with the Ozanne's.

But the king knows, and he is one step ahead. I'll try to find out," he said.

The Ozannes would not have had a castle witch as the kingdoms of darkness were known for having. Her mother would have been out of practice, to be welcome in the palace of Ozanna—in a kingdom of Light. Degare had called her a *counselor.* Ravenna remembered those piercing green eyes that Gerrin shared with her mother, and the eyes that she herself shared with both of the Ozannes. The woman who raised her had been a relative of some sort to her biological father, she assumed, since the witch had called her *Ashreya Ozanne.*

"One more thing, Ravenna," Zeph said, and Ravenna sat up a little straighter. "Jara and Degare are searching for something. They think Ashreya could have hidden your parents' gifts in some sort of a talisman. It would have to be of bloodstone. Pure. Bright red."

Her forehead wrinkled as she pondered. "The only time I ever saw my mother with one of those stones was on the night of her death. And that stone was not the one they search for," Ravenna explained. That bloodstone had been the exact one she had won in the Gauntlet. "And besides, you and your men took that one from me when you invaded Vestele."

At that, he flinched. "Okay. Just try to think. It would be helpful if we could find that talisman before the king does."

Ravenna nodded slowly, head propped against the wall as she pretended to fight sleep. The sun was setting and dimming the tower enough that the candle needed to be lit. No other guards came to relieve Zephaniah of his duties, and as Ravenna's mind secretly raced around Leith and the bright red stone in the hilt of her dagger, she was grateful for Zeph's company.

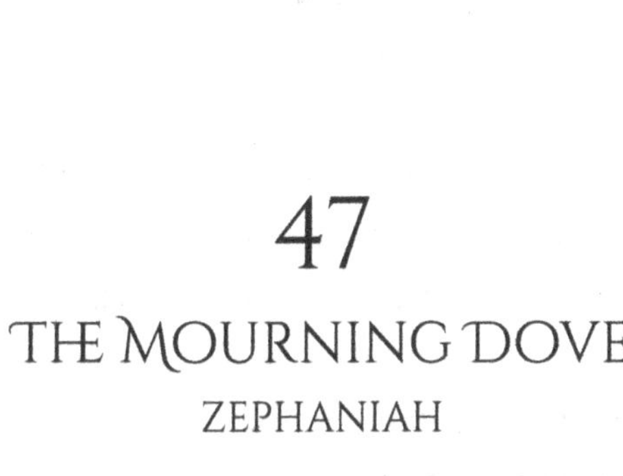

47

THE MOURNING DOVE
ZEPHANIAH

Ravenna now knew that he was a follower of the Light. Zeph knew he could trust her. But quite frankly, he did not care if he could trust her or not, did not care if her knowing this secret in a kingdom where the Light was forbidden got him killed. He would be glad to die for something as important to him as bringing Arresia out of the blackness. The persecution and hatred he had endured all his life had been enough to ensure him that he was on the right path, whether he had been gifted for his obedience or not. The darkness and war and death that had engulfed Arresia and all the Embers since Degare's rule needed to come to an end. He was only one person, ungifted, and weak—one person of little faith. But Ravenna could be powerful with the Light on her side.

Lightmarked or not, perhaps this was Zephaniah's purpose.

Zephaniah knew he had been seen by the Father of Lights,

that his prayer had been heard when he and Ravenna had traveled through the Valley of the Shadow unscathed, while his company was racked with debilitating fear. He had felt the protection around him, and though the valley was woven of thick darkness, he could feel the warmth of a light that guided him through, past the shadows of fear that attacked his men.

Ravenna was now slumbering beneath his cloak, eyelids fluttering in sleep. The wound on her cheek was healing, but he had noticed her limp had worsened.

Zeph needed sleep so very badly. The last few days standing and sitting on the hard stone of the tower floors had wrecked his body. He could only imagine how Ravenna felt. Their conversation before dinner was interesting, to say the least.

Ashreya Barrett—or Ashreya Ozanne—the woman who had raised Ravenna. *How was a witch involved with a family who followed the Light? How does she fit into the family tree?* That was the question. So, Zephaniah did what any insane person would do, and instead of taking his chance to get some much-needed rest, he walked nearly two miles across the kingdom to the library that towered above the city. The stone building overlooked the Black Sea. The knowledge held within those walls always astounded him. With every visit, he learned something new, something that could aid him in the slow process of defeating the king and the witch and all the Despiri. It was in this library that he had learned most of what he knew of the origin of the goddesses and the witches.

He still had not gained enough knowledge to even guess at a way to restore the Light to these lands, though. Between the stolen gifts that Degare held within his body in the form of dark magic, and the intense darkness that poured from Jara, he would need more power than both combined to even attempt to fight back. He had laid low for the seven years he had been here serving the king, trying not to draw too much attention to himself. But Ravenna was right. He had grown sloppy, finding it more difficult to hide his true intentions and emotions as he watched the king destroy each ounce of Light that came into the kingdom.

As he neared the several steps that climbed to the entrance, he strode between two pillars decadent with carvings of mythical creatures and legends only spoken of in the books inside. Sirens and dragons snaked up the massive structures. He pushed the heavy wooden door forward, and a gush of cool air rushed in behind him.

Tonight, he was after a new piece of information. Who had Ashreya truly been, and how had she gotten away with hiding the heir to the throne of Ozanna?

No one greeted him, not at this hour of the night. Instead, the warmth of the fires in the many hearths of the building caressed his skin, welcoming him in as they had done so many nights before. The building and the many stories it held were much more welcoming than the Despiri he was forced to share a barracks with.

He was thankful that no librarians were here tonight. The last thing he needed was a nosey worker reporting his whereabouts to the king. He snuck to the back wall of the library where a winding tunnel was hidden behind a tapestry. Slipping behind it, he lit a candle and began down the dark hall until he came to a wooden door.

With five taps at the door and two wiggles of the metal knob, he waited.

Magdalene opened the door of the secret passageway, blonde hair in a mess of curls around her tired face. She held a sleeping newborn and motioned Zeph in quickly with wide, forest-green eyes.

"Zephaniah. What are you doing here at this hour? Is everything okay?"

"I need help finding something. I'd like to look at the scrolls again if you don't mind."

Her face wrinkled in curiosity. "Of course." She placed her baby into a cradle and hustled across the room to the basket of scrolls beside her rocking chair. She and Zeph had spent many hours together lately studying the Light Scrolls and every ounce of information they could find on the origins of Arresia.

Magdalene was an Ember and Zeph checked on her often. Her husband had been hanged for defending an Ember at the Spring Trade, and luckily, Zeph had been able to sneak her into hiding here in the secret room off the tunnels attached to the library. This room was the home of the only known copies of the Light Scrolls in Oro and every surviving book on the origins and history of Ozanna. They had been successfully hidden here for years, and when her husband Henry had been killed, Zeph had known Magdalene would be safe here, too.

She set the basket down on the small wooden table. There were no windows in the small room, and the air was cool and stagnant, but thankfully the south wall backed one of the many hearths of the library, and the warmth of the stone bled into the room.

"How are you doing?" he asked, emptying his pockets with his rations for the month. Gratefulness shone through her face, and she offered him some water.

"As well as we can be. We were able to get out for a few hours earlier today…I just needed to see the sun."

"Don't we all," he said, taking a sip of his water. "Be careful to keep those covered," he said, gesturing to the lightmark on her wrist, and the baby with glowing marks beneath his swaddle to his right.

Magdalene nodded. "I am careful. We are hoping to leave soon. We could go to Eswen. Or Remont. Henry had family there. Perhaps they would take us in."

Zephaniah paused for a moment. "We are at war with Eswen and Remont. Voyage is almost impossible to find. Especially from the docks of Oro, unless you board with the armada. And even if it weren't suspicious for a young, single mother to be traveling to one of the kingdoms of Light, they'd check you for lightmarks before you boarded. You would never make it."

Magdalene sighed, wrapping her hands around her cup and looking at her newborn son.

"You're right. But we cannot stay here forever."

"Soon, Magdalene. I'll find a place for you to flee. It's just not possible right now." He had promised Galen the same things. That soon, he would get her out of this kingdom. Now, he had Ravenna to help, too.

He waltzed to the corner of the room, to a short shelf that held no more than a dozen books.

There.

HISTORY OF THE ROYAL FAMILY OF OZANNA. He pulled the dusty title from the shelf. The book was finished only a year before Ravenna was born, and he had high hopes that it held the information he sought.

He carried it to the table. "What is it you're looking for?" Magdalene asked.

"A few things," he said. "First, a witch by the name of Ashreya. I need to know how she was involved with the Ozannes. The king is looking for a bloodstone of hers, and I need to find it before he does." Magdalene's brows scrunched together.

"I'll help you look," she said.

"If you don't mind," he said, "just flip through that and see if it has any useful information. I'm going to read a bit from the scrolls." She nodded for him to go ahead, and he unrolled one on the table, smoothing his hand across the parchment beneath the candlelight.

The scrolls of sacred text, of prophecies and guidance—he had read them many times before his family had been brought to Oro in shackles. The texts had since been nearly eradicated from the continent. It had given him hope once, that he would find a purpose and that there was hope in returning Light unto the darkness. Now, he could only remember a few of his favorite scriptures. He repeated them daily, whispering them under his breath lest he forget them.

He rubbed a palm over his face as he came across the one particular section he was looking for. A scripture of prophecy and the Light to come.

Signaled by a cry to be heard across the three great seas.

The night of the mourning Dove is the Dawn of the Light's return.

Magdalene stopped flipping pages. "What is it, Zephaniah?"

He looked up at her as his heart plummeted to his chest. "I think it is beginning."

"The return of the Light?" she asked.

He nodded slowly. "We are in the beginning of the night of the mourning Dove."

"It is to get worse, then," Magdalene said.

"Much worse."

"But it *will* get better," she said hopefully. "When the seven will gather."

"Yes, Magdalene. Eventually," he promised, though he was not sure how long the night would last, before the fulfillment of the remainder of the prophecy she spoke of. "I need to go. But be safe and stay put. I'll come back every few days and make sure you're okay."

"You be safe, Zephaniah. Thank you," she said, gesturing to the food he had supplied. He nodded and gave her a grim smile, and he left the scrolls and collected the book from the table, knowing that Ravenna would love to read what lay inside the seams. He closed his eyes, breathing deeply.

Not smart, he told himself. But he concealed the book inside of his thin cloak anyway.

He followed the curve of the tunnel, and slowly snuck through the tapestry back into the library, careful that no one saw him exiting. But before he could leave, there was one more book he needed.

At the bottom of the steps to a loft, another set of shelves expanded across the entire bottom floor of the library, wrapping across the walls and towering to the rocky, cave-like ceilings. He followed along the edge of the wall. He knew where to look; could pinpoint the exact location of the text he searched for in his sleep. The librarians had placed all books that romanticized the origin of the new kingdom and Degare's rule in the front of the library. They were the first books visitors saw upon entrance through the giant wooden doors.

So, Zeph headed toward the door and grabbed the text on his way. He shoved it into his cloak with the other before heading out into the gray light of the morning in the miserable Kingdom of Oro.

48

LOVESICK WITCH

JARA

In the early hours of the morning, Jara lay alone, awake in her bed, listening to the racket in the streets below her window as Degare's men fought off the witch guardians. "Will they ever stop?" Her servant, Mirren, asked as she filled Jara's glass with tea.

"I know just as much as you, lady," Jara grumbled.

"But you're a witch. Don't you...control them?"

"Does it look like I control them?" Jara asked, and Mirren's hands began shaking as she grabbed the silver tray from Jara's bedside table.

"No, Miss Jara."

Jara rolled her eyes and threw a palm toward the window, shutting it with an enchantment. The witch guardians had kept her awake for a week now, thanks to Ravenna and the curse that followed her. That same curse had now attached itself to half a dozen of Degare's men, and the king expected Jara to find a solution to that, too.

She grabbed the only book on witch guardians that she

could find at the library from her bedside table, and began reading. The beasts' origins were unknown, but she assumed, by the ancient legends, that they had been created by one of the original witches to preserve the limited dark magic of the land.

"Do you expect to be here tomorrow evening, or should I meet you in the king's chambers?" Mirren asked.

Jara did not look up from her book. "Mirren. For the last time, keep to your own business." Mirren ducked her head, pocketing a peculiar piece of paper she had been holding in the palm of her hand and continuing to tidy the room.

While the sheets were slick and warm against Jara's skin, she longed for a different bed, wrapped in the arms of the one she loved. She had not been invited to the king's chambers since the Vestelian had arrived in the kingdom and ruined everything. Jara had been so sure Ravenna would be the solution to all her problems. But Degare continued to grow more impatient by the day, and though he had made Jara a promise over twenty-three years ago, that promise remained unfulfilled. The Delle Witches helped to overthrow Ozanna, and in return, Degare was to restore to them their land in the Hollow Coves. The witches were to be free to establish the territory as their own kingdom. Over two decades after the destruction of the old kingdom, the witches were still under Degare's law with no territory to call their own.

After Degare's initial betrayal, Jara's clan had abandoned her, and refused to plot with her or Degare any further. Some still resided in the Hollow Coves, but they provided Oro with half of their crops and were starving and dying off—much like many in this kingdom. Jara knew many had fled the kingdom completely, traveling east to the opposite coast, to The Kingdom of Brinland.

After her clan abandoned her, the king was all she had left. Degare only cared about gaining more power, and Jara could give it to him.

"Do you think he loves me?" Jara asked Mirren.

The servant stopped in her tracks. "Who, the king?"

Jara lifted a brow, awaiting her answer.

"How could he not?" Mirren said, gesturing toward her.

Jara missed the way Degare held her at night, but she would soon be back in his arms, feeling the soft caress of his kisses on her neck, his body pressed against hers. She needed only to convince him to allow her into Ravenna's mind once more.

"I will find that talisman, and soon, Degare will give me the Hollow Coves as he has promised." He would be so pleased with her that he would not be able to deny her what she deserved: a place on a throne of her own. The witches would bow to her once more, in their rightful home, which she *would* return to them. They would have their home to themselves, out from under the holds of Oro, and she would be their leader, as her mother had once been.

Queen of the Delle Witch Clan.

"I have no doubts. And I will help you if I can," Mirren said, still fidgeting with the curious paper in her pocket.

"I just need to convince Degare to let me search Ravenna's mind one more time. I can get the information from her," Jara said.

"Haven't you and Jio tried? What if she just doesn't know where the talisman is?" Mirren asked.

"It doesn't matter if she doesn't know. I am sure there is something in her mind that can help us find it. She is our only lead. Ashreya is dead, and so is all of Vestele."

Mirren twisted her hands in front of her, and Jara narrowed her eyes.

"Is there something you're not telling me, Mirren?"

"Nothing, Jara. It is just...I cannot tell if this woman is innocent, or guilty."

Jara hummed. "Ravenna is of Ember heritage, she is daughter of the Ozannes, and therefore, she is guilty of being an enemy to this kingdom."

"Why do you hate the Ozannes so much?" Mirren asked quietly.

Jara chuckled at Mirren's ignorance. "The Ozannes burned Degare's village, they killed my mother, and ran my clan out of their territory." When Jara had found Degare twenty-four years ago, she had been Ravenna's age—young and naive. Jara thought she had needed him, a powerless human, when all he had to offer was his charm and the ability to wield the staff. She had fallen for him, and the two of them had bonded over their hatred for the Ozannes. The Ozannes had stolen from them both.

Mirren's eyes widened. "So that is what started the war those years ago. Retaliation."

"And look what it has blossomed into," Jara said proudly, gesturing around her. "A kingdom more powerful than any other, and growing darkness—growing *power.*"

Degare and Jara's plan had played out flawlessly before them. Degare raised an army of Shades—ungifted ones who worshiped the darkness—and the Delle Witches. With the manpower of the Shades, and the clan who combined their power under Jara's command, the Ozannes and all the Embers in Ozanna's armies were weakened enough for Degare to take the throne. The witches all joined to spell the prisons, chains, and shackles, and began enslaving every Ember they could find. The slaves were put to work, mining across the land to locate what was left of the bloodstone the Ozannes had destroyed.

"It took us fourteen years of dedicated searching to gather enough stone for the staff to be created. Fourteen years I stood by him, aiding him in the creation of that staff," Jara said. She was growing angry with him, and with herself, for still loving him despite his lies. After those years, Degare had killed hundreds of Embers for himself before he ever began creating his own army of Despiri. Jara had been entranced in each kill as she watched the king continue to swell with more and more power—until eventually, he surpassed her. But still, she had been nothing but proud of her creation. "He had been so pleased with me," she said. "But he never made good on his promise."

"The Hollow Coves," Mirren said.

"My rightful kingdom. Where my clan—which has since abandoned me—lives in constant reminder of his betrayal. Now, once again, Degare is too concerned with the Ozannes to remember that promise."

As the Ember Trades kicked off and he began gaining a larger audience with each event, Jara convinced him that he should put on a show with the execution of the Ozannes. He had planned to do it at the upcoming celebration that would mark one year since the first trade.

It is finally time for retribution, Jara thought. But no retribution came. When the Despiri that Degare had sent out arrived with the ex-royals in tow, Degare realized almost immediately that they bore no lightmarks and had no gifts.

Since that wretched night, Jara had made it her duty to bring him what he searched for. She would find the gifts that

Gerrin and Willa had hidden, even if she had to literally tear their minds apart to do it. Her king wanted more power, and so she would give it to him.

"When I find that talisman," she said, "he will have no choice but to return to me my rightful home that was taken by the Ozannes. And I will lead the Delle Witch Clan."

Perhaps when the king saw the power she would behold with all the witches on her side again, he would agree to unite their kingdoms and the two of them would rule over all of Arresia together. Together, they would reign over every shadow and they would leave no light in the world—only darkness and power. Jara would ensure the entire race of Embers paid for what they had done to the witches and her homeland, and to Degare, *until there were none of them left alive.*

49

THE ART OF MANIPULATION
RAVENNA

Rest in this cell was just shutting her eyes for six hours and opening them more tired than she had been the night before. Ravenna never had the pleasure of sleeping through the night without either being awoken by a nightmare, the witch guardians, or by the uncomfortable stone rubbing against the bruises that painted her body. She had peeled her eyes open this morning at sign of first light, to a vaguely familiar guard propped against the wall.

He was the one who had carried her into the throne room on her first day here; the one who had laughed as she split her lip upon the floor when he had tossed her forward onto her face.

Callan.

Yes, that was the name Zeph had called him by. She breathed in deeply, gaining the strength to stir up just a little annoyance in him before Zeph was set to return. She had to time this just right.

"Sleeping on the job?" she asked, and he turned toward

her, rousing from his slumber. "I so easily could have escaped!" she mused, clinking her shackles. He only grunted in irritation. "Why don't you make yourself useful and bring me some breakfast? I'm *starving*," she drawled, prodding until he was visibly angry. It worked. Oh, yes. It had definitely worked. He had a temper, and she knew it. She smiled, willing it to rise just a little more.

Callan rose to his feet, his body larger than she remembered. He had carried her with such ease, and his body was two times her size. His thick arms and calloused hands proved him a soldier, and a strong one at that. As he worked to unlock the door, she shrunk back into the corner.

Anger rolled from him; his face was the picture of pure rage.

"You have no rights here. You eat when and if someone decides to bring you food, *Ember*," he spat.

"Not an Ember," she reminded him.

The cell door clicked open, and Ravenna climbed to her feet, readying herself. She could guess what was about to happen by the way he held his shoulders. It was no lie that he was one of the larger men she had ever fought, but that fact did not scare her. She was quick and knew just where to send blows on a man his size...when she was not in shackles. Callan stepped into the cell, sloppily. He left his entire body unguarded as he stalked toward where she now stood in the corner of her cell. With her body chained, he was feeling far too confident.

She would add him to her list of people to kill in this kingdom, whenever she got the chance. Today was not the day.

He swung a fist toward her face, and she ducked, barely dodging a blow that would have easily knocked her out cold.

His fist slammed into the stone wall, and it surprised him enough that she had an opening to ram her shoulder into his torso with as much gumption as she could muster. Immediately, he grabbed and tossed her. Her bones ached as they crashed into the stone and she slid to the ground. He turned from her, ready to lock her inside the cell once more.

Quickly, she leapt onto his back, thankful for the length of the chains at her ankles. She wrapped the chain from her wrists around his neck and pulled as tightly as she could manage. He fought her, twisting his body and doing anything he could to knock her off. He flipped her over top of himself, and Ravenna landed on the stone with a crack. It was then that she heard Zeph's voice echoing as he ran toward them, barking commands at Callan as he approached with Ravenna's breakfast in hand. She smiled from the ground as pain seared through her lower spine and across her sore thigh.

Though Callan towered over him, Zeph was able to shove him out, speaking to him with lethal rage. "Do not *ever* touch her." He backed Callan further out of the cell. "I *never* want to see you near her again." He shoved him once more and added, "The king wants her alive. Do not," he paused for a moment, then continued through gritted teeth, "lay a hand on her, until His Majesty says otherwise."

Ravenna scoffed, wiping the blood from her brow. When Callan stalked off and Zeph shut the cell door once more, she spit a mouthful of blood at the floor in his direction. "Really? Until His Majesty demands otherwise?" she said, carefully slipping the keys she had snagged from Callan's belt into the folds of her dress.

"Are you okay." Not a question, but a statement of

frustration at the inconvenience of the altercation, as if he suspected she had caused it. His grip was still tight on his blade.

She ignored him and wiped her lip with the back of her arm, adding more blood to the sleeve of her dress and propping her body up against the wall once more. He handed her a handkerchief and she took it, blotting the blood from her forehead. "Why do you look so exhausted? Did you not sleep well in your cozy bed with warm covers last night?"

"No, in fact. I did not sleep at all."

She did not hide her surprise at the unusual sass in his tone. He looked over his shoulder and his voice began again, this time in a whisper. "I was too busy traveling across the city in the dark to obtain texts that may be beneficial to *you*." She straightened as he threw two books into her cell. "You better not get caught," he added, "Or it's my neck on the chopping block."

The titles read: HISTORY OF THE ROYAL FAMILY OF OZANNA and THE ORIGIN OF THE KINGDOM OF ORO. Both books were fairly new, written within the last twenty-five years. She would guess the book about her family made no mention of her, as it was finished the year before her birth. But the things that were written inside, prior to her birth...those were the things she wished to know, anyhow.

As she turned the thick book about Oro over in her hands, Zeph said, "It's always good to know your enemies, Ravenna." He paused, nodding to the other book. "I think there are some answers in there...about Ashreya."

Ravenna released a breath.

She began thumbing through the pages about the Ozannes, looking for any signs of familiar names mentioned in the pages on lineage. The family tree was complicated, to say the least. It traced back all the way to the beginning of the Kingdom of Ozanna, when the land was founded by Joachim and Ahelis Ozanne, when they had traveled from Remont on a mission to spread the way of Light across Arresia. It told of how they centered their palace amid the continent, between the three present day kingdoms that now made up the land. Over the course of a forty-year rule, the couple had five daughters and two sons, two of whom went off to start their own kingdoms on the continent with their parents' blessings: Brinland and Edmaria. The two new rulers married natives in those territories. And so, the three countries on the continent became three separate Kingdoms of Light. It was written that the oldest son, Hugh, had hated the kingdom and sold his birthright to Oran, the younger, setting him on track to become King of Ozanna in his parents' old age. Through the years, by marriages of the descendants of Joachim and Ahelis with other Kingdoms, Ozanna allied with each kingdom in Arresia. The kingdoms of Remont, Eswen, The Isles of Volcania, The Dawn Islands, Edmaria, and Brinland.

Zeph hovered beside her on the other side of the bars, reading as her finger traced the words. "This book makes no mention of the early Ozannes being Embers," she noted.

Zeph shifted. "It was not until a few hundred years ago when the seven kingdoms were attacked by the witches and their dark armies that Embers were gifted. Before the followers of the Light were gifted, they were called Lumes. When the witches and armies attacked, they targeted the temples first in an attempt to stifle the Light and limit people's access to it. But then the Father of Lights...he put his Light within his followers. His people do not need temples for worship or to have access to his power. He is with them all the time.

Everywhere. Always," he explained. "The Lumes who had true faith in the Father received his Light and became Embers. His power within the Embers serves as a reminder of his love for his people, and as a sort of protection against the witches and those that walk in darkness—though recently it seems to be more of a death sentence," he said quietly. "There are different gifts. They all work together to strengthen his kingdom. The Ember race was born less than four hundred years ago."

"And why aren't you gifted, Zephaniah?" she asked. It was clear to her that he did not worship the darkness. He had shown her kindness, and he was filled with all the Light she had ever seen in this kingdom, yet he had none of its alleged power.

Where is his god...this Father of Lights?

His expression changed. "Those who have faith that the Father is strong enough to overcome any darkness—they are the gifted ones. They act as lights in this world—embers of hope—because they believe in his goodness...and that his Light will someday return to Arresia—for good."

Ravenna looked at him, trying to read his solemn expression. "And you do not believe that the Light will overcome the darkness?" His brows scrunched, and she watched his throat bob.

"I try," was all he said in response. "I mean, I do. But for some reason, I've never received a lightmark."

"And because of that, you fear you do not have enough faith," she said. He nodded, and she studied him for a moment before continuing down the lineage, tracing her finger over the names on the tree until it landed on one that caught her attention. *Delle Revere.* Like the book Jara had laying open in her chambers. *Spells of Delle: The Delle Witches.*

"What? What is it?" Zeph's voice echoed softly between

the bars that separated them. He had been silent for a few minutes, and she now heard him shuffle closer. Ravenna read further, heart pounding a little harder at what came next.

Right below Delle's name was the name of the woman she had called *mother* the entirety of her life. Ashreya Ozanne, illegitimate daughter of Arne Ozanne and Delle Revere. *Half-sister* to Gerrin Ozanne, the legitimate son of royals Arne of Ozanna and Vevila of the Dawn Islands. It would explain how Ashreya had been a witch, while her brother, Gerrin, was an Ember.

Ravenna slid the text forward, toward where Zeph strained to see at the edge of her cell.

"Ashreya is your biological aunt," he said. She nodded. It explained the similar features. The eyes. It explained how Ashreya was a witch and how Ravenna was not, just as Asta had said. It felt like a lifetime ago, that conversation with Asta in the village that had been wiped from the world. What had happened twenty-two years ago that had led to her being raised by her aunt in that village, hidden, yet so close to her birthplace of Ozanna?

"What do you know about the Delle Witches?" Ravenna asked, and Zeph's eyes shot up to meet her pensive stare. He shifted to lean on his right shoulder, pressing up against the black stone wall. Ravenna adjusted too, scooting closer to where he sat, leaving no space aside from what the bars demanded. She pointed at the page once more, directing his attention to the name that had stood out to her.

"Delle Revere," she said quietly. "She was a witch, correct?" He nodded. "I saw Jara's spell book...the Delle Witches." Zeph scratched his head, and she wondered if he was debating between giving her the truth or a lie.

"Delle was Jara's mother." Ravenna shifted to face him.

"Mother? So, Jara was my mother—Ashreya's—half-sister? Why did she hate her so much?"

Zeph shrugged and shook his head. "All I know of the Delle Witch Clan is that Jara is their rightful leader by blood— because her mother was their queen. But they have excommunicated her from their clan for her dealings with Degare. He was supposed to grant them their land back in exchange for their help in the war, but he kept taking and taking and never held up his end of the deal." Ravenna watched him closely as he skimmed further on the page of his own book, the ORIGINS OF THE KINGDOM OF ORO. "It says here that the Ozannes killed Delle. Jara would have been a child at the time."

"Does it say why they killed her?" Ravenna asked.

"No, it doesn't."

"Convenient," she muttered. "I'm sure she deserved it, then."

"Probably," Zephaniah said. "But seeing your mother killed changes you. I can sympathize with her that much, at least." Ravenna's throat bobbed. Like Jara, like *her*, he knew this pain. This unrelenting grief.

Ravenna's forehead creased as she studied his expression.

"Tell me of your family, Zephaniah. Tell me why you are here."

50

UNBURIED HISTORY
ZEPHANIAH

"I come from a village on the far northeast side of the country called Usholk. It was one of the first territories invaded by Degare after he finished the bloodstone staff seven years ago." His voice began to shake, and he willed it to steady, twisting the small, ripped paper in his hands. "My parents, my older brother—Samuel," he choked on the name, and Ravenna could feel his grief trying to merge with her own, "and myself were taken by Degare's men. We did not fully understand why they were taking us, until we arrived here at the castle." He clenched his jaw.

Ravenna swallowed, face grave as she predicted what he would say next.

"We thought maybe they were enslaving us to work in the mines."

His voice had gone cold. "They stripped us bare of our clothes in the throne room and examined us for lightmarks." He shook his head at the memory. "As you know, I am not lightmarked. I still do not understand why I bear no mark—I know the Light is within me. I can feel it." Ravenna narrowed her eyes, trying to process all he was telling her.

"They killed Samuel first," he said. "They wanted our parents to watch us die, as a punishment for worshiping the Father. When they examined my body, they found nothing. No evidence of my allegiance to the Light." Ravenna tilted her head, looking him up and down as if she expected to see a faint light somewhere upon him, glowing from his skin. "Something like remorse washed over Degare's face when he saw that I was not marked. There was just a split second of it, before he ordered the soldiers on to my mother."

He did not lift his gaze from his lap, his hands, the torn paper. He shuddered, remembering how Degare had stood over his mother's body where she lay crumpled on her side, golden brown hair a mess, her hand reaching for him.

Zephaniah, my son, she had said. *You are hidden by the Father for a reason.*

And then Degare had flipped her onto her back, driving the bloodstone staff through her chest, the lightmark fading along with her breaths as her gifts of Light were turned to shadow, and then twisted with dark magic into the body of the king who had killed her.

Those last words from her lips had given him purpose all these years. They ignited a flame in him that he refused to let die until his purpose had been fulfilled, whatever it may be. He wanted nothing more than the promise of safety for his people, a world free of darkness. Whether Zeph lived to see it and walk the lands of Arresia with the Light—or passed on, he would live in eternal Light—he hoped. Along with the Light in

Arresia, his faith was dwindling, and as an unmarked and ungifted—he could not help but feel forgotten by the Father of Lights.

"My father," he continued, "did not even fight them after my mother was gone." He had watched his father's lightmarks fade away too, the glowing marks down his chest and over the skin on his arm going dark.

"And then it was only me. They searched my body again to be sure," he said grimly. "I had never wanted to be lightmarked more than I did in that moment. I wanted them to kill me, too. When it was clear I was unmarked, Degare—he had some sort of feeling of responsibility for me after he'd killed my entire family."

Zeph leaned his head up against the wall. He peered up at the darkness of the underside of the stairs that snaked around the tower. "At fifteen, I could have cared for myself. But Galen had been taken from her home in the city of Ozanna in a similar fashion after her village had burned. She had become a castle healer in Oro and was ordered to take me back to her home in the slums of the kingdom for a few weeks, to help me heal and adjust."

Ravenna poked her hand through the gap in the bars, squeezing Zeph's hand in comfort, just as he had done for her in the Valley of the Shadow. He ran a thumb over her knuckles in response.

"Galen quickly became my only family. We were all each other had. After two weeks had gone by, you can imagine I was still grieving, but I had moved on to anger. I was ready to act on what had been done to my family, and I joined the king's guard, as Degare had ordered." He halted, biting his lip. "I quickly learned Galen's secret, that she too, is a follower of the Light." Ravenna sat up straight.

"Galen talked me down from my anger. Told me I would only get myself killed trying to take down the king, especially with the witch by his side."

You must play it smart, she had said. *We need Light on the inside of this kingdom, even if it is concealed for a time.*

"I worked for a cartographer in Usholk and learned much in those short months. I did my best to exhibit that knowledge when I joined the guard. I wanted to stay out of the war—I wanted to avoid killing innocents. Soon, I became one of Degare's top navigators. I hoped I would have the chance to help some others to avoid the outcome my family had been given."

Zeph shifted again. He had not done enough to stop Ravenna from being dragged to this kingdom against her will.

"Why would Degare believe you are loyal to him after he killed your family?" Ravenna asked.

"He had wrongly assumed me to be a Shade, since I bore no marks. He assumed my loyalty was to the darkness, and therefore, to him. His pride swelled when he spared my life, and I think he thought I saw it as a kindness. He allowed me to live and gave me an opportunity to make a living as one of his soldiers." He shook his head.

"I've been playing the game for over seven years, watching his *every* move. Learning his weaknesses." The only one of which was sitting right in front of him. "I have been trying my best to save a few innocent victims in the process."

He let his head turn to where she sat, still listening intently. Her eyes were saddened and empty after all that had been taken from her, and he so badly wanted to open the door and hold her. His hands flexed in his lap.

"I have not done a very good job with you, I'm afraid."

Ravenna's dark eyebrows furrowed slightly as she faced him, but her eyes flashed with an unexpected, fiery rage.

"I am going to help you kill them all," she said.

51

BY THE BLOOD OF HIS OWN VEINS

RAVENNA

Whatever was left whole inside of her, Zeph's story had broken it—shattered it into a million shards of glass ready to cut, maim, and kill. Ravenna wanted a slow, prolonged death for Degare and the witch. They deserved nothing less for all they had done to her and her people, her family, and Zeph. Her vengeance was sweltering, and she was growing impatient.

Her days in the cell now consisted of scheming and dreaming of ways in which she would accomplish the task, and when exactly she would use the key that she had pilfered from Callan's belt to free herself.

If she were somehow able to break free, she doubted Zeph would try to stop her after all he had confided in her throughout the last week. He would probably even unlock her shackles. Though if she wanted Zeph to be involved in the escape, she would have asked him for the key herself. It was too dangerous. She would not risk his life for her own selfish vengeance.

Even if she was successful and lived, she would travel far from here and never allow herself to think twice about him. He did not deserve the cruel death a friendship with her would bring. She could not wait too long, or she may lose her chance. But right now, against Degare and Jara with all their dark magic, she had no chance of success. How could she?

The two books were open in front of her, and Zeph had generously given her a small candle to read by. She could only read when he was on duty, as the other guards would likely punish her *and him* for bringing her the texts from the library. The other hours of the many days she spent in this cell, the books, candle, and flint stayed concealed under Zephaniah's cloak. It stayed wadded up in the corner where Ravenna had been sleeping these past weeks.

"I'm tired of looking through all this useless nonsense," Zeph said, leaning against the stone. He was right. Much of the words in these texts jumbled together and did not seem to aid their cause at all. He had come early this morning, rousing her and telling her it was a good time to read.

No other guards would be coming up the tower for at least a few hours, as they had officially started prepping for the Summer Ember Trade that would occur next month. Ravenna had taken a deep breath at that realization, at the looming death sentence for any of the gifted who were unlucky enough to be discovered by Degare. Had she truly been at the castle for two weeks?

"Keep looking," she ordered, as she searched the hundreds of words for anything that could help her find the location of the Ozanne's gifts. There were no hints of bloodstone relics or talismans within the pages, and she grew more and more anxious that perhaps Leith had a reason for taking her dagger. She traced her lineage back nearly four hundred years; her ancestors were all greatly gifted Embers. From Ravenna's line, were some of the first documented Embers with the fall of the Temples of Light those centuries ago—when the Father of Lights had risen triumphantly within his people.

Could she have had a chance, if she had been raised to know the Light, to become a gifted Ember? Maybe. But that was not how she had been raised. She had been raised on the edge of darkness, ironically between mountains of black and towering hills of gold that glittered in the light. She had lived a life not knowing, not understanding the full extent of this world she lived in, or what lay beyond it. She did not have a good idea of what truly lurked across the seven kingdoms outside of Vestele, and had not understood the true reasons why her mother had never wanted her to leave the village. She had not known that there were two walks in life—the way of Light or the way of darkness—and her choice had been taken from her.

She slammed the book shut, tired of reading about the family she had never known.

"If the Ozannes were gifted, why had they not been able to stop Degare when he took the kingdom?" She did not understand, could not fathom how a kingdom full of Embers with gifts and strongholds of all kinds could be so easily suffocated under the reigns of an average man, who was completely ungifted at the time.

Zeph pondered on it for a moment, and then answered. "Degare had aid from the witches, remember? And I read that the darkness itself bowed to him. That's why they planned their attack on the darkest night of the year. For more power."

Ravenna still did not understand. *Isn't the Light supposed to overcome the darkness?*

"I don't think you'll ever truly know the answers you seek, until we find a way to restore the Kingdom of Ozanna and make it safe for the Embers to live freely again. Maybe then, you can speak to your parents about what really happened that day." He paused, hesitant to speak further. She knew it was because he, too, wondered if she or her parents would even make it out of Oro alive. "But I do know that your aunt—mother—Ashreya," he stuttered, "was the daughter of a very powerful witch, and though she was a member of the Court of Ozanna and likely steered clear of the darkness for the years she lived alongside your parents in the kingdom..."

What is he implying?

"Look. I think maybe your family turned from the Light in fear on the day Degare attacked. Maybe they saw no other way out, and Ashreya stepped in to help in a way she knew would work."

Ravenna wanted to be angry with him, but she could not be. Not when the words he said were likely true. She had spent hours in her cell thinking up scenarios and trying to imagine how she had ended up in the shadows of Vestele.

He spoke again, breaking the silence. "I think Ashreya turned her face from the Light that day to save your life in the only way she knew how."

Zeph must have seen her mind turning, because he said, "One who is born a witch is not doomed to eternal darkness. They still have a choice in who they follow. Perhaps Ashreya turned to the light in her final moments."

"She died practicing dark magic," Ravenna said hoarsely, remembering the way her mother's arms had been raised and the unfamiliar language she had spoken into the night, entrapping those soldiers. The darkness that had swirled around her. Consumed her. Ravenna had only distracted her enough for her exposed throat to be cut, and she had fallen to her knees right before death claimed her, whispering something Ravenna could not hear over the sound of her own bellowing scream.

No.

She refused to believe her mother was doomed to the shadows forever.

"What happened that night?" Zeph said carefully, extending his hand through the bars.

She did not take it. Sympathy welled in his gray eyes. She had never spoken to anyone about that night. Never had the chance to, really. But something about the way his face softened like he knew her heartache and wanted to help her bear it, made her want to share. He did know her heartache, she realized. He had watched his entire family be killed right before him and had then been forced to serve the man who had done it. The two of them were not so different. She did not speak for a long moment.

"My mother—the shield-maiden—had gotten word somehow of the prison wagon coming through. It seems that Xan had known of the plan, too." She remembered how Xan had seemed so on edge that evening, how his pack had been a little more full than usual, as if he were planning to run—*with her.*

"Xan, was he your husband?"

She breathed in, and her voice came out in tremors. "No. I am not married. Well, technically I am—was—betrothed. But not to him. Xan was my best friend, and I loved him. But not in the way he loved me. If I could go back...if things hadn't been kept from me, with a mutual trust...perhaps things would have been different."

"He is the one who you came out of the fire with."

Ravenna nodded slowly in response, trying not to think about that night too long.

She continued. "The clan was acting strangely. I think my mother was planning to free Gerrin and Willa, and they all knew it, somehow. Everyone but me. Xan and I were put on watch in the Dead Wood as opposed to the safer option of the Sunstone Forest. I was a fool for not realizing then, that something more was going on. My mother would have never put me on watch in the Dead Wood if she could have helped it, especially not my very first watch."

Her mother had tried to keep her from all dangers and horrors of the world, and she had done a decent job of shielding her all this time, but Ravenna did not think that was necessarily a good thing. Being blissfully unaware of the threats to her life had been inconvenient, to say the least. She wondered what would have been different if she had been given a fighting chance in this world of Light and darkness.

"Somehow, the soldiers entered from where Xan and I were on post. I could have taken them all out on my own, but there was something *off* about them." She knew now that it was the dark magic that they possessed that made them so aware of her presence, that gave the leader enough speed to catch that arrow in his hand. "They were Despiri, of course. But I didn't know that until I made a move. It was too dark to see their shadowmarks. They spotted me in the treetops while Xan was racing back to the clan to warn everyone of their approach. He blew the horn, and by the time he returned, I had already made the mistake of sizing them up, and one used his gifts on me." She remembered the pain that had seared through her body from head to toe. "It was like fire, burning through me."

"Elam," Zeph acknowledged the Despiri's name quietly and let her continue.

"They ordered us to deliver them to our village where they could find rest and a hot meal. I refused at first, but Xan insisted that it was what my mother wanted." She had been so livid at that moment, at the pure negligence. But she had not understood what was at stake. If she had known that her true parents—or even just known that the king and queen of Ozanna were being held and tortured all those years—maybe she would have helped. Maybe the mission would have been successful if she had not messed it up so badly. Zeph listened intently, his eyes still soft and full of sorrow.

"Once we led them all the way to Vestele, they had hot meals waiting for them and a fire on the edge of the village. I remember being so angry with my mother for making the decision to welcome them in. We never welcomed outsiders. That was a *very* strict rule." Ravenna fiddled with the fabric of her dress. "I was exhausted. Xan insisted I get some rest. I thought he was just being kind, but he was trying to get me out of the way, so I would not witness what was about to happen."

It was only mere moments before her entire world shifted and she began to learn of the presence of dark magic and of the problem that *was* the Despiri of Oro, and of the Light that had been so cruelly kept from her throughout the entirety of her life. "I refused to go to sleep, and soon our friend—Tenille— came with tea for each of us. I thought it too, a kindness, until I blacked out after the first sip. They sedated me." Her cheeks grew hot. "I awoke in my bed to that same searing pain again. It was so severe it had pulled me out of my induced sleep. I realized it to be the Despiri, and I rushed out as quickly as I could through the pain. My mother stood there, in a trance of some sort, casting a spell that seemed to paralyze the men. No one helped her." She swallowed. "My people—all just stood there watching her do the spell."

Zeph's eyebrows scrunched in the center.

"When she saw me, she paused for a moment. Long enough for one of the men—Elam—to break free of the holds of the spell. He had drawn me out to distract her. I couldn't make it to her in time. He killed her, and I *caused* it." Her voice grew hollow as she stared at the wall before her.

She had not yet said it out loud, that she blamed herself for her mother's death. It had been eating away at her all the weeks since it happened. "I caused the massacre of my entire village, just by existing," she said. "And I have only taken one life in return."

Elam's life was not enough for what had been done to her. Ravenna felt the key in her pocket. She swore that Degare would pay by the blood of his own veins, and she would be the one to draw it.

DEATH SENTENCE
ZEPHANIAH

Zeph had not quit thinking about Ravenna since their talk yesterday. He enjoyed speaking to her, despite the circumstances. He wondered if she would enjoy spending time with him if it were not her only option of entertainment throughout the day. She had returned his trust by sharing details with him of her life in Vestele, and though he was unable to imagine it entirely, he could relate to the guilt she bore within. He had let his own grief nearly kill him.

Survivor's guilt was what Galen had called it. She had noticed him digressing and plummeting into his emotions, still many months after the incident. Eventually, he had broken entirely, and she had given him the words of advice that he needed most.

"It was not your fault in any way, but you need to forgive yourself for surviving when they did not. You are here for a reason, and maybe that is to honor them by helping to assure this does not keep happening." Her words of wisdom seemed to amplify his mother's.

Zephaniah, my son. You are hidden by the Father for a reason. After all these years, his purpose had still not been made clear.

Screams of pain bellowed down the hall from the torture chambers. He knew who was beyond the door, and he wished he could turn and go back to Ravenna. But Faxon had relieved him of duty and directed him to the bottom of the tower, where the greatest horrors of the kingdom lurked behind closed doors. He was only thankful Callan had not come in his place, or Zeph would not have been able to leave her.

Zeph walked through the door of the torture chambers and around the winding hall, taking note of the tools that had been selected for use today, whose spaces now hung empty on the stone walls. He breathed in deeply, neutralizing his facial expression before turning the last curve of the tunnel. Before him was a large stone altar, stolen in mockery from a destroyed Temple of Light, and spread upon it were the bloody bodies of Gerrin and Willa Ozanne.

Thankfully, Ravenna had been sleeping when the two of them had been dragged down the steps of the tower and past her cell just before dawn this morning. He wondered if she could hear their screams echoing up the tower now. If so, he only prayed she did not know who they came from. She needed no more guilt added to her already-suffocating pile of it.

Not surprising to Zeph, Jara was overseeing the torture. It seemed she was ordering the two men who stood in the chambers with her to make cuts upon the Ozannes' skin. One of the men was Jio, the mind reader, and Zeph knew to immediately guard his mind.

When they were weakened by the cuts Jio and the other guard had made, Jara then attempted to infiltrate their minds.

Zeph only stared straight forward past the torture, as he did often when in the presence of Jara and her antics. Ignoring it did not make it go away, but watching it was sickening to him, and he would be rendered unable to keep the disgust from his face. So, he stood there, arms stiff at his sides awaiting orders. His face was the picture of an obedient soldier.

As Jara placed her hands over their heads, worming and shoving her dark magic into their minds, she looked up to Zeph for only a moment. He knew it must take great concentration to infiltrate the human mind as she did, and he could tell she was already growing tired of the day's endeavors. He only hoped she would not make Ravenna watch this or endure torture to try and coax the answers she sought from Gerrin and Willa. He wondered if it would work.

After all the two had done to protect Ravenna, he doubted they would stop here in these chambers. Though, he had noticed a great decline in the stability of Willa since she had been made aware that Ravenna was in the tower. Gerrin—he too appeared thinner, if that were even possible. His face was a little more haunted, but Zeph knew he tried to remain strong for his wife and for the daughter he had never known. Gerrin's hand never left Willa's if they were within arm's reach of one another, and when his lips could reach, they were placing kisses upon his soulbound's fingers. Even now, upon the altar together, they bled and held tight to each other's hands. It was an offer of comfort, and maybe even a tie to reality that they were still here, together, fighting for the same thing they had been for years. The safety of their daughter.

But Ravenna had now been found by the king, and all they had fought for was crumbling before them. How much longer would Ravenna be allowed to live without that power Degare so diligently sought? Once Degare found the talisman, would he kill Ravenna?

Zeph shifted ever so slightly on his feet, unwittingly gaining the attention of the witch he hated so much. She smiled at Jio, then looked back to Zeph. "You know Zeph, you have such great ideas." His breath caught in his throat at the wickedness in her tone.

As if Jio had read his mind and given Jara the information he had found, she said, "The girl is of no use unless she helps us find what we search for. Why don't you go get her, so she does not have to die in vain?" Zeph stumbled back a few steps, quickly correcting his balance and nodding his head in an attempt to portray agreement as he quickly turned to exit through the hall.

His heart pounded against his chest as if it searched for a way out. How long had the two of them been within the walls of his mind? He had not felt them there. He had unknowingly given Jara the idea to bring Ravenna to the torture chambers, to be *tortured* in front of her parents. If he had any sense, he would run now. He could exit the castle and never come back. He could grab Ravenna, but he would never make it out of the kingdom with her in tow, especially not with her infected leg. She would be recognized before they made it to the square.

No, no, no. What have I done?

His body fought each dreadful step up the tower to retrieve Ravenna. *What am I doing?*

For seven years he had been in this castle, serving a king who hated his kind. He had made no progress in saving the lives of anyone other than two young boys in a village of Embers he had been ordered to raid. Even then, the two boys had been orphaned in that raid.

The darkness was all around him. He stood no chance against the dark power within the king, against the dark power that weaved its way through nearly every crack of this kingdom. He reluctantly climbed the steps of the tower. With each step closer to her, his feet seemed to grow heavier.

Zeph found Ravenna and Faxon staring at the wall, completely ignoring one another's presence. She looked miserable, but her mind was spinning behind her tired eyes. Though she showed some relief when Zeph unlocked her cell and ordered her out with a gruff voice meant to deceive Faxon of his allegiance to Degare, he doubted she would appreciate his rescue when she learned where they were headed.

A strange voice seemed to whisper to him. *Take her and run, now.* He ignored the obvious death sentence.

Once they were a few hundred steps down the tower, hovering outside of the chamber door, and he was sure their voices would not carry, he glanced around to be certain no one watched. Looking her in the eyes was the only option here, to get her to understand how sorry he was. She needed to see how sorry he was.

Now. Go, the voice seemed to say.

Ravenna turned to face him, shackles clinking and grazing against each other. His hands found her arms and he gripped them tightly, not breaking her stare. Fear began to bloom in her eyes at his next words to her, his only words before he opened the door.

"Forgive me."

Before his physical body could overcome his mind and force him to flee with her, this princess of hope, he pushed the door open.

AT THE POSTS

RAVENNA

Zeph led her into the darkness of the spiral tunnel, its narrow walls black and unnerving. Though he was visibly shaking, and remorse seemed to stifle the air around him, they continued through the hall, weaving in and out of the stone walls that held tools of many kinds. Watching his hands, seeing his face of conviction when he had apologized to her before opening the chamber door, witnessing his hesitant steps forward as he led her to her demise—she knew he had come to care for her over their last few weeks together. She would even go so far as to consider him her only friend.

Though he saw this as a betrayal, Ravenna could not be upset with him. He was doing only what he needed to survive the king and have his chance at a future. He longed for a purpose. She hoped he would find it someday, and she hoped that purpose was fulfilling. Zeph had been forcibly taken into this wretched kingdom and had suffered longer than her. Zephaniah, more than her, deserved a way out of these lands, perhaps into one of the two remaining kingdoms that were full of the Light he spoke of with such reverence and admiration. She was thankful he had chosen to be her friend, no matter the complexity of their relationship. He was a guard, sent to monitor and control her every move. She was his prisoner, and yet in the hours they had spent together, the two of them had become friends. It was perhaps one of the only mercies she had met in this kingdom.

She was almost certain she knew what awaited her beyond the circular walls of what she suspected was the torture chamber. The walls were covered from ceiling to floor in all kinds of tools used to inflict pain and pry information from the human body. Her skin crawled at the sight of the strangely shaped, sharp weapons and devices. Zeph's grip on her arm seemed to soften into a comforting touch as he led her around the last bend in the hall, before the warmth of the dim candlelight began to bleed into the blackness of where they stood.

All she could think as she surveyed the room was that she should have used the key.

She could not have prepared herself for what she saw, *who* she saw, lying on the altar. There, together, were Gerrin *and Willa Ozanne*. Above them, hovered *Jio*, and an unfamiliar guard with blades in hand. Beyond them was Jara, giving Ravenna a malicious smile.

Her biological parents laid on the stone, skin cut open and wounds still leaking red. She swayed at the sight of the wretched color, and her vision blurred. Ravenna's eyes followed the many cuts across their bodies, the many *scars* she had not noticed before in the darkness of the tower halls. They had been dragged passed her cell many times, enduring torture while she lay helpless in her cell. Frail, weak, and unable to do anything to help them.

She imagined that was how they felt now, as both of their eyes bore into her with years of sadness and pain. They had done so much to protect her, went as far as giving her up as a baby when they had longed for a child for nearly a decade. All for her safety, Gerrin and Willa had endured this, *years of torture*—apparent by the hundreds of blemishes upon their bodies. *Only to ensure her safety*. Ravenna's knees buckled, and Zeph only steadied her enough to lead her forward. His hands were clammy, shaking against her arms, and she nudged him— a careful reminder to remain indifferent.

"Ravenna, my dear," Jara's cold voice rang out into the chamber, too chirpy for the scene playing out before her. Her long, spindly fingers motioned for Ravenna to join her at her side, and as Ravenna did, Jara's hand wrapped around her shoulder and pulled her in close. The witch's tall, thin body towered over her.

Ravenna was average height for a woman her age and had never felt this small next to someone. Not even Roarke or Xan, who had more than a foot of height on the witch. Jara's nails pressed into the skin on Ravenna's arm.

"Your parents, as you've heard," she motioned toward them with her opposite hand, "have done so much to protect you." Ravenna knew where this was going. "They committed treason to their own kingdom—your kingdom—saving *your* life. I doubt there is little they would not do to ensure you survive. The precious child they tried so many years for. How many years was it, Willa, that you prayed and just hoped the *Father of Lights*," she said in a mockery, "would bless you with a child?"

Jara paused, as if waiting for an answer from the broken woman on the altar, whose hand was entwined with the man's beside her. A single tear slid down her face, and she closed her eyes. No sound came from her lips as they formed the word, *seven*. Ravenna's heart was pounding. It seemed to plummet down to her stomach and back up to her throat with every beat.

Anything.

She would do anything to take their place on the table. She was not worth the years of torture they had endured. She was not worthy of this—of their love. If they only knew the things she had done and the deaths she had caused. She was no daughter of Light. No, she was far from it. Where she walked, darkness always followed.

"The child you longed for is here before you, and there you lay, unwilling to give me what I want. You can be with her, if only you'll tell me where you have hidden your power." Jara seemed to grow angrier with each word. "Do tell, or your beloved daughter will experience what you have experienced here today."

Ravenna could have sworn Gerrin's grip tightened around Willa's hand, and she wondered for a split second what it would have been like to be raised by them in the Palace of Ozanna, as a princess, *an Ember*, with gifts of light. Why had the Father of Lights abandoned her? The life she envisioned was such a far cry from where she had ended up.

She was deserving of whatever Jara could do to her. There was no cold table of stone available for her, but across from the table where her parents lay, were two posts. Whipping posts, perhaps. They were like those in the Brunts, where Ravenna had once witnessed a thief receive ten lashes for stealing a coin back from the betting basket after he had bet against the wrong opponent in the tavern. He had bet against Ravenna, and it had cost him. Back then, she never lost. She breathed a deep, unsteady breath.

Sure enough, when Ravenna turned back to face Jara, she was handing a whip to the guard who now stalked forward to tie her to the post. They did not bother removing her clothes to reveal bare skin. It was understood that they would be here awhile. By the time they were finished, she was sure her dress would be mere shreds of bloody fabric caked against her skin.

"I have been inside your daughter's head," Jara said. "She knows nothing of a talisman." She clicked her tongue. "So it will be up to you to tell me, or she'll die."

A small noise escaped Willa as they kicked Ravenna's knees and she fell forward, her bones instantly crashing against the stone. Ravenna winced, but kept her composure for Zeph's sake, grateful that Jara had not ordered *him* to be the one to restrain her wrists to each post. Ravenna did not think he could bear it.

"Anything?" Jara asked the Ozannes, awaiting a spill of information.

Nothing.

Jio started the lashes.

One.

Two.

Three.

Four.

Ravenna refused to scream and add to the panic that had set into her parents' hollow faces the moment she had stepped foot into this room. If they had done everything to protect her and were still able to resist telling the secret of where the gifts were hidden, even while she was tortured in front of them...

well, maybe that was the more important task: protecting the location of those gifts.

Five.

She would not add to their conviction with cries of pain. She could handle the torture. Her back began to bleed, and she hung her head in an attempt to hide the fear that spread there. She winced at the anticipation of each lash, and she hated herself for it. Her teeth clamped down on her lip, drawing blood. She lifted her head to look at the former queen of Ozanna, her mother, whose eyes were wide and whose face was being stroked by her companion—Ravenna's father with the kind eyes. At the sight of those eyes, she was back in the valley, riding Fintah alongside the woman who had raised her, *shielded her*. And then she was thinking back to the book in her cell, to those same green eyes in the portrait of Ashreya, and then to the spherical brass pendant she always wore around her neck. The pendant Delle wore around *her* neck.

In this kingdom you wear a noose around your neck.

Perhaps Leith did not have the gifts after all.

Ravenna breathed out and another lash crashed upon her skin. She felt Jio prying his way into her mind, and she fought against him with all the might she had left.

Six.

Seven.

There seemed to be an unspoken word between Gerrin and Willa, and then they prepared to speak.

No. Not after all these years. She would not let them give up anything else for her. Certainly not for the king and the witch to use their gifts of Light for darkness. The witch would surely kill them the moment she got what she needed.

Eight.

Nine.

Ten.

Ravenna willed her head to rise, stirred up a smirk from the depths of her soul, and flicked her gaze to Jara before saying, "Perhaps they do not know where the gifts are, because Ashreya hid them. Did you not think of that, *witch*? How would they know, if they've been imprisoned all these years?"

Ravenna spat blood at the wicked woman, painting her expensive gown red. She was foolish to wear such finery here.

Jara held out a hand, an order to halt the whippings. Ravenna loathed herself for the sigh of relief that rushed out of her lungs. "And what do you know of it? I've searched your mind. You have no recollection of the events that took place when you were an *infant*."

"Well, it is not hard to guess," Ravenna said in as condescending a tone as she could manage in her compromising position. She hated the witch. If she made it out of these chambers, she would kill her at the first opportunity. And until then, she would conjure up the many ways it could happen.

"Ashreya took me in as her own. I would start by looking in the village that you burned. But you likely will not find whatever it is you are looking for. You know, because it's probably been burned."

Jara grabbed the whip from the broad-shouldered man. Then, the witch stiffened slightly and ordered Zeph to leave— and Ravenna knew it was because she planned to kill her. Little hesitation hounded him as he turned to exit like he had no choice, like his body had to obey her every command. Ravenna was glad he had been granted permission to leave. The agony on his face as he beheld the whip slicing into her repeatedly was too much. She could not take it. She needed him to leave before his true allegiance was discovered.

Jara stepped forward and began lashing uncontrollably, whip after whip, ripping through Ravenna's clothes, slapping, and thrashing against her skin.

Twenty-three.

Twenty-four.

Her skin tore, and tore, and tore, the wounds that spread across her back widening and filling with red.

Oh, how she loathed the color.

Twenty-five.

Screams began tearing from her lips, but she willed herself to look at the former king and queen of Ozanna, begging them not to speak.

Twenty-six.

Twenty-seven.

Thrash, after thrash, she swayed between the posts until her body hung limp between them. To her surprise, Gerrin and Willa kept their mouths shut aside from the sobs that broke free of their lips. They said nothing of importance, only begged for mercy as Ravenna was whipped into blackness.

54

DISCOVERING LIGHT
ZEPHANIAH

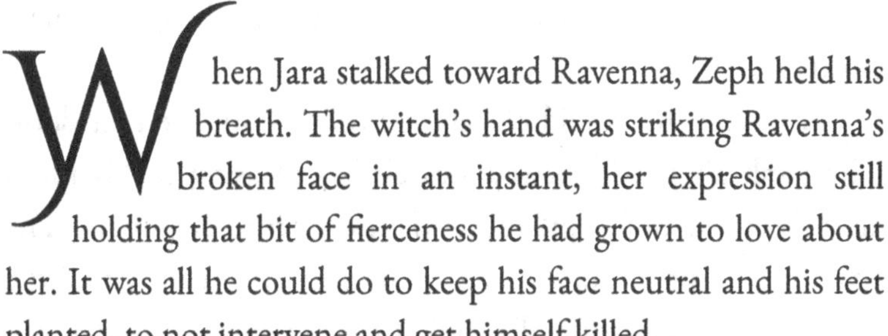

When Jara stalked toward Ravenna, Zeph held his breath. The witch's hand was striking Ravenna's broken face in an instant, her expression still holding that bit of fierceness he had grown to love about her. It was all he could do to keep his face neutral and his feet planted, to not intervene and get himself killed.

He had dreamt many times since Ravenna's arrival of the ways he would help her kill this witch that had caused them so much pain. At first, the dreams had frightened him. But after getting to know the woman before him at the whipping posts, he would do anything, including handing over his life, to make sure she found hope again and that she forgave herself for even the things that were not her fault. He had always longed for lightmarks—proof of his love for the Light, but more than that, he wished for a purpose, and he would be satisfied if his purpose was helping Ravenna to find hers.

It surprised him when Ravenna had spoken, mocking the witch and her ignorance, while spitting in her face. He thought maybe he loved her for it. That fire would get her killed in this castle though. Zeph had barely stopped himself from moving forward and drawing his blade on the witch. He had almost done it, though his chances of winning against her and two guards were zero.

Zeph had shifted on his feet in anxiousness and right as he did, Jara stiffened. She did not bother turning to face him when she said, "Zephaniah, you are relieved of your duties for the evening." The words hit him and moved through his body, pulsating with every second longer he spent in the chambers. She seemed to have some sort of grip on him, some access to his mind. Her words had control over him, and without even one more glance to Ravenna, he had turned to exit the room where darkness reigned.

Normally, he would be relieved to step outside that door. The fresh air that followed was always pleasing to his lungs after being in the stagnant air of the torture chambers. The space reeked of old blood and even death, from the times the torture masters accidentally took it too far. He prayed that did not happen to Ravenna, but Jara had asked him to leave for a reason.

It was difficult to leave her, but it was more difficult to stay.

He lingered outside the door, the witch's command still seeming to entrance him and push him further away.

Go. Go. Go, it seemed to whisper.

His eyes stung as he barely managed to choke back tears. Where would he go? Not to the barracks. No, he could not go there right now. Could not bear the idea of making small talk with the sorry soldiers who would already be drinking for the evening. He could not deal with their incessant chatter about the Embers they hoped to kill in the upcoming trades.

Ravenna's name had been whispered on the wind since she arrived, and tonight, he did not wish to hear it.

Her screams began to echo from the chambers behind him, and he stalled, only for a moment before that awful magic shoved at his back again, urging him on. He clutched his stomach, swallowing the bile that worked its way up his throat.

He found himself at Galen's house across the kingdom when the darkness of the night was approaching. Galen opened the door and rushed him in.

"Zephaniah? I haven't seen you in weeks. *Weeks.* What is going on?" She looked tired, as if she had not slept well in days.

Zeph said nothing as he took a seat at her cluttered table. Plants, jars, oils, and salves were strewn about every flat surface in her home. He had grown to love the mess over the years he had been coming here. Unlike the blackness of the kingdom this tiny house was nestled in, the clutter offered a sort of calming effect on his nerves. The colors Galen decorated with, her woven tapestries and the green in the plants that grew within these walls—only because of her gifts —all offered him a little bit of joy. An escape in a kingdom void of color.

The lovely scent of rosemary tickled his nose, and he glanced past Galen to see where she had just sprouted some of the aromatic herbs. He had seen her bring a seed to a lush green plant in a matter of seconds many times before, but it never ceased to amaze him. Galen was the sunlight those plants needed. She gave them life.

Much like the Father did for his followers.

"Zephaniah." He felt his cheeks flush at the mention of his name. "What is it that troubles you?"

Her speech was always proper but soothing. He heard the faint tap of her foot upon the wooden floors—another thing he loved about her home. The kingdom had been completely carved of stone, and every structure's floor made of the same black rock, while Galen's floors were crafted of wood from the trees of what was now known as the Dead Wood. The forest had been full of life before the darkness had snaked across the land and cursed the ground that stretched from the castle to the Valley of Vestele.

Perhaps the black sliver of land was like a tether— beckoning Ravenna to this kingdom. Begging her to fulfill that prophecy and end the night. Or maybe it was a promise—a curse that had been born when the Ozanne's had chosen the darkness.

"Zeph. Tell me."

His shoulders shook, and he could not look her in the eye as his lip quivered.

Galen reached for his hand across the table, her slightly wrinkled skin covering his with a soothing stroke. He inhaled and lifted his head to meet her gaze with teary eyes.

Panic bloomed on her face. "Is the princess alive?"

How did she know Ravenna was the princess? Degare had not yet released that information.

He managed a slow nod. "What is it, then? I haven't seen you in weeks," Galen said.

It was true. He had not come to visit her in nearly three weeks—since Ravenna had arrived. With every passing day, he risked his true motives being discovered. He was afraid to get her involved in his schemes. Galen was far too precious to him, and he would do anything to protect her. One could have once called her his only weakness before Ravenna had been added into the mix.

How was he going to get Ravenna out of this mess?

Galen continued. "I tried to visit her, but they would not allow me up into the tower. They are barely allowing outsiders into the west wing. That gauze needed to be removed a week ago. Is she well, Zephaniah?"

He ignored her question. "I need you to be honest with me about how you knew who Ravenna was the first day I brought her here. Because you did, know, didn't you? Before anyone other than the king and Jara realized she was the princess. Why did you keep it from me?" he asked.

Galen closed her eyes, swirling the tea in her cup with a small spoon. "You know I have secrets, son." Zephaniah awaited her explanation. "This kingdom needs Light, even if it is concealed for a little while."

She had said those words to him for the first time many years ago. He motioned for her to continue.

"I am not just an Ember in hiding, Zephaniah. I am a spy—for Ashreya Ozanne."

"For Ravenna's mother? For Vestele?" he asked.

She confirmed with a duck of her head. "We have been in communication since the destruction of Ozanna." His face twisted. "I lied to you about how I came to Oro. My village did burn, and I did lose my husband in the war, but I came to Oro voluntarily."

"You *volunteered* to come here?"

"For the kingdom," she said, and he knew she was talking about the prophesied Kingdom of Light that would come when the Father returned for his people. "To help conceal Ravenna, until it was her time."

"Until it was her time to what? When were you going to tell her of the Light? You let her live unaware—completely *unaware* of her destiny! With the gifts that were prophesied, she could have defeated Oro by now. Brinland. Edmaria. The Dawn Islands. Volcania. Arresia could have been brought back to the Light. Her destiny was to prepare the way for the Father!"

Galen winced. "Zephaniah, what we did will not stop the Father's return. He always makes a way, whether that way is through Ravenna or not."

Zeph licked his lips and propped his arms behind his head. "I don't believe this. You knew the whole time, and you said nothing? Not even when I marched her to her death?" he spat, rising from the stool.

"She is dead, then?" Galen asked quietly.

"Not yet. I don't know. Maybe," he said. Galen held back tears.

"Zephaniah, I wanted to tell her. Ashreya was supposed to hide her but still raise her to know the Light. She was going to tell her eventually when Ravenna was eighteen. But she never did out of fear that she would lose Ravenna to the king's bloodstone staff. She feared he would come for her."

"I don't care what Ashreya was supposed to do. What about you? You let me deliver her straight into the arms of the enemy."

Galen recoiled. "I wanted to say something. But I physically could not, Zephaniah. I took a blood oath."

"As did everyone in Vestele." Zephaniah scoffed. "To

protect Ravenna," he muttered, running a hand over his face. "Well, look where it landed her."

"Look, now that you know—now that she knows, I can tell you everything. I never meant for this to happen."

Zephaniah could not stand to see the hurt on her face, and he grimaced. "I know, Galen. I know. Just start from the beginning, please."

She took a deep breath and crossed her ankles. "I worked in the palace as a healer for the Ozannes when I dwelled in the city with my husband. I was brought in on the night Ravenna was delivered. Gerrin and Willa had been trying for a baby—an heir—for years. They came to me for herbal remedies and potions. We tried *everything*. The queen had a handful of miscarriages and stillbirths. I felt for them because I was never able to have a baby of my own either." She paused, and there was a catch in her throat.

"Some of the people in the kingdom were beginning to wonder if the Ozannes had been cursed. They wondered why the Father of Lights had turned his face from them, and why they were producing no heir. Soon, Willa was given the nickname of *The Barren Queen*. But the Father had not abandoned them. After seven barren years, they were blessed with Ravenna." She smiled at Zeph, a sparkle in her eye.

"Just as the prophecy says," Zephaniah said. *A once barren queen shall birth a daughter, and she shall become a bright light, a crackling flame. Burning brighter than any Ember before her.* "The first half of it, anyway."

"She shall *become*, Zephaniah. *Become.* There is still hope." She patted his hand gently. "Willa chose to hide the pregnancy in fear of having another miscarriage." She smiled again, remembering. "Willa had a smooth pregnancy with Ravenna, though she was riddled with anxiety and fear that something would happen to her baby. Understandably so. I could not imagine losing child after child before they had even taken a breath." Galen looked down at her hands.

"I was sleeping one evening when a man—a soldier—by the name of Reid Barrett, burst into my home, begging for help."

"As in Ashreya *Barrett*?"

"Lover," Galen said. "They were to be married." Zephaniah raised his chin in understanding.

"He practically pulled me from my bed where I laid alone. My own husband was out fighting in the battle between the Embers and the witches just outside the kingdom walls. Reid was frantic. I feared he brought news of my husband." Horror swept across her face, and she calmed her shaking hands, continuing. "But it was the queen he sought to help. We ran all the way to the castle, quicker than I'd ever run. Along the way, he explained what had happened. Reid had been at the battle fronts...things weren't looking good for Ozanna. Ozanna couldn't hold Degare and the witches off much longer. The kingdom would be taken...and with it, all possible heirs. The darkness had closed in, and all Light was going to be suppressed."

Zeph's mind was working, putting together the information he and Ravenna had discovered together in her cell. "They used The Darkening to gain a foothold." He had already known as much.

"Yes." Galen began again. "Degare was coming for Gerrin and Willa's gifts—not Ravenna. He did not even know about the pregnancy. Against better judgment, Willa had chosen to deliver Ravenna early through surgery."

"Ashreya—she had already begun the procedure when I arrived. Willa was begging her to get the baby out. I could not stop it, so I helped." Her voice softened as sadness clouded her vision. "It was awful for Willa. We got Ravenna out and she was beautiful. Radiant. A true gift from the Father of Lights— a promise of hope. But because of the prophecy, and because even Degare and the witches knew of it, she would not be safe. Willa begged us to do something, anything."

"She was persistent, and Gerrin, well he just looked at me with those sad eyes, begging to appease his wife's wishes. To do anything to calm her while she lay cut open, only begging for her child to be given a fair chance at life."

"So, Ashreya agreed to take her into hiding? But if she was able to escape with Ravenna, why couldn't the Ozannes go with her?"

"Degare was coming for the Ozannes. They knew he would stop at nothing, and they wanted Ravenna as far from danger as possible. They only wanted her to be safe. It was a sacrifice they were willing to make."

To be separated from the daughter they had waited seven long years for.

"What of their power?" Zephaniah asked. "Where did it go?"

Galen clenched her eyes, as if it pained her to remember.

"They knew Degare searched for bloodstone, and they knew it was a possibility that he would someday have the ability to steal their gifts. They could not let him get that powerful. Against better judgment, Ashreya was convinced by her sister-in-law's pleas to turn to dark magic." Galen's voice shook. "Ashreya found a spell from her mother's spell book which explained how to bind gifts or magic to an item—a talisman. The item had to be of enough strength to hold such depths of power, and bloodstone was hard to come by for a reason. Gerrin and Willa had ordered it to be mined out of the lands and destroyed to weaken the dark magic. But one known remnant remained that was pure enough—Delle's necklace. Ashreya used it to place Gerrin and Willa's gifts into the stone."

"And then what did she do with it?" Zephaniah asked. Galen tapped her fingers on the table, seeming to avoid the question.

"Ashreya took it with her. They hoped that Ravenna would have use of them someday when she reigned. They prayed she would take the throne again someday and reign with the great power they had given her. A power so great, she could defeat the darkness almost entirely."

"The prophecy already promised that, without the help of their gifts," Zephaniah said.

Galen ignored him.

"Until she was older and ready, Ravenna was to live a life, protected and unaware of her birthright."

"Unaware of the hope we have in the Light," Zeph muttered.

Galen continued, waving him off. "Ashreya was to raise her as her own, and Gerrin and Willa would pretend they had never known her, if only to protect her and keep her from her fate."

"Her fate to save an entire kingdom? To *pull* Arresia out of the shadows of death?"

"I regret it every day, Zephaniah." She wiped a tear from her cheek. "I promised them I'd keep their secret, that if I ever saw Ravenna again, I would tell her nothing," Galen said. "But if it is her life on the line, I am done being silent. Tell the girl everything I have told you. And tell her to remove the gauze from the wound on her thigh." Galen grabbed a small jar of salve. "She'll need this."

Zephaniah took it from her and placed it into his pocket.

"And Zephaniah?"

He looked up at her desperate face.

"Keep our hope alive."

55

IT DIES WITH HER
RAVENNA

Ravenna awoke in her cell, not surprised that she lay in a puddle of her own blood upon the grime that was sure to cause an infection. She could barely move. Every inch of her body stung and burned like fire coursing through her veins. She had withstood great injuries before but, thanks to her parents, had been kept from torture such as this until she had been dragged into this kingdom. She could not imagine what life had been like for them, enduring torture in prison for over twenty years. Degare's rage was personal.

When the guards left her, Ravenna moved her arm just slightly. Scraps of her dress lay upon the floor around her, hanging off her in mere threads that were soaked in blood, just as she had anticipated. She had not, however, anticipated the amount of disappointment she would feel when she awoke in her cell without Zephaniah beside her.

She slowly shuffled through what was left of the folds of her dress. Her mind had been spinning out of control as the guards dragged her up the stairs and into her cell. They did not bother staying to guard her, as if they expected her to die soon anyway. As her thoughts had wandered and woven a path to where she may find the necklace that once hung from her mother's neck, she remembered that it had hung from hers until her arrival in this kingdom. She had last held it in her fingertips, just moments before Zeph had carried her into Galen's home. Galen had admitted to her in the note that she knew who she was, and Ravenna wondered if she knew what must lay inside the pendant as well.

Her fingers found the open gash on her leg. She breathed through the pain. Infection had started, and it was sore to the touch. As her fingers wrapped around the gauze and pulled, the small pendant rolled out of it onto the floor. The brass necklace had been concealed in the pocket of her flesh, wrapped in gauze.

In this kingdom you wear a noose around your neck, Willa had said. She had been trying to warn her, trying to tell her of the necklace.

When she was tied to the whipping post, she had connected the dots. The Ozanne's gifts were inside of Delle and Ashreya's pendant. They had to be. Ravenna pulled the bloody pendant into her hand, rubbing its spherical brass shape between her fingers. Her body shuddered with waves of pain.

She lay there, face down on the cold floor. At least the coolness of the stone helped to sooth her. Turning the brass over and over again in her palm, she wept. She brought it to her face and looked upon the fine details of it. It encased minuscule jades and meticulous designs of rushing waves entangled with vines and two birds. A raven and a dove. The emblems of Oro and the witches, and the old kingdom of Ozanna. She had admired it a million times, but never this closely. There, between the two birds, was a tiny latch, almost too small to see. She lifted it with her blood crusted fingernail and popped the charm open. Out came a stone of red. *A bloodstone.* She squinted her eyes and examined it closely for only a moment before footsteps began to sound behind her. She quickly concealed the stone in her fist.

Zeph unlocked the cell door, opening it quietly and cursing under his breath. "Oh, Ravenna," he whispered. "Oh, no." He crouched down beside her, gently brushing the hair from her feverish forehead. She did not look up at him, it took too much effort. "I am so sorry." His voice was racked with guilt. "I am so sorry." He kept repeating the words, again and again, unsure of where to start tending to her. All this time, he truly had wanted to help her.

He pulled some salve out of his cloak and before he could open the jar, she extended her open palm to him, revealing the bloodstone.

"I've had it all along," she rasped in disbelief. He staggered back, examining the gem in her hand as if it were the most frightening thing he had ever seen.

"Let me help you first," he pleaded. He knew she had lost too much blood. They both knew she was dying. "Then we'll figure out what to do with it..."

"There is no time," she rasped. "We do it now."

"Do what, Ravenna?" Zephaniah's voice was filled with concern.

While Jara had tortured her in her chambers that day after the bath, she had unwittingly given Ravenna a seat with a plain view of the spell book that was open on the table. If a talisman is broken, the power within is released into the breaker. A fool, the witch had been.

"You need to break it." She needed him to claim the gifts. He would have a chance at survival if he had the power to fight back, and she was going to die either way. Vengeance was his.

"What? No. Just let me help you." His gaze was frantic as he hovered over her in shock.

There would be no helping her. She was of no use to the king now. If she did not die today, he would just kill her later.

"I am not breaking that stone, and neither are you," he said. She would die before the hour was up.

"If one of us doesn't claim these gifts, Degare will," she said through gritted teeth. The pain was unbearable.

She would do anything to keep these gifts from the hands of evil, and if Zephaniah was not going to break the stone and take revenge on the king, then the gifts would die with her.

"Wait, Ravenna!" Zeph blurted, but it was too late.

She cracked the bloodstone against the hard floor where she lay and bled, and with one single whack, a force burst from the rock, engulfing her in a haze of intense power.

<h1 style="text-align:center">56</h1>

KEEPING HOPE ALIVE
ZEPHANIAH

Extreme force threw Zeph backward into the wall. The bloodstone turned to powder, and the power that exploded from it was overwhelming. The castle shook around them, the quake shivering through the deepest crevices of the world. Panicked breaths escaped him and he looked around from where he lay on the floor next to her.

Galen had not told him, though she must have known, that Ravenna possessed the bloodstone necklace all this time. Ravenna had come to the kingdom wearing it, and it had disappeared from her neck after he had taken her to Galen. Galen had hidden it for only Ravenna to find—when she was ready.

Why did she not warn me? How did Jio and Jara not see the pendant in Ravenna's mind? Because they had been looking for bloodstone, and this stone was wrapped in brass, he realized.

Zeph was sure the new and unfamiliar power that ravaged her weak body would kill her if the blood loss did not. Ravenna had known it too. She would rather the gifts die with her than fall into the hands of the king. Zeph swayed with dizziness as he sat up beside her.

Rocks fell from the ceiling above them, and he immediately placed his body over top of hers, shielding her from the tumbling shrapnel. Ravenna's body had gone still, but her heart pumped blood from her destroyed flesh.

There was a strange shimmering light that swirled over her body like steam, and Zephaniah reached out a hand to touch it. It curled around his fingers and crawled across his pale skin, seeming to caress him, and then it rose, vanishing out of the high windows in the cell, leaving them in utter darkness.

"Ravenna," his voice rasped. *Shadowmarks*—not lightmarks—bloomed across her skin, swirling across the ripped flesh of her back and her arms. She did not stir.

No. No. No.

"Ravenna," he pleaded once more, his hand finding its way to her face, the only visible skin left untouched by blood. "You're alright. You're alright." He brushed the hair from her cheek. "Father, help her," he begged as she bled. He rose to his feet and Ravenna stirred beside him. "Don't let her die," he begged the Light.

Claiming such power took a physical toll on the body. Zeph had seen it bring Degare to his knees many times, and he did not wish to see Ravenna die from it. The new markings were not those of Light—no. The Light had been detached from those gifts when Gerrin and Willa had placed them into the bloodstone. Ravenna bore gifts only through dark magic. Only when—*if*—Ravenna turned to the Light would she be freed of the chains of darkness that were now wrapped tightly around her soul.

If Zephaniah accomplished anything in his life, he wished

for it to be that he gave hope to this woman in front of him—a nudge toward the Light. Some sense of purpose, despite the life she had been born into. He knew what it was like to live with no feeling of purpose. He wished for her to know that she was more than what had happened to her, and for her to have the strength to fulfill this prophecy, and to find the great purpose he suspected she had had all along.

He had to at least attempt an escape to buy her more time. He was certain he was already dead, anyway. If Ravenna could wake up, the gifts within her, dark or not, could buy them some time, or better yet, make them untouchable. But did he truly wish for her to use such gifts, and welcome even more of that darkness within her? He needed somewhere safe for her to heal, or she would be killed in the king's attempt to take the power.

As he looked at her, near death, he remembered his family. *Everyone that had been taken from him.* He had wondered for years and years why he had not been gifted and lightmarked as his family had. He believed in the Father's power over the darkness, and he followed the Light. He *lived* in the Light, working and devoting his life to bringing people out of the thresholds of darkness. But did the Light live within *him*, if he had no gifts or lightmarks to show for it?

He had welcomed the light into his soul, and he had felt it fill him. He felt it with him every day, but there was no physical marking or proof. It was only when Degare had finally found the ingredients for the bloodstone staff, and the persecution and hunt for the Embers had begun, that he was somewhat grateful for his lack of lightmarks. While his lightmarked family was shunned and kept from working, buying, or selling by orders of King Degare, Zeph was able to continue working for the mapmaker in his village. He had worked as much as possible to shield them from hunger and death.

But then, everyone he loved was taken and killed before his eyes. Witnessing such horrors in this castle had broken something in him, and all these years he only craved a purpose. A reason that he had lived when so many had not. In helping Ravenna, he had found purpose.

The guards had been alerted by the explosion and the tremors that still snaked through the castle walls, and their hurried footsteps echoed up the tower. Zeph hauled her limp body up the stairs, continuing a silent prayer as he climbed higher and higher. There would be no place to conceal her, nowhere to run. Going up would only trap them, but perhaps it would buy her time to wake up and defend herself. Descending the tower would only guarantee a sooner meeting with the men that now tracked them. Oh, how he wished now that he could be gifted, so he could blow this castle to bits and get her to safety.

He climbed and climbed the steep steps, legs burning with each bit of incline. Thankfully, the tower had steadied, shaking no more. "I need you to wake up," he muttered under his breath.

Her blood. It dripped down his arms, leaving a perfect trail of red behind. His stomach twisted. Taking her into that chamber was the worst decision he had ever made, and he would hate himself for the pain he had caused her for the rest of his short life.

What would have happened if he had run with her? As he rounded the very top of the tower, it was clear that the guards were only a few levels below them. He frantically set her down outside the highest cells of the tower.

Gerrin and Willa fell to their knees, each in their own cell, adjacent to one another. They bore their own injuries, and he knew with all they had done for her that they would do it all again, if it meant hiding her from the darkness.

A whisper met the air around him. It was Willa. "It was not in our plans for Ravenna to ever need to fight. It was our intention to hide her from this dark world forever. But that would not be fair to those she was perhaps born to help. Now that she has claimed the power within the stone, she may be the only hope for the people of Ozanna. For *all* Embers."

They were the calmest and most clear sentences Zeph had heard the queen speak, and he was saddened as she noticed Ravenna's markings were of shadows—where the Light should be but was not. "We should have never turned to the darkness," she said under a trembling breath.

Willa's eyes dropped down to the key ring around Zeph's belt loop. Slowly, he left Ravenna's side and unlocked the grieving queen's cell door. A soft smile painted her worn, motherly face. Soon, they would all be dead. He would give her this one last moment with the daughter she had done so much for. He turned to unlock Gerrin's cell as well.

The Barren Queen touched his cheek. "Zephaniah. *Hidden by the Father.* You have been greatly blessed to be hidden in such a dark kingdom as this, and to help my girl catch a glimpse of the Light that we failed to assure she knew." A tear slipped down his face.

"I have failed," he said. Ravenna had not chosen the Light, not yet, and perhaps she may not receive another chance.

"There is still hope," Willa said softly, and Zeph could have sworn, just for a moment, that a faint mark briefly glowed on her cheek before fading, as she hovered over top of her daughter.

Her words had given him an understanding. He had been a part of something bigger all along. *Indeed*, he had been created for a purpose. Maybe his only *gift* was staying hidden from the darkness, but that was a gift he was indeed thankful for. If he were to live without any purpose other than this, to just help one person—Ravenna—*it was enough for him.*

57
SHADOWMARKED
RAVENNA

At the first crack of the stone, the world had imploded. Ravenna's vision had gone black. But then, a small hint of light had caressed her in a comforting manner, its warmth like a blanket of relief. It was a fleeting feeling, gone before she even comprehended it aside from the pain. As if it had wanted to stay, but there was no place for it.

The excruciating pain and the force of the power she had claimed pressed from all sides of her body, rushing through her veins, swelling and engulfing her. Consuming her. Prodding for a way out of containment. She had no escape from this feeling as the power raced through her. Filling, and filling, and filling, until she thought she would explode. When she thought her body could hold no more of the power, it continued pushing and shoving into her. The feeling was not as she had expected.

As if he were worlds away, a male's voice echoed into her ears, ricocheting off the confines of her newly darkened soul.

"Ravenna."

This was a power she did not wish to touch. It had crept inside her, welcome at first, yes. But it was all consuming, and stronger than she had ever imagined. It would kill her. She remembered that had been her plan—her hope. Her only hope at keeping such power out of the king's grasp. She had to die so the king could not claim this power as his own.

"Ravenna." The voice echoed again. "You're alright. You're alright."

Oh, the pain. Her skin was shredded, bleeding, from the whipping she had just endured, paired with the pain of the power that ravaged through her and changed her very being.

"Father, help her," a pleading, frantic voice addressed the Father of Lights.

Yes, he would be the only one that could save her from this, but she suspected he had left her long ago, when her parents had turned to the darkness to save her life—when those gifts of light had been tossed aside and hidden away through dark magic. When her family had denied the Light, lacking trust in the Father's plan. She wondered how things would be different if they had not abandoned their faith and had instead gone down the path of Light. She was not worthy of the goodness of Light.

Strong arms held her, and her body pressed against the one that carried her. Her eyes would not open, but she felt consciousness returning. Her head swayed and her arms hung, fingers grazing something like stone. She stirred, and something urged her body to wake.

She felt like she was being carried up a stairwell, much like she had been the night she arrived in the castle. Zeph. She would bet anything that was who held her so fiercely, yet gently, against his beating heart. He was her only friend left in the world.

Cold stone met her body as he sat her down. The darkness was so strong. Too strong for her broken body. She tried to surrender to it, but just as on the journey to Oro, her breaths continued to come, ignoring her own will to die.

A gentle hand brushed over her body, the touch followed by a whispered prayer. A woman, whose voice was so familiar, yet so far away. It was a voice that had screamed Ravenna's name the night Ashreya had been killed before her. It was a kind voice that Ravenna wished she could have grown up hearing, and a hand whose touch she wished she had to comfort and guide her.

Willa.

Things could have been so different.

The voices around her faded, and she clung tightly to the soft words Zephaniah spoke into her hair.

58

FIGHTING DARKNESS
ZEPHANIAH

Gerrin and Willa hovered over top of their daughter's mutilated body, weeping. They stayed between her and the door, shielding her from the guards that would enter through at any moment. Their own bodies were wrecked and bleeding. They did not look away from her.

Zeph sat against the wall, sinking and crumbling, as he really looked at Ravenna, whose shivering body was covered with his cloak. Blood pooled around her, the fabric of her dress lay in scraps, and a bruise now spread across her forehead. Half of her flesh had been marred by the whip, and his cloak did nothing to slow the bleeding.

He clenched his jaw, returning his gaze to the entry where the guards now neared. He would do anything for the broken, precious soul before him to have a second chance at a family. She deserved to know happiness once more and to find her own purpose. She had given him one, and he would forever be indebted to her. So, he rose to his feet and drew his sword.

Ravenna did not stir as he leaned down where her parents cradled her and placed a kiss atop her head. He ran one hand down her hair and whispered into it between shaky breaths. "Wake up. Fight the darkness that consumes this kingdom. Choose the Light, Ravenna. *Please*." And then he stood, stalking toward the door.

He knew the guards were close as their yells echoed louder and louder. Four of them, at least. He stayed hidden behind the wall, and as the first one entered, he swiped his sword. The man fell to his knees.

Zephaniah had just committed a true act of treason in killing one of his fellow soldiers. He knew the moment he vowed to help Ravenna, that it would likely end this way. He did not care. He knew the moment he chose to carry her up those stairs, that there was no turning back. He knew that for this, he would be sentenced to death. None of it mattered.

As more guards tunneled in, he fought and swung his blade until it was ripped from his hand in a cloud of shadow that quickly dissipated to reveal the witch in the doorway.

Her orange eyes burned with rage. Her slender neck and dark hair accentuated her bony face, and her pale skin seemed to crawl with a faint black smoke. Behind her, to Zeph's surprise, entered Degare.

"I suspected you would betray us from the beginning, but Degare had a soft spot for you," Jara spat, throwing a deadly stare at the king, who coughed *blood* into his sleeve as he wheezed from the tiring ascent.

Zephaniah could assume Jara's distrust in him had been the only thing saving him from having to kill an Ember with each passing trade. That, and the fact that he had never successfully and individually delivered an Ember to the king before, aside from Ravenna. In the king's eyes, Zephaniah had not earned such a reward.

The guards chained Zeph within seconds, and he watched as Ravenna's parents were yanked from their daughter and thrown back into their cells. Screams echoed from all around him in mass chaos.

Unauthorized release of three prisoners. Plotting with a prisoner. Killing one of the king's men. He glanced down at the body of the soldier. Killing a *Despiri*. Planning to kill his king. Leading this woman to her certain death. Zephaniah was guilty of it all.

Degare stalked toward Ravenna as the guards placed chains upon her without kindness. The metal clasped over her marred skin, tightly rubbing into the exposed flesh. He could have sworn he saw her wince even in her sleep.

"Let her go!" Zephaniah yelled. Ravens scattered from the windowsill, flying over the vast kingdom in a flutter of shadows and wings. He struggled against the chains until his wrists were bruising. The metal clanked against the stone, sending shrill sounds echoing up the bars of the cells. Willa's cries were haunting as she watched. Gerrin was across the tower, kicking the bars of his own cell with all the strength he had left, eyes on his wife—his *soulbound*.

Zephaniah did not know if he wished for Ravenna to remain in her slumber into death or to wake. Which would be worse? Now would likely be her last chance to speak to her parents, who loved her so much but had been given no time to show her. His eyes remained on her. If she awoke right now, it would likely only bring more pain.

So, he prayed she stayed unconscious. He prayed it did not hurt, and that she was not scared. All he could do was stare ahead at her laying in her own blood. Zeph could not decipher where Ravenna's red hair ended and where the blood started. He looked at her beautiful face one last time, before Degare pressed the bloodstone staff to her chest.

59

A BREATH AWAY
RAVENNA

She awoke in a new space. One she had not seen before. From where she lay confined on a bed, she could see that the window faced the town square. Strange marks coiled across her skin. She examined the shadowy swirls and her wounds, squinting against the dim light of day that hurt her head. Her skin was healing, though still very much open and sore. By the level of improvement, it appeared she had been here for several days. Weeks, even.

Have I been asleep for that long? What happened?

Her fingers twitched. A twinge of that power started rushing, clawing its way through her. The power was still there, then. The king had not yet taken it. Well, of course he had not. She was still alive. If he had used the staff on her and taken her gifts, she would be dead.

Zephaniah.

What had happened to him? He had whispered to her, begged her to choose the Light.

Fight the darkness.

But she could not remember anything else that had happened while she was sleeping.

"Good morning." A feminine voice called from the corner of the room. Ravenna turned her head as much as she could manage against the stiffness in her neck. Across the room was the blonde servant who had shown her kindness in Jara's chambers.

Ravenna's eyes scanned the room for any sign of Zeph. "Where is my guard?" she asked. Cove shifted on her feet.

"You have guards posted outside," she answered, still standing in her corner of the large chambers with her hands crossed at her waist.

"I do not inquire about *those* guards," Ravenna said flatly, taking in each exit of the space she was in and every object she could use as a weapon if needed. She had been moved to a chamber like Jara's, though not as spacious. It was an obvious upgrade from her cell, though she now bore *more* chains. The shackles around her wrists seemed to burn her skin, which had been rubbed raw beneath the metal. Thankfully, the tears in her flesh had been tended to, and some were beginning to close.

Cove walked toward her, hands raised, as if she feared what Ravenna may do. Even in the restraints, the servant feared her. "I am here as your servant until Jara can figure out a spell to remove the vast amount of power from your body."

And transfer it to Degare, Ravenna supposed.

"Do you remember what happened?" Cove asked.

A few moments passed, and then she remembered. Degare had pressed the golden tip of the staff into her and shoved it so hard against her sternum that she had felt a crack inside her chest. Her eyes had flown open, and she had wondered if that would be the end. The last thing she saw before entering darkness was Zeph, brought to his knees in chains before her.

In their cells, her parents had screamed and begged for her life, just as they had in the torture chamber only hours before. Ravenna had only laid upon the floor, barely enough energy to open her eyes, her skin and clothes in shreds, blood pouring out of her.

Too much blood.

A rush of that power had flowed through her, being sucked out by the bloodstone staff. Then, the staff had shattered. Yes, she remembered. Somehow, before it had penetrated her chest completely, the king's beloved weapon had shattered against the immense amount of power within her. The king had cursed at the witch, blaming her for his failure to retrieve the power once more.

"How long has it been?" Ravenna asked quietly, staring blankly at the black stone of the ceiling. She was so tired of seeing black. Even the lifeless Dead Wood would be better than this black castle, but truly, she craved the golden hills of the valley and the Sunstone Mountains. Though, even if she got the chance to return some day, there was nothing left of the life she once knew. The people she loved.

"Eleven days." Cove did not look at Ravenna as she changed her bandages, removing each one carefully and replacing them with new ones. "Your body has endured much..." she paused, looking for the right words, "trauma." Indeed, Ravenna's body shook with weakness at minute movements, bore bruises and swelling, and an array of open flesh wounds.

Cove continued with the small talk in a soothing voice. It was the kind voice that had inspired Ravenna to fight Degare when she had nearly given up that day in the bathing chambers. "Some of your wounds were infected." Cove lifted a piece of gauze from Ravenna's shoulder, and the skin slightly pulled up with it. They both winced. "The salve I've been using has helped. Only a few more days and you should be able to move around and get out of bed."

"And go where?" Ravenna asked, unhopeful that her life would last long enough for her to ever be free again. She would join her clan in death the moment that Jara figured out a way for Degare to access her power.

What had become of her biological parents? The king now had no use for them. They were likely dead, too. And Zeph. He would be hung for treason if he had not been already.

Cove was staring at her, eyes swelling with tears as if she cared about Ravenna and knew the trouble she faced on a personal level. It was only then that Ravenna felt the wetness on her own face, streaming from her eyes. The kind servant squeezed Ravenna's hand in a comforting gesture.

"Zephaniah—I haven't seen him," said Cove sympathetically. She used his name as if he were a friend. "I only heard him once...in the torture chambers." The servant broke eye contact, averting her gaze back to Ravenna's wounds. "I am sorry."

Saying nothing, Ravenna only kept her gaze on the ceiling. She had failed her mother and her clan, her biological parents, and Zephaniah. She had not been able to avenge all the wrongs that had been done to them. The wrong that had been done to them because of her presence in their lives.

"There is still hope," Cove offered. Ravenna did not look at her. "I am an Ember, Ravenna." Ravenna straightened, moving her eyes to meet Cove's icy-blue ones. The servant's face was full of something like uncertainty as she pulled her collar to the side to reveal a glowing lightmark right above her collar bone. It formed the shape of a small wave and seemed to pulsate as it glowed. She hovered a dainty hand above the glass of water next to Ravenna's bed, and a few droplets rose into the air. She released them, and they dropped into the glass once more. "I am on your side. You can trust me."

"What are you doing in this castle?" Ravenna demanded in a whisper. "You could be killed. Helping me could get you killed."

Cove huffed out a small laugh. "I am not only here for you." She paused, blinking tears from her eyes. "There is a grand scheme that is much greater than you, but you *are* a part of it."

Ravenna's face crinkled. *Is she saying there is a resistance? How could anyone stand against the king?*

Once again, Cove answered Ravenna's inner thoughts. "Yes. There is a rebellion of sorts. And no, I cannot read minds," Cove explained, smiling softly. "I can feel emotions, and to a degree, I can influence them. I try not to be too invasive, but yours are very easy for me to feel." Cove motioned for Ravenna to sit up, and she aided her in the painful, dreadful movement. Cove began changing the bandages on her back. Ravenna was so *tired*. "I can help ease the torment in your mind, if you wish," she offered.

"No." Ravenna answered quickly. She deserved to feel it all.

Cove opened another jar of salve, gently kneading it into each gash on Ravenna's back. "Guilt is a tough one," Cove said. Ravenna shot her a look of disapproval at the repeated invasion of her emotions and the servant quickly changed the subject.

"The witch has been searching non-stop for a new way to

take your power, but the darkness has limits. The bloodstone in the staff was not enough to contain your power for the transfer. They will stop at nothing, and they do not care if you die in the process."

Neither did she.

Cove paused. "You may not care, but others are depending on you."

"Who? I have *no one* left," Ravenna said.

"I seek a way to shift the power the king already possesses, to someone else. *You*."

Ravenna stiffened. "Why me?" she asked. She was not the right candidate.

"He is far too powerful with his magic, and we have been searching for a way to dampen it enough to have a chance against him for years." Ravenna assumed by *we*, she meant the resistance she was working for. "I see it fit to jump at the opportunity when I see one," Cove said, "whether I have had time to discuss with my leader or not. If we are successful, you'll possess enough power to bring the entire kingdom and all its Despiri to their knees."

Ravenna sat up straighter. "I'll do it." She would do *anything,* for a chance to destroy this kingdom.

A look of surprise fleeted over Cove's pretty and delicate face at Ravenna's agreement. "Don't you need to hear the plan first?"

If Zephaniah was still out there, if Gerrin and Willa were still out there, she would find a way to save them whether it got her killed or not. In the process, she would avenge her people. Cove mapped out the plan for her.

"The witch is working on creating a spell that will work. I know a little about dark magic. Once she has completed it, I can sneak into her chambers and alter the words to work in our favor."

"How?" Ravenna asked. "Won't she notice it has been tampered with?"

"It will be a matter of a few words, and this spell must be in the ancient language of the witch goddesses. Jara doesn't speak it. She won't notice," Cove assured her. "And if she does, at least we can say we tried. What other option is there?" Cove asked.

"And you speak this ancient, witch goddess language?"

"I know enough," Cove said, fidgeting with her hands.

"Here's a thought: you could unchain me," Ravenna muttered.

"There is no key. They're spelled to keep you from accessing your power, and the lock is enchanted. It took the entire Delle Witch Clan to gain enough strength to subdue your power with those things." Cove nodded to the chains.

"The witches are working with Degare again?" Ravenna asked.

"Not just for the shackles. They agreed to help fuse his bloodstone staff together again. I heard they made it more powerful this time by adding the stone they retrieved from you in Vestele." Ravenna cursed. That wretched stone—she should have let Leith take it home.

"I thought the witches hated Degare," Ravenna said. "Why would they allow him the chance to achieve more power?"

"That alliance has been unstable for years. He's made them

a promise to grant them their land if they help with this one final thing."

"And they came crawling back, just like that?" Ravenna asked. "Has he not promised them that a dozen times before?"

Cove shrugged, spinning a thin silver ring on her finger. "Perhaps they are as desperate as we are to get out from under his grimy claws."

Ravenna lay there, utterly defenseless for three more nights, concentrating on the call of the witch guardians, which the king's Despiri battled in the streets below her window.

Finally, Cove came with stirring news. "Jara has completed the spell," she said as she walked through the door of Ravenna's chambers. Her blonde hair was so light, it almost looked white, illuminated by the glow of the moon through the window. She clicked the door shut.

If their plan failed, at least Ravenna would not be alive to reap the consequences of the unmatched power that would run through Degare's veins. The havoc he would reap on the world would be devastating to all Embers and followers of the Light. It would be heartbreaking for Zephaniah to witness, if he even had the chance. He would be the first person she would run to, the first person she would save if she were able to kill Degare and the witch. If Cove's plan worked, the world of Arresia would look a whole lot different. Ravenna would make sure of it.

"Today, Degare and Jara are headed to the prison to choose the stock for the Summer Ember Trade. I'll sneak in to change the spell while they're gone."

"It's that simple?" Ravenna asked from where she sat, still chained to the wooden frame of the bed.

Even Ravenna's part of the plan seemed simple. Participate willingly in the spell, offer up her hand, and her blood. It was the binding they would use to complete it. The spell would create a tie between herself and the king, and from there, Jara would begin the ritual.

But if Cove was successful, the outcome would be altered. Instead of Ravenna's power flowing down the tether to Degare, the king's power would flow to her, weakening, and hopefully *killing* him in the process.

They would all be weakened by the spell. Jara's strength would dissipate enough for Cove to kill her. As Degare was disarmed of his great power and his witch, Ravenna would bring him death. She only hoped her body could handle more of the darkness, and that she maintained consciousness long enough to kill him. If not, she was confident that Cove would be able to finish him in his weakened state.

"The spell will be done tonight, when the three moons are new and black," Cove explained. "When Jara can pull from the darkness. It has to be done this evening. Jara is not strong enough on her own for a spell of this magnitude on any other night."

"And what of the Delle Witches?" Ravenna asked.

"Refusing to help further until they have received their land," Cove said.

Ravenna grunted in response, and a small smile crept upon her face at the plan as she replayed the scheme repeatedly in her mind. Vengeance was a breath away.

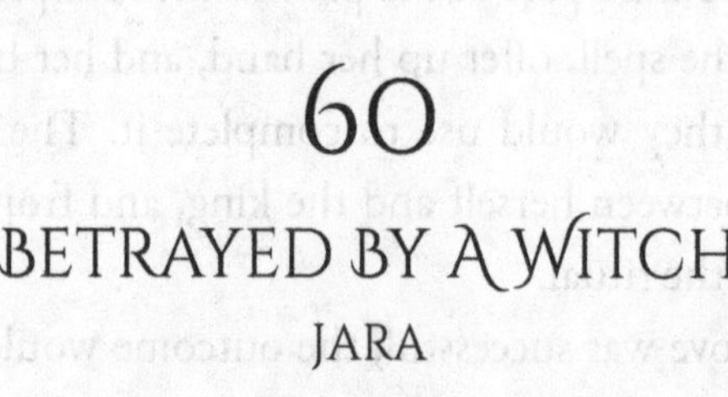

60

BETRAYED BY A WITCH

JARA

"We have done what we will to help you get our land back. But you have failed us, time and time again. You let your feelings for him cloud your vision. You have no right to be our queen," Norell spat.

Jara gritted her teeth at the straight-haired witch who had taken her place. The same witch who had raised her when Jara's mother had left to seduce Arne Ozanne and had never come back.

"Not anymore, Jara Delle. Your name means nothing to us. We aided in the recreation of the staff because it is obvious that your king fades further into death with each kill. His body cannot take any more power. When his own greed kills him, the Hollow Coves will be ours again, and we will claim his throne, too. Unless you prove your loyalty to our clan—by ensuring he dies in this spell, you have no place with us. And we will not be there to help you. This is your decision, and it is final. Your last chance," Norell hissed. "The bloodstone staff is a safety net because we do not trust you. Either way, your king dies. Choose wisely."

Jara only shoved the spell she had created into the other witch's hands and waited for her to examine it.

"Degare will not die by use of the bloodstone staff," Jara said coolly. "It will be my spell that kills him. He *will* die tonight when he takes Ravenna's power."

"Jara. You *assure* me you have enough strength for this spell?" Degare asked. She sighed. Her own strength would not matter if she had the aid of her clan—but now, they were ready to wage war on Oro. If Degare did not have the numbers in his armies and access to all the bloodstone in Oro, the witches would fight back. But they were not stupid—and now, they just waited for him to die.

"I assure you, Your Majesty. When the three moons are in shadow, nothing will stand in my way." His eyes crinkled, and she recognized a few new wrinkles spreading across his paling face. For a moment, she was lost in thought.

He tilted his chin, and a smile tugged at his lips. "If you succeed, you just might find your place on the throne of the Hollow Coves." She studied him.

"Truly?" she asked, her voice echoing through the vast, empty throne room. He did not mean it, did he?

"Truly," he said, slipping a hand behind her neck. She should not have fallen into his touch so easily, but underneath the warmth of his hand, she always melted. She was awaiting the feel of his kiss on her lips when the familiar thrum of his power buzzed over her skin. She stiffened. His stormy gray eyes gazed into hers, flashing a warning of what he could do to her if she failed.

Then, he kissed her. Slowly and passionately, and her body melted beneath his addictive touch.

Her heeled boots cracked against the stone of the streets while she walked next to her king. She was tired. She had prepped the spell and studied it a hundred times. She had memorized every word. Tonight, the moons would be in shadow, and she would earn her place as queen.

"What do we have in this shipment?" Degare asked as they advanced toward the carriage. Jara searched for the inventory papers in her sack. In all her exhaustion, she had forgotten them.

"Y-your Majesty," she stuttered. "Let me go back. It'll only take a moment. I—I've forgotten the list in my chambers."

"Unnecessary," he said. They climbed into the fancy wagon, and she could not help but blush as she caught him admiring the way her black satin dress hugged her curves. "I am certain they have another copy at the prison," he grumbled.

Yes, she knew they did. There were over a thousand Embers in the new prison just across the city, and each one was documented in detail. From the color of their hair, where their lightmarks were located—to each gift they possessed, the strength of those gifts, and their starting bid for the trade.

"I do not wish to be at the prison long. We'll choose the stock for the Summer Ember Trade, and then I wish to return to the castle immediately." He smiled a wicked smile. "We have a big night ahead of us." Jara returned his smile and then looked out the window at the foggy city that passed them by.

When they arrived at the prison, they were greeted by four Despiri who corralled the most physically robust and healthy Embers with the least impressive gifts. These men and women would not offer much value to the Ember Trades and were better suited in the mines, where they would live out their days swinging picks and searching for more bloodstone. Only when the end of their lives neared, and they were too weak to work, would Degare sell their lives for a low price. Jara watched as the Embers were marched north toward the Black Sea Docks, where they would board a boat and be shipped to Edmaria to work in the most promising of the bloodstone mines.

The four Despiri guards escorted the witch and the king toward the cells and cages. Some Embers spat at the king's feet as he waltzed by, and Jara sent waves of pain through each perpetrator.

Wretched people.

The cavernous prison reeked so badly it made her eyes water, and all she could focus on was the drip from the ceiling. They descended further into the prisonous pit, and the air grew cooler, but it was still suffocating. She hoped the king was quick at choosing which of the inventory he wanted for himself and which to be put into the trade so she could stop holding her breath.

"We have these ones saved for the big celebration," one of the Despiri said to Degare, regarding the Autumn Ember Trade that would mark one year since the trades began. Those Embers were not for *this* trade, but the next. "They are some of the strongest we've come across. They should bring in a lot of money. People from all over will be traveling to get their hands on one of these."

Jara surveyed the stock. There were about fifty of them set aside for the Autumn Trade so far, and each one of them stared at her with defiance. "The ball will be crowded with royals," the Despiri said.

"It will be quite the celebration," the king said proudly. He was known for throwing extravagant parties, and she figured he had something up his sleeve for the anniversary ball. He would make a show of his power to all the guests that would travel from across Arresia. Ravenna's gifts would officially make him untouchable—if the immense amount of power did not kill his weakening body, and if Jara allowed him to live. She bit her cheek as she continued to follow him through the tunnels.

He walked slowly, leaning heavily on his staff and occasionally pointing at certain inventory. "What can this one do?" he asked. The Ember was a young girl—age twelve or so. She was one of the youngest in the prison but not the youngest gifted one Jara had seen. She had met lightmarked children as young as five—though that was very rare.

"She can move things with her mind," the Despiri said contemptuously.

"Well, we can't have anyone else having *that* ability, can we?" Degare looked to her as if awaiting her opinion on the matter. His gray eyes gleamed with the mischief Jara had grown to love, and for a moment, guilt panged in her gut as she remembered her promise to Norell.

"Oh, *Majesty*. Why don't you sit this one out?" She covertly gestured to his shaking limbs, and the way he relied on the bloodstone staff to keep him upright, and then returned her gaze to his. His nostrils flared, but after a few moments, he begrudgingly walked away from the Ember, averting his eyes from hers.

Jara took a breath and turned to face the Despiri guard. "Set her aside for next time," she said. The guard warmed an iron in the fire that was adjacent to the cell and proceeded to brand the Ember's flesh with the mark that symbolized Degare's ownership. To Jara's surprise, the young girl did not so much as wince when the hot iron seared her skin. She only stared through Jara's soul, as if trying to collapse her throat with her mind, despite the spelled shackles around her wrists.

Jara, the Despiri, and the king continued their stroll through the tunnels and halls, listening to the lists of Embers and gifts that were read off to them. When they had chosen a stock of a hundred for the Summer Ember Trade, they finally exited the stagnant air of the Ember prison.

61
RISE
RAVENNA

It was getting easier to move her arms and legs. To walk, even. But currently, she laid in the bed, staring at herself in the mirror and studying the new marks that painted her skin. She ran a finger over the shadows on her arm and trailed them all the way up to the back of her neck.

She had slept considerably well lately. She was actually beginning to prefer sleep over being awake—the opposite of how she had felt in Vestele just a month ago. She had been so exhausted from the immense power within her, it was as if her mind completely shut off in sleep, unable to conjure any nightmares at all.

Cove had helped her out of bed many times in the days since she had first woken up. The mysterious servant had even provided her with a dagger from who knows where. It was the dagger Ravenna would hide under her clothes and use to stake the king after the spell.

"They'll come to get you at dark," Cove said, twiddling her thumbs in her lap. She had just returned from Jara's chambers where she had altered the written spell. "They plan on using the throne room." Ravenna kept picking at the food on her plate, wondering if Zephaniah had been fed, wherever he was. Had he been wounded worse than she had been in the torture chambers?

What had they done to him?

"Are you sure you can do this?"

"What is there to be sure about? I have no choice. Degare will not be the first man I've killed. I've killed many for less," Ravenna said.

It was true. She had killed many men for doing less than what he had done to her. One in the Brunts for abusing his wife and children. They were better off without him. *Two,* on the rooftop the night of the Gauntlet. She had nearly killed Leith that same night, but had instead given him a dagger to the leg. She had killed another the night of her mother's death. And on top of all that, her mere *existence* had caused the death of hundreds.

Cove leaned forward from her chair to brace her elbows on the bed. "None of this is your fault, Ravenna. You were born into this world of darkness and never shown the Light. It was bound to consume you sooner or later. All you can do is hold onto that ember within your soul, the one that I can feel. I can *feel* the Light working within you. *That* is you. Not the darkness."

What if I am not deserving of anything the Light has to offer me? Ravenna thought.

The guards came to retrieve her that evening, dragging her shackles and chains along the floor behind. "If you removed these, it'd be a lot easier to transport me," she said. They ignored her. They were not as easily riled up as Callan had been the day that she had stolen his keys. Unfortunately, that ill-thought-out plan of escape had never happened.

She was tired of feeling weighed down, both physically and metaphorically. The pressure built inside her with every breath. She could feel the power moving throughout her body, begging for escape. But with the shackles, she could offer it no release. Not that she would know how, anyway.

The plan was in action, and Cove would be tending to Jara's needs before the spell. Apparently, the witch needed to be catered to more so than usual today, to salvage all her strength. It was a big spell, Ravenna had learned. She sighed as the throne room grew closer. They passed the old tower and the torture chambers that were settled at the bottom of the stairs. Thankfully, no sound echoed from them. Still, she could not help but wonder if Zeph was inside on the stone altar or at the posts where she had been two weeks ago. Or if he was dead.

In the throne room, Degare lounged on his black velvet throne, newly mended bloodstone staff in hand. She knew he would not dare try to use it on *her* again. She marveled at the insane amount of power that must be thrumming through her veins to burst it like she had. She could not bear to think of such power in the king's hands.

This plan better work.

There was nothing she wanted more than to skin the king that sat on the throne of Oro.

The throne of Ozanna.

Cove was situated behind Jara with a platter of food and

deep, red wine. She looked innocent, but her hands trembled slightly. Ravenna wondered if the fear was an act. Cove had seemed confident this morning, but maybe that had been an act too, an attempt to ease Ravenna's mind. Jio was also present, standing to the left of the king with a smirk on his face.

I know your secret, he had said. Now, she did not allow him into the depths of her mind.

She would kill him, too, at first opportunity.

Ravenna was surprised there was not more of an audience. A servant stood stiffly in the back corner of the room, face gaunt behind wild, golden curls. Aside from her, only Jio, Cove, and the soldiers—whether Shades or Despiri, Ravenna did not know—were there to witness.

The guards brought Ravenna forward, kicking her to her knees before the king. A gruesome smile painted his lips.

"Ravenna, my dear. Come forward." He motioned her toward him with his left hand, keeping his right upon the staff.

She took eight long, agonizing steps forward. Once she reached the bottom of the dais, where the floor turned to mirrored tile, with guards at her back, the king gripped her hand and led her up to the platform. His fingers were cold and shadowmarked, and trembled against hers. They walked to the right, where Jara awaited them with a shallow golden bowl before her, a knife in hand. Her face was pure evil, no sympathy at all for the life she was about to ruin. She grabbed Ravenna's hand and sliced her palm before she could prepare for the sting. Degare offered his up willingly.

Jara added a drop of her blood as well. It pooled at the tip of her pale, slender finger and dropped into the bowl. Ravenna's heart beat against her chest so hard that she thought she might fall over from the force. Then, a wave of calm rushed over her. She took a deep breath and silently thanked the Ember servant that stood in front of her.

Jara began.

The chants were strange, of a different tongue. They were like the chants Ravenna had heard her mother saying the night she had been killed. A knot grew in her throat, and her chest heaved, but she remained focused on her surroundings and the waves of peace that circled around her.

Cove's alert but innocent face still hovered behind Jara, waiting for the chance to strike. When Jara got to one specific phrase, the servant stiffened, and Ravenna breathed tightly.

This has to work.

Ravenna felt a tug inside her, a rushing of power. Something strong and unfamiliar. The tether that would transfer the gifts had been completed.

In an instant, she felt her body changing, filling *more*, as it had that night in the cell. She was *overflowing* with power. Still, taking more, and more, and more. The color drained from the king's face, and the witch grasped her chest. Jara gasped between chants.

Thank the Light, *it was working*.

Ravenna's body felt strong, and new, and tired at the same time, as Degare's power entered her bloodstream and flowed through her. *Encapsulating her.*

And then the witch stopped chanting and slowly looked to Degare, who had collapsed upon the floor. He lay there, eyes wide, flexing his hands and muttering.

"My power. It is *gone*." His eyes looked to Ravenna in horror. "She took it. She *took* my power!" The witch looked to

Ravenna and then back to Degare, still clutching her chest. She braced herself on the small table that held the golden bowl.

"Fix this, or your clan will never see their homeland," he spat.

Jara looked at her, falling to her knees between breaths, as Ravenna closed the distance between herself and the king. Dizziness threatened her as the king's power rooted itself within. Ravenna crouched, hovering over Degare as Cove closed in on the witch from behind. Jio was stiff, and his distant, panicked gaze was on Ravenna, as if he were deciding whose side to take.

Ravenna was on the verge of blacking out, but one quick movement and a downward motion to the king's neck, and he would be dead. She heard the guards racing up behind her.

The king's gaze turned to Ravenna with widened eyes. "Please. Don't kill me."

Ravenna laughed as he begged for his life after taking so many for himself. She wondered how many Embers had begged him in the same manner before he had plunged his staff into their chests.

His eyes welled in fear, and she took a deep, shaky breath before she readied to stab him—but the dagger would not move. She was frozen in place, *unable to move*. Under wrinkled brows, she examined her hands. She wanted to kill him so badly. Wanted nothing more than to watch him bleed out upon the floor, but it was as if her body was not her own. It obeyed none of her silent commands to plunge the dagger into his throat.

She backed up a step and tried once more.

"*No*," he begged.

She halted again and dropped the dagger onto the floor. What was happening to her?

At the sound of a panicked sob from Cove, Ravenna looked toward the witch. Cove was out of sight. She had *fled* and was no longer behind Jara. She had left in such a hurry that she had spilled the wine.

Something had gone utterly and terribly wrong.

Degare furrowed his brow, beginning to understand something that Ravenna did not.

The witch laughed. "You can alter my spell, Ravenna, but I am always one step ahead."

Degare and Ravenna both stared at the witch in confusion.

"Jara, what have you done?" Degare demanded.

Jara smiled at Ravenna then, fully and terrifyingly, without turning to face the king who addressed her. "I've given her your power, *yes*. But you have full control over it. She is *sired* to you. Like a blood oath—but stronger."

Ravenna fell to her knees, chains rattling against the stone.

"The power will no longer ravage your aging body. You are *free*," Jara said to the king with pride. "I found a way to let you keep the power without it killing you. I *saved* you, Degare."

Ravenna looked from the king to the witch. Jara had planned this all along—Degare had been dying from the power, and she had found a way for him to continue his reign. She was trying to convince him to give her more power *still*, when she could have just let him die.

Degare examined the back of his aged hands, and the grayness of his shadowmarked skin seemed to brighten into a dull pink. His face seemed to become more youthful, and his cloudy eyes cleared. All the power he had stolen had made him ill, and with it gone, he was *healing*. His shadowmarks faded as Ravenna's grew.

Degare was intrigued, and lifted his hand from where he lay, weakened on the floor. Ravenna retreated backward a few steps, and then fell to her knees again. The new power tore through her, exhausting every bit of her strength. It was even darker than what she had felt before. This was power that had been forged through death.

"Ravenna, *rise*," the king spoke, watching her closely. As much as she fought against it, her body *rose*. The king smiled a malicious smile, and Jara watched pridefully. "Now bow before me." Ravenna did.

A sob broke from her throat.

"Lower," he demanded. Her nose touched the ground of the throne room floor.

She had cheated death so many times, only to end up here, bowing before a king she hated. Degare broke into wicked laughter and clapped his hands together. He ordered the guards that stood in the audience.

"Bring the boy in." Ravenna's heart thudded in her chest and climbed up her throat. She willed herself to do *anything else*, but her nose stayed pressed to the cold ground.

Footsteps sounded a few minutes later as guards approached, dragging someone behind them.

"*Up*, Ravenna."

She obeyed, and turned to see *Zephaniah*, utterly broken between two guards. His bloody, bruised body mirrored her own.

Red.

Two more sobs broke from her as her legs fought the urge to collapse.

No. No. No. No.

The king chuckled at her back, his laughter intertwining with the darkness that seemed to wrap around her, keeping her upright. The guards brought Zephaniah before her, then pushed him to his knees. All light seemed to flee the spinning room.

Degare's voice cut the air once more as the bloodstone staff clashed onto the floor beside her.

"Ravenna, kill this man for treason."

EPILOGUE
COVE

The night was misty, and Cove's boots splashed through puddles of murky water as she fled through the cobblestone streets of the kingdom to the edge of the Black Sea. A raven met her there on the beach. It watched her from its perch on a washed-up tree, rain rolling from its slick, dark feathers. Hurriedly, she pressed the tear of paper into its talons and watched as it took to the skies to meet the rush of ravens flocking south from the bordering Dead Wood, carrying a message that had the potential to start or end a war.

Do not come. Your little Dove is too far gone.

About the Author

Abigail Brier is the American author of the epic fantasy novel *Rush of Ravens*, which is book one of her *Til Kingdom Come* series.

Aside from writing, Abigail enjoys quiet time in nature, bird watching, flower gardening, and spending time with her family in the midwestern United States. She finds herself very busy with her many creative hobbies, which include painting, design, and photography. She can often be found sticking post-its on the walls or working on her laptop to the background noise of cinematic music or worship songs, snuggled up with her cats and dogs.

Abigail's love for storytelling blossomed when she was in middle school. She started (and abandoned) many stories until she came to the idea for the Til Kingdom Come series. In the midst of grief, she was reminded of the hope she has in Jesus, and this story became an outlet for her to share the good news with others. She began pouring little pieces of her own story into her characters, many times unintentionally, until the story came to life. If readers take away anything from this story, Abigail hopes it is this:

There is light in the darkness. There is hope in despair. There is joy in the midst of grief. There is redemption when you feel irredeemable, and you are loved beyond measure.

MORE BY ABIGAIL BRIER
DON'T MISS OUT THE NEXT BOOKS IN THE TIL KINGDOM COME SERIES!

Sea of Sorrows, book 1.5 in the Til
Kingdom Come series.

Dawn of Doves, book 2 in the Til
Kingdom Come series.